Frances Anne
lives in the town of Scarborough, North
She has worked in shops, in a coffee bar, as a clerk in a
building society and as secretary to a headmaster in a
private preparatory school – and at present she works
in the Social Services offices. She is married and has
two grown-up daughters. She has been writing since
she was a child and has previously had articles and
short stories published. *Dance Without Music* is her
first novel.

Dance Without Music

Frances Anne Bond

'He that lives in hope danceth without musick'

George Herbert

HEADLINE

Copyright © 1989 Frances Anne Bond

First published in 1989
by HEADLINE BOOK PUBLISHING PLC

First published in paperback in 1990
by HEADLINE BOOK PUBLISHING PLC

ISBN 0 7472 3189 3

Typeset in 10/12¼ pt English Times
by Colset Private Limited, Singapore

Printed and bound in Great Britain by
Collins, Glasgow

HEADLINE BOOK PUBLISHING PLC
Headline House
79 Great Titchfield Street
London W1P 7FN

For my mother.
A promise kept.

I would like to thank my husband and my daughters
for their love and support during the writing of this book,
and express my deep gratitude to dear friends,
who never failed to give me their time,
help and endless encouragement.

Chapter One

The curlew wheeled dizzily through the fierce blue skies arching over the moorland, then it dived. Its cry shrilled through the still air as it sped away from the high places to pass over fields of heavy-headed corn, ribbons of road and dried-up streams. Finally, its brown wings rested and it hovered over the pit village of Swaithdown.

Tight-pressed buildings sweltered in the heat. The only visible movements came from an unlucky horse as it struggled to pull a wagon up a cobbled street and from the plumes of smoke rising like prayers from the chimneys.

'Hottest summer in history,' agreed the old men taking their ease beneath the shade of the chestnut tree – but still, the fires had to be lit. The day shift would end soon and the colliers, coal dust streaking their faces like black tar, would return home to their tin baths before the fire.

The torpor of the village was broken when a bell clanged and the children spilled out of the tiny school house. Immediately, a circle formed within which a tall, lumpish boy taunted a much smaller child, a girl. Sycophantic jeers and whistles rose from the onlookers as the girl knuckled her eyes, but then surprised silence fell as she suddenly flew at her tormentor and struck him in the mouth with her clenched fist. The boy reacted by slapping the girl across her face but a spurt of blood from his split lip then sent him blubbering down the street. Disappointed at the cessation of excitement, the spectators drifted away and the girl was left alone.

Above her, the curlew opened his long curved beak and again his bubbling song filled the empty sky. Startled, the child looked upwards, wincing at the pain from her bruised cheek, but she saw nothing.

The curlew had already left the village behind him. He climbed the sky, escaping to the moors, where a breeze could always be found, where bilberries grew sweet amongst the heather, where rabbits played and the enduring landscape belonged to nature and not to man.

There was no such escape for Mary Armstrong. Beneath her long skirt she felt the heat prickling her legs as she bent to take more clothes from the wicker basket near her feet. How she hated ironing. Heaven knows, she had enough of it with keeping the bairns clean and tidy but now she was reduced to doing other folks' washing, too. She sighed and slapped the heavy iron down on to Bessie Hatton's Sunday shift as if it was the mine manager's bald head and she was cracking it. If only the accident hadn't happened.

A cry from the wooden cradle nearby distracted her.

'Hush, darling,' she crooned and gave a gentle pull to the piece of cord which attached the cradle to her belt. The rocking soothed the cry to a sleepy murmur. Mary worked steadily, transforming the tumbled piles of clothing into neatly stacked symbols of her clients' prosperity. Why, Bessie even possessed some lace-edged handkerchiefs.

The back door banged. That would be the children. Mary listened for chattering voices, the sound of boots on the scullery floor but there was silence.

'Florence?'

Again, nothing. Mary rested the iron on its stand. She untied the cord at her waist and crossed to the door and pulled it open. It was Sarah, not Florence who stood, flushed-faced and mute, beside the mangle in the darkest corner of the scullery.

None too gently, Mary caught hold of her younger daughter and pulled her forward in order to see her more clearly. 'What have you been up to?'

'Nothing.'

'Looks like it.' Mary's dark brows met in the middle as she frowned. She observed the torn pinafore, the drops of blood on the bib. Sarah's dark hair was a wild tangle of curls and a bruise flowered on her left cheek.

'You've been fighting, haven't you? Now, tell me the truth.'

The child hunched her shoulders and scowled. 'It's that Hughie Brownlow. He was teasing me – about Pa, so I thumped him. Then he hit me back, but it didn't hurt.' Her sooty lashes swept upwards and her eyes, brilliant with unshed tears, stared defiantly at her mother. 'He won't be such a big mouth now.' She blinked away the tears and grinned: 'I think I've knocked one of his teeth out.'

Mary did not smile back. Her face was set and angry. 'How can you behave so? Fighting is a sin. And look at you – you look like a gypsy!'

The grin faded. Sarah dropped her eyes and shuffled her feet. Staring down at her, Mary felt a confusion of anger and guilt. What was she to do with the child? She had a wild streak that must be tamed, for her own good. And how pretty she was getting; too pretty. Even now, with her face smeared with dirt, the ugly bruise showing, her looks set her apart from the other children.

'You must learn to control your temper, Sarah.' Seeing

3

the droop of the soft pink lips, Mary's voice softened. 'Well, we'll leave it now. Go and tidy up. I shall want you to take some of the laundry round soon.'

She went back to her ironing. Five minutes later a much tidier Sarah entered the kitchen and began stacking the freshly ironed clothes into their waiting baskets. She glanced across at her mother.

'Has the minister been, Mam, about Harry's christening?'

'Aye, he has. It's all fixed up. After the service, first Sunday in August.'

Thinking of the minister, Mary felt guilty again. Mr Brown, she knew, thought of her as a 'godly' woman. What would he think if he knew how often Sarah bothered and irritated her? Mary stared at the flat iron heating on the hob. And what about the way she positively hated Clayton, the mine manager? The minister would say the man had simply done his job. He had done that, all right. Joe had received a bit of brass in compensation for the accident and now drew a few shillings pension each week, but still she hated to come face to face with Clayton in the street.

She remembered his weaselly face the day he had spoken to her at the hospital. The day she had not known whether Joe would live or die.

'Act of God,' he had said. 'These things happen.' And then, 'Be thankful it's 1913 Mrs Armstrong. In the bad old days thee and thine would have been headed for the Workhouse. Pity Joe had never been a saver,' he had added.

No. Joe had never been a saver. And even if he had, with a bairn practically every year and his liking for a pint on an evening, there had been precious little left to save. They had never worried about money then. She had been so proud of her strong, handsome husband: drawing top wages at the

mine, champion wrestler of the district and always a joke in
him. He'd come swinging down the street with a whistle
sweet as a blackbird and Mary knew all the womenfolk had
envied her. Now they pitied her.

She pressed her lips firmly together and wiped the sweat
off her hands before taking up the fresh iron and pressing
Mrs Meadley's white linen tablecloth.

The door of Number 29 Joshua Street slammed again
and Florence and Arthur entered the kitchen. Mary's
expression softened as she looked at Florence. Florence was
sober, hard working and sensible. Mary understood her
eldest girl.

'Our Sarah's been fighting, Mam.' Red-haired Arthur
had a smirk on his face. 'Mrs Brownlow says . . .'

'Set the table, Arthur.' Mary pressed her hand to the
small of her back and straightened to ease the stiffness. 'I
don't want to know what Mrs Brownlow says. Florence and
Sarah are taking the laundry, so you can help me.'

She filled the kettle at the stone sink and placed it on
the hob. 'I'll just have a cup of tea before I see to the
meal.'

The two girls left the house and Arthur clattered about
laying the table with ill grace. With an easing of her spirits,
Mary glanced about her kitchen. Times might be bad, but
she had managed to keep her brass candlesticks, now
twinkling away on the high mantelpiece. Between them
stood the willow-patterned teacaddy which her mother had
sworn came from foreign parts. Her brightly coloured
hooked rugs scattered on the spotless red brick floor made
the room look cheerful and homely.

The ring of the miners' boots on the cobbles outside
made her aware of the passage of time. The day shift was
over.

Had Joe been to the office to pick up his pension money? she wondered.

'Get the crock pot, Arthur,' she said. 'I'll cut the bread and you can spread the dripping.'

The tea was being mashed in the brown teapot when the girls returned.

'My, it's awful hot.' Sarah had recovered her high spirits. She skipped across the room and sat in a chair by the table. 'Can I go and meet our Jim after tea, Mam?'

'He's working late,' replied her mother. Thank God, she thought to herself. If Florence was her favourite child, Jim was an absolute godsend. After the accident her fourteen-year-old eldest child had assumed the mantle of provider for the whole family.

There were squeals from the table. Arthur and Sarah were at each other's throats again.

'Will you two stop it!'

Mary moved swiftly and boxed their ears. Sarah's face assumed its mulish expression and Arthur burst into tears. Mary shook her head. Such a crybaby he was. Sometimes she thought he should have been born a lass.

'What's the matter now?'

'It's my turn for the chair, Mam. Tell her. Tell her to let me have it.'

'No. It's me. It's my turn, honest.' Sarah had clamped herself on to the kitchen chair like a limpet. She glared at her brother, defying him to dislodge her.

The things they quarrelled over! Three good chairs, apart from their father's, and every night they argued who would sit in them. Mary had five children, counting baby Harry, and sometimes she felt like murdering the lot of them.

'Don't fret, Mam. I'll sort it out.' Florence grabbed Arthur's ear and pulled him backwards. At the same time she jerked the chair and dislodged Sarah. Then she calmly sat herself down and reached for the teapot.

Eh, she is a good lass, thought Mary. What a wife and mother she'll make. But Florence was clever too. Mary knew how much her elder daughter wanted to stay on at school. Well, she'd do her best to grant that wish.

Mary checked on the baby then looked at the clock ticking away on the shelf. 'When you've finished your tea, Arthur,' she said, 'nip down to the corner and see if your Pa's coming.'

The boy reached for the last piece of bread and rammed it into his mouth before leaving the room. Florence rose and re-filled the kettle and Sarah's dark blue eyes grew guarded. Mary rocked the cradle. A quietness slipped over the room; a sense of waiting. Arthur re-appeared. He was breathless.

'He's just coming, Mam.'

They listened. There was a faint sound which grew sharper. The tap, tap of a walking stick. The back door opened. There was a thud, then a muffled curse.

Mary moved to the table. 'Florence – take Arthur and Sarah over to Mrs Fenton's,' she said. 'Go the front way. Here.' She picked up a freshly baked loaf and a twist of paper. 'Ask if you can stay a bit and give her this tea and bread for your supper. Go now.'

Florence bit her lip. 'But, Mam . . .'

'Go on. I'll be all right.'

With a backward glance at her mother, Florence took her brother and sister by the hand and hurried them from the room. Mary waited. Her hands pleated, then smoothed the coarse material of her apron. The inner door crashed open and Joe Armstrong swayed on the step.

* * *

At first glance, Joe was still a handsome man: broad-shouldered and tall, with the dark blue eyes and glossy hair Sarah had inherited. His strong white neck rose from the open-necked shirt he wore now that he was no longer a miner down the pit. A fine figure of a man; until you noticed other things. He leant heavily upon a stout stick and, when he moved, his left leg dragged. He was running to fat, and there was a blurred look about him: his shirt front bulged against the broad leather belt which had once clinched his lean waist; his cheeks were puffy and the added flesh caused his eyes to narrow. His eyes had once been beautiful. A strange description for a man such as Joe Armstrong, but true nevertheless. The deepest blue they had been, sparkling with life and a hint of devilment like sunshine glancing off fast-moving water. Now they were dull pools of bewilderment.

He looked towards his wife and scowled. He passed his hand uncertainly over the bald patch at the back of his head. 'Am I late, then?'

Not waiting for a reply he limped into the room and made for the cradle. 'Now then, lad. Been a good boy?'

Mary's tense figure relaxed. She gave a brief nod of welcome.

'I met some of the lads, Mary. Been to the Bull with them. Am I late? You know I can never fathom the time.'

'It's all right. Your meal's not ready yet. I had to get the ironing finished.'

The spark of animation in Joe's eyes was quenched. He dropped heavily into his chair then leant forward, his large hands dangling aimlessly between his knees.

'Bloody shame,' he muttered, staring at the rug at his feet. 'You shouldn't have to work so.' He coughed. 'Not a proper man anymore, lass. That's the trouble. No bloody use to man nor beast.' He sighed.

Mary frowned but made no reply. She disliked Joe in maudlin mood but that was infinitely preferable to the way he usually came back from the Bull.

'Did you go for the money, Joe?'

'For God's sake, woman, let me get me boots off first.'

'I'm sorry.' She crossed to stand beside him. 'It's just I'm right out, love. You gave me short last week. Remember?'

Joe groped in his trouser pocket and threw a handful of coins on to the table. 'Here – take it. Take the bloody lot. It's all there is. I've spent some of it.'

He darted a quick look at her then averted his eyes. 'Aw – don't give me that "cow" look. You don't understand.' He put his face in his hands. 'A couple of pints, that's all. I was one of the lads again, Mary. Just for a bit. One of the lads . . .'

Mary rested her hand on his shoulder. 'I know. But we need every penny, Joe, and . . .' she hesitated. 'You know what the doctor said.'

Joe turned towards her and put his arms around her waist. 'What does he know! Oh, Mary. There's only you knows, only you cares . . .' His voice thickened: 'You do care don't you? You still love your old fellow. I'm still some use to you?'

Mary stiffened. She tried to free herself from his grasp but he held her tighter, running one hand down towards her thighs, feeling them through the folds of her skirt.

'Stop it, Joe. The bairns will be back soon.'

He ignored her, pulled her roughly down on to his knee. His hands fumbled at the buttons of her high-necked blouse.

'Aw – come on, lass. You used to want it as much as me. Remember?' His breathing quickened. His hand slipped inside her bodice and he squeezed her breast.

'No. Stop it. You're hurting me, Joe.'

9

She tried to break free but he held her easily. He was laughing softly now and his eyes held a red spark she had learnt to dread. She struggled silently for a moment then, realising this aroused him more, submitted. He pushed her down to the floor and clumsily lowered his heavy body on top of her. Mary shut her eyes. Desperately she tried to remember how it used to be. Times they had loved in the past. Times when she had offered herself eagerly, knowing her husband would respond with tenderness as well as passion. Would he ever be like that again? A tear squeezed from her tightly shut eyes. She withdrew herself in spirit from the grunting creature swaying above her. She willed her mind on a prayer to the Almighty. A prayer she silently repeated over and over again: 'Please, God, don't let the bairns come back until it's over and please, God, don't let me get pregnant again.'

'But I don't want to go with you. I don't want to go.'

Florence took a firmer grip on her wayward sister's arm and pulled her down the street. 'Do as you're told, Sarah – or I'll clip your ear.'

Sarah's eyes blazed. 'Do that and I'll tell Pa. You can't hit me. You're my sister, not my Mam.'

Florence changed her grip so she could give her sister a good shaking. 'You just behave. We've got to do as Mam says.'

'You've dropped the tea.'

'What?' Florence turned her head to stare at Arthur who was following moodily behind the two girls, his hands in the pockets of his knickerbockers.

'You've dropped the tea.' He pointed: 'There – it's all spilled out on the ground.'

Florence's pale face tinged with pink. 'Well, frame

10

yourself. Help me to pick it up.' She shook Sarah again. 'It's your fault.'

Sarah was unrepentant. 'I don't care.' She freed herself from Florence's grasp. 'What's a bit of old tea. Ma Fenton will give you her tea. She'll enjoy that. She'll go on about "you poor youngsters".' Her small frame assumed a belligerent stance. 'Well, I'd sooner be me than one of her kids, 'cos her Janey picks her nose and they all have spots. You go to the Fentons, I'm off to wait for our Jim, so put that in your pipe and smoke it!'

Florence had withdrawn her attention from Sarah. She was trying to scoop up the tea and replace it in the screw of paper. Arthur answered for her.

'You're daft. Jim won't be finished for ages yet, and you can't go home till Mam says so. You'd better come with us.'

Sarah pulled a face at him and ran off down the street.

'Oh, leave her be, Arthur. There's no arguing with her in that mood.' Florence admitted defeat over the tea and straightened up, shaking out her skirts. 'Come on, then.'

They walked reluctantly towards number 23 Joshua Street; towards the inquisitive though kindly eyes and the veiled questions they knew were awaiting them there.

Chapter Two

Sarah ran until she could run no more. When she reached the top of Joshua Street she turned instinctively away from the pithead and the surrounding slag heaps glowering over the village and ran towards the cornfields and the stream; towards the east, towards light and colour. She was breathless when she reached the stream. She threw herself down on the parched grass, pillowed her head on her arms and gave herself up to the luxury of being unhappy.

What was the matter with everyone? It wasn't just having to go to the Fentons. It was everything. Why did things have to alter? At nine years old Sarah could remember happier days. When Mam didn't have the stupid baby to care for and used to sing about the house. When Florence would play with her and not behave like a fussy old woman all the time. As for Arthur . . . she dismissed Arthur; he had always been a misery. Thank goodness Jim never changed. But now he worked all the time and when he was home he seemed tired. But mostly, it was Pa.

Sarah rolled on to her side and watched as an ant made heroic attempts to drag a stick three times its size through the grass. She flicked a pebble in its path and watched as it scurried about frantically to find a way around the new obstacle. Pa was like the ant; but whereas the ant would find a new way, Pa became increasingly confused and strange.

She flopped over on to her back and made a cave of her hands. The sun, now dipping in the sky, formed a stream of golden dust motes between the shapes of her fingers. The dazzle was blotted out. She removed her hands from her eyes and saw her best friend.

'What you doing, Sarah?' Lucy Smailes demanded.

'Nothing much.' She squinted through her fingers again. 'Just think, Lucy. If you could drift up through the sunshine you could see what it's really like in the sky.'

'Eeh, you do say some daft things.' Lucy looked down at Sarah, perplexed admiration in her mild eyes.

'Don't ever call me "daft".' Sarah showed her small white teeth in a grimace. She snatched at Lucy's ankles and brought her plump friend down to lie spread-eagled on the grass beside her.

'There was no need to do that.' Lucy hastily assumed a more decorous position and glared at Sarah. 'What's biting you?'

'Nothing.' Sarah turned her head away and stared at the dried-up bed of the stream.

Lucy settled herself more comfortably. She was of a placid disposition and well used to Sarah's moods. 'Phew. Hot, isn't it?'

'I like hot weather.'

Lucy stared at the bruise on her friend's face but made no comment. She turned and peered down into the stream.

'Not much water left. Bet all the minnows are dead.'

'Bet they're not. They are deep down, keeping cool.' Sarah jumped to her feet and, picking up a twig, stirred the mud vigorously. 'Look,' she said triumphantly.

A fragile shape quivered into view then disappeared again.

'How did you know?'

14

'Jim told me. He knows all about fish and animals and birds.'

'Didn't think lads were interested in such things. How does he know?'

'He just does. Our Jim's clever. Cleverer than Florence, though everyone thinks she's the brainy one 'cos she's always reading.'

Lucy scratched a midge bite. 'Don't suppose he likes it down the pit, then. No animals and things down there.'

Sarah's face closed into a tight mask. 'He never talks about it.'

'Still, all the menfolk have to work in t'pit, don't they? All except for my Pa and yours. I mean, my Pa being the milkman and yours . . .' Lucy's voice trailed off and there was an awkward silence.

'Look!' Her face brightened with relief. 'I've got some humbugs.' She produced a crumpled bag: 'Want one?'

Sarah accepted graciously and they sucked in silence. When the sweets were finished Sarah rose to her feet.

'Have to go now,' she said. 'I'm going to meet our Jim. See you tomorrow.'

Knowing she would be early, Sarah still hurried towards the pithead. She was anxious to be near her brother. She threaded her way through the outskirts of the village. Here, the houses were well built and somewhat smug, sitting in the middle of self-conscious gardens. They belonged to the professional folk of the village: the doctor, the mine manager and the lady who managed the only dress shop for miles around. She passed the squat church and the gloomy burial ground where weathered gravestones leant wearily towards each other as though seeking mutual support and plunged into the black streets herringboning the hilly area close by the mine.

15

Frances Anne Bond

Outside the colliery gates was a dispirited patch of grass.
Here, Sarah seated herself ignoring the gritty layer of coal
dust which immediately sullied her clothes. Mam would be
cross, but then she always was. Sarah's expression became
blank. Like a small sphinx she waited. Almost an hour
later, a handful of men came into view. They grinned at the
girl, their white teeth splitting their black faces like piano
keys. She smiled back. Sarah liked the colliers. They were
almost frightening figures, work stained and slouched with
fatigue, but their rumbling voices were kind. Working in
the earth as they did, they acquired a solidness and stead-
fastness with which the child instinctively identified. It was
the same feeling she experienced up on the moors sometimes. Her eyes strained past the men. Jim should be
coming soon. A gangly lad of about fourteen came into
view. Sarah frowned. Her brother stumbled along like an
exhausted crow. He rested and his thin chest heaved as he
drew gulps of fresh air into his lungs.

'Jim.' She shouted and waved.

Immediately the boy's shoulders went back and his chin
came up. He strode towards the gates, swinging his water
bottle and trying to whistle.

'Now then, Sarah. What are you doing here?' Then,
more sharply, he asked, 'Something up at home?'

'No. I wanted to meet you. That's all.'

He looked at her dubiously and she shrugged. 'Well,
Mam sent us to Ma Fenton's but I wouldn't go. I came here
instead. It's all right,' she hastened to add, 'Florence knows
where I am.'

She fell in step with him and together they walked down
the hill.

'Pa home?'

She bit her lip. 'He was just coming when Mam sent us

out. Jimmy?' Her voice wobbled: 'What's the matter with Pa? Is he loonie?'

Jim's head jerked involuntarily and he stopped and faced her. 'Of course not. Who said he was?'

'Hughie Brownlow said it. He said the accident's made him daft and the other lads laughed. And he said we're the loonie's kids, and we'll go daft too.'

Jim started walking again so fast Sarah had to run to keep up with him.

'Don't be mad, Jim.'

The boy took her hand. His face was serious. 'I'm not mad at you, Sarah. They're the ones who are daft. They don't know what they are talking about.'

Sarah clutched his hand tightly. 'I know Pa's lame now and can't work but he'll get better, won't he, Jim?'

He looked into her anxious eyes. 'Look Sarah, he was awful sick after the accident. Most men would have died but Pa's real strong and he started to get better. But they had to put a kind of steel plate in his head and that's why he gets such terrible headaches and he gets mixed up.' He sighed: 'You've got to remember that when he flies off in a temper. It's the pain I reckon. And,' he paused, 'Pa used to be a kind of hero down the pit, the men looked up to him. Now it's all changed and he can't even work. Can you understand what that means to him?'

'I suppose so.' Sarah walked along quietly for a moment then her face brightened. 'Still, he'll get better, Jim. Some days he's fine. Just like he was before.'

Jim looked fondly down at the pert little face. He smiled and tugged at her long hair. 'Maybe he will, Sarah. Maybe he will.'

* * *

17

'Why do you never do as you're told? You should have stayed with Florence.' Mary's voice sounded strained and tired.

'She came to meet me, Mam. I was right glad to see her.' Jim's eyes flickered from his mother's face to the bulky form of his father, seated in his chair and staring silently into the embers of the fire. 'All right, Pa?'

'Right as I'll ever be.'

A smouldering resentment showed in the older man's eyes as he saw his son wearing the pit-stained clothes which proclaimed the visible badge of manhood Joe could no longer attain. He averted his gaze then saw Sarah, his favourite child.

'How's my darling then?' Clumsily he rose from his chair and opened his arms wide. With a shriek of joy Sarah rushed into them. At this moment he was 'her' Pa again. He tossed her high in the air and gave a bellowing laugh and she laughed with him. Then he glanced defiantly towards Mary.

'See,' he was silently saying, 'here is one who still loves me.'

He tickled his girl under her chin and around her ribs and attempted to toss her up into the air again but stumbled and nearly fell.

'I've got her.' Jim stepped forward and caught Sarah as her father's arms slackened. Mary went to Joe's side and pressed him back into the chair easing him against the crocheted-wool cushion. He sank back with a baffled expression and his head dothered like that of an old man.

Mary turned towards her daughter, her mouth folding into a thin line. 'How many times do I have to tell you? You are too big for such games.'

Sarah shrank against Jim for protection. He gave her a

18

warning pat on the shoulder then moved across to his father.

'Come on, Pa. It's late. I'll help you upstairs.'

Mary placed a plate of stew and a hunk of bread on the table then turned to Sarah. 'And upstairs with you, Miss. Florence and Arthur are already in bed and next time I tell you something, see you do as I say.'

With downward glance Sarah followed her brother and father upstairs. After a few moments Jim re-entered the kitchen and crossed to the sink to wash his hands.

'I've covered him up. He's almost asleep already. Been to the pub, has he?'

'Aye. He has.'

'Have you got his pension money?'

'Most of it.'

Before sitting down at the table, Jim felt in his pocket and produced a brown envelope. He pressed it into his mother's hand. 'Well, put this away somewhere safe. Where he can't find it.'

Mary's hands closed on the envelope gratefully.

'Eat up, lad. I'll get your bath ready. You'll be glad to be out of those mucky clothes.'

Jim ate his food slowly. He was almost too tired to eat at all. His mother set out the tin bath and moved to and fro filling it with steaming water from the copper. She chatted on, refraining from watching her son as he shed the too-large pit clothes which had once been worn by her husband.

'Minister's been. Christening is to be beginning of August. Oh, your Aunt Blanche and her husband will be coming. Eh,' she paused for a moment, 'I'll be right glad to see her. It's been years.'

Jim stepped gingerly into the hot water, flinched, then sat down with a sigh of relief. 'Sarah will be pleased,' he commented. 'She's always telling her friends she has a "posh" auntie that owns a shop.' He laughed and for a brief moment his perpetual worried 'old man's' face fell into more youthful lines. 'She'll be bringing them round here to admire Blanche's fur coat I shouldn't wonder.'

'Fur coat she may have,' responded his mother, 'but I reckon that antique shop she says she has is more likely to be a junk shop. What does our Blanche know about antiques? Still,' she sighed. 'I'd not say no to a trip over to York to see it.'

She knelt on the hooked rug by the side of the bath. 'Come on lad. I'll do your back.'

She soaped his thin shoulders. Pity each of her sons had her small, thin frame. Still, a man didn't need to be six feet tall to inspire respect. She rubbed away with a rough flannel. The coal dust sloughed off and through the rivulets of water Jim's white skin showed, smooth and unblemished.

'Why, Jim,' she teased. 'You've got a skin as fine as a lassie.' She laughed when she saw him blush, gave his back a final scrub then stood up and shook out her apron. 'Reckon that will do,' she said and lingered a moment, her hand resting on the nape of his neck where his hair had curled in the dampness and rested like a question mark on his pale skin.

'I hope Harry turns out something like you, lad,' she said quietly. 'If he does, I'll be well pleased.'

She picked up the paraffin lamp from the table and went upstairs. Jim sat for a few moments in the warm, scummy water. There was a lump in his throat. His mother had rolled up the sleeves of her blouse above her elbows to wash his back and he had seen the livid bruises forming on her upper arms. The thought of her life these past months sickened him. Bile formed in his mouth as he thought of his father.

'He can't help it. He can't help it,' he told himself desperately but the sickness remained.

He shivered. The water in the bath was cold now. He could feel the gritty dust beneath his toes. He rose and dried himself. Shadows in the room were lengthening but there was still light to see by. He pulled on his drawers and went into the scullery to empty the dirty water. This done and the bath put away, he stretched out on the truckle bed in the corner of the kitchen. He was so tired but his thoughts kept him awake. He'd get up even earlier in the morning, he decided, and scrub the floor for Mam before he left for work. He'd sort Arthur out and make him help more. His mind skimmed to his little sister. His lips turned upwards in a smile. Always in trouble, she was. She hadn't mentioned that nasty bruise on her face but he had seen it. He frowned. If Pa . . . but no, she could still twist the old man around her little finger.

He moved into a more comfortable position on the narrow bed. His tense limbs relaxed. He tried to prolong the delicious moment before sleep finally overcame him, but his treacherous body betrayed him and his tired eyelids closed. Tomorrow – at six thirty – he'd be going down the pit again.

Chapter Three

During the first week of August Britain entered what was to become known as the Great War, and Harold George Armstrong was christened. The latter event was infinitely the more important to the Armstrong family, though the war news temporarily disturbed the even tenor of the village. Doctor Robertshaw discussed the matter gravely over port and cigars with his cronies but general interest in the subject soon died. For the colliers' world was Swaithdown and they preferred discussing the forthcoming brass band competition; the bloody three foot high seam they were working in; and the fact that Joe Armstrong might not be the man he was, but by God he sired some bonny bairns.

The sun shone on Harry's special day. And so did his home. Mary had indulged in an orgy of cleaning. The lace curtains at the small windows showed pristine white, the brass candlesticks were polished within an inch of their life and, thanks to much scrimping and saving, a decent high tea had been set for the occasion. Now the day was drawing to a close. Guests had departed and little remained on the embroidered teacloth except for a jar of pickles, a few slices of Mary's currant bread and the centre-piece of wild flowers that Sarah had insisted on placing there.

Mary had almost removed the flowers. They were really weeds as everyone knew and she wondered what insects lurked amongst them but, seeing Sarah's hurt expression, she had changed her mind and left them there. She had noticed a couple of the neighbours smirking at the sight of them but the minister had remarked how bonny they looked which had put the couple firmly in their place.

'Well, Mary . . .' Mr Brown, the minister, had picked up his hat and was preparing to leave. 'It's been a grand afternoon. But now your Harry has been properly welcomed into the family of Jesus I must be off.'

Mary moved to see him out but her sister, Blanche, forestalled her. Hurrying forward she laid her hand on his arm and accompanied him to the door.

What a shock Mary had received on seeing Blanche again. She remembered her sister as the slim, attractive bride of seventeen years ago. Now Blanche was huge. Oh, her complexion was still pink and white and her hair black and glossy but now her tiny high-arched feet looked ludicrous beneath her ballooning body – and her hands. Glancing down at her own workworn hands adorned only by her wedding band, Mary wondered if Blanche did any housework. Her sister's fingernails were long and hooked and none too clean. She wore rings on practically every finger and they appeared to be fighting a losing battle against sinking into her lardy, puffy flesh.

Mary glanced around her own spotless home. It took effort to keep things clean in a pit village but she managed it. All the women did. It was a matter of pride. Each day a relentless battle was waged against the encroaching grime. Windows were cleaned constantly, fire grates and ovens blackleaded until they gleamed like jet. The flagged scullery floors were washed daily and, always, the doorsteps were immaculate with decorated white-stone edges. Why, sometimes, the street cobbles shone as if they lay under water, so often were they swilled and brushed by the womenfolk. Still, things were different for Blanche. She no longer belonged to Swaithdown.

'I'll see you later, then. About the other matter.' The minister spoke directly to Mary over the bobbing head of her sister. His long horsey face showed an expression of irritation and amusement in equal measures.

Mary moved to Blanche's side and looked at her severely. 'Would you get another cup of tea for Joe please, Blanche. I want a word with Mr Brown before he leaves.'

'Oh, all right.' Blanche patted her hair and gave an arch smile. 'I was just saying to the minister here, you'll soon have enough bairns for a choir.' She sighed dramatically: 'And me, blessed with just the one. He's a grand lad, mind, but with all I have to do . . .'

Mary ignored her sister's prattle and went to stand outside on the front step to take her leave of the minister.

'I'm seeing a member of the education board on Wednesday, Mary,' Mr Brown said. 'Rest assured, I will do my best for Florence.'

He shook Mary by the hand and left, walking briskly down the drab, heat-ridden street.

Mary returned indoors to find Blanche flopped in a chair, fanning her face with a paper. 'Thought he'd never go, Mary,' she said. 'And the thing is, I want a word with you before we leave.' She glanced across at her mild little husband sitting quietly in the corner of the room. 'You got those train times, didn't you, Ted?'

He nodded.

'But you can stay a while surely,' protested Mary. 'It's so long since we met. I want to hear all your news. That's why I sent the children off for a walk, so that you and I could talk.'

'Well, it's a fair way to the railway station, Mary, and we

mustn't miss our train. We've left Jack in charge of things and we don't want him on his own too long, poor lamb.'

'He's old enough, surely?'

'Oh, aye. But there's valuables in the shop, you see. You can't be too careful.'

Joe, who had been sitting quietly in his chair, stirred and touched his head in a familiar movement. 'Bloody lucky you have something worth pinching,' he muttered.

'Anyways,' persisted Blanche, 'I want to talk to you.'

Joe reached for his stick and struggled out of his chair. 'If it's women's talk then I'm away,' he said. 'Come on, Ted. I'll show you my allotment. It's just up back lane. I can do a bit of gardening and I've a grand pig fattening up for you to see. Reckon I'll pick up a prize with her next fair day.'

He limped from the room followed by Blanche's husband who looked for a nod of permission from her before he hurried after his brother-in-law. The two women were left alone. Blanche looked at her sister in silence.

'Well,' said Mary, smiling a little.

'I must say, Mary,' began Blanche, 'you did us proud today. It can't be easy for you now with Joe out of work.'

'We manage.' She went to pick Harry from his cradle and tried not to think of the week ahead to be got through. 'Now what is it you want to talk about?'

She opened her blouse and smiled at her son as he eagerly nuzzled her breast, then she looked across at Blanche, surprising a strange expression on her face.

'You look thoroughly worn out, Mary. I suppose you know that?'

She shrugged. There was nothing to say.

'You were always soft,' Blanche continued. 'You had the looks. You could have got a chap with a bit of cash, someone with a profession like my Ted.'

Spots of colour appeared in Mary's cheeks but she answered calmly: 'Joe had a trade, or profession, as you call it. I reckon a collier is as good as a monumental mason any day.'

'Aye. But I used my head. I knew Ted's auntie would leave him everything. After all, he was her only relative. Oh, you may sniff. Ted's not much to write home about but he's a fair husband and I've got security.'

'I loved Joe.' Mary spoke in a low voice.

'Love! Well, all I can say is, look what you have landed up with.'

Mary glared at her sister. 'I'm glad you came to the christening, Blanche. I was looking forward to seeing you again and you brought Harry a lovely christening spoon but if you keep on like this, I'll be asking you to leave.'

Blanche lowered her voice to a more conciliatory tone: 'I'm sorry. I didn't want to upset you. But what is going to happen – with Joe?'

Mary smoothed down a tuft of hair on her baby's head. 'We manage. Joe gets a pension and Jim brings money into the house.'

'I don't mean just the money, though that's a problem I'm sure. It's these,' Blanche paused delicately, 'these moods of Joe's. I've heard things, Mary. Oh, he's been all right today but he's not always so calm, is he?'

Mary bit her lip. 'He gets terrible headaches. The doctor thinks they may wear off in time.'

'And if they get worse?'

'They won't.' Mary moved the baby to her other arm. 'You've seen him today. He's fine. Anyway, I have good neighbours.'

Blanche stirred in her chair and Mary heard her corsets groan.

'Well, it's your affair. But I'd be thinking if I were you. If he gets really violent you could see about having him put away. No,' she raised a fat hand, 'hear me out. You want to watch you don't have more bairns too.' She sighed. 'I don't know, seems like every time he hangs his trousers on the bed end, you've caught again.'

Mary lifted Harry to her shoulder and made no reply. She pushed from her mind the thought of the last time Joe had made love to her. Made love! She gave a wry smile.

Meanwhile, Blanche was continuing her own line of thought. 'Now listen, Mary. I've an idea. That Florence now, she looks a useful girl. What if I took her back with me?'

Mary stared at her.

'Think about it,' urged Blanche. 'It would be one less mouth to feed and I'll look after her. She can help me and she'll have a much better chance of finding a young man in York than she would have here.' She paused expectantly: 'What do you think?'

'*No!*' Mary was angry. 'My young 'uns stay with me.' She took a deep breath, striving for calmness. 'Anyways, Florence's future is being taken care of. She's clever, Blanche, really clever. The minister wants her to try for a scholarship. Go to Grammar School.'

'Much good that will do her.' Blanche snorted. 'And how would you afford all the expense, uniform, books and suchlike?'

'There's a fund, to help such as Florence. We'll manage somehow. I want her to make something of her life, Blanche.'

There was the sound of voices outside. Joe and Ted had returned. Mary put the baby back in the cradle and Blanche heaved herself up and smoothed her dress.

'Oh, well,' Blanche said. 'I tried. I had my heart set on Florence, but bear in mind, Mary, I might be prepared to take the other one, Sarah. She's a bit young and flighty but she seems sharp enough. Think on it.'

'What's that?' Joe had overhead the last part of the conversation. 'What's that about our Sarah?'

'Nothing, Joe. Blanche was offering to take one of the girls back to York for a bit. Be a change for them and give her some help too.'

The vein on Joe's forehead throbbed and his hand trembled on his stick. 'They're going bloody nowhere, do you hear? Especially Sarah.' He glared at Blanche. 'If you wanted more bairns you should look to your own man for them; not come here, pinching ours.'

Blanche gave him a killing look but did not reply. She crossed the room and picked up her hat and coat.

'I'll write, love,' she said, turning to Mary and, pointedly ignoring Joe, she hurried to the door where an alarmed Ted hovered, waiting for her.

As the sound of their footsteps clicked on the cobbles outside, Joe gave vent to his rage.

'She's not to come here again, understand,' he shouted to Mary. 'Fat, stupid cow. I told Ted. I told him. Stand up to her. Be a man and tell her what for.'

The noise disturbed Harry who began to cry. Mary crossed to the cradle and Joe stared at her thin frame as she bent over their son.

'Aw, well.' He limped over to her and dropped a heavy hand on her neck. 'Reckon I got the best sister in your family,' he said and, for a moment, the ghost of the old Joe looked at Mary. She smiled and straightened up and, together, they admired their child.

Chapter Four

Later in her life Sarah was to remember the day of Harry's christening as the last truly happy day of her childhood. On her return home she had been disappointed to find her Aunt Blanche gone. The line of children she had positioned in the street outside would not now be able to appreciate the ornate rings and ear-rings she had so graphically described. They would disbelieve the existence of the solid gold fob watch pinned to the massive bosom, and the hat with blue feathers. She sighed and shrugged. Life was unfair.

Sarah entered the kitchen. Her mother and father, arms interlinked, were smiling down at Harry, gurgling in his cradle. She stood and stared. Her mother's face was rosy and gentle. Her father's dark head bent in a protective manner over his wife and child. A stubborn ray of late sunshine had forced its way through the thick net curtains and rested benedictorily on the little group and upon the pot of wild flowers Sarah had placed upon the table. The rich gold of the buttercups gleamed brighter than Blanche's fob watch and the delicate perfume of the bee orchids permeated the room.

Her parents looked up, saw her. They moved apart. The scene fragmented but in her heart she carried the memory. Perhaps that is why the following months were so difficult to understand.

As the glorious summer coloured into autumn the mood of the village changed. A poster appeared outside the village hall. It was the picture of a man with glaring eyes and a heavy moustache pointing his finger and pronouncing: 'Your King and Country need *YOU*'. Groups of young men began to congregate nearby. They laughed and scuffled with each other. They boasted of how they would sort out 'the Hun'. They were good humoured, but there was a tension about them which caused Sarah to hurry by.

Older men bought more papers and looked gloomy as they read them. A frail gentleman, Mr Blatchford, who was a Quaker, spoke out against the war and that night his windows were smashed. Worse still, a lady who lived in Station Road had a little dog, a dachshund, and late one evening a gang of drunken pit boys kicked it to death. Sarah cried all night when she heard the news.

Joe Armstrong took to spending more and more time at the Bull. But even when he was out of the house his presence was felt. Sarah watched her mother become quieter. She was harsh with the children. Florence did not help so much with the chores. She had been given a vision of another kind of life and spent all her free time with the minister's family or at her teacher's home. She would return, her eyes glowing, to tell Sarah all about the exciting life she would lead once she went away to school. Jim worked every hour he could at the pit and watched his mother with anxious eyes. He seemed to have little time for Sarah. Sometimes she was surprised to see a look akin to hate on his face when he looked at his father.

Joe would stump home from the pub, excited and incoherent, his temper uncertain.

'I'd have shown them,' he would shout, banging his stick. 'I'd have made a bloody good soldier. If only . . .'

Then his face would darken: 'For God's sake, shut that bugger up, will you.' And Mary would hurry across to little Harry, grizzling with teething pains, and rock him into silence.

Only Sarah could coax her father from his black moods and sometimes even she failed. She would flinch when he swore and raised his hand, but on her the blow never fell.

One night in the November following Harry's christening, Sarah awoke crying with toothache. She left the bed she shared with Florence and crept downstairs to find her mother. Mary was sewing by the fire. Sarah glanced across at her father. He must have recently returned from the Bull. He was snoring in his chair, his feet propped up on the fender. The steam was rising from his stockinged feet in the heat from the fire. Because Pa was an ex-miner, at least they had coal.

'What is it, Sarah?'

Sarah explained.

'Um. Your face does look swollen. Just a minute.' Mary rubbed the afflicted gum with oil of cloves. 'That should soon feel better.' She felt Sarah's hot forehead. 'You pop into Jim's bed for a little while. It's cosy down here and Jim won't be back until late. I don't want you disturbing Florence. She has an important exam tomorrow.'

Sarah curled up in Jim's bed. She watched the leaping flames of the fire, listened to her father's snores and gradually drifted off to sleep.

'Joe!'

The short, sharp cry disturbed her. She rubbed her eyes and stared towards her parents. Her mother stood in front of the recumbent form of her father. She was clutching the blue jug in which the rent money was kept. Sarah blinked at the expression on her mother's face. She had never seen her look so.

'Joe!' Mary repeated his name. She raised her foot and

pushed his legs so they slipped off the fender and hit the floor. He awoke with a cry of pain.

'What the hell?'

'How could you?'

His expression bewildered, he looked up at his wife. In the flickering firelight Mary seemed to have grown. She glared at him and for a moment Sarah thought she was actually going to strike him.

'You've had it, haven't you? The rent money. I've scrimped and saved to keep a roof over our heads and now you've spent it. How many pints, Joe? How many pints did it buy? Enough to keep you warm when we're out on the Parish?'

Joe rubbed bleary eyes. Comprehension dawned on his face. 'What are you blithering about, woman? You'll get it back. Next week, I'll have some brass then.'

'Next week's no good. We're behindhand as it is. We're in debt, Joe. Can't you get that through your thick head? Everything costs more since the war started. Everything! I promised the back rent this weekend.'

Joe shook his head. 'They'll wait. They've waited afore.'

'Not this time. I have to pay tomorrow. Dear Lord – what have you done to us?'

Sarah watched, wide-eyed, as her mother sank into her chair.

Mary wrapped her arms about herself and rocked backwards and forwards in despair. Then she paused: 'The pig! You can kill the pig.'

Joe struggled to his feet, his expression outraged. 'That pig's staying where she is; until the fair. She's nowhere near ready for killing yet.'

'It doesn't matter. The butcher was asking me about her last week. He said he would give anything for a good bit of

34

pork. You'll have to, Joe. It's the only way. We have nothing else. We can't go out on to the street.'

Joe reached for his stick and Sarah saw her mother's form grow tense but, once he was steady on his feet, her father sighed and rubbed his head.

'You're always bloody right, Mary. Do you know? Sometimes I hate you for that.'

He closed his eyes. 'My head,' he complained. 'It's bursting.'

He looked round. 'Where's the lantern?'

Mary's expression changed. 'Not now, Joe. Tomorrow will do. First thing in the morning.'

'By God, no.' Joe straightened up. 'Kill the pig,' he mimicked. 'I'll kill the bloody thing. Might as well kill meself while I'm at it. Jim, where's Jim? He can help me.'

'You can't. It's dark, Joe. See Mr Mills in the morning. He wants the meat. He'll do the killing.'

'It's my pig. I'll kill it. Let me do that, at least.' He glanced wildly about the room. Sarah kept still but he noticed her.

'It's Sarah. Sarah's here. She'll help me.'

Mary put her hand to her mouth. 'I forgot . . . No, Joe, please.' She started forward. Her husband swung round and slapped her across her face. She fell against the table with a whimper of pain.

'Did you hear me, Sarey? Come on, get your coat on.' The bed covers were stripped from her and her father's face glared down at her. 'Hurry up!'

Sarah sat shivering on the side of the bed. She had never seen her father look so strange. His face was mottled with red and white patches and a thick vein throbbed and jumped at his temple.

'Me boots, Pa. They're in the scullery.'

'Well, get them.'

She fetched the boots, pushed her feet into them and clumsily knotted the laces with shaking fingers. She scuttled to the door and took down her coat from its nail, pulling it on over her nightdress. As her father crossed to take down a lantern from the shelf she looked across at her mother but Mary was slumped over the table and did not raise her head. There was no help there.

She flinched as Joe took her arm, propelling her through the scullery and into the darkness of the night. He paused and striking a match lit the lamp.

'Here. Carry this.'

It was a cold and lonely night with no moon. Just a few remote stars charted their shambling progress. Sarah had never been out so late before. She felt the chill dampness stroke her bare trembling legs. The boots were already rubbing a sore spot on her heel. She followed the huge figure of her father as he walked in front of her. His stick sounded sharp on the cobbles. He turned off the stubby street into a back lane which led directly to the allotments. She moved closer to him. Her father had frightened her tonight, but at least he was a familiar fear. The looming shapes which appeared and disappeared in the light of the lantern were infinitely more fearful because they were strange.

They were, she knew, merely outbuildings, piggeries and bushes, but at this strange hour they materialised into childish nightmares. They became ghosts, goblins and monsters.

The pig snorted at their approach, anticipating food. It slammed its heavy body against the gate, eyes gleaming. Sarah was glad of its nightmare strangeness. Deliberately she closed her mind to memories of scratching its back, feeding it peelings. She dreaded what was to happen next. The pig snorted and swung its heavy head towards the man.

'No, please. Don't, Pa!'

'It's your Mam's fault, gal. Always money. Poor little pig.'

He laughed, then spat and a globule of phlegm landed on Sarah's boot. She shrank back.

'We've got to eat, Sarey. We need money so the pig has to go. Pity. No prizes for me this year.'

Joe opened the gate and pushed Sarah before him. She shivered and the lantern she held swayed, throwing up wild dancing shadows on their surroundings.

'Hold the bloody thing still.'

Joe struck a match and lit the stub of a candle standing on a plank of wood. He put down his stick and felt beneath some old sacking at the rear of the shack.

'Here we are.'

He turned towards Sarah. In his hand he held an axe, the blade shone wickedly in the rays of the lantern.

He lunged towards the pig. The animal squealed and lumbered away from him. To the terrified child, the red-veined panicking eyes of the pig and the glare in the eyes of her father looked horribly similar.

'Hold the bloody light higher so I can see. Aye, that's better.' Joe was still strong. He grasped the pig by one ear and forced it down. Pulling at its snout, he dragged its head back then struck with the axe. There was a high-pitched screaming noise, then an enormous gush of blood. Joe stood back, satisfied.

'Grab that pail,' he ordered Sarah. 'Quick now. Catch the blood.'

For Sarah it was a scene out of hell. Her hand was shaking so much the light from the lantern wheeled crazily around her like a lighthouse beam gone mad. But more horror was to come. The pig had died instantly, but the message took time to reach the nerve ends. As Joe released the animal its head was hanging from its body, but the beast instinctively tried to flee, tottering a few steps towards where Sarah stood.

Her eyes opened wide with shock. She screamed. For one terror-stricken moment she was unable to move; then she dropped the lantern and fled. Leaving behind her Joe's curses, she raced down the back lane. The shadows now held no terrors worse than those behind her. She fell and scraped her knees, but was up in a moment, rasping sobs burning her chest. She remembered her boots clattering on the cobbles, her hands banging on the door, her mother's face, then nothing . . .

Cool hands sponged her face, placed a stone hot water bottle near her frozen feet. She sighed and opened her eyes to see her mother and Jim looking down at her. Her mother had an ugly red mark on her forehead and Jim's normally gentle face held a fierce anger. So much anger. She made a sound of protest, and his face changed back into the brother she loved. He stroked her hair.

'It's all right, love. Rest easy now.' He spoke across her to his mother. 'Let her stay there, Mam. I'll away to Bob Firman's for the rest of the night. No need to disturb the others. But what about him?'

Her mother sighed. 'You know what he's like. He's so mazed he doesn't know what he's doing half the time. Sarah's his favourite. He'll be so ashamed tomorrow. Best to leave it.'

'Well, if you're sure?'

'Aye.'

Mary bent down and kissed Sarah on the forehead. 'Go to sleep now, love.'

Sarah smiled and closed her eyes. It wasn't often Mam

kissed her. She heard the murmur of their voices then, worn out, fell into a deep sleep. Her dreams were restless. She awoke near morning and saw her mother asleep in a chair nearby.

Again she slept. Through her dreams she heard the click of the latch as the door opened. She stretched, she felt so tired but comfortable. But there was something she should remember. She half opened her eyes. Her father was looking down at her. Her mother's chair was empty.

She wondered vaguely why his face and hair were wet. His thick dark hair had formed into tight curls on his forehead. She yawned. He lowered himself quietly on the bed. His lovely blue eyes were full of tears.

'Oh, Sarey,' he said. 'I'm sorry, love. So sorry. Your old Pa didn't mean to frighten you.'

He touched her face. 'I wouldn't hurt you for all the world. My bonny little Sarah. My favourite lassie. You know that, don't you?'

She smiled.

He gave a sigh of relief and slid his arm beneath her shoulders.

'Still love your Pa, do you? Remember the games we played when you were little. Bears, we played, remember?' He growled softly and tickled her behind her ear. She smiled again and put up her hand to his damp hair. But something was surfacing in her mind, something troubled her.

'That's right, darling.' His voice was soft. 'Such a bonny baby, you were. Like an angel.' He laid his lips on her forehead and the weight of his body rested half across her. Sarah smelt the male smell of him, tobacco, beer and something else. Something sweet and cloying.

'Pa, get off. You're heavy.' She put her hands against his chest and pushed ineffectually.

'God you're dainty, so soft,' he breathed. His body started to move rhythmically and his hand touched her beneath the covers.

'Little Sarah,' he whispered.

She remembered. Her eyes snapped open. His face and hair were damp because of the pig. He had to wash, the blood had sprayed all over. Her body arched away from him. She could smell the blood. She remembered his eyes. She struck out blindly. This creature, his hands feeling her body, it wasn't her Pa. It was one of her monsters come horribly to life. She screamed.

'Joe. My God, stop . . .'

She heard her mother's voice. Mercifully her Pa's body shifted from her and again, there was nothing but blackness.

Chapter Five

'Don't worry, Sarah. The guard will look out for you and Aunt Blanche will meet you at York. See, you've got a corner seat.' Jim paused and bit his lip. He had never seen Sarah's eyes look so enormous, dark patches in her white face. He attempted a smile. 'Wish I was coming. Could do with a change.'

Sarah swallowed and grasped his hand tightly. 'I wish you was coming too,' she whispered.

The guard blew a whistle and they both jumped. Jim stood up.

'I'll have to go. Oh, come on, Sarah. Don't look like that. It's an adventure. There's big shops at York and you can go in a boat on the river. And there's the Minster. By, I'd like to see that.'

'You'll come and see me. Promise?'

Sarah's gaze clung to her brother's face. He hesitated. Then seeing her look of dismay, he pulled her towards him and gave her a violent hug.

'I promise. It will take time. I'll have to save up. But I will come and I'll write, often.'

Doors were being slammed. There was a warning hiss of steam. Jim opened the carriage door and jumped down. Sarah leant out of the window.

'Our Florence should be going. She's the eldest.'

'Aw, Sarah. Don't start that.' Jim looked up at her. 'Florence is going away to school. You know that.'

Sarah nodded. 'I know. But it's not just that. It's Mam, she wants me to go.'

'That's daft.' Jim thrust a packet towards her. 'Packed you these sandwiches didn't she? She'll miss you.'

'She didn't come to see me off.'

'You wanted me to. And you know she has a lot to do.'

'She didn't want to come,' insisted Sarah. But she took the sandwiches. With a jerk the train began to move and Jim stepped back and started to wave.

'Remember,' he shouted. 'I'll come to see you, Sarah; as soon as I can.' He watched until the train became a memory, a smudge of smoke lingering in the slate-grey winter sky. Then he left the station and trudged back along the road leading to the village.

There *was* something queer about the speed with which Sarah had been sent off to York. Mam had been so mad about Blanche's suggestion, yet now Sarah was going there, even though she had been so poorly. After the business with the pig she had raved in a fever. Dr Robertshaw had muttered about brain fever brought about by inflammation from her abscessed tooth.

Jim frowned. Mam had acted queer these past weeks. At least Pa had been quieter. He'd not been drunk since that night. But he'd been strange too. He avoided looking at people. Sarah had always been his favourite and yet he had hardly spoken to her, poor kid.

A chill breeze blew round Jim's thin figure and turned the tips of his ears red. He turned up his jacket collar and quickened his pace. Well, they wouldn't tell him anything, that's for sure. He felt a spurt of anger against his parents. There was something about Blanche – he hoped Sarah would settle there. He would have to tell Mam he intended saving a bit from his wages. He was determined to keep his promise and go to York as soon as he could.

Sarah sat up straight and listened to the clickity-click of the train wheels. She still couldn't believe she was going to live with Aunt Blanche. Things had changed so quickly. She remembered feeling ill. The doctor had come, so she must have been bad. But she was better now. If only she could remember. There was something about a lantern in the dark and she remembered banging on the door of the house but that was all.

She looked round the empty railway carriage. It smelt musty. She fixed her eyes on the picture of mountains above the seats opposite her and tried to remember. It was a bit like the time she had lifted a stone by the stream and underneath had lain a nest of grass snakes, all sticky, writhing and twisting in the mud. She had dropped the stone back on top of them with a cry of alarm. Now her mind was doing something like that, refusing to let her lift up the stone.

She looked out of the train window. The fields lay bare and forlorn. The noise of the train disturbed a flock of cawing rooks and they whirled into the sky like an explosion of soot from a chimney.

'I've done something,' she said aloud. 'Mam and Pa don't love me any more.'

Tears welled in her eyes. Mam had never been one for cuddling but she would re-tie your ribbons, twitch at your dress and rest her hand on your shoulder for a moment. And Pa, what had happened to his bearhugs and kisses? Now, he wouldn't even look at her.

She rubbed away the tears, then looked down at the

comic Jim had given her. It was called *Funny Wonder*. The corners of her mouth turned upwards as she saw the front page bore a strip featuring Charlie Chaplin. He was her favourite. Dear Jim. He would never change.

She glanced across at the opposite window. Her reflection stared back. She was awful pale. But she was pretty. Much prettier than Florence who had a big nose. Her spirits rose. Maybe Aunt Blanche chose her because she was pretty. After all, she had only the one boy. Perhaps she wanted a girl to dress up and take about with her. Maybe York would be good after all, and Jim could visit her then go back home and tell them all what a good time she was having.

York Station was huge. The high-vaulted ceiling and mass of people intimidated Sarah. She waited anxiously by the ticket barrier, clutching her battered suitcase and the packet of sandwiches she had not eaten. Suppose no one came? Her legs, unsteady after her illness, felt strange.

'Sarah? Sarah Armstrong?'

'Yes.'

'Thought it must be you. Come on.' A tall youth with greasy hair and pimples on his chin was staring at her.

She stared back. 'I have to wait for my auntie.'

'That's all right. Mam sent me. I'm your cousin, Jack. Let's be having you then.' Without waiting to see if she was following him, he dashed off. Sarah had to run to keep up with him.

'Wait,' she pleaded.

'You're a slowcoach, aren't you. Still, country folk are all slow.'

Sarah felt a flash of temper. 'I'm not slow. I've been ill.'

Her cousin slowed down. 'Thought you looked a bit

washed-out,' he said. 'Mam won't be pleased. You're coming to give her a hand, after all.'

'I'll be all right. Oh!'

They were outside the railway station now. Sarah caught her breath. She had never seen so much bustle; heard so much noise. Tram cars clanked their way along the road, motor cars honked and boys on bikes weaved their way through the traffic ringing their bells loudly. She was pleased to see a carthorse clop unconcernedly by.

She looked upwards at the stone walls gleaming in the fast-gathering dusk. 'Is that the Minster?'

Jack looked at her in amazement. 'Lord, where have you been? Them's the city walls. They go all the way round York. Minster's that way.'

He waved his arm vaguely towards the left. 'Our house is this way.'

When he eventually turned into a terrace of high, cramped houses Sarah felt nothing but relief. She had a stitch in her side and her case had banged against her knees as she had hurried after Jack, terrified in case she should lose him. She followed him down a dark alley leading to the rear of the house. They went through a backyard and in through a door.

'This way.'

She followed him down an oil-clothed passage smelling of damp and into a kitchen. Her first impression was one of clutter. The large dresser and table were burdened with boxes, ornaments and packages. 'Mottoes' – coloured strips of paper about nine inches long attesting to domestic joys: 'East, West, Home's Best' and 'Bless this House' – jostled with cut-glass scent bottles and pottery animals. Used to the sparse furnishings of her home, the colourful confusion seemed to Sarah's bemused eyes to resemble

Aladdin's Cave, but something was wrong. The objects, even to her young eyes, were tawdry. The colours were too bright, the materials cheap. A smell of tobacco smoke hung in the air overlying a fainter, more unpleasant smell of cheese or mice. Still, the fire was blazing and a kettle was singing on the hob. She put down her case with a sigh of relief.

'So Jack found you all right, did he?' Aunt Blanche rose from her seat by the fire. With heavy tread she approached Sarah.

Perhaps she will hug me, thought the child, or even kiss me.

Blanche did neither. She clicked her tongue and shook her head. 'I hope you are stronger than you look,' she said. She gestured towards the teapot perched on the corner of the table. 'Pour yourself a cuppa. It's second brewing but you have to expect that. The bloody war, everything scarce now. There's a piece of bread too. That will have to do you. When you've eaten you'd best go to bed. Look worn out, you do. Jack will show you where to sleep and he'll knock you up in the morning.'

Duty done, her aunt picked up a newspaper and returned to her seat by the fire. Sarah drank the tea thankfully but left the stale bread. She smiled shyly at the silent figure of Uncle Ted who sat opposite his wife. He blushed and his Adam's apple jerked nervously in his skinny neck as he nodded back to her, but he did not speak. Jack watched her mischievously. He didn't speak either. Only the ticking of the clock disturbed the silence.

'Finished?'

Sarah nodded.

'Come on then. I'll show you upstairs.' Jack rummaged on the dresser and produced a candle-holder with a stub of candle. 'We'll need this. We don't have gas on the top floor.'

She followed him up a flight of narrow stairs.

'Mam and Dad have that room.' He gestured towards a dark-brown door. 'I'm in here.'

Sarah looked round hopefully.

'You're up here.' They climbed another flight of stairs. He pushed open the door at the top. 'In here.'

Sarah hesitated in the doorway. She looked at the dingy attic room. The light came from an unscreened skylight set high in the roof. A few wispy cobwebs stirred in a draught. Patches of damp disfigured the plaster walls. The only furniture was a small bed in the corner of the room and a dilapidated chest of drawers. A rickety cane stool was by the bed and a marble-topped corner unit held a wash bowl and jug.

Jack watched her with malicious eyes. 'Home from home, isn't it?' he said. 'Don't look so worried. Mam will probably find you a rug and a few other things. It was all a bit of a rush, you see. We didn't know you were coming so soon. And she's been busy in the shop and hasn't much time. That's why you have to help her. Dare say you'll fix things up a bit. Well, sleep well.'

Placing the wavering candle on the chest of drawers, he clattered downstairs.

Sarah listened. It was quiet. She shivered – cold, too. She opened her case and took out a flannel nightdress. The water jug was empty and her fingers disturbed a thick film of dust on the rim of the basin. She climbed, unwashed, into the creaky bed and pulled the covers over her head. The bed felt damp. At home she was surrounded by family noises. Harry, whimpering or crowing in the next room, snatches of half-heard conversation from below. She

47

would have been spooned up against Florence's back listening to her faint snoring. Instead she was here. There was only silence. Or was there? She strained her ears. There was a faint scuttling noise. Was it a mouse or a huge hairy spider? She curled herself into a tight ball and put her fingers in her ears. Finally, she slept.

Chapter Six

She awoke with a start, rolled over and stared upwards. The sky showed blue through the attic window. It was June. She had been in York for six months and she was late again.

'Sarah!'

Jack bawled up the stairs: 'Come on, Sarah. Get up!'

She yawned and forced her reluctant body out of bed. She shook each item of clothing before dressing. The winter nights had been cold and miserable but warmer weather brought greater problems. The room had bugs. On discovering them she had been transfixed with horror. On being told Aunt Blanche had listened, then laughed.

'For goodness' sakes, lass, these are old houses. You get things like that in old houses. They'll not hurt you. What do you think they do, bite?' She had laughed again. 'Don't tell me your Mam never had a few bugs in that pokey house of yours.'

'She never did. We never had anything like that. Mam was always cleaning.' Not like you, Sarah had wanted to say but she kept silent, her eyes downcast.

But maybe Blanche could read her mind because her eyes went bright and hard as little glass buttons. 'There's worse things in life than bugs, madam. The sooner you realise that, the better.'

But there wasn't. Sarah loathed the brown crawling

things. She would sit up in bed, unwilling to blow out the candle, watching the scuttling little bodies and praying they would stay away from her. Then a boy at school told her, in graphic detail, about someone hc knew who had got a flea inside his ear.

'It jumped and jumped,' he said, his eyes gleaming, 'and almost drove him mad. They held a candle to his ear at last, and it hopped nearer and nearer the light until it jumped into the flame and crackled.'

Every night after that Sarah propped herself upright in bed and sat with her fingers in her ears, dozing off to sleep then starting awake again. No wonder she awoke each morning exhausted.

After dressing she looked into the water jug and pulled a face. She had forgotten to bring up fresh water again. The drop remaining in the jug gave off a sweetish odour. She dipped her fingers into the water and patted around her mouth. Her dark hair, dulled now from lack of washing, she tied back with a piece of string. Then, her scanty ablutions completed, she went downstairs.

'So, madam's decided to get up, has she?' Blanche padded across the kitchen with heavy steps. 'I'm away to the shop. A customer's calling in early. There's porridge ready. Ted made it afore he went out, but get Jack his packout done first.' She paused at the door: 'And tidy this place up afore you to to school. You're getting a lazy slut, Sarah. I didn't bring you here to stay in bed.'

The shop was really the front parlour of the house with a large window fitted. It, too, was a place of clutter. Cheap china ornaments jostled with shabby dining chairs. Candlesticks peered from behind dusty picture frames and stuffed birds, trapped forever inside glass-domed cases, glared wild-eyed at the depths to which they had descended. Sarah

hated the place and wondered how her aunt made any
money. But Blanche was shrewd. Amongst the confusion
lay the occasional treasure, a string of cool amber beads or
a delicate miniature. Many a knowledgeable dealer made it
his business to call in on Aunt Blanche. She also engaged in
a brisk business amongst the more humble of her neighbours: if the pawn shop was closed, Blanche Colley's place
was always open.

'Done me pack-out, Sarah?' Jack appeared in his work
clothes. Sarah noticed he had slicked back his hair with
water. Jack fancied himself as an expert on 'birds', both the
racing variety and the female sex. He was at present walking
out with a young woman who worked at the Penny Bazaar.

'It's here. Your Mam's managed to get some decent
bread.'

'Mam's got her connections.' Jack winked and went out,
slamming the door behind him.

Jack wasn't too bad, reflected Sarah as she fetched the
dustpan and broom from the cupboard. Nothing like Jim
of course, but at least he was cheerful.

She swept up then, to save time, lifted up the edge of the
faded Turkish carpet and deposited the dust underneath.
Then she washed the breakfast things, making little attempt
to remove the stubborn tea rings at the bottom of the cups.
Mam's standards didn't apply in this mucky place. Her
aunt never noticed whether she had done her tasks properly. As for Uncle Ted and Jack, they never bothered. They
were used to the dirt, she supposed. Her chores done, Sarah
put a dollop of porridge in a bowl and, standing by the
kitchen table, bolted it down. Blanche always managed to
acquire reasonable food although you never saw her standing for hours in the queues like everyone else. Uncle Ted
made good porridge.

Sarah couldn't make up her mind about Uncle Ted. He was a shadowy figure, slipping in and out of his own house and speaking only when spoken to. Blanche treated her husband with irritated affection. She never consulted him about anything but she always cooked him a meal and had it ready for him when he returned home from work. He would eat it silently, pour his tea into his saucer, slurp it back, suck the last drops from the ends of his gingery moustache and sit back with a contented sigh.

'That was champion, love,' he'd say.

Only once had Sarah seen another side to Uncle Ted. She had run down to Blossom Street, where he worked, with a message from her auntie. He was chiselling letters on a headstone and when he saw her watching him he had put down his tools and shown her round. He told her about the different kinds of lettering, Roman, Square Block and Medieval and about the different marble and granite he used. His eyes had lit up as he caressed the blocks of stone.

'This is the best, lass. Finnish Red they calls it. Beautiful granite, beautiful.'

He had straightened his shoulders and smiled at her, and he didn't look at all like the meek little man he was at home.

Sarah dropped her bowl on the table with a clatter. She was going to be late again. She grabbed her schoolbooks and ran towards the shop. Normally she left the house the back way, thereby avoiding her aunt and the stuffed birds because the latter always made her feel sad, but the shop way was quicker. Aunt Blanche stood by the window showing some hand-painted plates to a well-dressed gentleman. Sarah noticed that the drawer in which Blanche kept her money was open and she paused. A parsimonious woman, Blanche was also curiously careless in some ways. Sarah knew Jack often helped himself to the shop money and if

Blanche noticed she never mentioned it. Sarah hesitated then, almost involuntarily, she snatched a handful of silver coins and hurried past her aunt and the man, almost bumping into them in her panic to get away.

'Stupid fool,' Blanche raised her be-ringed hand then, remembering her client, changed the gesture to one of patting her smooth hair.

'My sister's girl. I'm raising her. Well, you do what you can, don't you?

Sarah caught the words as she fled through the open door. She ran towards the school until the pain in her side forced her to slow to a walk. She felt the weight of the money in her pocket and tears stung her eyes. What would Mam say if ever she found out? They had sent her away because she was bad and now she had proved them right. God would surely punish her.

The school came into sight. She could hear the sound of the assembly bell. She began to run again. God could do what He liked. He had put her in this rotten place. Being here had made her wicked. She hated her auntie. She hated the children at school. They laughed at her and said she was stupid because she sometimes fell asleep at her desk. She knew they whispered about her being dirty. Well, she was.

Tears of self pity filled her eyes. They would be dirty, too, if they had to blacklead the grate and clean the house and sleep in a room running wick with bugs. Their mams looked after them. Her mam had sent her away. She raised her head defiantly. God could forsake her for being a sinner. She was better off without Him.

The school day was drawing to a close. Miss Russell, a pretty young woman and teacher of IIB, paused before ringing the leaving bell. She looked across the rows of desks, the studiously bent heads of her pupils, to Sarah Armstrong seated at the back of the room. The child was becoming more unkempt and miserable looking. Miss Russell made up her mind.

'Sarah. Stop behind the others. I wish to speak to you.' Then she swung the hand bell. 'Class dismissed.'

The forty-odd pupils made their usual dash to freedom. Seconds later the room was empty except for Sarah, immobile in her seat, a scared expression on her face. Miss Russell walked up to her and sat on a nearby desk.

'Now, Sarah. We need to sort a few things out.'

'I got the money for my birthday, miss. My mam sent it.'

'Money?' Miss Russell remembered. She had seen Sarah earlier in the day passing out sweets to the other children in the tiny playground. She had noticed particularly because it was strange to see the girl in the middle of a crowd. Normally she was hanging about on the fringe of any activity.

'Two shillings, miss. From my mam.'

'I'm not interested in money, Sarah. I want to talk about your work.'

Instead of looking worried Sarah looked relieved. 'Yes, miss.'

'You were late to school again.'

'Yes, miss.'

The teacher felt a spurt of annoyance. It was like addressing a stone wall. She looked at the grubby pinafore, the rough hands with the finger nails bitten to the quick.

'No wonder you are so far down the class, Sarah. You miss such a lot.' She hesitated. 'You are quite a pretty girl, you know. Why don't you take a little more pride in your appearance. Brush your hair, things like that?'

Sarah gazed impassively in front of her.

Miss Russell floundered on. 'Do you like it here in York?'

'It's all right.'

'I saw your auntie yesterday. It is the first time I have met her. I believe she doesn't get out much?'

Sarah's eyes narrowed. 'She's usually in the shop, and . . .' her voice flattened, 'she's too fat to walk far.'

'She says you come from Swaithdown. Do you manage to see your family often?'

The girl bent her head. 'No.'

Miss Russell looked at the thin vunerable neck showing a definite tidemark of dirt and felt a pang of sympathy. She decided to pay a call on Mrs Colley.

'That's a pity. Still, your aunt mentioned that your brother is coming through to see you on Saturday. You will be looking forward to that?'

Sarah looked up and Miss Russell caught her breath. The child wasn't just bonny, she was beautiful. Her blue eyes sparkled and a delicate pink tinged her pale face.

'Saturday? Jim's coming Saturday? Oh, miss. Can I go now?'

Miss Russell assented and watched her pupil run from the room. Obviously she had over-reacted over the welfare of the child. She was probably just moody. She certainly looked radiant now. She dismissed Sarah from her mind and returned to the front of the classroom to clean the chalk from the blackboard. The small worry of Sarah was replaced in her mind by a much larger one. She wondered again if Robert, her fiancé, had embarked yet for France . . .

Sarah burst into the kitchen and halted in front of Blanche who was making a cup of tea.

'Jim's coming, isn't he?'

'My God, news does travel fast.' Blanche picked up her bag and extracted a letter. 'Here you are.'

Sarah grabbed the envelope from her. 'It's addressed to me. Why did you open it?'

Blanche fixed her niece with a cold eye. 'I open all the letters that come to this house. You know that.'

Sarah did not reply. She was painstakingly shaping the words with her mouth. 'It's right. He's coming. Saturday.' She grinned at her auntie and disappeared from the kitchen as rapidly as she had appeared.

Blanche sighed and scratched beneath her huge bosom. 'She's getting to be a looker, that one,' she muttered. 'Have to watch our Jack and no mistake. Leastways, I'll not have to worry about Ted.' And she sighed again as, with a touch of regret, she contemplated the quiet little man to whom she was married.

Chapter Seven

After the darkness of the cinema the afternoon sun dazzled the eyes. Sarah blinked and grasped her brother's arm as they left the picture house. Her face was soft with dreams. Her thoughts were entangled with the magical world they had just left.

'Oh, Jimmy. It was wonderful. When Pearl White was fastened to the railway line, I nearly died!'

'Don't be silly. It was only pretend. Don't think they would really risk her getting killed, do you?' Jim spoke with the worldly cynicism of a fifteen-year-old but he, too, had been awed by their trip to see moving pictures.

They walked down the street and turned into Whip-ma Whop-ma Gate. An open-topped, horse-drawn bus passed them and Sarah turned hopefully towards Jim but to no avail. He had just caught sight of an ornamental clock in the front of a watch-maker's shop and his face sharpened as time punctured his daydreams.

'We'll have to go back, Sarah. My train goes at six and I've hardly seen Auntie Blanche and Uncle Ted.'

Sarah ducked her head and her fingers tightened on his sleeve. He gave her a troubled look. 'If we go down these steps we reach the river, don't we? Let's go there and have a bit of a talk.'

They descended the stone steps, passed a riverside pub

and strolled along the grassy banks edging the river. A woman walking her dog passed by and smiled at them, otherwise they were alone.

Jim stole another glance at Sarah. He had been reassured when she had met him at the railway station. She was thin, but she had grown a couple of inches and her expression had been happy. Her ill-spelt and unhappy letters had, he thought, merely been brought about by homesickness. Sarah had always dramatised things and it was obvious she had made up her mind not to like York.

But now his doubts returned. His once vivacious little sister looked pale and listless and none too clean. Saving for this day had been difficult, but he had done it because he had wanted to reassure himself of her well-being. Now, he thought, he would go away more anxious than before.

'You've not asked about home?' he said in an abrupt voice.

Sarah picked up a stone and threw it into the river. She answered his question with one of her own. 'Have they said if I can come home?'

Jim sat down on the grass. He reached for her hand and pulled her down beside him.

'Oh, Sarah, you know it's not that simple.'

'Why?'

'Because it isn't.' He frowned. How could he explain? 'We all miss you.'

She sniffed, disbelieving him.

'We do. But home's not like it used to be. Money's real tight, Mam's at her wits' end. There's rows all the time.' He swallowed but went on steadily. 'Pa's bad, Sarah. He drinks most of the time and shouts and goes on. Florence is away now, but poor Arthur and Harry – it's rotten for them. Arthur's got a stutter now. It's all because of Pa.'

'He'd be better if I were home. He was always good with me.' Sarah was staring down at her hands, her face crimson.

'No. You're much better here . . .'

'*I'm not!* I hate it here.' Sarah spoke in gasps. 'You don't know; Aunt Blanche is mean and dirty. She sends me to school in old clothes. I get teased. Nobody likes me. The teachers think I'm a dunce. I can't seem to think. Pa would get better if I were home. You know he would. Why can't I come home?' She put her hands over her face and wept.

'Oh, don't cry, love. Don't cry.' Jim pulled her into his arms. His own eyes pricked with tears. She should be home with the rest of them. It wasn't fair, he thought.

'Come on. It can't be so terrible. Does she hit you? Do you get enough to eat?'

Sarah gulped and rubbed her nose with the back of her hand. 'Well, there's enough food. She hits me sometimes.' A glimmer of a smile showed. 'When she can catch me. But I have no friends here, Jim. And I have to do all the house-work and . . .' she paused dramatically, 'there are bugs in my room!'

Jim's eyes crinkled. 'Well, I reckon we can do something about that,' he said. 'And I'll have a word with her about your clothes. But you are going to have to try too.'

She looked at him, silent, her eyes large.

'Now listen, Sarah. This is important.' He stared across the calm river a moment, then said, 'You know I'm still down the mine?'

She nodded.

'You probably know I hate it, too. But you can't know *how* much I hate it, Sarah.' His voice deepened with emotion. 'It's so black and hot. It smells awful down there. Sometimes the seams are running with water. Sometimes you feel you will never come up again. In the summer, it's worse. You leave the sun and the wind and go down there.'

He bent forward, hugging his knees. His face was sombre. He had almost forgotten his sister.

'It's not right. We're like animals down there. We're almost naked you know. It's so hot we strip off to our drawers. We look like savages or,' a bleak smile flittered across his face, 'lost souls in hell.'

He was silent a moment then, recollecting his audience, attempted a smile.

'They don't all feel like me, of course. They compete to see who can cut the most coal. They sing and joke. I suppose Pa was like that. They're hard, but they rely on each other. I like that, but I have to get out, Sarah.' He turned to face her. 'I've started going to classes. They are held at the Mechanics' Institute in the evenings. There's a teacher; he was once a collier. If he can do it, I can too.'

His eyes brightened with excitement and Sarah smiled in sympathy.

'But it will take years to be a teacher, won't it, Jimmy, and what about money?'

He sighed. 'I don't know if I'll be a teacher exactly. I just know I have to get more education. Then I'll be ready. I'm going to do something with my life, Sarah. And you have to do something with yours.'

'But I'm not clever. What can I do?'

They stared at each other then Jim grinned and tousled her hair.

'You'll land on your feet. You're that kind of person. Don't you know that?'

Sarah grimaced. 'Not in York, I won't.'

He gave her an exasperated look.

'That's up to you. Look, I trail off to classes after work

when I'm tired out. The pit lads think I'm crazy but I still
go.'

She looked at him blankly.

'You say Blanche is dirty. Think, Sarah! You don't have
to be, too. Tidy yourself up a bit. Look at you! I bet it's ages
since you washed your neck properly.'

A tide of colour spread over Sarah's face. 'I did tidy up,'
she mumbled. 'Because you were coming.'

Jim longed to hug her, but he kept his voice stern.

'Well, you didn't do a very good job. Come on, Sarah.
You can get your hands on a bit of soap and water, can't
you? You'll have friends if you look a bit better. You've got
to fight. Think of the chaps in the trenches fighting the
Germans. I'm fighting by going to night classes. You can
fight Blanche by being polite but not giving in to her.'

Sarah's eyes were beginning to dance. Jim was delighted
to see a hint of devilment in them. He had thought perhaps
it had gone for ever.

'I'll try, Jim. I really will. But she is nasty.'

He nodded. He sensed a bad atmosphere around his
aunt. She seemed on first acquaintance to be a jolly, plump
woman, but there was an emptiness within her. He shook
his head then sprang up and pulled Sarah to her feet.

'So remember. When I'm gone – keep fighting. Now,
come on.'

'Where are we going?'

'Back to Blanche's, but first . . .' he grinned, 'I've
got my train ticket and three pennies. Do you know what
we are going to do? We are starting as we mean to go on.
We are going to the nearest grocer to buy a packet of
"sulphur candles". We are going to kill off those bugs of
yours.'

* * *

Blanche breathed heavily as she rested in her chair. That little tyke Jim Armstrong had upset her. So his precious sister needed new clothes, did she? Well, she'd fettle her. She threw a vindictive glance towards Sarah who was peeling potatoes at the kitchen sink. There was a pert tilt to the girl's head. Blanche swallowed. She felt queasy. The meat at dinner time; it must have been off. Even her contacts in the black market were letting her down nowadays. Dark red, it had been, probably horsemeat. Ted constantly worried her, reading aloud from the newspaper about the bloody war. Conscription was coming, he said. Single men would be called up first. If it went on much longer her darling Jack would be taken. A giant hand squeezed her chest.

'Gawd love us,' she said, and belched.

Blanche was a selfish woman. All her life she had pursued one goal, her own bodily comfort. To this end she had married Ted Colley. A woman needed a husband; preferably an easily managed chap with a bit of brass. Ted had suited the bill admirably. He now danced to her tune and she rarely thought about him. But Jack was different. He was flesh of her flesh, a part of her. Jack was the chink in her impenetrable armour. He was her joy. He was exactly like her. He didn't give a damn for anyone including his mother and she rejoiced. Jack was strong. He'd be all right so long as the bloody war didn't get him.

She rubbed her chest. A feeling of impotence weighed down upon her. That pipsqueak of a collier wouldn't be forced into the trenches. He was safe down the pit. He'd made her feel right uncomfortable. She was bringing up his sister wasn't she? That skinny lad looking at her with contemptuous eyes. Why, her Jack was twice the man he was.

As if on cue, Jack swaggered into the room. He wore his

best jacket and the aroma of cheap brilliantine hung about him.

'Lend us a few bob, Ma. There's a new show on at the Music Hall and I've said I'll take Mavis Wright.'

'Me bag's there, son. Help yourself.'

The pain eased slightly. Jack's careless confidence in his own invincibility chased away her bleak thoughts. The war would never get Jack.

'Watch what you're up to with that lass,' she called after him.

He winked at her before closing the door.

She listened to the sound of his footsteps retreating down the passage. Mavis Wright was a stupid girl, but no doubt Jack would have a few like her before he finally settled down. Blanche leant back in her chair and her thoughts returned to her grievances.

That Jim Armstrong, precious few lassies would look his way. She sniffed. With his wrists sticking out of his outgrown jacket and those blue marks on his hands, scars from minor mishaps down the pit, he'd find it hard to get himself a sweetheart. Perhaps that's why he fussed around Sarah so much.

'I've done the veg, Auntie. Is that all?'

'Aye. But don't go running off yet.' Blanche stared at the girl and rubbed her chin with fat fingers. 'That brother of yours, he says you need new clothes?' She waited but Sarah remained silent.

Blanche smiled. 'Reckon he's right. I've been too busy to notice how much you've grown. Anyways, I know where there is just the thing.' She waved her hand in the direction of the shop.

'There's a brown paper parcel on the back shelf. Fetch it.' Sarah hurried through the shop. She returned a moment later clutching a large parcel. She turned an expectant face towards her aunt.

'Is it for me? Can I open it?'

'Yes, yes. You open it.'

Blanche folded her hands together and watched. Her face expressionless, she saw the dismay dawn in Sarah's face. The girl lifted the clothes from the brown paper.

'But, Auntie . . .'

'What?'

Sarah held the costume jacket against her meagre chest. 'I can't wear this. People don't wear clothes like this anymore.'

The velvet suit had been made for a mature woman. The blue material had once been handsome, but parts were now scuffed and faded. The style was of the turn of the century. The jacket was fastened with dozens of tiny buttons and bands of tarnished gold frogging embellished the sleeves. Sarah picked up the long skirt and shook out the folds of material.

'I can't wear it,' she repeated.

A faint smile flickered over Blanche's face. 'Nonsense. It only needs a bit of alteration. Take that gold stuff off and take up the skirt. There's a lot of wear left in that suit. Quality stuff, it is.'

A nerve jumped in Sarah's cheek. She grasped the skirt so tightly her knuckles cracked. 'I won't wear it,' she said.

There was a cough and the rustle of a newspaper. Both Blanche and Sarah looked round in surprise. Ted Colley was such a silent man he was apt to be completely overlooked.

'It does seem a bit old for Sarah, love.'

Ugly red patches flared on Blanche's face. Her eyes narrowed. 'What do you know about it, Ted? It's me that has to clothe the child. Me that has to scrimp and scrape to keep this household going. The amount of brass you bring home wouldn't keep a mouse.' She stood up and pressed her hand to her side. 'I do my best!' she shouted. 'Now me own husband's taking against me. Do my best for everyone and what thanks do I get, tell me?'

Ted cast a terrified glance at his wife and disappeared behind his newspaper again. 'See there's been a raid on London,' he said in a muffled voice. 'Zeppelin, it was. Seems not even civilians are safe now. Terrible thing, war.'

Her eyes gleaming with the joy of battle, Blanche looked away from him and back at Sarah. Her feeling of satisfaction ebbed slightly and was diluted by a sense of unease.

The girl stared straight back at her and the expression in her eyes was as hard and implacable as her own.

Chapter Eight

Sarah and her uncle drank their tea in comfortable silence. She glanced across at the little man and smiled. You could always tell when he was relaxed: his Adam's apple ceased its jerky dance. Blanche was visiting Jack, his wife Doris and their new baby. How lovely it would be, thought Sarah, if she stayed there. But the idea was foolish. Blanche would not close the shop for more than a couple of days, even for Jack.

'Oh, Lordie.' She noticed the time. 'I'll have to dash.' She jumped up, draped a scarf around her neck and put on her coat.

'Wrap up when you go, Uncle Ted. It's cold this morning.'

'I will, lass.'

'Bye, then.'

As she left the house Ted looked through the window at the lowering sky. By the look of things, she was going to get wet. He sighed. She was a good 'un and no mistake. Over five years she'd been living with them. He could hardly believe it was so long. But there it was, life slipped away like a swallow of ale and to prove it, he now had a grandson. Funny little scrap. He wished the new arrival luck. He'd need it with Jack for a dad and Doris – well, she was all right but not the brightest of girls. Blanche would rule that

67

roost. Still, a grandson would please his wife and maybe make Sarah's life a bit easier.

She was sixteen now, but still a slip of a lass. Right bonny, too, with those huge blue eyes. Ted sighed again. Blanche had been fifteen when he had first met her. She'd been bonny, too: pink and white with soft curves and hair so dark it held the sheen of a blackbird's wing. He'd never understood why she'd taken him. Five years he had courted her then, suddenly, she had accepted him. He'd been so happy. She'd picked him, plain, dull Ted Colley. He'd soon realised why. She'd never loved him at all. The light in her eyes had been greed, not love.

He pulled the newspaper out of his boots and felt inside. Aye, they'd dried out all right. November was a miserable month, nothing but grey skies and rain. He pulled them on and bent to lace them up. Funny how he kept thinking about the past. It was the baby coming, he supposed. Blanche might have been different if she'd had more bairns, but she wouldn't. Didn't hold with that side of marriage at all. My God, when he'd been younger, a right state he had got himself into sometimes, but it wasn't right to force a woman, not if she was unwilling.

He rubbed his chin in a state of perplexed agitation. If he had been a strong, rough kind of bloke maybe she would have been happier. As it was, she'd grown meaner through the years.

Sarah, now, she was little but she had guts. She stood up to Blanche, but it caused a lot of hassle and, he guessed, a few tears. Pity she'd never gone back home to live. Funny business, that. Still, she'd spent the last two Christmases there, so that was something.

He stood up and reached for his cap. Human beings were too damn complicated. He was better off at work chipping away at the granite. Knew where you were with marble and suchlike, much simpler than flesh and blood.

Sarah hurried down the street, glad the wind was keeping the rain at bay. She crossed Lendal Bridge and paused to look down into the sluggish pewter-grey river. Much more of this rain and the town would be flooding again. A slap of wind ruffled the water into vicious little waves. She shivered. A feeling of foreboding swept over her. It was strange, she had felt a similar feeling on waking. She chided herself. She was being ridiculous. But a shadow of fear remained as she passed beneath Bootham Bar.

The Minster loomed before her; a symbol of man's struggle for spirituality, a psalm in stone. Sarah did not appreciate the soaring towers, she looked instead at the old and handicapped men congregating near the steps, clutching their trays of matches and bootlaces. Two years since the war had ended and they were still waiting for a land fit for heroes. Sarah dropped a few pennies into a box held by a one-legged man and shook her head as he offered her a box of matches.

Goodbye to the new pair of gloves. After Blanche had taken her cut from Sarah's wages and four shillings had been sent off home, there was precious little left. Still, she was one of the lucky ones, she had a job.

She turned into the entrance of Preston's Bakery. It was good to be out of the wind. She washed her hands and donned her overall, pushed open the door into the packing room and went in. She had worked here over two years, ever since leaving school. It wasn't so bad. On Saturdays she had to be in by six because the bread, cakes and biscuits had to be in the shops early but the rest of the week she started at seven. It was hard work, but she enjoyed dashing about packing the orders and checking them off from the large printed sheets pinned up on the walls.

'You cut it fine.' Ruby Tyler dumped a box of biscuits on to the work table and grinned at her. 'Mrs Harland's been looking at her watch and tut-tutting. She'll be docking your wages if you don't watch out.'

Sarah glanced towards the window behind which the supervisor watched her girls with an eagle's eye.

'She kept me late yesterday so I don't see she has any need to complain.' She pulled a tray of bread loaves towards her and, with practised hands, flipped them into the waiting boxes.

Ruby lowered her voice to a conspiratorial whisper. 'Can you get out tonight, Sarah? Go on, say you will. Come into town.'

'Why, what's happening?'

'There's Mormons in town. You know, those blokes who have a lot of wives.' Ruby giggled. 'They are from America and they are preaching in town tonight.'

'What are they doing in York? Run out of women in America, have they?'

Ruby looked hurt. 'Aw, don't get sarky. Wouldn't you like to see them, Sarah? It will be good fun.' Her eyes grew round with excitement. 'They have long beards and some of them wear cloaks. The younger ones are quite handsome.'

She put her head close to Sarah. 'Ron Webb, from packing, says they are holding meetings at the corner of Coney Street and they might go near the Monkey Run. If they do, Ron says there will be trouble because they're out to pinch York girls to take them back to America and he says why can't they stick to one wife each like decent folk do.'

'Why indeed.' Sarah smiled to herself. She thought briefly of Uncle Ted. What would he do with four wives? 'I might come, Ruby. I'll tell you later. Now, you'd better get on. Mrs Harland's tapping on the glass.'

Ruby scurried away and Sarah continued her work. Her thoughts moved as deftly as her fingers.

She didn't often walk the Monkey Run, the place for meeting members of the opposite sex, with the other girls. That was why some of them considered her 'stuck up'. If only they realised she didn't go because she had nothing to wear. It was all right for them, dressed in their shorter skirts and new lisle stockings. Proper frump she'd look in her working clothes and black stockings. What bloke would look at her?

She frowned. They'd notice her if she had a decent frock. Oh well, at least she wasn't a laughing stock, like she had been at school. She had Uncle Ted to thank for that. Her lips curved into a smile as she remembered. Was it really five years ago?

That terrible velvet costume. She had been draping it from the mantelshelf, deliberately allowing the sleeves to fall near the fire when her uncle had entered the room. He had approached her quietly and her heart had almost jumped out of her mouth when he had spoken.

'My, that's a pity,' he had said. 'Bit of good material, that.' Together, they watched the cloth smoulder, char and dissolve into a gaping hole.

'Don't reckon it will be fit to wear no more.'

He had looked at her, a glimmer of amusement in his watery blue eyes. 'Bit careless of you, lass.'

'I did it on purpose.' She had stuck her chin out in a defiant pose. 'They laugh at me when I wear it. The boys at school . . .' she choked, hatred for the costume and her aunt welling within her. 'They pretend to hobble after me, like I was an old woman. I hide, Uncle Ted.

71

Stand in back alleys where no one can see me.' She had clasped her hands together and looked at him with tragic eyes.

He had cleared his throat. 'Aye, well. Reckon you'll need something to wear for school.' He had put his hand into his trouser pocket and produced a banknote. 'Here, take this. It's not a lot, but it will buy you a skirt and jersey, or something.'

She had hesitated. Uncle Ted, she knew, had one secret vice which he had succeeded in keeping from Blanche. He loved a flutter on the dogs, and about every three months he managed a couple of hours at the dog track. He was giving her his stake money. He gave her a push.

'Go on, lass. She'll be back soon and if this is to be an accident I reckon we'd better scarper. If she asks about the new stuff you can say your Jim sent you the brass, but she'll probably not bother.' He sighed. 'As long as she don't have to foot the bill.'

She had taken the money, given him a brief smile, then left the house like a whirlwind. Dear Uncle Ted, what would she have done without him?

The whistle for the teabreak broke into her thoughts. She stretched. She was ready for a rest. Lifting heavy trays and wire baskets about was no joke. The tea was strong and hot, just as she liked it. She sipped appreciatively. Ruby threaded her way through the other girls and came to sit next to her. A big-boned, jolly girl, she regarded Sarah with affection and a touch of awe. Her friend's shifts of mood disconcerted her, but Ruby enjoyed her liveliness and good looks. Because Sarah was definitely a 'looker' even if she did wear dowdy clothes.

'Are you coming? Aw, go on, Sarah?'

Sarah laughed. 'Oh, all right.'

Ruby squeezed her arm. 'Tell you what, come for tea. Mam won't mind, honest.'

Ruby's workmates couldn't understand her friendship with Sarah Armstrong, but Ruby had a mind of her own. And her mam knew Blanche Colley. Ruby's family were noisy and rough but they were happy. Ruby's younger brothers and sister were slapped, cuddled, shouted at and kissed in equal proportions. Ruby would see Sarah's normally tense figure relax, her expression soften when she visited them.

'I'll buy one of the damaged cakes if you're coming,' she said.

But Ruby never got to buy the cake. Early in the afternoon, when the rush of work had ceased and the girls were scrubbing down the tables and stacking the cake racks for the following day, the supervisor tapped on her window and beckoned to Sarah.

'What's up?' Ruby mouthed to Sarah.

She shook her head. She remembered her feeling on the bridge, and her fingers trembled as she tidied her hair and crossed to the office.

'There's been an urgent message for you.' Mrs Harland's expression was mask-like and the light, glinting off her spectacles, threw back an eerie blankness. 'You are to return home immediately. Bad news, I'm afraid. I don't know the details.'

Sarah's face turned paper white. She stared at Mrs Harland then, without replying, turned and ran from the room. She pushed through the staring girls, snatched her outdoor things and left. A murmur spread through her workmates. Something was up! There was a lip-smacking buzz of conversation. Their lives were drab. A bit of drama was welcomed as long as the bad news was for someone else. Only Ruby remained silent, her heavy features screwed up into an expression of concern for her friend.

Breathing jerkily Sarah half walked, half ran down Nunnery Lane. She was desperate to know what had happened, but her first headlong dash had given her stitch in her side and she had been forced to slow down.

Yet in one way she was reluctant to reach home. What had happened?

Pa was ill, she decided. Her childhood adoration of her father had long since faded. On her last visit, eleven months ago, she had been shocked to see his deterioration. To observe the be-fuddled, raving tyrant he had become had proved painful. She preferred not to think of him at all.

She crossed the road and the strong wind caught her slight figure and buffeted her across the pavement. The ends of her scarf broke free and whipped across her face, imitating the flying autumn leaves which were being snatched from the trees by the careless hand of nature.

Maybe Florence had been involved in an accident? Florence was teacher training now and was lead singer in a famous church choir. Perhaps that was it. Her footsteps slowed. Perhaps Mam? The thought of Mam being seriously ill was unimaginable. Mam had sent her away but now Sarah was old enough to realise Mam was the one who held the family together. One name she would not allow herself to formulate. An abyss yawned at her feet. She began to run again.

Aunt Blanche was waiting when she let herself into the house. Sarah glanced fearfully into her face. Blanche stood in the middle of the kitchen. She was still wearing her hat and coat. Her face betrayed nothing but annoyance.

'You took your time.'

'I had no money for the tram. Tell me, Auntie?'

'Bloody telegram boy, running about, knocking on doors. The neighbours will love that.' She sniffed. 'Anyway, Mrs Rush sent him to our Jack's. Give us a right turn and poor Doris still in childbed.'

Sarah thought she would scream. 'For God's sake,' she said, 'tell me.'

Blanche pressed her lips together. She stared coldly at the girl. 'There's no need to blaspheme,' she said primly and then handed Sarah a crumpled telegram.

Sarah smoothed out the flimsy paper: COME HOME AT ONCE. JIM VERY ILL.

The telegram dropped to the floor. She swayed. There was a roaring sound in her ears. I must not faint. I must not faint, she said to herself.

'I've got to go home.' She moved to pass her aunt but the older woman caught hold of her wrist and held her.

'So you'll be dashing straight off, will you?'

Sarah gave her an uncomprehending look.

'Going – just like that. You know I'm staying at Jack's. Who'll see to things here?'

Sarah pulled away. 'Let me go.'

'Five years I've looked after you, and a right trial you've been too. You don't just go dashing off. You can go tomorrow when I've sorted things out. And where's the money coming for your fare?'

Sarah's anguish ignited into passion. She swung her free hand back and slapped Blanche hard across her face.

'You old bitch! I'm going right now and I'm never coming back, do you hear? You looked after me! I've been your unpaid skivvy for years. But no more. I've finished.' She pulled her arm free from Blanche's suddenly flaccid hand. Her aunt's face had gone slack with disbelief.

'I'm catching the next train home,' continued Sarah, 'and I'm taking the money for the fare and five pounds from the till.' Her dark eyes gleamed venomously: 'You owe me that.'

She brushed past her aunt and ran upstairs. Her breath came unevenly as she flung her few belongings into a case. Without a second glance she slammed shut the attic door and rushed back down the uncarpeted staircase. Blanche stood in the same position, her podgy hand resting at her throat. The light from the lamp on the table caught the fine stones in her rings causing them to sparkle and flash.

If Mam had owned just one of those, thought Sarah, everything might have been different. I'd have stayed at home and Jim . . . A gush of nausea filled her mouth and she turned away. She went through to the shop and opened the drawer.

'One five-pound note, Auntie.' She returned and waved the money in front of Blanche. 'One pound for every year – fair enough, don't you think?'

Blanche had recovered some of her equilibrium. 'Go, and good riddance to you,' she whispered. 'Nothing but trouble, you and that brother of yours.' She fell silent at the look in Sarah's eyes, but the girl did not speak.

Sarah turned and walked out of the house. A tram was slowing at the end of the street. She ran to board it. The conductor glanced curiously at the young woman with the case and the stricken look in her eyes.

'All right, love?'

'Yes. Railway station, please. Do you know when the next north-bound train leaves. I must get to Swaithdown.'

'Oh, they're pretty frequent. My lad, he works on the railway. There'll be one in about half an hour, I reckon.'

Sarah nodded her thanks and turned to stare out of the window.

She strove to calm her worse fears. Jim couldn't be that bad. Why, she hadn't even known he was ill. They would have told her. Her fingers drummed on the suitcase. Jim was a fighter, he was tough. He had endured all these years down the pit. And he had studied so hard. In his last letter he had mentioned final exams. He was making all kinds of plans. A sob rose in her throat. He had to get well. Why was the tram so slow? Childishly she knuckled her eyes. Please God, she prayed, let Jim get better. I'll be good for the rest of my life if only Jim gets better.

Chapter Nine

'Thanks for giving me a lift, Mr Smailes.'

'That's all right, lass. Lucky I saw you at t' station.' The milkman turned his weatherbeaten face towards her. 'Your Mam'll be right glad to see you. And our Lucy will, too. I'll tell her you're back. She'll be coming round to see you no doubt. That is . . .' His voice faded away and he gave an embarrassed cough.

'How is Lucy, Mr Smailes?' Sarah gripped her hands together and strove to keep her voice steady.

'Fine. She's fine. Got a young chap dangling after her now. Jackie Lawrence. You know him; used to be in your class at school?'

'Yes, I think so.' Sarah shifted upon her wooden seat restlessly. In a few moments she would be there.

'Here we are.' Mr Smailes jumped down and held out his hands to steady Sarah as she alighted from the milk cart. 'Wish it were a happier home-coming for you, lassie.' He shook his head as he climbed back on to the cart and took up the reins. 'Give my regards to your Mam. Tell her . . . anything I can do.'

'Thanks, I will.'

He clicked his tongue and the old horse pricked his ears and ambled down Joshua Street. Darkness was gathering and the white-stoned steps glimmered bravely in the gloom.

Sarah took a deep breath and turned towards Number 29. The door opened.

'Come in, quickly. I'm trying to keep the place warm.' The normality of her mother's voice reassured her. She stepped inside and looked around the familiar room. Everything was spotless. Indeed, Mary Armstrong, when threatened with disaster, cleaned with increased ferocity. The lamplight glanced kindly off pots and pans, the rugs looked newly washed and a pleasing tangy scent freshened the air. By the side of Jim's bed stood a blue earthenware jug holding three shaggy-headed chrysanthemums.

Jim was asleep. His face was turned towards the wall. Sarah noticed how his gaunt figure barely raised the crisp white bed-cover and his erratic breathing rasped through the quiet room.

Mary said, in a quiet voice, 'Doctor came this morning. He says it's pneumonia. He wasn't too hopeful but I must say, the lad seems easier now.' She shook her head as she saw the spark of hope leap in Sarah's eyes. 'Don't build too much on it, lass. He's awful bad. Still, we must hope and pray.' She bent over Jim and listened to his breathing then straightened and looked at Sarah.

'Get that coat off and sit by the fire. You look nithered. I'll get some tea.'

Sarah put down her case, slipped off her coat and sat down. She stretched her hands gratefully towards the fire.

'Where is everyone?'

'Florence is home. I've fixed for Harry and her to stay next door though, keeps it quieter here. Arthur came yesterday, but seeing how Jim seems a little better he's gone back to the Hall. He's getting a couple of hours off tomorrow.'

Sarah nodded. She knew Arthur had recently gained

employment as an under footman at Hazelbury Hall and was shaping up well.

'Where's Pa?'

Mary brought two mugs of tea and sat down opposite her. 'He's chasing round seeing if he can get something off next week's pension money. Without Jim's wages, it's difficult.'

'I have some money, Mam.' Sarah thought briefly of Blanche and the five-pound note. 'But tell me about Jim. Why didn't you write and let me know he was ill?'

Mary looked towards her son. 'He wouldn't let me worry you. He's had trouble with his breath for weeks. You know how his chest plays him up?'

Sarah nodded. Two years ago when the Spanish flu had spread through the country Jim had been ill for ages. 'But he was fine last time I saw him?'

Mary shook her head. 'These last weeks, he's been doing extra shifts. He kept on about earning more money. Then he was charging off to Union meetings. Weather's been terrible lately, he was always coming in soaked. On top of all that, he's walked over to Danby twice a week to see a mate of his. Seems like this chap lost his only bairn, meningitis, I think, and you know Jim.'

Sarah's fingers tightened on the mug of tea. 'Why, Mam? Daft, that's what he is. Who'll thank him in the long run?'

Mary gave her a troubled look. 'Done a bit of running about for you, Sarah. Don't forget that. Anyway, it's his way. You'll never change him. He was just the same as a little lad.'

'Who you talking to, Mam?'

The weak voice sent them both hurrying to his side.

'I've a surprise for you, Jim. Sarah's home.'

Jim's boney face lit up at the sight of his sister. 'Sarah, love. Can you stay?'

'I'll stay until you're on the mend, Jim.' She pulled up a stool and sat beside him. 'Seems like you need me to talk some sense into you.'

'Mam does that.' He smiled and tried to pull himself up on his pillows but the effort was too much for him.

'Here, let me do it.' His mother put her arm beneath his shoulders and bolstered him up. 'I'll leave Sarah with you while I do a few jobs but not much talking, mind.'

She turned and whispered to Sarah, 'Don't tire him.'

Sarah nodded, her eyes on her brother. He looked so frail. It made her feel the elder of the two. He looked back at her affectionately and gave a rusty chuckle that turned into a cough.

'How's the war between you and Blanche?'

She took hold of his hand. 'I can manage Blanche,' she said. 'Fancy you remembering that.'

'While I've been sick, I've been thinking about that day I came to see you at York. Long time ago now.' He coughed painfully. 'Glad you're here, Sarah. Passed my final exam. Knew a month ago, but didn't write. Wanted to tell you.' He coughed again and a red stain spread over his cheeks. 'I'll get out of the pit now, Sarah. I've got such plans. But money, I have to get more money first, for Mam and the others.' His head moved restlessly on the pillows.

'Why do I have to get sick, now?'

Sarah pressed his hand. 'Please rest, Jim. We can talk later.'

'No.' He clung to her hand and gazed at her intently. 'I have to talk. I can tell you things, Sarah. The others don't understand. But you understand, don't you?'

He paused, his eyes bright with fever. 'So many wonder-

ful things, Sarah. If we bother to see them. Things you will
learn about. Last month, I went to a concert. A man from
the Institute took me, he had some free tickets. By, it was
grand.' He tried unsuccessfully to suppress another bout of
coughing.

'Never heard anything like it. Full of colour, it was. Not
like the pit. Black as hell down there. But I'll get out . . .'

'I'm fetching Mam.' Sarah pulled her hand away.
'You've got to rest, Jim. You're making yourself worse.'

She called her mother. Mary hurried in from the scullery.

'For pity's sake, what are you doing to him?' Anger
showed in her face. 'Fetch a bowl of tepid water and a
towel.'

Sarah bit her lip. 'I'm sorry. I couldn't stop him.'

Mary ignored her. She smoothed Jim's hair back from
his forehead. 'Rest now. Rest.'

Jim's noisy breathing quietened. 'I wanted to explain,'
he whispered.

'Tomorrow. You can tell us tomorrow.'

Sarah was dreaming. She was running down a hill, a huge
boulder rolling behind her. She ran faster but the boulder
gained speed. It would crush her. She ran and somewhere
she heard Blanche's voice: 'Come to no good, that one.
Come to no good.'

She awoke with a start. Someone was bending over her.
Through half-opened eyes she looked at the thick plait of
hair hanging over her mother's shoulder. Mam's getting
quite grey, she thought. She had never before seen her
mother with her hair down.

'Wake up, Sarah.'

She sat up in bed. 'Jim?'

'He's real bad. Hurry, now.'

She couldn't stop shivering. She pulled the bedcover around her shoulders and followed her mother downstairs.

It isn't really happening, she thought. It's just a dream. Her father was sitting in his usual chair. Joe Armstrong was bald now and, with his face distorted with weeping, he looked like a grotesque baby. He held out his hand towards her but she ignored him. Teeth chattering, she walked towards Jim's bed.

It's a nightmare, she reminded herself.

But the normality of the scene clutched at her heart. The clock ticked on the mantelshelf, two o'clock. The fire glowed. She stared at the cluster of people around Jim's bed. Mam was stone-faced and white with fatigue. Florence was in tears: she's beginning to look like Mam, thought Sarah. Harry, his face fearful and bewildered, clutched at Florence's skirt. A neighbour hovered in the background. Eliza Fenton, was it? Sarah shook her head. It didn't matter. None of them were real. They were cardboard cut-outs to be brushed aside as worthless. Jim was the reality.

She fell on her knees at the side of his bed. The others drew back slightly. She wished they would all go away. She watched his thin chest fluttering as each ragged breath tore its way out of his body. She bent near his face. His lips were cracked, his breath fetid.

He smelt of death. Pain ripped through her. It was not a nightmare. It was real. The person she loved best in the world was dying.

She rested her head close to where his hands lay on the cover. 'Jim,' she whispered. 'You can't leave me.'

His eyes opened slowly, as if the effort was too much for him. 'Poor Sarah.' He moved his face slightly towards the window. 'Can you hear it?'

She stared.

'The music. You must hear it.' His head moved restlessly on the pillows. All Sarah could hear was the ominous bubbling sound his chest made. His fingers plucked aimlessly at the bedclothes and she covered them with her own warm hands.

'Listen. Isn't it wonderful?' Beads of sweat stood on his forehead. Sarah heard someone give a choking sob. She blinked.

'Yes, I hear it,' she said fiercely. 'I can hear it, Jim.' He muttered something. She bent closer: 'What did you say, love?'

'Live in hope, Sarah.' He smiled at her.

'What? I don't understand.' She rested the palm of her hand against his face in an agony of loving. She was rewarded with the faintest flicker of a smile.

'Dance for me,' he said. His head fell back. The tortured breathing stopped. The room was silent.

Mary looked across the open grave at her friend, Eliza. People disapproved of Eliza. She had slipshod ways, they said, and they were right. But at times like these, there was no one she would rather have near her. Look at her now, whispering to Harry, keeping him quiet and occupied. Mary's gaze moved on to her grown-up children. Florence, prim and serious in her black dress; and Arthur, his red hair slicked down, the tip of his nose glowing in the cold wind; Sarah stood a little apart from the others, her hand gripping the arm of Ted Colley. Blanche had not come. Mary's mouth tightened. She would not forgive her sister in a hurry. Still, they could do without Blanche. The number of people who had turned up for the service in the Chapel had surprised her and a goodly number had followed the hearse to the churchyard. So many people, eager to pay their respects to her eldest son.

She must not think of Jim, not yet. She raised her head defiantly. She would not cry. Joe was crying for both of them. He was shaking with suppressed tears now, as he stood beside her. She dare not look at him. Their firstborn was being laid in the cold earth. The day Jim had been born, Joe had gone all the way to Skelderby Market and brought her home a bunch of roses. It had been the talk of the village. Joe had laughed.

'Why shouldn't I?' he had cried. 'I've got the finest son in the North of Yorkshire. You deserve roses.'

Oh, Joe! From the corner of her eye she could see his hand clutching his stick. He was shaking as if he had the palsy. The tears she refused to release blinded her eyes and it seemed, as she looked into the faces of her neighbours, she saw ghosts: a broad young fellow with dark curly hair smiling down at a slim, serene-faced girl. Why God, why?

It was finished. The minister made his way towards them, his face dulled with sorrow and the need to comfort.

'Leave me be,' she wanted to shout. 'Leave me to grieve my son alone.'

'You'll be coming back to the house with us, Mr Brown?' she said instead.

'Yes, Mary. If I may?' His eyes met hers with a curious mixture of grief and embarrassment. She felt eased by his friendship.

'Aye, well.' She turned. 'Come along, Joe.'

Her husband stepped from her side and stood swaying at the side of the grave.

'It's wrong. It's bloody wrong. It should have been me.' He sobbed aloud, raised his stick and shook it at the sky. There was a collective intake of breath. The group of mourners, anxious to save the family from further pain, scattered and fled.

'Come on, Pa. Let's go home.' Sarah was at her father's side. She took his arm and motioned Ted Colley to the other side. Joe's shoulders sagged. A bemused, baffled bull of a man, he allowed the two slight figures to lead him away.

Mary stood in the scullery and pressed a hand to her throbbing head. From the next room came the hum of conversation. She felt the cold from the stone floor strike through the thin soles of her shoes and she shivered, yet she couldn't bring herself to return to the company. Her gaze roamed around the workday utensils of her life. Everything reminded her of Jim. The tin bath hanging on the hook behind the door; the blacking for his boots; the bucket and scrubbing brush he would wrestle from her hands when he came home from work. What was it he used to say? 'You're on your knees too often, Mam. I'll finish that.'

She straightened her back. They'd not see her on her knees today, any of them. She started as Eliza poked her head round the door.

'I've brought you a cuppa, Mary.'

A wintery smile flitted over Mary's face. 'Another one! I'll be swimming in tea afore long.'

Eliza came into the scullery. 'Get it down you,' she said. 'It will do you good.'

She was about to continue when Sarah appeared. She was wearing a coat and scarf. Mary gave her a scandalised look.

'You're never going out. Not today?'

Sarah's mouth set in a thin line. 'I can't stick it any longer. They make me sick. How can they behave so?'

'They'll soon be away.' Mary spoke more gently; she did not like the wild look in Sarah's eyes.

'It's us as well as them. I've been in there watching them. Florence – talking to the minister and full of airs and graces. Arthur, he's telling folk about his "posh" job. As if it matters! Pa's in a corner with his cronies, supping brandy in his tea.' Her voice broke on a sob. 'Harry laughed just now, Mam. He laughed!'

'He's only a lad, Sarah. You mustn't blame him. Anyway, we have to try and act normal, for the neighbours. It's expected.'

'Expected!' Sarah spat the word out. 'Why is it expected? When has this family ever done what's expected? Pa's the town drunk and those who say he isn't think he's daft. Didn't you know that, Mam?'

Mary stepped towards her daughter but Sarah flung up her hands.

'Our Florence is a snob. Arthur and her will be ashamed of us soon, can't you see? As for me. What's expected of me? Seeing how I've not been part of this family for years, I can do what I like.' Resentment showed in her eyes.

'Jim was the only one who cared about me. He was worth the lot of us put together. He worked himself to death for this precious family and to better himself and much good it did him.'

'Sarah, please . . .'

'No.' Sarah pushed past her mother. 'I'm off. And next week I'll be leaving for good. It's all fixed up. I saw Lucy Smailes yesterday. Her sister works at Harrogate. There's a job going. I don't care what it's like so long as I can leave here.'

'But what about your job in York?'

Sarah gave a bitter laugh. 'You really don't know anything about me, do you Mam? I hate your sister. She's an evil woman. I shall never speak to her again, never go back to York.' She rushed out of the back door.

Mary stared after her. 'What have I done?' she said.

Eliza put her arm about her friend. 'Now don't take on. Sarah's young and thoughtless. She was always headstrong. She's lashing out at you because she's hurt. She'll come round.' She shook her head. 'Could do with her backside smacking, that lady.'

'No.' Mary looked at her friend. 'I was wrong to send her to York. I know that now. I should have realised; I thought she was making things up. But I was wrong.' Sadly, she shook her head.

'Seems like I've lost two bairns today.'

Sarah ran down the street and glanced briefly towards the pithead looming in the distance. Jim had always feared an accident down the pit. How he had hated the dark. The pain swept through her and she closed her eyes.

'Dance for me, Sarah.'

What had he meant? She shook her head. Maybe she would understand everything more clearly later, when the anguish had ebbed. It would, everyone said so. But part of her resisted the thought. While she hugged her pain to her heart Jim was still part of her.

She walked swiftly along the well-known route up to where the stream ran. She welcomed the bleak wind on her face, it matched well her mood.

It was so cold, hoar frost had gilded the bushes by the water. She walked on, following the narrow path up to the farmland. Jim had brought her here when she was a child. He had piggy-backed her when her short legs had become tired. Under this hedge they had eaten bread and cheese and gathered the blood-red poppies from amongst the corn. They had walked and he had listened to her chatter, quietening her to point out a lark, rising on one long note to disappear into a bright blue sky.

Chilled to the bone, but driven onwards by the ice in her heart, she walked on. The light was fading as she reached the beginning of the moors. Sarah always thought of the moor as a summer place. A friendly wilderness in which to hunt for birds' nests and pick the harebells rustling in sheltered places beneath outcrops of rock. But now it was winter. Purple shadows sprawled across the bleak terrain; ghostly thorn trees showed black against the misty landscape and the silence was absolute. Yet here she stopped. Like a slender young birch tree she remained motionless for a moment, then the storm of tears broke. Alone, under a bruised sky, she wept for the end of her childhood and the sadness of life.

Chapter Ten

Hammond House stood majestic behind elaborate iron railings. Sarah pushed open the gate, then hesitated. The massive front door, the pillars flanking the wide stone portico, looked too impressive to allow the entrance of a possible housemaid. Fortunately, her eyes rested upon a discreet notice indicating the direction of a tradesmen's entrance. She followed the direction of the pointing arrow and pressed the bell.

A woman of about twenty years of age opened the door. Sarah became acutely conscious of her own appearance, particularly the patch on her shoe, when she saw the young woman's smart uniform and pleated apron but a glance towards her face reassured her. Alice Smailes was the image of her sister, Lucy. At the sight of Sarah her face broke into a smile.

'Oh, good. We were wondering where you had got to.' She stood to one side and motioned Sarah to enter the house.

'Sorry I'm late. I'm afraid I got lost.' Sarah followed Alice down two steps and along a passage.

'In here. We're just going to have tea so you may as well have a cup before I take you up to see Mrs Linford.' Alice paused. 'If anyone asks you where you've worked before, don't say too much.' She giggled. 'I've told them you've been with a family in York and that you are an experienced housemaid.'

Sarah frowned but, before she could remonstrate, Alice swept her into the kitchen rather like an amiable sheepdog shepherding a stray lamb home.

'This is Sarah,' she announced to the room as a whole. Everyone stopped what they were doing and stared at Sarah. A blush mounted her cheeks but she held up her head and stared back with what she hoped was a pleasant but serious expression.

'This is Mr Osgood, Sarah.'

Alice's voice sounded most respectful so Sarah surmised the gentleman was of some importance.

'Mr Osgood is the butler. And this is Mrs Harman. Best cook in all Harrogate, aren't you, Mrs Harman?'

The cook's appearance was so comic Sarah had difficulty in suppressing a smile. Which was a pity, she thought, because it was the first time she had felt like smiling in a long time. Mrs Harman closely resembled a cottage loaf in shape and her grey hair, skewered into a tight bun on the top of her head, enhanced the likeness. Beneath her rounded figure and voluminous skirts her feet protruded, large and flat and shod in old-fashioned black boots. Despite her appearance it was obvious she was a kind-hearted woman for she immediately flapped her way across to Sarah's side.

'Take off your things, dearie,' she said, 'and sit you down.' She placed Sarah's coat on a nearby chair, a solemn expression flitting across her face when she saw the black mourning band on the sleeve.

'This is Betsy,' intoned Alice, who was obviously taking the task of introduction seriously. A tall, pretty girl smiled briefly in Sarah's direction and continued placing cups and saucers on the table.

'Betsy's the parlourmaid. Very posh,' continued Alice,

winking at Sarah, 'but she still has to do her bit down here. And that just leaves Dora.'

A skinny woman enveloped in a coarse apron nodded. Looking at her careworn expression and work-roughened hands Sarah presumed Dora was the skivvy.

Following their momentary pause the staff resumed their various tasks and Sarah looked about her. The kitchen was the largest room she had ever been in. Nevertheless, it had a comfortable, homely feel.

The floor was stone but covered with strips of coconut matting so it was warm to the feet. One wall was completely taken up with a huge dresser which was laden with dishes. On the other side of the room stood a large kitchen range and next to the range there stood another, smaller stove. Sarah discovered later this was a gas cooker used for keeping dishes hot. There were white muslin curtains at the windows, the paintwork was green and the wallpaper lurid, but cheerful.

Mrs Harman called to her to come and sit at the table and she was given a cup of strong tea which she drank gratefully and a piece of fruitcake which tasted delicious. To Sarah's relief no one questioned her about her previous employment. They ate and talked between themselves but refrained from conversation with her, merely giving her a friendly nod when they caught her eye.

Of course, she thought, there is no guarantee I shall be working with them, especially if Mrs Linford finds out I haven't worked in service before. She realised, with a jab of surprise, she would be disappointed if she failed to get the job. She had travelled to Harrogate rather like a leaf caught in a wind, desirous only of leaving Swaithdown and of escaping from York. But here, in the kitchen of Hammond House, the atmosphere disarmed her. Why, she thought, it would be almost like being in a proper family, working here.

'Finished?' Alice pushed back her chair. She looked at the large clock ticking solemnly on the wall. 'It would be a good time to catch the missus now.'

'Let the girl wash her hands and tidy up a bit,' snapped Mrs Harman. Her voice softened as she spoke to Sarah. 'You'll find the mistress a kind lady and easy to talk to.'

Five minutes later Sarah followed Alice upstairs to the family's apartments.

'This is Mrs Linford's own drawing-room' Alice spoke in a whisper. 'Wait here a moment.' She tapped on the door, waited, then, on a spoken command from inside, entered.

Sarah listened to the low rumble of voices and smoothed back her hair. If only it would stay tidy instead of escaping into bouncy curls. She glanced about her. The richness of everything intimidated her. Working here would be vastly different from working at the bakery. She studied the velvet curtains at the windows. There was a cabinet of shiny black in the corridor. It had a number of silver-framed photographs on it. For the first time she felt understanding for the affectations adopted by her brother, Arthur. Coming home after what must be the greater magnificence of Hazelbury Hall would not be easy.

As the drawing-room door opened she realised, with a pang of painful pleasure, she felt tense and excited. Since Jim's death she had moved through the days like an automaton. Now she felt she was coming alive again. She frowned. If only Alice hadn't fibbed about her being in service.

'You're to go in,' said Alice.

Wiping moist hands on her skirt, Sarah did as she was bid. The first thing she noticed was the picture. Behind a writing desk at which her prospective employer was seated, hung a huge canvas. It portrayed, in graphic detail, the death of some Saint. Arms outstretched, a gaunt figure riddled with arrows, strained towards a rosy light. He looked ecstatic.

Oh Gawd, thought Sarah. A bible thumper.

'Sit down, my dear.'

Averting her eyes from the dying Saint, Sarah did as she was asked, and looked instead at Mrs Linford. She made a much more attractive picture.

Sarah's prospective employer was middle-aged and threads of silver ran through her fair hair which was drawn back from her broad brow and knotted simply at the nape of her neck. Yet she looked young. Her blue eyes were as guileless as a child's and her pale face was unlined. She wore a simple yet expensive-looking dress and a gold cross rested on her ample bosom.

'I'm pleased to meet you, Sarah.' She placed her large, well-shaped hands before her on the desk. 'You are sixteen years old, I believe?'

'Yes, ma'am.'

A well-thumbed bible lay before her and Sarah noticed more photographs, this time of two young men. Her sons, she guessed. A spray of white chrysanthemums shed petals on to the figured walnut desk. Sarah averted her eyes. She hated the scent of chrysanthemums.

'You are rather small.'

'Yes, ma'am. But I am strong and healthy.'

A smile touched Mrs Linford's pale lips. 'Are you well trained in a housemaid's duties, Sarah?'

A short silence.

Mrs Linford continued. 'Alice assures me you would be ideal for the post?'

Sarah cleared her throat. 'I think I would be, ma'am. I am used to working hard and I soon pick things up.'

'But you have never been in service before?'

'No. I worked in a bakery in York. The dispatch

department.' Sarah looked apprehensively at the older woman but Mrs Linford's expression remained unchanged. She went on: 'I had to be quick and efficient. I can lift heavy things. I'm sure I could do the job, ma'am.'

Mrs Linford looked thoughful. 'But why leave a good job in York? Since the war it is proving difficult to get good girls to take this kind of work. They prefer to work in shops and factories. But you want to come here?'

'The work was all right. It was other things. Anyway,' Sarah's voice grew husky, 'I was called home suddenly, ma'am.'

'Ah, yes. Alice mentioned a bereavement.'

'My brother . . .' The words fell, heavy as leaden stones. Misery flooded Sarah's face, sharpening her features, presentiment of her old age.

'Yes.' Mrs Linford leant towards her. 'You must not grieve, Sarah. There is no death in the Lord. Rejoice, your brother is free of this vale of tears.'

Sarah raised startled eyes. Mrs Linford was definitely barmy. Still, she meant well. She straightened up in her chair, conscious once more of her surroundings.

'Yes. Thank you, ma'am.'

Mrs Linford sighed. She straightened one of the photographs. 'Very well. I will take you on three months' trial, Sarah.' She held up her hand to forestall Sarah's thanks.

'I need a maid and I think you will suit. Twenty-four pounds a year, paid monthly; one afternoon and one evening off fortnightly and alternate Sundays. I think that's fair.'

She waited for Sarah's nod of consent. And then went on, 'I will see Mrs Harman as to your uniform. And I must speak to Alice.'

'She only did it to help.' Sarah was worried for her new-found friend. 'Her sister, Lucy, is my best friend and Alice knew it was important I found a job.'

'I realise her motives were good, Sarah. I shall not be too unkind, but falsehoods are wicked.' Mrs Linford pushed back her chair. 'I need hardly add, my dear, that you must always be back indoors before ten o'clock in the evening and gentlemen suitors are not allowed to call here at the house.'

Sarah stood up. 'Yes, ma'am. Thank you.'

Once outside the drawing-room Sarah leant against the wall, her heart pounding.

It's a new start, she said to herself. I'll have a posh uniform and money and proper times off. No more Aunt Blanche. No more skivvying. Things are going to be different for me from now on.

'Fires all laid, Sarah?'

'Yes, Mrs Harman.'

Sarah washed her hands at the sink, removed her coarse apron and replaced it with a white one.

'This is the time of day I hate,' she whispered to Alice.

'Why, for goodness' sake?'

'I can stand getting up at six and laying the fires. I can stand blackleading the grates and dusting eight bedrooms that are never used, but I can't abide morning prayers.'

Alice grinned. 'I can see Mrs Linford's going to have a hard job converting you, Sarah Armstrong.'

The two girls tagged on behind the rest of the staff as they trooped up the back stairs and into the main drawing-room. Mr and Mrs Linford awaited them there. Sarah watched as Titus Linford eased his stiff collar away from his neck and pulled a face.

'He don't reckon much to them, neither,' she said under her breath. Alice muffled a giggle. The staff bent their heads as the mistress launched into the first prayer. Sarah closed her mind to the words and thought about the last weeks. Things were not quite as she had anticipated but, on the whole, she thought, she had been fortunate. She worked hard but she was used to that. Her wage was fair and Mam must be blessing the money she was able to send home. Mrs Linford was a real lady though some of the things she expected you to do made your mind boggle; ironing bootlaces, for example! Don't suppose Mr Linford even noticed.

She peeped through her fingers at him. A wonderful man and a fine doctor was how Mrs Harman described him. Sarah couldn't help wondering what had drawn him and his wife together. Titus Linford was powerfully built, with coarse features and a beak of a nose. But his eyes were merry and his mouth, half hidden by his luxuriant moustache and short beard, was generous. He looked a man of vigour and strong appetites, hardly suited to be the husband of the pale, tranquil figure beside him.

'Amen.'

Just one more to go, thought Sarah as she shifted from foot to foot.

Funny thing, couples. Look at Aunt Blanche and Uncle Ted. How ever had they got together? It was like mating a mouse with a ferret. She stole another look at Mr Linford. He caught her eye and winked. She blushed. He was nice, was Mr Linford. He would have a joke with you, but you didn't have to worry about his hands. She thought of the manager at the bakery, like an octopus, he had been. She shivered. She hated men touching her. She wondered briefly if there was something wrong with her. Lucy was courting and Alice and Betsy talked of nothing but boys. They thought she was queer because she said she was in no rush to get married. Mr and Mrs Linford had separate bedrooms. They had two sons though, so they must have been in love once.

Mrs Linford closed her bible and dismissed them. Thank goodness! They could go and have a cup of tea before tackling the rest of the chores. Back in the kitchen she asked Mrs Harman, 'Have you worked for the Linfords for long?'

'Ever since they came to Harrogate. Oh, it must be nearly six years now. This house belonged to Mrs Linford's mother. It came in useful when they decided to leave London.'

'London? I didn't know they lived there.'

'Oh yes, indeed. Mr Linford is a very superior doctor. That's why he's called Mr and not Doctor. He had a practice in, what's it called? Ah, yes, in Harley Street. Very exclusive. I believe he had a Member of Parliament as one of his patients. His younger son, Mr Redvers, is in London now, training to be a doctor.'

'Why did they leave?'

'The war, dear.' Mrs Harman hesitated. 'It was the war and then there was Mr Martin, their elder son.' She jumped as the butler, Mr Osgood, entered the room. He gave her a hard look as he replaced his black jacket for the grey one in which he worked.

'I was just telling Sarah, Mr Osgood, that the master and mistress originally came from London.'

'I believe Mr Linford finds Harrogate suits him well enough.' Mr Osgood's voice held a repressive note. 'It may not be Harley Street but the gentry come from far and near to sample the Spa water and partake of the hydro-therapy at the Royal Baths.'

'Just what I was saying,' flurried the cook. She looked about her. 'Where's that Alice? It's time she got on with her work.'

'I'm here, Mrs Harman.' Alice came hurrying in. She

looked flushed. Sarah guessed she had been hovering by the side entrance waiting for the boy who delivered the daily vegetables.

'There's all the glass and silverware to be washed and polished. Get on with it straight away. Sarah can help you.'

Alice collected a tray of silver and motioned Sarah to follow her into the pantry. There were two sinks in the pantry and most of the cleaning and washing up was done in this room.

'Put plenty of soda in the water,' Alice intoned. 'Then add the soft soap.'

Sarah rolled up her sleeves. 'What's the mystery about their son, Martin?' she whispered. 'And why did they leave London?'

Alice glanced behind her and added more hot water to the bowl. 'It's him that turned the mistress towards religion,' she said. 'Awful, it was.'

Sarah was intrigued. 'Go on.'

'Well, I wasn't there, of course, but I've heard things . . .' Alice tapped the side of her nose with a wet finger: 'Beginning of the war, it was. Poor Mrs Linford, nearly died of grief so she did. After that, it was the bible or the bottle.'

'Alice!'

Alice jumped. So did Sarah. Mr Osgood stood behind them. His voice was cold as ice. Sarah was surprised the glass she was holding didn't shatter.

'Stop this chattering. Get further behind with your work and I'll cancel your day off.'

'Yes, Mr Osgood.'

Alice grimaced at Sarah and raised her voice. 'When you've washed the silver, pour hot water over it then leather dry. Like this.'

And Sarah could extract nothing more from her.

Chapter Eleven

In March Mr Redvers brought a party of friends over to
spend a few days at Harrogate. They descended upon
Hammond House like a flock of chattering starlings. Sarah
watched their arrival from an upstairs window. She spotted
Mr Redvers immediately; he resembled his father, and she
decided he seemed quite nice. Later, bringing in the bags
from the cars and bustling about dealing with extra household tasks, she revised her first impression. True he was
handsome and had a genial manner with his companions,
but towards the servants he was curt and impatient. Sarah
observed how he treated his mother with an exaggerated
politeness bordering on insolence and she also noticed that
Mr Linford was not over-enamoured with his son. Suddenly the good doctor found a great many reasons to dine
with colleagues at his Club.

The female members of the party were, to Alice and
Sarah, exotic creatures.

'Did you see the girl in blue?' marvelled Alice. 'Her hair's
as short as a boy's and her underwear is crêpe de Chine.'
She laughed. 'Betsy says you can roll up a pair of her knick-
ers and hold them in the palm of your hand.'

'It's called an "Eton crop",' said Sarah. 'Her hair, I
mean. Don't you remember reading about it in Betsy's
magazine? It's terribly fashionable.' She sighed and

fingered her own curling hair. 'Mine would never go like that,' she lamented.

'Pooh, who wants to look like a boy.' Alice tossed her head.

'Maybe not. But they all have lovely clothes, don't they. Those dresses. And they're all so skinny.'

Both girls sighed again. Alice was well endowed in every respect and Sarah, although still slender, was flowering from shapeless adolescence into shapely womanhood.

Sarah stared down at her burgeoning breasts. She feared she would never be able to wear the new-style tubular dresses.

'They all smoke, you know – and talk about cocktail parties.' Alice raised her eyebrows. 'Wonder what Mrs Linford makes of it?' Sarah wondered, too, but, before their delicious conversation could continue, a bell tinkled, indicating service was required upstairs.

'You go, Sarah.' Alice held up her hands. 'I'm all mucky from doing the brass and Betsy's ironing in the pantry. Since they arrived she hasn't had a minute.'

Sarah approached the drawing-room feeling a mixture of anticipation and nervousness. She could hear music and laughter and when she entered the room she saw that the carpet had been rolled back and that the three couples were dancing.

'Ah, Sarah. It is Sarah, isn't it?' Redvers Linford broke away from his partner and approached her. 'We need more gin, Sarah. I've been ringing for Osgood but there's no sign of the damned fellow.'

'It's his afternoon off, sir.' From the corner of her eye Sarah saw Redvers' dancing partner lounge over to the gramophone. The woman placed a cigarette into a long holder, lit it, glanced at Sarah, then turned to study the pile of records.

'You'll fetch us some, won't you? There's a good girl.'

Redvers breathed over her and she recoiled slightly.

'Mr Osgood has the key to the drinks cupboard, Mr Redvers, but I'll see what I can do.'

Redvers pouted. 'Pity when a chap can't get a drink in his own house,' he drawled. 'Still, you'll find us some, Sarah. An intelligent girl like you.' He paused. 'Damned pretty too. In fact, more than pretty.'

Sarah turned to leave, but he stepped quickly in front of her. 'Do you dance, Sarah?'

'No, sir. At least, I've never tried.' Glancing away from Redvers' fixed stare, Sarah felt uneasy. A haze of blue cigarette smoke drifted in the room and a sudden frenetic blast came from the gramophone.

'Never tried. What a pity. All pretty girls should dance.' Redvers caught her by the hand. 'Come on, I'll show you. It's easy.'

'No. Please let me go.' She tried vainly to release herself from his grasp. His hand felt damp and unpleasant.

'Oh, don't be a spoilsport. It's ragtime, Sarah. Wonderful, wonderful stuff. Just follow me.' He pulled her towards him, jerking her upright as her unwilling feet slipped on the polished floor.

'Please . . .' The colour mounted in Sarah's face as the two other couples stopped dancing and gathered to watch, laughing and calling out ribald comments.

'Oh, she nearly went then, Redvers. Not such a good teacher as you thought. Can I have the next one, miss?'

Welcome fury replaced Sarah's feeling of humiliation. Exerting her full strength she broke free of Redvers.

'You've no right,' she cried, her face tense with anger, 'no right.'

The record finished and the sudden silence was emphasised by the hiss of the needle.

'Just a joke,' Redvers said. He turned to his friends, smiling and turning the palms of his hands upwards. 'Different kind of humour, I suppose.'

One of the young men gave an embarrassed cough. 'Put something else on, for God's sake,' he said.

The jaunty strains of *Sunny Side Up* dissolved the frozen tableau and Sarah turned thankfully towards the door.

'Put some coal on the fire, will you?' drawled Redvers' partner.

'Sorry?'

'The fire. It needs mending.' The woman examined her brightly painted finger nails.

'Yes, of course, miss.' Sarah crossed to the fireplace, brushing past the dancers without a glance. She replenished the fire. Then she left the room. Once outside she took a deep breath. She felt no desire to cry. These flimsy, rickety people, what were they to her?

That evening she curled up in bed and prepared to have her usual chat with Alice. Since her arrival at Hammond House the two girls had shared a bedroom and a firm friendship had grown up between them.

'I've been thinking, Alice, I may go home for a visit soon. What about you?'

'Forty-two, forty-three.' Alice was brushing her hair. She stopped and gave Sarah a look of surprise. 'That's the first time you've mentioned Swaithdown for ages,' she said.

Sarah linked her arms behind her head. 'I know. But Mam and me, we parted on bad terms, you know, and I'd like to go and see her.'

'But you've written to her since you came here and sent her money.' Alice gave up on her hair and flung the brush on to the washstand. She leapt into her bed and pulled up the covers. 'I'm not going. I've got better things to do with my free time.' She gave a self-satisfied smile. After weeks of lurking outside the house she had made the acquaintance of the vegetable boy and now, each alternate Wednesday, he waited for her, hair flattened down, cap in hand, to take her for a stroll.

Sarah came to a decision. 'Well, I'm going home, first chance I get.' She waited for a reply but when none was forthcoming, she sat up. 'Alice – don't go to sleep yet. I want to talk. Tell me about Martin Linford?'

'No. I'm tired.'

'Oh, go on. What's the secret? You have to tell me.'

'Shut up, Sarah. Mr Osgood had a real go at me after he caught us talking about Martin. He more or less said he'd sack me if he caught me discussing it again. I'm not risking that. Anyway, I *am* tired.'

'I won't *tell* anyone. Please, Alice.' Sarah waited hopefully but when Alice remained silent she flounced out of bed and turned out the lamp. 'Please yourself. I don't want to know, anyway.'

The room was quiet for a few moments then Alice said, in a conciliatory tone of voice, 'Did you hear Mr Redvers today, grumbling about us still having lamps. Couldn't understand why his father wouldn't have electricity put in the house.'

Sarah scowled into the darkness at the thought of Redvers Linford. 'Mr Linford thinks the electric wiring would spoil the panelling,' she said. 'He's right. Who wants new-fangled electricity, anyway?'

Alice laughed. 'You are funny, Sarah. You sound about thirty, sometimes.' She rolled over and soon gentle snores vibrated her sleeping form.

Sarah stayed awake longer. Funny how she suddenly

needed to go home; see Mam and the rest of them. A wave of homesickness swept over her. She chided herself. She was being stupid. Where was home, anyway? She pulled the bedclothes over her head. She didn't really sound as though she was thirty, did she?

Redvers and his friends departed and the household resumed its usual staid pattern. Yet things were different. Mrs Linford's manner became more unworldly. She spent longer over her prayers. Mr Linford's temper frayed more readily. Sarah would catch him looking at his wife with a perplexed expression. Sarah pondered on these things as she polished the doorknocker of Hammond House one bright April morning. Having plenty of money, she mused, didn't seem to make much difference as to whether you were happy or not. Mind you, she grinned as she gave a final rub to the brass, money meant you could be miserable in comfort. She put her duster back into the box and turned to look about her.

Spring had come to Harrogate and Montpellier Gardens, towards which Hammond House faced, had exploded into dizzy green. Sarah smiled with pleasure. It was not as beautiful as the moors, of course, but the outlook was most pleasant. A passerby, walking his poodle, raised his hat to the girl and she dimpled and smiled again. To the young man approaching the house the little maid looked as fresh and dainty as spring itself. He paused, the worried expression on his face easing a little, then he looked up at the imposing façade of the house, shook his head slightly then clicked open the gate.

'Hello.'

Sarah looked with interest at the early morning visitor. She noticed his shabby jacket and the battered case he carried.

'You'll do better at the side door,' she said. Whatever he

was selling she didn't reckon he stood much chance dressed as he was. He had a nice smile though, so she would help if she could.

'Pardon?'

'The tradesmen's entrance,' she gestured, 'round there.'

'Oh, yes.' He nodded and took the direction she had indicated. Sarah took up a broom and swept energetically down the path. She paused to admire the primulas, then hurried back indoors. Spring looked beautiful but the wind still had a sting in it and her hands were freezing. The young man had not reappeared. Perhaps he was a better salesman than he looked. As she entered the kitchen, Alice grabbed her.

'Come in here, and keep your voice down.' She hurried Sarah into the pantry.

'Why, what's happened?'

Alice looked ready to explode with excitement. 'Guess what? He's turned up.'

'Who?'

'*Martin!* Martin Linford. Walked into the kitchen just now, bold as brass.'

Sarah had a dreadful thought. She stared at Alice. 'But I thought he was dead?'

'Dead? Why on earth did you think that?'

'I don't know. Mrs Linford always looks sad, and you would never tell me what happened. I just thought . . .' She swallowed. 'Is he thin and fair-haired with a nice smile?'

'Well, he's got fair hair and yes,' Alice gave a short laugh, 'he's bound to be thin, where he's been.'

Sarah gave an impatient sigh. 'Where *has* he been? For goodness' sake, tell me. All this mystery, will you tell me what's going on?'

Alice took a swift peek outside the pantry door then shut

Frances Anne Bond

it again. 'I'd better be quick,' she said rapidly. 'They're in such a tizz they haven't thought about us yet, but they will.' She paused. 'Mr Martin was called up to go in the war and he refused to go.'

'You mean he was a coward?' Remembering the young man's steady gaze Sarah felt unaccountably let down. 'I've heard there were men like that,' she said slowly. 'They gave a white feather to a man at home when he refused to fight.'

'Mr Martin got worse than that,' said Alice. 'There was an awful row.' She lowered her voice to a whisper. 'Mrs Harman told me all about it, one day when Mr Osgood was out. He was there, you see, working for them in London. They came and took Mr Martin,' she paused dramatically. 'They put him in prison. It almost broke his mother's heart. Although it was partly her fault, on about turning the other cheek, stuff like that. And his poor father. You can imagine, all the whispering that went on. Some of his patients left. That's why they came to Harrogate.'

Sarah was quiet. No wonder Mrs Linford turned towards religion. 'He looked quite nice,' she said. 'Not like a coward at all.'

Alice pulled a face. 'I wouldn't say that word near Mr Osgood,' she warned. 'He thinks the world of Mr Martin. He says he was more brave refusing to go. Anyways, we'd best show our faces before they start hollering for us.'

Sarah followed her friend. 'Maybe,' she said. 'But it's a good job all the men didn't do what he did.'

'So there you are.' Mrs Harman's face was scarlet. 'Get upstairs and light a fire in the blue bedroom, Alice. It's still a mite cold. You'd better put some bottles in the bed, too. Sarah, take up some clean linen and towels.' She waddled over to the dresser. 'Where's my best recipe book? I must do something special tonight. We must celebrate.'

Sarah went to fetch the linen. She hoped Martin would prove less troublesome than his brother had been. Her heart sank when she remembered how she had directed him to the tradesmen's entrance.

By four o'clock her fingers felt red raw. Mrs Harman insisted on serving chestnut soup for dinner. For hours Sarah had been rubbing pounds of chestnuts through a fine sieve.

'Haven't you finished yet?' The cook's voice rose a further decibel. 'I want you to do the mint sauce and Alice can prepare the redcurrant jelly. They'll go a treat with saddle of lamb, and then there's cheese aigrettes and charlotte russe. I think that sounds all right, don't you?'

'Wonderful, Mrs Harman.'

But the cook had already rushed away. Busy, happy and completely in her element, surrounded as she was by pans bubbling and succulent smells filling the air.

'You'd think the blooming King was coming to dine,' grumbled Alice as she staggered past Sarah steadying a pile of the best china.

'Might have been worth it for him,' replied Sarah. She pushed back the hair from her forehead. 'I hope Mr Martin appreciates all this fuss.' She thought longingly of her next day off and her visit home.

Martin stuck a piece of paper over the cut on his chin. That's all he needed, blood on his shirt. His mother had unearthed a dress shirt and one of his old suits. She must have brought them with her from London. He looked at himself in the mirror. The suit was rather loose, he had carried more weight when he had last worn it, a carefree youth of eighteen. However, he had grown considerably and the jacket sleeves and the trouser legs were now too

short which made him appear slightly comical. He smiled
wryly. That was the last thing he was feeling, comical. He
glanced at the clock. Almost time for dinner. He hoped no
one would make a fuss. He felt like the prodigal son
already. He had intimated to his father that he had no desire
to meet with anyone outside the family. Not yet. His father
had looked relieved. Of course, probably no one would
wish to meet *him*. The war was still uppermost in their
minds. As for himself, he was sick of it. Sick of the guilt; the
pain he had caused his parents; the heart-tearing doubts he
had experienced, was still experiencing.

Gingerly, he removed the paper. Good, the flow of blood
had stopped. As the unbelievable rivers of blood that had
flowed in France had finally stopped. Now it was time to
look forward. Forget the bleak past. It was the 1920s – time
to start living again. He thought briefly of the little maid he
had spoken to on his arrival. How young she was, too
young to have war memories. He sighed. He could be
wrong, perhaps she had lost a father, a brother. He hoped
not. She looked like the future to him, vivid, strong and
resilient. He glanced again at the clock. Time to go downstairs and face his parents. Down to the people he loved and
who loved him back. Why was it so hard to talk to them?

Chapter Twelve

There were ten minutes to spare before the train left. Impulsively, Sarah bought presents, a shaving mug for Pa, embellished with a picture of a sailing ship, a *Chatterbox Annual* for Harry. Choosing a present for Mam was more difficult. Sarah couldn't ever remember her mother asking for anything for herself. A lifetime of 'making do' had stripped from Mary Armstrong any desire for 'fripperies'. With five minutes to spare, Sarah rushed into a flower shop and bought a plant.

Ever capricious, Spring had withdrawn her favours and after the spell of beautiful weather it had become cold and wet. There was no one to meet Sarah when she arrived and, as she trudged along the road to the village, her skirt became wet and heavy about her legs. The rain turned to sleet and, turning into Joshua Street, brown slush, like thin porridge, squelched beneath her feet and penetrated the thin soles of her shoes. With relief she entered the house and wrinkled up her nose at the remembered smell of freshly ironed clothes.

Her mother lifted her head from her work and spoke, a note of apology in her voice: 'I'll only be a moment. I thought I would have finished before you arrived, but with all the rain . . .' she clicked her tongue. 'Terrible drying weather.'

Frances Anne Bond

'It doesn't matter.' Sarah placed her bag and parcels upon the table and crossed to her mother. 'How are you?'

Awkwardly, she put her arms about her mother. Mary's figure stiffened, then relaxed. She pressed her cheek briefly against that of her daughter.

'You're looking well,' Mary said. 'You've put on weight. Harrogate must agree with you.'

'It does, Mam.' Sarah felt a strong desire to stay there, within the circle of her mother's arms. Mary smelt so fresh and clean. But already her mother was dropping her arms, turning away, back to the iron and the next item to be smoothed into submission. Sarah turned towards her parcels, forcing brightness into her voice: 'Where's Harry, and Pa? See, I've brought some presents.'

'There was no need.' Mary's face was expressionless.

'I know. But I didn't get home for Christmas and,' Sarah's voice faltered, 'I wanted to, Mam.' She picked up the book: 'This is for Harry. I'm so looking forward to seeing him.'

'He's round at his friend's house. He'll be back soon enough, don't you fret.' Mary continued ironing. 'Can you stay?'

'Until tomorrow. I have to be back for tea time.' Sarah replaced the book on the table and picked up the plant. 'I didn't know what you'd like, Mam. Then I saw this.'

Mary rested the iron back on the stand. She stared at the plant. 'It's right pretty,' she admitted. 'But then, you were always one for growing things, Sarah. Thank you. Now get them wet things off.' She look at Sarah's feet. 'You don't have to bring presents,' she said. 'You might have done better to have those shoes of yours repaired.'

Sarah did not reply. She walked across to the window and looked out at the sleet. 'I wouldn't have thought Pa would

112

have gone out in this weather. Where is he – at the pub?'

Mary did not reply, so Sarah after a quick glance at her mother, began to tell Mary a little about her life at Harrogate. As she did so, she removed her shoes and stuffed them with newspaper before placing them before the fire to dry. She filled the kettle and made tea. As she worked she stole glances at her mother. Mary Armstrong did not change. Her hair was, as always, neatly pulled back from her face, her mouth was held in disciplined lines, her eyes direct and sharp, seeming to look right through you.

Sarah stirred her tea, her fingers unsteady. Why did Mam always make her feel guilty? She handed a cup to her mother and noticed her red, work-worn hands. She looked again at her face. How fine-boned and spare were her features. Mary was as hard on herself as she was on others. Looking at her you could see how life had pared away all the vanities, the irrelevancies of her life, leaving behind a bright blade of honesty. A lump rose in Sarah's throat.

Oh, Mam, she wanted to cry, I want to be like you but I can't. But please, please love me.

Instead, she said, 'How's Florence and our Arthur?'

A spark of animation showed in Mary's face. She stacked away the piles of laundry and sat down. 'Florence is doing real well at her school. She's very highly thought of.'

Sarah nodded. She understood her mother's pride in Florence's escape from Swaithdown and her post as a teacher in Leeds.

'Has she written to you lately?'

'Yes. There's a letter on the shelf. She's courting.'

'Never!'

'She is. I told you she had joined a choir; well, she's walking out with the chap who plays the piano. He's got a

113

good job; works in an insurance office. There's a picture in with the letter. Take a look.'

Sarah stood up and reached for the letter. 'He's not much to look at, is he?' she commented, staring at the photo.

Mary sniffed. 'He's a good steady man and he thinks the world of her.'

Sarah studied the picture of tall, determined Florence arm-in-arm with her short, bespectacled, middle-aged 'young man'. Well, Florence had never been romantic. But then, neither was she. She did hope, however, that if ever she got married, her husband would prove a mite more dashing.

'That's not the only news.' Mary's face grew animated: 'See the postcard, behind the clock?'

'This one?' Sarah took the gaily coloured card. 'Oh, it's a picture of the Eiffel Tower.'

'It's from Arthur.' Mary's voice was proud. 'I was going to write and tell you but then I thought I'd wait until you came through.'

'What on earth is he doing in France?'

'Old Mr Trenton, up at the Hall, he's taken a real shine to Arthur. Reckons he's a smart young man.'

Sarah's face assumed an expression of scepticism.

'Oh, you may look like that but it's true. Arthur's a sort of companion to him; reads *The Financial Times* out loud, and plays card games with the old gentleman. Anyway, Mr Trenton has taken Arthur with him abroad and now your brother's learning to speak French and all kinds of things.'

'*Comment allez-vous*?' Sarah spelled out. 'What does that mean?'

'I don't know – but it's a wonderful education he's getting, isn't it?' Mary gazed into the fire, lost in thoughts of her son travelling the world.

'Seems like we are all doing fine,' said Sarah. 'Florence is teaching, Arthur is in Paris and me an understairs maid in Harrogate.'

Mary's brows drew together at the derisory note in her daughter's voice. 'There's nothing wrong with being a maid, Sarah.' She spoke quietly. 'You're earning your keep, your employer seems happy with you and Harrogate's a beautiful place to live. I went there once, you know.'

'You did?' Sarah looked up in surprise. To the best of her knowledge her mother had never left Swaithdown.

'It was only a day trip when I was a girl but I did enjoy it.' Mary's lips curved in a reminiscent smile. 'I wore a tartan silk blouse and went window shopping in James Street. Then we went to West Park Stray where there was a Band Stand. There were all kinds of entertainers about, jugglers, minstrels and a pierrot show. Lovely, it was.'

A door slammed and there came the sound of boots being scraped. Mary jumped out of her chair. 'Your Pa's back.'

'Has the lass arrived? Sarah, are you there?' A heavy form darkened the doorway.

Sarah jumped to her feet and went to her father. She was enveloped in a huge bear hug. She felt the blood sing through her and she laughed and hugged him back. The masculine smell of beer and tobacco swung her back to childhood. Her father was home. Then she looked up into his face. The once-merry blue eyes were red-veined and held a glazed look and bloodhound-like bags pouched beneath them. The once-sensitive mouth was loose and slack and heavy lines scored the fleshy planes of his face. She pulled back, affronted. At a distance she could sometimes re-create the father of her childhood, but reality splintered the image.

115

Half drunk as he was, he felt her recoil. 'What's up, lass? Haven't you a kiss for your dad?'

She smiled through stiff lips. 'Of course I have. It's just . . . I want to fetch your present.'

'A present.' He looked towards his wife: 'Our Sarah – she's brought me a present.'

Mary took up a basket of laundry and peered through the window. 'Yes, I know. It's stopped raining now. I'll nip these down the road and call and collect Harry then we can eat and have a good natter.'

'Shall I come with you, Mam?'

'No.' Mary shook her head. 'You keep your Pa company. I won't be long.'

Joe limped his way to his chair. 'You'll find she's grown into a hard woman, Sarey,' he complained when Mary had left. 'No comfort for an ailing man at all.' He patted the arm of his chair. 'Come and sit near me and tell me your news.'

Sarah brought his present.

'Well, will you look at that,' he marvelled. He turned the mug in his large wrinkled hands. 'Just what I need. I can spruce myself up now.' He passed his hand over his whiskers, making a rasping sound. 'Hard to believe, but I was a grand-looking fellow once, Sarah.'

'I know, Pa.' Sarah put her arm around his humped shoulders.

He reached up and patted her cheek. 'You have a look of me, you know, especially around the eyes. Florence might have the brains, but what chap is interested in brains?' He laughed and his hand wandered to her knee and rested there. A nest of snakes stirred in Sarah's mind. She jumped up.

'I'd best set the table for Mam,' she said.

116

Her father's mouth drooped and animation left his face, leaving it slack and drained of expression. 'Aye you do that,' he said. 'I'll have a kip.' A few minutes later he was asleep.

Sarah went into the scullery and stared out of the small window. The spring day was ending and darkness crept forward, hugging the buildings and making familiar objects strange and indistinct. Somewhere a dog howled and next door water from a broken guttering tapped insistently upon the lid of a dustbin. She sighed and leant her forehead against the cold glass.

Why, oh why, had she been in such a hurry to come home?

Damn the rain. Martin Linford tilted his umbrella in a vain attempt to divert a stream of water which was running down his back. As he did so, he bumped into the figure of a girl hurrying past him.

'Sorry. Oh, it's you.'

She was soaked. Her dark hair was plastered to her pale face in wet streaks and her coat was wet through.

'Quickly, get under my umbrella.'

Sarah's face was unsmiling: 'I don't think . . .'

'For goodness' sakes, girl – be sensible.' He took her arm and pulled her under the precarious shelter. 'We'll still get our feet soaked, but it's better protection than none. Here, you hold this and I'll take your case.'

'Oh, but it's not heavy . . .'

'Do you have to argue about everything?' He took hold of her case, reclaimed the umbrella and they walked along the road. She had to run to keep up with him. 'Sorry. I forget. You're so small, aren't you? Haven't got great long legs, like mine.'

'Do you have to keep saying sorry.'

He paused, then laughed. '*Touché!*' He slowed his steps

117

and they splashed along in silence. The streets were deserted. A peal of thunder rent the air.

'It's getting worse. Look – let's pop into this teashop. It's stupid to be out in this lot.'

'Oh, I don't know. It doesn't seem right.' She looked at his quizzical face, then nodded. 'All right. I won't argue.'

The entrance to the teashop held the scent of wet waterproofs and toasted muffins. Inside, the tables were covered with crisp white tablecloths. Two young women with shingled hair chatted and smoked, creating a hazy cloud over their table in the window, and in a corner a lady of indeterminate age peeped over a large potted plant and tinkled away at the keys of an ancient piano.

'It's quite nice in here, isn't it?' Sarah, divested of her coat, pushed back her hair and smiled at Martin. He was amused to see she was now entirely composed. Having voiced her doubts as to the propriety of them being seen together, she obviously intended to enjoy herself.

'Have you never been here before?' He beckoned the waitress who hovered in the background wearing a pained expression.

'Goodness no. Bit too genteel for us. Oh!' She put her hand over her mouth to suppress a grin but her eyes sparkled and he found himself smiling in sympathy.

'Where do you go on your days off?'

She shrugged. 'Different places. If it's nice, I walk in the Winter Gardens. And Alice and me go to the pictures.' She stopped as the waitress approached their table, pad in hand.

'We'll have a pot of tea, please, and some Dundee cake. That all right?' He looked at Sarah. She nodded. The waitress noted down the order and departed, throwing Sarah a suspicious look.

'Not very welcoming, is she?'

Sarah shrugged. 'No, but she's probably coming to the end of her shift. I expect her feet are killing her.'

Martin smothered a smile. 'I never thought of that.'

'Well, you wouldn't – would you?'

'Now what does that mean?'

'Nothing.' Sarah picked up a spoon and trailed it across the tablecloth.

'I'll have you know, young woman,' Martin spoke with mock solemnity, 'I know all about working for a living. This past year I have worked at all kinds of jobs, including that of a waiter.'

Sarah looked up. 'Honest?'

He nodded.

'Fancy that. Of course,' her voice dropped. 'I suppose it was difficult for you trying to get a gentleman's job straight away.'

Martin's smile faded. She gave him a startled glance then looked away. The waitress brought their order and left.

'I'm sorry, Mr Linford. I don't know why I said that.' Sarah fixed her gaze on the silver-plated teapot.

'No, it's all right.' A nerve jumped in Martin's cheek but his gaze was level. 'It *was* hard when I came out of prison. They kept us locked up until 1919, you know. I still can't vote. "Conchies" aren't human beings to some people.'

'But,' Sarah fiddled with the spoon again, 'it wasn't as if you'd killed anyone. Nothing as bad as that?'

'A lot of people thought it was worse!' Martin's voice was morose. He leant forward and looked at her intently. 'What do you think, Sarah?'

'Me? Goodness, I don't know.'

'Go on, tell me the truth.' It was suddenly important to Martin to know what this little maid with the dark blue eyes thought about him.

'I don't like . . .'

'Tell me!'

'All right.' She looked into his eyes. 'I don't know much, but I think you should have fought.'

He sat back and gave a short laugh. 'Thanks,' he said.

She saw the white line about his mouth. 'Shall I pour the tea, Mr Linford?' she said.

'Yes. Yes, of course. Pour the tea by all means.'

'Do you want some cake, sir?'

'No. And stop calling me sir.' Irritably he ruffled his drying hair and although she was nervous she couldn't help smiling at the figure he presented.

'What's so funny?'

'Nothing.' She looked at the cake. 'It seems an awful pity to buy cake and then not eat it.'

He capitulated. 'Go on then. Just a small slice.'

Sarah cut a thin slice and a larger one for herself.

'How was home?'

'Pardon?'

'I missed you. My mother said you went home for a short visit.'

'Yes.' She put her piece of cake carefully on her plate. 'It was very nice, sir.'

'Nice is a terrible word and I asked you not to call me sir.' He was watching her intently. 'Home was "nice", was it?'

'Yes . . . Mr Linford.'

'You're lying,' he said quietly. 'Mother would be disappointed in you, Sarah.'

Ridiculously, her eyes brimmed with tears. He looked away, patted the pocket of his jacket. 'Do you mind if I smoke?'

She shook her head.

He lit a cigarette and watched the thin trail of smoke.

'It's never so good, is it?' he said. 'When you're actually there.'

'What isn't?'

'Anywhere,' he replied. 'Home for instance.' He was silent for a moment, then continued. 'All the time I was in that hell of a prison I kept thinking of home. That was the house in London, but it was Mother and Father I kept thinking about. Mother with her serenity and soft voice. You know, I don't think I have ever heard her shout. And Father, so cheery, a real gentleman.'

He squashed his cigarette with a savage gesture into the ashtray . . . 'When I was finally released, I couldn't face them. I *was* a coward then, Sarah.' He smiled briefly and gazed towards the steamed-up window of the café as though visualising a far-off place.

'I couldn't tell them, you see; just how dreadful it had been. They would never be able to understand – how it changes you. They never understood why I refused to fight.'

He fell silent and Sarah, unmoving in her seat, watched him.

'Then I came back, to Harrogate, and I found Mother lost in a world of her own and poor old Father gamely trying to pretend everything was the same. And it's all my fault. I've messed things up for everyone.'

'Don't say that!'

He blinked and stared. Sarah's face was bright with anger.

'I *hate* those words. It's not all your fault. Things happen, people change. You can't be responsible for everyone.' She shrugged her shoulders in an angry, helpless gesture. 'My brother, he tried to do his best for everyone. He was so good. And he wore himself out trying to keep everyone happy. You mustn't let people claim you. Just look after yourself, that's enough.'

He looked at her in surprise. 'Poor Sarah,' he said. 'That's a bitter philosophy for one so young.'

Her face closed up. 'I don't understand long words, sir.' She glanced towards the window. 'I think it's stopped raining. We'd better go now. Mrs Harman's expecting me back by five o'clock.'

He followed her to the door and held her coat for her. She waited as he paid the bill.

'I did enjoy the Dundee cake, Mr Linford,' she said.

'So did I,' he answered.

'I think,' she paused before opening the door, 'it might be better not to mention our meeting, up at the house.'

He felt another spurt of irritation. 'I couldn't care less whether they . . .' he started to reply, but she was already out of the teashop and walking briskly down the road. He shook his head and started after her.

Chapter Thirteen

Sarah grabbed the carpet sweeper and dusters and bolted into a nearby, unused bedroom on hearing Martin's voice in the corridor. She waited with bated breath until his footsteps passed the door before she relaxed. She liked Martin much more than his brother, but he confused her. Since their visit to the teashop he seemed purposely to waylay her. He would engage her in conversation when she was polishing the windows or clearing away the breakfast things. The conversations were impersonal, but he watched her so intently she became flustered and wished he would leave her alone. She supposed she had become a sort of curiosity to him because she had spoken her mind. Life had been simpler before his arrival.

She put down the cleaning things and went towards the window. The room she was in smelt fusty, it could do with an airing. She drew back the curtains and flung open the window. That was better.

It promised to be an idyllic summer's day. Sarah leant over the window-sill and breathed deeply. Somewhere, an unseen thrush sang its heart out and, in their borders, the bright flowers shone like silk. The smell of the sun-warmed earth rose upwards and permeated Sarah's senses, awakening a corresponding glow within her. She wrapped her arms about herself to contain the strange, sweet sensation.

She thought back to the scene in the library two days ago. Martin had entered and found her holding a book of poetry. She had tried to replace it, but he had rested his hand on hers, restraining her.

'Do you read poetry, Sarah?'

She had seen the surprise in his face. It had angered her. 'Of course not.'

'Then why?' He had raised his eyebrows.

She was conscious he still held her hand.

'I was just looking. My brother used to read poetry. I wanted to see what was special about it.' In a belligerent voice she added, 'I don't read much at all.'

She did, of course. Every week she and Alice called at Smith's Circulating Library to search for the latest Ethel M Dell or Berta Ruck novel. But obscurely, she recognised Martin would not consider such books 'reading'. She found them rather silly herself, but Alice loved them.

'And what did you think of the poetry?'

What business was it of his? she thought. 'Not a lot. I couldn't make head nor tail of it.'

She pulled her hand away and left the room. It was the truth. The poems were full of words she couldn't understand and talked of Grecian urns and pilgrimages. Yet, some of the lines had rung in her mind and, as she turned to resume her work, she remembered them:

'That's the wise thrush; he sings each song twice over
Lest you should think he never could recapture
That first fine careless rapture!'

Her feeling of restlessness continued. Later in the day she coaxed Mrs Harman into letting her off work for an hour. She walked into town and, feeling guilty, bought herself a coat dress of blue light-weight gaberdine. She was so sick of wearing dowdy old clothes. She had enough money left for a pair of artificial silk stockings and, with her last sixpence, she bought a box of pink face powder from Woolworths.

Alice expressed approval. 'Time you smartened up. I know, swap your next afternoon off with Betsy then you can come out with me. We'll go to the Crescent Gardens. We'll listen to the band and see if there's any good-looking blokes about.'

Sarah hesitated and Alice wagged a finger at her.

'You should get yourself a boyfriend. I hope you're not getting ideas about Martin Linford, Sarah. I've seen you two in huddles together. You want to be careful.'

'Don't you dare say another word.' Sarah's eyes flashed dangerously. 'If you've seen us, then you will have seen me trying to avoid him. I don't even like him. Anyway, you're a fine one to talk. What about Percy?'

Alice looked slightly shamefaced at the mention of her faithful swain, then she brightened up. 'It does no harm to have a bit of fun now and again. After all, you're only young once.'

Alice was right, thought Sarah as she lay in bed a few nights later. She had enjoyed her afternoon off. The sun had shone and the young bandsman had told her she looked 'smashing' in her new outfit. They had strolled among the crowds, eaten ice cream and she had adroitly dodged his clumsy kiss as they stood behind the bandstand. He wanted to see her again though. She smiled. She guessed *he* didn't read poetry.

Mrs Harman munched reflectively on her seedcake. 'Sweet-breads en caisse,' she mused. 'Perhaps caviar canapés for starters.' Martin's return home had transported the cook to seventh heaven. During the last weeks, Mrs Linford had held two luncheon parties followed by a small dinner party. Now Mrs Harman was preparing for '*la pièce de résistance*'!

'Pity you've not got proper training, Sarah,' she lamented, popping the last few crumbs of cake into her mouth. 'Because you'll have to wait on, you know.'

'Oh, no!'

'What's the matter with you, girl? Nobody will bite you.'

'I just hate it, Mrs Harman. I don't know why. I go all fingers and thumbs. Why can't Alice do it?'

'Because Alice is clumsy and like as not she'll break out into giggles. No, you are quick and quiet. You'll manage all right.'

Sarah was silent, her face downcast.

The cook shook her head. 'No good looking like that. You'll have to get used to it. Mr Osgood says Mr Redvers is qualifying soon and Mr Martin's going back to his studies so there will be lots more entertaining. In fact,' Mrs Harman lowered her voice, 'there's talk of them returning to London to live.'

'London?' Both Sarah and Alice, who was stacking pots on the dresser, repeated the word.

'Just a possibility, but a strong one.'

'If they do, what will happen to us?' Alice asked the question; Sarah was staring into space.

'I will probably go with them.' Mrs Harman smoothed her apron. 'Mrs Linford values a good cook when she sees one and there's nothing to keep me here. As for you two,' she looked thoughtful, 'I don't know.'

'London.' Alice sighed. 'It's a long way isn't it, almost like another country.'

Sarah's face was expressionless. 'We don't even know if they're going yet so I shouldn't bother about it.' She walked towards the pantry. 'I'd better take up the hot water, Mrs Harman.'

'Funny lass.' The cook stared at her retreating back. 'I like Sarah but you never know what she really thinks, do you?'

The dinner guests had arrived. Two old gentlemen who had tutored Mr Linford at Oxford were staying in the house, the rest had booked into the Prospect Hotel for the night.

'They must have pots of money,' commented Alice. 'Did you see their cars? Percy says one of them is a "Roller".'

Percy once more figured in Alice's affections. After a couple of dates with the bandsmen Sarah and Alice had agreed that good looks were not everything. Wearing uniforms made young men vain and inclined to demand too high a payment for the occasional ice cream and afternoon tea.

Sarah did not respond to her friend's chatter. She was dreading the dinner party. Redvers would be present, and Martin and all the important-looking gentlemen and their well-dressed wives.

At least she enjoyed preparing the table. When it was finished she touched the crystal epergne which was the centrepiece, the long-stemmed sparkling glasses and the embossed silverware with gentle fingers. Everything looked wonderful. She checked the time then slipped away to don the special organdie apron and coronet cap Mrs Linford had bought for her to wear. She would try hard not to let her employer down.

Under Mr Osgood's guidance she managed the soup course but, following the fish course, disaster struck. As she came forward to clear, she tripped over the edge of the carpet. She recovered quickly but she heard Mr Redvers mutter something to his neighbour and they both laughed. At that moment, she hated him, hated all of them: the men in their dress suits and stiff collars; their women, with their flashing earbobs and brooches. Scarlet-faced she approached the table and reached over to take an elderly gentleman's plate. It was heavy and her hand was shaking. Horror-struck, she watched the fishbones slide off the plate and on to the guest's long white beard.

'What the . . .' He stared downwards in disbelief.

'Sorry. I'm sorry sir.' Sarah put the plate back on the table and, biting her lips, attempted to pull the bones from his beard. She met with singular failure. The only one she managed to extract brought with it a tuft of white hair.

'Leave it. You stupid girl.' The old man looked apoplectic.

Sarah stepped back. She was on the verge of tears and dare not look at the faces watching her.

'Clear off.' A voice hissed behind her.

She jumped. 'What?'

'Go – now!' Mr Osgood caught hold of her elbow and gave her a none-too-gentle push. She ran. Outside the dining-room she stopped. She wanted to be sick. The door opened behind her. She braced herself.

'Come on, Sarah. Don't look so tragic. It's not the end of the world.' It was Martin. She looked at him in bewilderment; he looked amused.

'It's not funny,' she stuttered.

'But it is. The look on the old buffer's face.' He laughed.

She slapped him.

'I'm glad you're amused.' Her words were forced from her in gasps. 'But then, that's what we are here for isn't it – to wait upon you and occasionally amuse you, stop you from being bored?'

His grey eyes darkened. He put his hands on the wall on either side of her and looked down at her. 'Do you really think that?'

128

'I don't know what to think. I know I've let your mother down. Oh,' she put her hand to her mouth. 'You shouldn't have followed me out. You've made matters worse. Please go back in there.' She ducked under his arm and rushed away from him. In her bedroom she flung herself down on the bed and cried.

Why did things have to change? Why couldn't things stay the same?

Next morning Mrs Linford sent for her. She looked with concern at the pale, shadowed face of her maid.

'You mustn't upset yourself, Sarah. It was partly my fault. I knew you had not been trained in silver service and yet I expected you to cope.'

'I'm very sorry, ma'am.' Sarah's voice was low. She did not look at her employer.

'You are a good maid, my dear. The trouble is,' Mrs Linford tapped a pencil on the desk, 'we are thinking of returning to London. I would suggest you go with us but we will be entertaining a good deal. Mr Redvers is to practise as a surgeon and as he is unmarried he will live with us.'

'I would prefer to stay in Yorkshire, ma'am.' Sarah stared down at her linked fingers. 'When will you be moving?'

'Two, perhaps three months' time. We have our London house, you see.'

Sarah looked up at the picture of the dying Saint. She never had found out his name. How long ago was it since she had first seen him? Not so long really, yet Hammond House and its inhabitants had come to mean a great deal to her. Now everything was disintegrating.

'Would you like me to enquire as to another post for you, Sarah?'

'No, thank you.' She smiled shyly at her employer. 'I

would welcome a reference though. I've loved being here, but I think I would like to try some other form of employment. I'm not sure what. But a reference . . .'

'Yes of course. I shall write you an excellent reference.' Mrs Linford's voice was kind but abstracted. She was consulting a written list in front of her. Sarah realised she had already been crossed off and Mrs Linford was moving on to the next item. Feeling a little chilled, she stood up.

'Before I go, Mrs Linford, I just want to say again how sorry I am.'

Mrs Linford looked up from her list. Her lips twitched. 'It was unfortunate,' she agreed. 'Still, I suppose it will be one dinner party which will always be remembered.'

Sarah stared at her. Did she think it was funny, too? Strangely enough, the thought of Mrs Linford smiling over the affair did not hurt her as much as Martin's amusement. But no, she was mistaken, her employer gazed back at her with her usual serene expression.

'Run along, dear.'

Alice decided to stay in Harrogate. She would find work somewhere and Percy was talking of marriage.

'But Alice, you'll need some money to set up a home.' Sarah was worried for her friend. She thought of her mother's ceaseless battle against poverty. 'Percy doesn't earn much, does he?'

'No, but we can get a couple of rooms easy enough. It's having some cash to buy furniture that's the problem.' Alice laughed. She was not one to worry about the future. 'Me dad will see us all right. So long as I keep working, we'll manage. He'll be glad to see me settled. I'm not getting any younger and life's galloping by, Sarah.'

It certainly was. Day by day the familiar surroundings

were changing. Curtains and carpets were removed from unused rooms, cleaned and packed for transportation to London. Prospective buyers arrived to view the house. Sarah felt a pang of sorrow when the anguished Saint was shrouded in canvas.

There had been few occasions to see Martin since the night of the dinner party. Sarah had heard an altercation between father and son one afternoon and Martin had rushed out of the library dark-browed. He had passed her without even seeing her. Sarah experienced the same chill she had felt when Mrs Linford ticked her off the list of 'things to be seen to'. Her employers were a fine family, but obviously their paternalistic attitude did not extend to real friendship. She had been a fool to think otherwise.

Martin was to spend some time in Oxford on some course or other. The day before he left he came looking for her. For the first time in her life, Sarah played the coward. She took refuge in a broom cupboard until he gave up the search. Why, she could hardly explain to herself. She just wanted a bit of peace. The Linford family had caused her too much hassle. She was better away from them.

The day following his departure she felt depressed. Even Alice noticed.

'You need cheering up,' she said. 'Why not come with us tonight.'

The imminent departure of the family had led to a slackening of the house rules and the maids were allowed out for the occasional evening.

'Betsy knows where there's a fortune-teller. We're off to get our palms read. Come on, Sarah. It will be fun.'

She went. The fortune-teller, satisfyingly foreign-looking, plied her trade in the back room of a boarding house. Alice was told she would marry young and bear four children.

131

'Not too soon, I hope,' she muttered to Sarah, but she dimpled and laughed.

The woman stared down at Sarah's palm.

'I see a parting of the ways,' she whispered.

Sarah sniffed. It was obvious she had heard Alice and Betsy babbling on in the next room.

'You will move to a place where there is much water. There will be tears in the night and a tall, dark man.' She glanced at Sarah. 'You'll not have an easy life but there will be sunshine as well as tears.'

'Thank you,' Sarah said politely.

The woman dropped her hand. 'That will be two shillings,' she said.

Next day Sarah was perusing an old copy of *The Lady* which Mrs Linford had given to the cook.

'Situations in Branswick,' she read. 'This beautiful seaside resort offers much in the way of employment for smart young ladies who are willing to work hard. Write to the Information Centre, Branswick for details.'

Seaside resort. Sarah had never seen the sea. She stared at the magazine in mounting excitement. *The Lady* was a respectable magazine. And what had the fortune-teller said? 'A place where there is much water.' She went to find a writing pad and envelope. Jobs were hard to come by in Harrogate, unless you were a maid, and she wanted a change. She couldn't park herself on Mam, so Branswick it was going to be. Seated at the kitchen table, her tongue poking from the corner of her mouth in concentration, she started to write.

Chapter Fourteen

The blue-jerseyed fisherman lurched towards the door completely oblivious of the chorus of jeers and catcalls which followed his progress. He cannoned into tables and stumbled over stools before reaching his objective. He fumbled with the door handle, fell outside and retched into the gutter. A card-school, seated near the doorway, cursed as the howling north-east wind roared gleefully into the pub and sent their cards flying but Sarah, sweating behind the bar, was grateful for the rush of clean air. The sounds issuing from the groaning figure sprawled outside did not disturb her. Five months spent working in the Flower in Hand had extended her education amazingly.

'Not long to go now, ducks.'

Her fellow barmaid, a buxom woman with red, recently marcel-waved hair, grinned at her as she deftly pulled pints for the vociferous crowd demanding last orders.

'I'll get the glasses.' Sarah scurried between the tables avoiding, with good nature, a few groping hands. A wave of laughter came from the men standing at the bar. Some cheeky remark from Maisie, no doubt. Sarah glanced her way and smiled. Good old Maisie. What would she have done without her?

Green as grass she had been on her arrival in Branswick. She winced at her memories. She had arrived at the end of

October, naïvely expecting blue sea, holiday-makers and a choice of jobs. The reality chilled her; in more ways than one. Branswick lay on the north-east coast of Yorkshire. As she left the railway station, a freezing wind tore into her and buffeted her through near-deserted streets and into the Employment Exchange.

The woman who answered the bell obviously thought she was mad.

'But it says here,' explained Sarah, waving the now tattered magazine and the slip of paper the Information Centre had forwarded, 'plenty of work.'

The employment clerk, a thin lady, her neck bowed beneath the weight of two rows of chunky glass beads, read in silence.

Finally, she spoke: 'These advertisements were put out at the beginning of the season. Of course there were plenty of jobs then. But now it's out of season.' And she stared in mingled irritation and pity at Sarah.

'But there must be something.' Sarah was appalled. She had exactly ten shillings and ninepence in her pocket. With a patient sigh the clerk pulled a square box to her and opening the lid flipped through the cards. She shrugged. 'The hotels are closed down, the cafés too.' She paused, extracted a card and looked at Sarah. 'No, I don't think so.'

'What is it? I'll take anything.'

'Ever worked as a barmaid?'

'No – but I'm a quick learner.' Sarah did not even pause before she replied.

The clerk looked dubious. 'I don't know that you would wish to work at the Flower in Hand.

Sarah felt a lift in spirits. 'What a nice name.'

'The name is the best thing about it. It is quite a small place but frequented by the fishermen and people who work near the harbour. It's below the Bar, you see.'

Sarah didn't. It was the first time she heard the expression she was to hear so many times in the future.

'If there's nothing else, I'll give it a try.'

The woman sniffed. 'I'll give you a note, then.' She stamped a printed card and passed it to Sarah. 'Turn left at the end of this street. That will bring you to the main street. Turn right and you'll come to Foreshore Road. The Flower in Hand is just around the corner.'

Sarah walked to the bottom end of the main street. So this was a holiday resort out of season. She passed gift shops and kiosks. They were boarded up, only grime decorating their windows. Torn posters flapped in the biting wind exhorting non-existent visitors to enter the 'nail-biting Chamber of Horrors' or have their fortunes told by Gipsy Rose Lee. This part of town was deserted. Sarah walked briskly onwards.

She heard the sound of the sea before she saw it. The tide was in and grey waves pounded the beach where, half sub-merged in the sand, rusting iron swing supports waited stoically for spring and a coat of new paint. Sarah shivered. Branswick, out of season, reminded her of a sad clown's face devoid of greasepaint.

The pub sign creaked noisily. It was an old-looking build-ing with small windows. Sarah pushed at the door. It opened. Inside it reeked of stale tobacco smoke and beer. Sarah stared at the scarred bar tables embellished with glass rings and burns from cigarette ends.

A woman came through and stood behind the bar. 'Yes, love?'

'I've come about the job.' Sarah handed her the card the employment clerk had given her.

'The boss is out just now and we're closed. Still, if you want to wait?'

'Yes please.' She looked about her, wondering where to sit.

'Fancy a drink?'

'Oh, no. I don't drink.'

'That's good for starters.' The woman laughed. 'You wouldn't believe how many boozers try and get jobs in pubs. What's your first name?'

'Sarah.'

'I'm Maisie. Maisie Hooper. Pleased to meet you.' The woman thrust out her hand and grinned. Sarah put out her own hand and felt more cheerful.

To her surprise she was offered the job and Maisie helped her find digs.

'Mrs Smith is a trawlerman's widow and very respectable though a bit po-faced,' she explained to Sarah. 'Since her old man drowned, she's taken in lodgers. You'll be all right with her.'

Maisie steered her through the first week of work when Sarah thought she would never survive pub life. 'They are only big kids, Sarah. Don't mind them.'

Sarah did mind them. She hated their swear words, the way they spat and missed the spittoon. She hated the eye-stinging smoke and the way her feet stuck to the floor which was tacky with spilt beer.

'I'll find something else,' she said to Maisie as they cleared up after her first evening. 'I'll go back into service.'

She shuddered as she thought of her Mam or Mrs Linford seeing where she worked now.

Maisie sighed and stuck a fresh Woodbine in her mouth. 'You're not at Harrogate now, ducks. Here it's all boarding houses and b & b. And it's out of season. Oh, in the summer you'll get a job. They'll be crying out out for you. And they'll work you to death and pay rotten wages. I know.

I've had some of it. No, you stay here. I'll learn you the ropes. Oh, Gawd.' She stubbed out her tab-end as she heard the landlord's voice.

Maisie kept her promise. She taught Sarah to pull a good pint and add up in her head without making mistakes. She tipped her the wink about putting the odd coppers in a glass beneath the bar instead of taking the drinks they were offered. Sarah also learnt how to handle amorous customers without offending. She was so adept at this she became quite popular. 'Little ice girl' the customers called her, consoling themselves with the thought that if they got nowhere with her, well, neither did anyone else. There was always Maisie.

Maisie was the most popular barmaid below the Bar. In drink the seamen became sentimental, comparing Sarah to daughters or long-ago first loves. Maisie was different. They swopped jokes with her, delighted in her crude wit, confessed their sins to her when they were full of drink and, whenever possible, slept with her. Maisie liked men.

'I don't know how you can,' said Sarah when she knew Maisie well enough to be honest with her.

'It's easy.' Maisie laughed, her big warm laugh. 'They deserve a bit of comfort. Terrible life they have at sea, you know. Many a good bloke has sailed out of that harbour and never come back.'

'But some of them are married.'

Maisie looked thoughtful. 'It's a strange thing, lass, but wives often forget how to be women, haven't you noticed?'

Maisie took her about and showed her the town. Bar Street was a narrow street leading off to the right of the main street. Years ago it had been the boundary of the sea port and each evening a huge wooden gate had been closed at curfew time. The gate had long gone and the town had grown and sprawled in all directions away from the original fishing community.

Below the Bar, lay the beach; the cockle and whelk stalls; the fish-gutting sheds; the gift shops selling buckets and spades and paper Union Jacks; the donkey rides; everything, in fact, to gladden the hearts of the factory lads and lasses who poured into the town for the annual Wakes' week holidays.

'It's a great place, then.'

Sarah had to take Maisie's word for it. She waited longingly for the clown to don his make-up.

Above the Bar were the better shops, the theatre and the cinema. Further away still, on the South Cliff, stood the imposing Victorian hotels surrounded by verdant bowling greens and well-set-out public gardens.

'This garden – it's a picture in the season,' enthused Maisie, sitting down on an iron bench and easing her finger round a too-tight shoe. Sarah looked at the small pool before them, its rank water covered with a green slime. A morose statue of Pan crouched on his plinth in the centre of the pool playing his pipes for a couple of bedraggled sparrows.

'I can't wait,' she replied dryly.

'Aye, it's a bit depressing right now,' agreed Maisie. 'Come on, let's go back to the pub.'

In the evenings the Flower in Hand was noisy, smoke-ridden and scruffy, but at least it was boisterous and full of life.

'Come on you drunken sods, let's have you.' Maisie, drops of perspiration rolling down her cheeks, snatched glasses off the bar.

'Any time you like, Maisie.'

Sarah caught hold of the old man's elbow and he snorted

with laughter and held on to the bar. She gave him a gentle push in the direction of the door then lifted the bar stools on to the tables. As she retraced her steps a dark, well-built man finished his drink and handed her his glass.

'Thanks.'

'My pleasure.'

He wore a suit and was not a fisherman. Perhaps he was off one of the deep-sea trawlers. He nodded to her and left. Sarah returned to help Maisie with the glasses.

'Who was that chap, Maisie? Have you seen him before?'

'He's not a regular, but he comes in now and again. Why, do you fancy him?' She gave a cackle of laughter.

Sarah flushed. 'Don't be daft. He seemed to have nice manners, that was all.'

'He's a dark horse, that one, very quiet. You be careful.' She tossed a dishcloth over to Sarah. 'Wipe the bar, love – then we're finished.'

They collected their coats and left the pub.

'Walking my way, Maisie?'

'Not tonight.' Maisie turned up the simulated fur collar on her coat. She gave a half-rueful smile. 'Just popping round to see a friend.'

She flapped a hand at Sarah and, turning, disappeared into the warren of streets leading away from the harbour. Sarah walked back to the boarding house. She put her hands in her pockets and her fingers touched the postcard she had received that morning from Alice. She and Percy were formally engaged, she told Sarah. She hoped Sarah liked her new job. As an afterthought she put that Mrs Harman had written to her. Things were going well with the Linford family and Mr Martin had passed some important exams.

When Sarah reached her lodging she took off her shoes

before tip-toeing upstairs. She had promised her landlady she would not disturb the other residents when she was in late. Mrs Smith had two other lodgers, yet the house was always quiet. We're like shy mice, thought Sarah, hiding away in our rooms.

Once in bed, she listened to the sound of the sea. It was a lonely sound. She owed Mam another letter but it was difficult to write what Mam wished to read without lying. She sighed in the darkness. Florence was to be married soon and Arthur was off junketing abroad again. He was living the life of Reilly. Ruby Tyler, who still kept in touch, had written to say she now had a boyfriend. Sarah grimaced. Fancy papering a bedroom wall with mud-coloured paper, she thought suddenly. When I have a house, it will be white, and yellow and light blue.

She tucked the bedclothes firmly under her chin. A sneaky draught was blowing the curtains. She drifted off to sleep imagining her own house. Nothing too grand, but she hoped it would have a tiny garden. There was another figure in the house, a man. A blurred combination of grey eyes and a wide smile, overlaid by an older man's powerful form with a strong unsmiling face and dark brown hair. She slept.

Chapter Fifteen

Suddenly, it was Whitsuntide. At regular intervals trainloads of holidaymakers poured from the railway station, flowed down the main street and settled on the beach. Overnight, swing boats appeared by the harbour, donkeys plodded their patient path between the site of the crab stalls and the rock shop, and the Punch and Judy man drew record crowds. Some fishermen offered boat trips around the bay and the sea welcomed the landlubbers graciously, changing from sullen grey to a sparkling blue. Branswick, like Sleeping Beauty, had awakened and come down to breakfast, beautiful.

Landladies smiled and offered two kinds of jam for tea, the large hotels blossomed in new drapes and tea dances, and the Lyric Theatre was packed every night.

On Sunday afternoon, Victor Manvell whistled as he came down the stairs of his home and entered the kitchen.

'You're never going back to work?' Mrs Manvell's face showed consternation as she saw her son reach for his working jacket.

'I told you, Mam.' Victor patted his pocket to check on the existence of his keys.

'But Gracie Johnson and her mother are coming to tea.'

Seeing the storm clouds gather in her face, he sighed. 'I have to, Mam. The new show starts tomorrow and one of

141

the sets isn't finished. There's a couple of spotlights to fix, too.'

'But why is it always you has to do everything?'

He shrugged. 'That's the way it is. Anyway, sooner I'm off, sooner I'm back.'

He left the house with a feeling of relief. With a bit of luck he'd miss Gracie and her Mam altogether. When he turned the corner of the street he started whistling again.

Maid of the Mountains, he mused, that had been a grand show, lovely music. He wished he could live at the theatre. He loved everything about it: that special smell of grease-paint, dust and paint, the bustle before the show, the excitement of the audience. He didn't get hassled there, no women to bother him. Oh, sometimes a chorus girl would give him the eye but he had their measure and they never stayed long. He got his share of nagging at home, didn't he? He sighed. Mam had done a good job raising two youngsters on her own but it had made her bossy. Wasn't so bad when Ted had been around but since he had upped and gone to Canada she had been hard work.

He arrived at the Lyric and unlocked the stage door. If only she'd give up this idea of him marrying Gracie Johnson. At the thought of Gracie's pendulous bosom and pale, gooseberry-coloured eyes, Vic shuddered. It must be six or seven years Mam had been pushing Gracie at his head. Christ, he was thirty years old; you would have thought she would have realised by now he had no intention of marrying. The only thing he loved was the Lyric.

He walked through the echoing dressing-rooms and down the steps to the back of the stage.

'That you, Vic?'

He frowned. No other person should be here; it was his time. 'Yes. Who is it?'

There came the sound of a hacking cough. Victor's face cleared. It was only Micky Shand. The old man appeared from behind the fire curtains and shuffled towards him.

'I got the blue paint out. You said you might need it.'

'Yes, thanks, Micky.'

Micky scratched his bald head and hesitated. 'Want me to stay and help?'

'No, you get off. I can manage.'

Watching Micky's reluctant retreat Victor felt a pang of guilt. He knew the old man would have preferred to stay, but he didn't want him. He needed to be alone. By the time the stage door shut with a muffled bang Victor had already forgotten him. He walked to the front of the stage and looked appreciatively at the auditorium. The walls were coloured a deep salmon pink and crystal-drop chandeliers hung from the panelled ceiling. The Grand Circle curved lovingly towards the boxes at either side which were embellished with lush and fulsome drapery.

Box of Delights – that's what it was. When it was empty it was his own personal plaything. Full, the applauding audience swept him into god-like realms. He had never told anyone, of course. Asked about his job as stage manager he'd reply: 'It's all right.'

He returned backstage and stripped off his jacket. The backcloth did need brightening up. He'd put another coat of colour on the sky. He applied the paint happily. Thank God he'd miss Gracie's high-pitched voice. Why did women always talk so much? The chorus girls, in the dressing-rooms, they were the same. Yap, yap, yap. Unaccountably, the image of the dark-haired girl in the pub by the harbour rose before him. He rested his paintbrush. Could be on the stage, that one; wonderful eyes, she had. He shook his head and moved the paint pot. Nice low voice, too; God knows what she was doing in a rough joint like that. Still, probably not as innocent as she looked. He'd met girls like her in France. Looked like butter wouldn't melt in their mouths until you got them in a field with their skirts up.

He reckoned a number three spotlight would pick up that colour fine. He whistled softly through his teeth as he worked. When he had finished, he checked his pocket watch and frowned. He didn't want to go home yet. It was a fine day; he'd have a walk to give them time to clear away the tea things and get off to the evening church service.

After the hushed dimness of the theatre, the late afternoon sun felt good to Victor. He strolled along the Cliff Walk then went downwards, towards the beach. When he reached Foreshore Road it was quiet once more. The day trippers had departed for their trains and charabancs, and the proper visitors had trailed their sand-filled shoes back to hotels and boarding houses in search of high tea. He crossed the road and leant over the iron railings. A small boy enticed a shaggy mongrel into the waves creaming the yellow sands, and out at sea a lone trawler throbbed its way to its fishing grounds followed by a crowd of screaming, swooping gulls. He closed his eyes and breathed in the tangy salt air.

'Lovely, isn't it?'

Disconcerted, he looked round. The girl from the Flower in Hand had joined him. She put her hand on the railings and turned to smile up at him. When he made no response, the smile faltered, then disappeared.

'I'm sorry,' she said. 'I shouldn't have spoken, but it's such a beautiful day. It seems a pity not to share it with someone. And we have spoken before, don't you remember?'

'Yes, I remember.'

He guessed she was lonely. There was a wistful note in her

voice. He stared at her. She had cut her hair since he had seen her last. It curved gently about her shapely head giving her the look of a medieval page. Her dress was the usual low-waisted, straight unbecoming style but the breeze from the sea was moulding it to her body, clearly revealing her high round breasts and tiny waist. Victor's pulses quickened and annoyed with his own feelings, he frowned.

She coloured and put her hand up to her hair. 'Does it look awful?' she asked. 'I've been home for my sister's wedding and Maisie persuaded me to try a new style. It won't stay straight though, and I'm not sure . . .'

'No. It looks nice.' He shifted uneasily. He didn't know whether to go or stay.

She smiled again.

Abruptly, he asked: 'Maisie – is that the other barmaid, the brassy looking one?'

Her smile faded again and the strongly marked eyebrows drew together in a straight line. 'Don't say that. Maisie's a good sort. She taught me my job and is a friend of mine.'

He felt uncomfortable. 'Sorry. But she's a lot different from you, isn't she. I mean, you don't even look old enough to work in a pub, particularly one like the Flower in Hand.'

'I'm nearly twenty.' She tossed her head.

He looked out to sea again. He was sure she was lying.

'Anyway, I'm on the look-out for a better position.'

He felt easier. She was only a kid, after all. 'Are you a good barmaid?'

'Of course I am. Why? Do you know of a job?'

He hesitated. It would be better if he kept his mouth shut. He wasn't sure he wanted to keep bumping into this young woman.

'There may be a job coming up at the Lyric.' He heard

himself speak with a feeling of astonishment. 'One of the women who work in the bar is packing in.'

Her eyes sparkled. 'The Lyric, that's really posh, isn't it? It looks it; what's it like inside?'

'You mean you've never been?' He gave her a look of amazement.

'Well, I'm working most of the time and when I'm off, I usually go to the flicks.'

He shook his head. 'Do yourself a favour and go and see a live show. We do all kinds of shows: musicals, straight plays, reviews. Why, Stainless Stephen played the Lyric last month.'

'Did he?' she said politely.

He could tell she had never heard of him. 'Well, maybe I'm biased,' he said. 'I work there, you see.'

She put her hand on his arm. 'You will let me know?' she said. 'About the job, won't you?'

He straightened up and took a hasty step backwards. 'If I hear anything, I'll tell you,' he promised.

On the Tuesday evening he entered the bar. He saw her look up, blush, then start to polish glasses furiously. The plump one came across to serve him.

'I'd like to talk to her,' he said, gesturing towards the dark girl.

The fat woman gave him an unfriendly look.

He stared back. Whatever the girl said, it was easy to see this – Maisie was it? – handed out more than beer.

'Sarah, you're wanted.'

Sarah, it suited her.

'Is it about the job?'

It was hot in the pub and her sleek hairdo was dissolving into tiny curls about her ears and forehead.

'No. I haven't any news about that yet.' He put two tickets on the bar.

'They're for the Thursday matinée,' he said. 'I hope you can go. Everyone should go at least once to a theatre. Take your boyfriend, or someone.'

'I haven't . . .' she started to say, but he had turned and left the bar.

Chapter Sixteen

Sarah and Maisie went to the theatre and Maisie talked all the way home. The Lyric was posh but you could see the faces clearer at the pictures. The previous week she had visited the Roxy and seen Lillian Gish in *Broken Blossoms*. It had been lovely. She had cried all night.

Sarah did not listen, she was speechless. She had never seen anything so grand. The splendour of the rococo ornamentation, the leaf-scrolled architraves, the opulent velvet drapes appealed to an unrealised streak of sensuality within her. When the curtain rose and the expectant murmuring of the two thousand-strong audience hushed into silence, she was entranced and the glamour of it all mixed inextricably in her mind with the tall, dark man who had given her the tickets. The next time Victor entered the pub she rushed over to him.

'It was wonderful. I can't tell you how much I enjoyed it all.'

The ghost of a smile passed over his face. 'I thought you'd like it. I'll get you more tickets when the programme changes.'

He hesitated then, looking at her with a funny expression on his face, almost as if he didn't know whether to like her or not. When he finally suggested he meet her afterwards, she was delighted.

Maisie was not pleased. 'What about poor Jenks?' she asked.

'Oh, Maisie.'

Jenks was a tow-headed young fisherman who had been dangling after Sarah for weeks.

'I can't be bothered with Jenks. He's just a boy; surely you can see the difference between him and Victor.' She savoured the name, Victor Manvell. 'He practically runs the Lyric, you know. Everyone listens to him, even the stars. He's quite good looking, don't you think, a bit like John Gilbert?'

Maisie was not convinced. 'Why isn't he married already, that's what I want to know? He must be thirty-five, if he's a day. Not natural, a man that age living with his mother.'

'He's thirty. That's a lovely age. He's a gentleman. He doesn't swear or spit.' Sarah looked with disfavour at the spittoon by the bar. 'Anyway, I like him.'

But did he really like her? About once a week he would arrange to meet her. He took her to tea in a café which reminded her fleetingly of Harrogate and for a trip on a pleasure steamer. He listened to her chatter but said little himself.

'You're very quiet, Victor?'

'Yes, I know.'

He had looked at her so seriously, she had felt a flicker of alarm. Did he never laugh? Then one day he had shown her 'his' theatre. He took her round the huge expanse backstage, showed her the so-called 'demon traps' which were utilised during the pantomine season and explained the 'Chariot and Pole' which enabled smooth scene changes. She watched his suddenly animated face, noticed the sideways glances from passing stagehands, heard them whispering. They were obviously surprised at her being Victor's companion. He seemed a lonely, romantic figure to her and her young heart swelled almost maternally at his enthusiasm for his work.

'Were you in the war, Vic?'

His face smoothed into blankness. 'In France two years,' he replied, 'but I'd rather not talk about it.'

There were many things he would not discuss. She knew he had a younger brother in Canada and his father had died when they were both young. His apparent lack of ardour frustrated her and yet intrigued her. Feeling disloyal, she discussed him with Maisie.

'It's not as if I'm bad-looking, is it?' she asked, with a touch of complacency.

'Don't fish for compliments from me, madam.' Maisie gave her a shrewd look. 'You know the effect you have on most men. Still,' her brow furrowed, 'remember what I said, perhaps he's a "nancy-boy".'

'No. He's certainly not that.'

Sarah was positive Victor found her desirable. There was a tension in him when she linked his arm or touched him in any way. So why wouldn't he respond? She became determined to break through his reserve. She found herself playing the coquette and despised herself, but she was hungry for affection. All around her she saw couples. Young ones kissing and cuddling in the gardens; old ones strolling arm in arm. Florence was settled in her own home now and on her last visit to Swaithdown Sarah had found Lucy Smailes engaged to a young farmer. Why, Alice and Percy were expecting their first baby. Maisie wasn't worried about getting married, but Maisie was a law to herself. Besides, she had a different man every week.

'What's it really like, Maisie?'

'What kind of question is that? You know what's for, don't you?'

'Of course I do.' Sarah coloured. 'But you know – is it like in the books?'

Maisie chuckled. 'No, but it's a bit of all right.' Then she looked seriously at Sarah. 'Don't you go being silly. You've plenty of time left for that kind of thing.'

But Sarah was restless. She read *Wuthering Heights* and, thrilled by the story, imagined herself as Cathy. She wrote to her mother and told her of Victor's polite manners and his job at the theatre. Then she waited hopefully for the courtship to progress.

Nothing changed. The woman working at the theatre bar decided to stay on for a few more months, Victor still met her once a week and, as Christmas approached, she knew no more about him than the actors she watched strutting the stage of the Lyric. Until one evening in December . . .

Victor watched her as she waved and ran across the street to join him. She looked happy but he saw her smile fade as she approached him. He realised how grim he must be looking and he tried to relax and to force his face into a welcoming smile. He was obviously unsuccessful because as soon as she joined him, she asked, 'Is something the matter?'

'Nothing. Let's go in here for a drink.'

Without waiting for a reply he propelled her into the nearest public house and ordered a whisky for himself and a glass of port for Sarah.

She tasted her drink and pulled a face. 'I'd rather have had a lemonade.'

He ignored her and, downing his drink, went to the bar for another one.

His sainted mother, God, she had a tongue on her!

Talked to him as though he was a child. He was taking out a barmaid, was he? Barmaid – she had spat the word out as though it spelled 'whore'. What was he thinking of? What about poor Gracie? That girl had spent the best part of her life waiting for him. He'd shamed her. She'd gone on and on. His hand clenched on his glass.

'Are you sure you're all right, Vic?'

'Yes. I'll just get another drink.' He went back to the bar.

They all nagged, all of them. He'd actually raised his hand to his mother. He was ashamed of that. But why couldn't she leave him alone. He didn't want Gracie, not like he wanted Sarah. There, he'd finally admitted it to himself. God, *how* he wanted her. But no woman was ever going to tie him down. Not ever! He glanced back at her. She was watching him anxiously. He bought her another port. She was a bonny lass. He'd enjoyed seeing the stage-hands ogle her. That had been a smack in the eye for them. They thought he was strange because he wasn't always talking about women. He took a gulp of his drink. What would they think if they knew he frequented the street women down below the Bar. His mother would die. Yet it seemed clean enough to him. You paid your money and gained quick release. The whores didn't suck your lifeblood out of you. There was no talk of 'belonging' and 'loving'. He took the glass of port over to Sarah.

'I've got you another drink.'

'Oh, it's a bit . . .'

He glared at her.

'Right. Thank you.'

He sat beside her. The whisky was blurring the sharp edge of his anger. He smiled at her and she immediately smiled back. God, she was so pretty. He honestly believed she didn't realise the effect she had on him.

153

'This one tastes better than the last.' She dimpled.

'They usually do.'

They stayed in the pub until closing time and Victor drank steadily.

'You working over Christmas?' he asked.

'Yes. But I've got a week off in the New Year and I'm going home for a visit.'

'You ought to get out of that dump, you know.' He brooded. He'd show his mother. 'Mrs Olds, that woman in the bar at the Lyric, she's definitely going in the New Year. I'll fix you a job there, Sarah.'

'Oh Victor,' she clasped her hands together, 'that would be smashing.'

When they left the pub it was raining. Sarah shivered and clung to Victor's arm.

'I'd best walk you home.' Victor's voice was slurred. He had drunk far more than his usual ration of whisky.

'Oh, I don't feel like going back yet. I'm too excited. I'll get to talk to all the stars won't I?'

'Ivor Novello's coming next year.' Victor blinked and swayed.

'Can we go there now, Vic, see where I'll be working?'

He looked at her. Because of the rain, her dark hair was springing into a riot of curls. The three glasses of port had turned her eyes into stars and her cheeks to roses. He felt a slow throb of desire.

'Why not?'

Recklessly he hailed a taxi.

The bar at the Lyric was as ornate as the theatre. Their steps, muffled by thick carpets, did nothing to disturb the brooding magnificence of the red-plush seating and long mahogany bar. Sarah flopped into one of the elaborate couches.

'Have you keys to everywhere?' she asked in a whisper.

'Yes. Just me and Mr Benson, the owner. The staff have to put their takings and keys into an overnight safe so if anything happens they call me out.'

'You must be very important,' she said, and yawned, resting her head back on the couch and stretching her arms above her.

He came to her; kissed her, gently at first and then with increasing pressure. She returned his kiss gladly, but gasped a little as the force of his embrace increased. Her skin was damp from the rain and she smelt clean and sweet. He kissed her closed eyes and the tiny pulse that beat at her temple, then his lips moved downwards.

As he unfastened her blouse she made a token resistance, but he brushed her hands aside and caught his breath at the sight of her breasts. Her pink nipples hardened and peaked as he ran his fingers over them, then bent his head to suck and nuzzle them. She groaned with pleasure and, wrapping her hands in his dark hair, she pulled him to her.

His breath caught in his throat. He wanted her so much. His movements became rougher as he pushed up her skirt and pressed open her legs.

'No!'

Her head rolled back and her hands pushed at his shoulders but he couldn't stop now. The sight of her white skin and the tangle of dark hair drove him wild. He forced his way into her. She cried out. She was a virgin. He knew at once. He ground his teeth and slammed into her again and again. She'd asked for it. Beneath his pleasure, his satisfaction, he felt guilt, and guilt made him angry. He thrust again and again and, as he did so, Sarah's fingers scrabbled against the velvet covers and her eyes moved wildly from his swaying figure to the frieze of carved actors' masks bordering the ceiling. With blind eyes, they gazed back at her.

Breathing heavily he pulled away from her at last. She said nothing but her body trembled uncontrollably and her dark eyes were huge in her pale face.

Expressionless, he looked at her sprawled naked body. He was still angry. To lose one's control, in this place, it was like blasphemy. He rubbed his face. He'd had too much drink. Drink and women – he groaned.

At the sound she scrambled awkwardly upright and reached for her clothes.

'It's all right, Vic,' she said. Her voice was uncertain. 'I do love you.'

'You'd better get dressed,' he said, and turned away from her. He could not bear to look at her but she made a small noise and he was forced to face her again.

'I think I'm going to be sick,' she said.

He guided her behind the bar, to where the sink was. 'I'll wait outside for you,' he said.

It had stopped raining. They walked in silence through the deserted streets. Outside her lodgings, they stopped.

'I'll see you next week?'

He could hear the panic in her voice.

'Probably.'

He walked away from her, hating himself. He could feel her watching him until he turned the corner of the street and out of her sight.

Chapter Seventeen

The shelter, perched high on the Cliff Walk and facing the sea, was an attractive vantage point in the summer but, on a late afternoon in February with the boom of the sea beneath them and the damp air misting the iron seat upon which they were sitting, it was a forlorn meeting-place.

Victor glanced at Sarah. In the poor light her features were indistinct. He could see the outline of her short, straight nose and her determined chin, but not her expression. She was staring straight in front of her.

'I wish you hadn't come to the theatre like that,' he said.

'I'm sorry. But I had to see you, talk to you and,' her voice was low, 'you didn't come looking for me.'

He shifted uneasily. 'I thought you were visiting home.'

'Oh, Victor – I've been back ages. You must have known.'

He felt in his pocket for a cigarette, remembered he was out of them and swore softly under his breath. 'I've been busy. Two of the scene shifters have been off work with flu.'

'Too busy to see me.' She turned to face him. 'Didn't you want to see me?'

'I . . .' He started to speak but she interrupted.

'I'm expecting, Vic. I'm sorry, but I don't know what to do.'

His breath expelled in a long sigh. 'Just my bloody luck,'

he said. He felt, rather than saw, her shiver and was filled with compunction.

'Are you sure? It's not very long . . .'

'I'm sure.'

He looked at her properly this time. She was huddled in her coat, and looked small and scared. She reminded him of an animal caught in a trap, awaiting the hunter's knife.

Poor little bugger, he thought. He remembered the way she had looked when they had first met and talked down by the sea. Her face all lively, full of expectation that life promised good things. Like a little kid, really, and now she was carrying one. His kid. Well, he hoped it would have its mother's nature. A child. He'd never thought of having a child. A faint warmth grew within him. He smiled. 'Well,' he said, 'we'd best get married then.'

'Victor!'

The joy expressed in that one word caught him off-guard. She laughed out loud and flung her arms about his neck.

'I love you, I love you,' she said.

'Steady on, I'll not be much good to you if you throttle me.'

She laughed again and nestling close to him nudged his arm about her.

'You'll not regret it, Vic. I'll be a good wife.'

'I know you will.' He stroked back her curls. Maybe it will be all right, he thought. A sneaky wind blew round the shelter, causing them both to shiver.

'Come on, I'll walk you back. It's damn cold in here.'

Beaming, she stood up and tucked her hand into his pocket for warmth. 'I can tell my Mam, can't I Vic? I mean, we won't have to be too long, will we? We don't want people knowing . . .'

'You do that.'

Harsh reality chilled the glow inside him. Ma – she'd kill him; and there was Gracie and his Ma's church-going friends. He cringed inwardly. There'd be scenes, recriminations. He lengthened his stride in an unconscious attempt to escape the inescapable. Beside him, Sarah made a small sound of protest as she struggled to keep up with his fast pace. Her face still glowed with relief, but she tugged at his arm, made him stop.

'Everything's all right, isn't it? I mean, you *do* want to marry me?'

He took her hands and looked down at her. 'Yes, it's all right.' He cleared his throat. 'Look, Sarah, I don't know how to say this but . . .' he fumbled for the right words, 'I never saw myself marrying. It's not you; I just never saw myself with a wife, a family. Still, I promise you, I'll do my best, I really will.'

Through the bay window, Cissie Manvell watched her son and his 'intended' approach her front door. She cast a sharp eye on the windows of the houses opposite. Yes, the lace curtains were twitching. She smiled thinly. The gossips were enjoying a field day.

The door opened.

'We're here, Ma.'

The great lummox! A surge of irritation rose within her at the sound of his voice. To be taken in at his age. She clasped her hands and turned to meet them.

So this was her future daughter-in-law; not what she had expected. The girl's head was bent, but she could see her face was pale and unblemished by the thick make-up she had feared. Small in frame, she was neatly dressed with small hands and feet yet, Cissie saw, those hands were square and capable looking, the nails short, the fingers work-reddened. Cissie felt the first stirring of hope.

Then the girl looked up and the hope died. The full wanton mouth, the firm chin, the gleam in her eyes, swiftly veiled by sooty lashes as she glanced downwards again, confirmed Cissie's worse fears. There was going to be trouble ahead. She forced her thin lips into a smile.

'Pleased to meet you,' she said, untruthfully.

'I'm glad to meet you at last, Mrs Manvell.'

'I'm sure you are.' Warmed by a flicker of satisfaction at the look of uncertainty in the young woman's face, Cissie turned to her son.

'Don't just stand there, Victor. Take her coat.'

He flushed and waited until Sarah had shrugged out of her coat and then left the room to hang it on the hallstand. Cissie didn't like things out of place. The two women stood and looked at each other until he returned.

'The table looks very well, Ma.'

Cissie's eyebrows rose. Victor was actually making conversation. She thought of the many times Gracie and Ivy had been to tea and he had sat there, dumb as an ox for hours on end.

'Well, this is an occasion, isn't it?' She waved towards the laid-out meal. 'Sit down then.'

No one had much appetite, which was a pity considering how much food cost. When the pretence of eating ceased, Cissie pushed her chair back.

'Time for some straight talking, I think.'

The girl, no, Sarah – she had to think of her by name, hadn't she? – folded her hands on the table.

'Victor and I want to get married as soon as possible,' she said.

'I'll not argue with that; seeing how things are.' Cissie

spoke directly to Sarah: 'He tells me he's sure the child is his.'

'Ma!'

She ignored his interruption. 'That being the case, he must do the right thing, of course.'

Sarah looked across at Victor, but he was staring at the bread he was crumbling on his plate.

Cissie continued: 'I'll not pretend I'm pleased, but what's done is done. Now – are you still at *that* place?'

'The Flower in Hand, do you mean? Yes, I am.'

'Well, the first thing to do is hand in your notice. No daughter-in-law of mine should work in a place like that, and particularly in your condition.'

'But the baby won't show for a while and I thought,' Sarah swallowed painfully, 'we'll need to save to get a place to live.'

There was a shocked silence.

'A place to live?' Cissie turned to her son.

He glanced up from his plate. 'We haven't really discussed everything, Ma.'

'But Vic!'

Cissie's voice cut through Sarah's appeal. 'You'll live here, of course. Do you think my son's made of money?'

Without waiting for a reply, she swept on: 'Victor and his brother were born in this house. On my own, I struggled for years to keep a roof over our heads. Still, I'll not dwell on that. Ted's in Canada now, but Victor's been a fine son. He pays the rent, sees to things. There's plenty of room here for all of us. We'll be all right.' She sighed. 'And when my time comes, you'll be able to take over the tenancy without any trouble. The furniture will be yours, everything.'

Ignoring Sarah's reddening face and the looks she was

sending Victor, Cissie reached for the teapot. Now she'd had her say, she felt more comfortable. 'Let's have another cup of tea. Have you been to see the vicar yet, about the wedding?'

'We thought, the Registry Office, Ma.'

At her son's remark, Cissie dropped the teapot on to the table. 'Oh! Now look what you've made me do! Oh, dear, my best cloth!' Her complacency shattered, she covered her mouth with her hand. 'You *must* have a proper wedding, Vic. I'll never live it down if you don't. The Registry Office! You might as well live in sin.'

She gazed at her son then at the spreading tea stain. 'That tablecloth's ruined.'

She began to sob.

'Don't Ma, please.' Victor sprang to her aid. 'It'll be okay. Soak it in cold water, it will come up good as new.' He placed his arm about her shoulder. 'Don't fret. We'll have a church wedding, if that's what you want.'

Cissie leant against his shoulder in weary relief. She didn't even notice the bewildered expression on the face of the girl as she sat by the table, forgotten.

Late in April, Sarah and Victor were married in the parish church. There were few guests. Despite Cissie's disapproval, Maisie was the bridesmaid dressed in a pink woollen stockinette jumper suit which clashed violently with her hair. Maisie was the one dash of colour in a sombre occasion. It was Maisie who arranged a collection at the pub and, on behalf of the staff and customers, presented Sarah with a flamboyant mirror decorated with carved cherubs and bunches of grapes. It was Maisie who went to church to hear the banns called and Maisie who produced a posy of flowers for the bride to carry.

'Hold 'em well down, ducks,' she advised. 'You're beginning to show a bit, see.'

Sarah, suffering from pregnancy sickness and torn between feelings of doubt, anticipation, pleasure and despair, clung to her friend. Mrs Manvell, once the date was set, took no further interest in the wedding. She invited no guests. Sarah was aware of her feelings. The wedding was just something that had to be got through.

The final blow was when Mary Armstrong was unable to attend. At least, Sarah comforted herself, her Mam had met Victor. They had visited Swaithdown in March. As usual, Victor had said little, but he had listened to Joe's rambling tales and told Mary he would do his best to look after her daughter. Strangely enough, he had got on well with Harry, now a boisterous lad of ten years. As she watched them together, the reality of her own baby strengthened and she felt more at peace with herself. She, Victor and their child would be a true family and nothing Victor's mother could say or do would spoil things.

She told her mother the truth of course. One did not lie to Mary Armstrong. Her response heartened her.

'He seems a good steady man,' she said. 'Maybe a bit old for you but that could be a good thing. You were always one for getting in a pickle, Sarah. His ma sounds a bit of a tartar, but once the bairn arrives you'll not have time to worry about her. Like as not, she'd made her own plans for him, mothers are like that. She'll get used to things as they are.'

'I know, Mam. We'll be fine. I do love him, only he's hard to understand sometimes.'

A spark of amusement lit Mary's eyes. 'You don't have to understand your man, Sarah. Just be thankful if he comes home on a night and gives you the rent money every

163

week.' She shook her head, 'I don't know where you get your fancy notions from.'

Sarah didn't either, but deep inside her lurked an ominous feeling that all was not as it should be and, try as she may, it wouldn't go away.

A couple of hours before they had to return to Branswick she left the house alone and climbed up the hill to the moors.

'Jim,' she whispered. 'Where are you? Tell me what to do?' She watched the white clouds scudding along in the March wind. There was no Jim, no easy answer. There was nothing she *could* do, except be grateful. She walked back slowly. What was it Jim had said, about dancing? She grimaced. She doubted whether there'd be much dancing at her wedding.

Mary Armstrong was all ready to travel to Branswick but the day before the wedding Florence suffered a miscarriage. She was very ill and Mary went to nurse her. Poor Florence. She was desperate to have a child. When she was recovering Mary told her about Sarah. Her face soured. Trust Sarah – some people couldn't wait until they had a wedding band before they were at it!

There was no reception. After the service, Victor, Sarah and Cissie went back to 82 Victoria Street. Cissie put her coat away.

'I've already moved my things into the back bedroom,' she announced.

'Aw, Ma.' Victor ran his fingers through his hair. 'You shouldn't . . .'

'No. It's right you have the big bedroom. There's a good wardrobe and chest of drawers; plenty of room for your things.' Her eyes passed over Sarah as though the girl was not there. 'I'll go and start tea.'

'Oh, let me do that.' Sarah started forward. 'I'll just put this in water.' She touched her posy with gentle fingers.

'No. I'd prefer to do it. You sit down. You don't know where things are.'

Cissie's ramrod figure swept from the room.

Sarah shrugged. She crossed to Victor and sat beside him on the uncomfortable slippy couch.

'Hello, husband,' she said.

He took her hand. 'She'll get used to things, love,' he said. 'Just be patient. She's a bit upset, that's all.'

As dawn broke the next morning, Sarah lay beside Victor and wished she could cry. If she cried perhaps the painful ache in her throat would go away. Fingers of light poked through the curtains, touched the dark wallpaper and the heavy, looming furniture and sought vainly for motes of dust to dance in its rays. The room was sterile in its cleanliness. Victor's head was burrowed in the pillow, his arm lay over her, a dead weight. She shifted slightly and looked at him, critically, as one would look at a stranger. For he was a stranger.

Last night she had reached for him in love and gratitude. She was now his wife. They could start their life together.

He had repulsed her. It was late, he had said. She must be tired. They must think of the baby.

'But we're married,' she had cried.

Best sleep now, he had said. There's plenty of time. Anyway, it was difficult. Listen how the bed squeaked, even when they just turned over. Sleep tight, he had said.

Sarah shifted on the lumpy mattress. The bed was noisy. She squinted at her left hand. Yes, it had happened. The ring was there to prove it, and the flowers. She looked towards the posy on top of the chest of drawers. Mrs Manvell hadn't approved of flowers in the bedroom. Sarah had flared up then, insisted. The daylight caressed the blooms, freesia mainly; how pretty, delicate, they looked. At last the tears flowed; silent tears.

Chapter Eighteen

'You've got a visitor.' Cissie Manvell, her face expressing a mixture of distaste and hauteur, stepped aside, and Maisie Hooper swept into the bedroom.

Sarah, lying uncomfortably in bed, her body still sore from the trauma of childbirth, was delighted to see her. She pulled herself up on the pillows and grinned as Maisie pulled a face behind Cissie's back. The older woman placed a wooden chair next to the bed and, without speaking again, left the room. She still wore the long dark dresses of a former decade and beneath her breath, Maisie hummed a chorus from *One of the ruins that Cromwell knocked about a bit* as the sombre, upright figure departed. Then, disregarding the chair, she plumped herself down on the side of the bed.

'Right. Where's this week's wonder, then?'

'Here.' Beaming with pride, Sarah reached into the cot beside her and lifted out her three-day-old son.

'Edwin Victor Manvell, nine pounds three ounces,' she boasted.

'My God!' Maisie poked her finger through the layers of clothing. 'That's a big 'un for the likes of you, Sarah.'

The baby twisted his face into a grimace.

'Not much in the looks field, is he?'

Sarah laughed out loud. 'He's beautiful,' she protested, smiling at the pink-rouged face of her friend.

167

Victor Manvell, entering the house, heard his wife's laughter and his faced relaxed into smiling sympathy. When had he last heard Sarah laugh like that? he mused. Not for a long time.

'It's *that* woman,' hissed his mother. 'That hussy from the Flower in Hand.'

He looked at his mother's furious face and his shoulders hunched. 'It'll do Sarah good to have a visitor, Ma,' he said.

Upstairs, Maisie was telling Sarah the latest news from the pub. 'We've got a new landlord,' she said. 'Great big fellow with a funny name, Leif Svenson. His dad was a foreigner but he's from Hull. Been at sea for years but now he wants to settle down. He's a good man. When he calls time, they're all out in ten minutes.' She stopped talking and delved into her handbag. 'Mind if I have a fag?'

'Oh, no.' Sarah's face clouded. 'Sorry, but if she smells cigarette smoke near Eddie she'll hit the roof. Even Victor can't smoke in the house anymore.'

Maisie shrugged and put the Woodbines away again. 'Well, love,' she said, 'how do you feel?'

Sarah stroked her son's tiny hand. 'Oh, I'm coming round now,' she said.

'You still look peaky but you've got it over with now, so that's a good thing. That husband of yours, treating you well?'

There was a short silence then Sarah blurted out: 'It's not Vic, it's her, his Ma. We're never on our own, Maisie, except in this room on a night and even then she's in the next room, listening. I'm not allowed to do any housework and I don't have any money. Victor gives it to her because she does all the shopping.'

Maisie frowned. 'I suppose some folk would like having

nothing to do and lots of couples do live with their in-laws,' she commented. 'Perhaps now he's arrived,' she gestured at the baby, 'things will be different.'

'Worse, I should think. She's already started.' Sarah mimicked her mother-in-law: ' ''Don't keep picking him up all the time, you'll spoil him.'' ' Her eyes flashed. 'He is *my* baby.'

'Doesn't Victor say anything to her?'

'I don't know,' Sarah rocked Eddie as he whimpered softly. 'He's not strong, like I thought, Maisie. And he's so quiet, I just don't know what he's thinking. When his Ma and I have a row, he just gets up and walks out. He won't discuss anything, and he . . .' she stopped.

'Go on, love. You might as well get it off your chest,' Maisie encouraged.

'He doesn't seem interested in me. I didn't expect . . . when I got big . . . but even before.' She bent her head to kiss her baby and her hair fell forward across her face obscuring her expression.

Maisie's expression was incredulous. 'You mean, you've never . . .?'

'No. Of course not. It's not as bad as that. It's just . . .' she could not finish. How could she explain their infrequent, yet violent couplings to Maisie? How he would ignore her for weeks then turn to her and without a preliminary kiss even, force his way into her unready body; and always silent, aware of the woman in the next room? How, once he had finished, he would roll to the far end of the bed, still wordless, leaving her bruised from his roughness, yet her body clamouring for something unknown, unexperienced?

'I don't mind really.' She hurried to reassure Maisie. 'I think this sex business is over-rated anyway, don't you?'

Maisie did not answer her immediately and her plump face held a troubled look, then she said, 'When you're on your feet

169

again, you have a go at his mother. Victor's had her bossing him about all his life, but you're different. You're Vic's wife and now you have a kid so give her what for and bugger the consequences.'

She's right, thought Sarah. After Maisie's departure she lay in bed cuddling her son and felt new strength flow into her. She was a woman now, not a silly girl, and Cissie Manvell wasn't going to walk all over her.

Victor came to see her. 'You look better today, Sarah,' he said. 'Maisie's visit has done you good.'

'It has.'

She considered him. He avoided her gaze and looked instead at their son.

'How is he?'

'Beautiful. Here,' she sat up higher in the bed and thrust the child towards him. 'You hold him.'

'Oh, I don't know. He's so tiny.'

'Tiny – he's enormous! Go on, Vic, he won't break.'

She watched as he rocked the child. Eddie yawned and Victor's face broke into a smile.

'Are you happy, Victor?'

'Eh, what?' He looked up, his smile fading. 'What kind of question is that?'

'It's important Vic.' She pressed on: 'It's lovely, isn't it? Just the three of us.'

'Aw, don't start that again. We have to stay here.'

'But I don't see why.'

He put the child back into her arms. 'Look Sarah, Ma would kill me if she knew I told you, but our dad didn't die young. He walked out on us. I was four and Ted was only two years old. Ma's proud, you know that. Well, she grafted, worked at anything she could find and she brought us up proper. She even found the sixpence a week it took to keep us at school. She's had no pleasure in life, Sarah, and that's why she seems hard at times.'

He turned away from Sarah and looked out of the window. 'Ted's gone now and I'm left and I'll never desert her. Anyway it would be stupid to pay two lots of rent. There's plenty of room here. You'll just have to learn to get on with her.'

He stalked from the room. Sarah hugged Eddie to her chest.

'No wonder Ted went off to Canada,' she whispered. 'Well,' her face hardened, 'we'll have to make some changes, won't we?'

A month later, Cissie Manvell was surprised when a delivery man knocked on her front door.

'New bed and mattress, missus. Sign here please.'

'Bed? I haven't bought a bed. You have the wrong house.'

A voice called down the stairs: 'It's all right. I ordered it.' Sarah came to the door. She smiled at the man. 'Up the stairs and in the front bedroom, please. Can you manage?'

'You never told me about this? And who's paying for it, pray?'

'That's my business, isn't it?' Sarah brushed past her and helped the man as he manoeuvred the mattress along the narrow passageway. Cissie retreated to the kitchen and slammed the door shut.

Victor got it at teatime.

'You should have asked me, Sarah,' he said. 'Where's the money coming from to pay for it?'

Sarah reached for another slice of bread. 'It costs seven pounds, ten shillings,' she replied. 'I had four pounds saved up so I put that down and the rest is on the never-never. The tally-man's going to call for four shillings a week until it's paid for.' She put some jam on her bread and took a bite.

171

'A tally-man, calling here? Never!' Spots of colour burned in Cissie's cheeks. 'This is the kind of woman you've married,' she hissed at Victor. 'I've never bought a thing I couldn't pay for.'

Victor was also angry. A white line showed round his mouth. 'You shouldn't have done it, Sarah.'

She kept the tremor out of her voice. 'If you gave me some money of my own,' she said, 'I could call at the shop and pay it every week, then he needn't come calling here.'

'You don't need money. Ma does all the shopping.'

'Exactly!' Sarah pushed her chair back and jumped to her feet. 'I'm your wife, Victor Manvell. I should do the shopping, not her.' She was shouting now. 'If Edwin's teething and needs some Fennings Fever Cures, I have to go and ask her. It's not fair.' She glared at her husband.

'*Women*, bloody women!' Victor stood up. 'I've had enough. You can sort it out between yourselves.' He walked out of the kitchen.

There was silence, then Sarah asked: 'Shall I make a fresh pot of tea, then we can talk?'

Cissie did not answer her daughter-in-law. 'A tally-man, coming here,' she muttered instead. 'You don't even need a new bed.'

'But we do, Ma.' Sarah placed her hands flat on the table and stared into the older woman's face. 'The one we have is lumpy and uncomfortable and I hate it. And,' she narrowed her eyes, 'it creaks something awful.'

Cissie looked away from her. 'I'll give you the difference tomorrow,' she said. 'You can go to the shop and pay it up.'

She left the room. Sarah poured herself a cup of stewed tea and looked around the pokey little kitchen.

'Won that time, Eddie,' she said to the baby, kicking and cooing in his pram in the corner of the room.

'Cheers!' She lifted the cup to her lips. The tea tasted bitter.

A few weeks later, Victor began giving Sarah a few shillings a week for herself. He hoped that would solve his problems. It didn't. Whatever he did was wrong. If he pleased Sarah his mother sulked. If he favoured his mother Sarah flew into a temper. The constant rows were driving him crazy. He spent less and less time at home. Even his delight in his son was dulled by his unhappiness. He buried himself in his work.

Lilac Time was about to open at the theatre. The leading lady was Evelyn Jeans, a star he had worshipped for many years. She was expected to arrive any minute and he hung around, like a callow youth, for his first sight of her. She entered the Lyric swathed in furs, her smile was irresistible. The first night was a terrific success. The cast took nine curtain calls. Victor whistled to himself as he straightened the props after the show. Most of the staff had scarpered, but he was in no rush to return home. He checked some fuses and turned off the remaining house lights. What a picture Evelyn had looked on stage, like an angel. He climbed the stairs to the dressing-rooms. It paid to have a last look. Despite the no smoking rule backstage there was always some idiot who stole a quick drag. A muffled giggling came from one room and there was a shuffling sound. He frowned. Everyone should have left the building by now. He pushed open the door.

Evelyn Jeans was there with a young man, the juvenile lead, a slim youth called Lionel Tindall. They turned startled eyes towards Victor. He took in the scene in silence. Close to, Evelyn Jeans looked her age. Without the disguising stage make-up her skin showed coarse and ageing. Lipstick was smeared across her mouth and her dressing-gown gaped, revealing sagging flesh. Her hand was on the young man's trousers which lay open. A cloying scent made Victor's nostrils flare. He backed away from the silent couple and clattered back, down the stairs. He rushed from the theatre and stood in the alley outside. He wanted to cry. He should have known better. They were all the same. Not Sarah, though.

For the first time in weeks, Victor really thought about Sarah. The girl she had been, not the tight-faced young woman battling daily with his mother. He thought of her feeding the child, her eyes tender. Sarah didn't wear make-up, didn't need it. And she never rebuked him, even when he used her badly. Why did he do that? He hung his head, ashamed. He took his wife as he had taken the street women he used to associate with. He'd make it up to her. She was a good mother. She'd be a good wife if only Ma would give her a chance.

He walked home through the lonely streets, thinking of Sarah, needing her. The house was in darkness. He took his shoes off in the kitchen and crept upstairs. He looked at Sarah, asleep in their new bed. He undressed and slipped in beside her.

'Sarah,' he whispered.

She turned towards him, her face rosy with sleep. He bent to kiss her.

'You're late,' she murmured. 'I waited up for you.'

The waft of perfume hit him. He pulled away from her. 'What in God's name?'

She sat up, rubbing her eyes. 'I bought it today; with the money you gave me. I thought you'd like it. Do you?' She held her wrist to his face. 'It's called June Roses.'

'It smells cheap.' He spat the words out. 'Cheap. You want to know how it makes you smell, Sarah?'

She stared at him, wide-eyed.

'You smell like a bitch in heat.'

Chapter Nineteen

In 1924 Maisie married her boss, Leif Svenson.

'We've been "friends" for months,' she explained to Sarah, her eyes twinkling with happiness. 'And he's a socialist, see.'

She laughed at Sarah's bemused expression. 'Once, when we'd had a bit to drink, he says: "If ever the Labour lot get in, Maisie love, I'll marry you".'

She laughed. 'So as soon as old Ramsay MacDonald took office as Prime Minister, I reminded him. He started muttering about "minority Government", or something but I talked him round.'

Sarah hugged her friend. 'I wish you every happiness, love.'

Maisie hugged her back. 'He knows about me,' she said. 'I told him and it's all right.'

Sarah took pleasure from her friend's happiness, but a small selfish part of her felt sorrow. Maisie had been her escape route when things became too bad at home. Although Eddie was now over a year old, she still felt an unwanted guest in Cissie Manvell's house. If she did any household tasks, Cissie would say nothing but re-do the work as soon as possible. Sarah had suggested she take over the washing. Heaving sheets out of the copper and scrubbing them on a board was heavy work for a woman of Cissie's age, but again her offer was refused.

'I'd rather do things my way,' was the reply.

When the weather was fine, Sarah took Eddie out in his pram for long walks. She wheeled him round the Italian Gardens, pointing out the colourful flower beds and the birds to him. Eddie was a placid, quiet child. Like a stoic Buddha he sat in his big pram and observed the world. He did not like too much cuddling. When Sarah's frustrated emotions overflowed into an orgy of mother-love, and she kissed and hugged him, he would struggle away from her exuberant affection.

The evenings were endless. Vic left for the theatre at six and Eddie was put to bed at six-thirty. Sarah read every book she could get her hands on. Then she sat opposite her mother-in-law and watched her knit. The steel needles flashed like rapiers and, watching the dour, silent figure – Cissie never spoke unless spoken to – Sarah raged inwardly. Was this to be her life from now on?

'Why can't I get another job?' she demanded of Victor.

'Married women don't work. Do you want people to think I can't support my family? Anyway, there's Eddie to see to.'

'Your mother does that.'

Cissie was strict with Eddie, but it was obvious she adored him. The only time she really smiled was when she was talking to him.

'Chip off the old block, aren't you, Edwin. You're a Manvell all right.'

He was. Each day that passed he grew more like his father. What's more, he loved his Granny. Sarah was chilled to see how readily he would smile and hold up his arms to her. One day, when she was feeling particularly depressed, she received a letter from her friend, Alice. She showed it to Victor.

'I'd like to visit her, take Eddie for the day. May I?' she asked.

He gave her the money.

Alice met her with open arms. 'By, it's lovely to see you, Sarah. Come in.'

Alice and Percy still lived with his parents. Sarah hoped her face did not reveal her feelings as she looked round. The family occupied the top floor of a dingy Victorian terrace house. Percy's father, mother and sister lived cheek by jowl with Percy, Alice and their two children. The room they were in was cluttered with cheap furniture, and nappies hung everywhere. They filled the room with an ammoniac stink.

Alice must have noticed something in Sarah's expression. 'Well,' she said, raising her shoulders in a shrug, 'what can you do? We have to go down two flights of stairs to get to the sink.'

Her young baby cried and, when Alice picked him up, Sarah saw his bottom was red raw. She felt almost ashamed of Eddie's rosy cheeks and neat clothes. She moved a pile of laundry from a chair and sat down, holding him on her knee.

After attending to the baby, Alice made a pot of tea. She smacked her toddler's arm when she reached for a crust of bread then, when she howled, picked her up and hugged her, dipping the bread into her teacup and placing her back on the dirty hearthrug where the little girl sucked at the crust with great enjoyment.

'How's things, Sarah? I must say, you look well.' Alice gestured at Sarah's dress.

'Fine,' replied Sarah lamely. How could she complain about her life when Alice lived like this? 'What about you?'

'Aw, it's not so bad.' Alice waved at the chaos about her.

'Percy brings fresh veg from the shop every night and his Mam and Dad are great. They work so I'm on my own most of the time. Percy's Mam has a little job on the market. It brings a few more coppers in.'

'Are you happy with Percy?' Sarah dared to ask.

'Happy?' Alice looked surprised. The baby cried again and she picked him up, opened her blouse and thrust a great breast at his little face. 'We rub along all right.' She laughed. 'He's a sexy sod when he's had a drink,' she said fondly. 'I'm off to the clinic next week. They've opened one at the new Health Centre. His Mam says I shouldn't go. It's against nature, she says, but I'm damned if I'm going to have a kid every year.'

She extracted her infant from her breast and tapped him on the back. He gave a noisy burp.

'Eh, Sarah,' she continued, fastening up her blouse. 'I can't get over you. You don't look any different from when we were at Hammond House, remember?'

'Of course I do. But it isn't that long ago.'

'No.' Alice looked thoughtful. 'It just seems it, don't it? Remember all the fuss when Martin Linford came back? I wonder what happened to 'em all?'

'I thought Mrs Harman wrote to you?'

'Not any more. She got hitched you know, to old Osgood.'

'She didn't!'

'True as I'm sitting here. Gawd, can you imagine the two of 'em in bed?' Alice went off into peals of laughter.

Sarah smiled. She was glad to see her friend had retained her sense of humour but looking about her she felt a pang of sorrow for the life Alice was now living.

They talked for a long time but eventually Sarah stood up. 'I'll have to get back for the train,' she said.

'Oh, can't you stay a bit longer?'

'No.' Sarah noticed the look of relief that flickered over Alice's face. She guessed, rightly, that Alice had worried in case she was staying for tea. 'I just wanted to see you again,' she said.

'Well, keep in touch,' said Alice, waving her off from the top of the staircase. She waved again, then slapped the grizzling toddler hanging on to her skirt. 'Bye.'

Sarah hitched Eddie up in her arms. He was a heavy baby, but she had kept him on her knee during the visit. She hadn't fancied him crawling about on the dirty floor. Fortunately, it wasn't far to the station.

She passed Montpellier Gardens, but did not even glance at Hammond House opposite. That part of her life was over. She looked instead at the fashionable clothes, the people crowding into the Pump Rooms to sample the Spa water and she admired the new War Memorial.

In the train she held Eddie to the window to see the passing countryside. She sighed at the thought of the house she was returning to, but then she shuddered. There were worse ways of living. She supposed a few people had interesting exciting lives but she didn't know anyone like that. She smiled at her son and played pat-a-cake with his starfish hands. Thank goodness, he still had sparse hair. It occurred to her she had better search through it looking for nits.

Indirectly, the visit to see Alice led Sarah to make another acquaintance. Every evening, after Cissie had retired to bed, Sarah stripped down to her underclothes and washed herself thoroughly at the kitchen sink. After Harrogate, she felt in need of something more. The next day she announced she was taking soap and towel and visiting the public baths.

179

'You don't want to go there.' Predictably, Cissie disapproved. 'You could pick up something nasty.'

Sarah went. The surroundings were shabby, but the luxury of stretching out in a bath full of steaming hot water was exhilarating. Leaving the building Sarah made the acquaintance of another young woman. Violet Willock was blonde, bubbly and what Cissie Manvell would have called 'common looking'. But she was fun.

The two women liked the look of each other and went to a café for a cup of tea. Violet laughed a lot, smoked a lot and was intensely curious.

'Eh, you don't look old enough to have a kid,' she said. 'You look about seventeen.'

Vi went to the Baths regularly. She made rock and, as she said: 'After a day working that stuff, you feel like a lollipop yourself!'

'I wouldn't mind,' replied Sarah wistfully. 'I'd do any kind of work, but Vic won't hear of it.'

'You should get out and about more,' urged her new-found friend. 'I know. Come with me one night to the Astoria. You could tell the old misery you were going to the flicks.'

Sarah had told Vi about her mother-in-law.

'I don't think . . .'

'Oh, go on! You're only a kid. You have to get a bit of fun, now and again.'

Sarah was charmed by the vitality of Violet. Eventually she agreed to meet her on Saturday. Cissie raised her eyebrows when Sarah announced she was going to the pictures but said nothing. Victor told her to enjoy herself and gave her money to buy the ticket which made her feel dreadful. She wore the gaberdine coat dress she had bought in Harrogate and her wedding ring. She enjoyed herself. She sipped a sherry and enjoyed the admiring glances she attracted, but refused to dance. She felt young again. Two weeks later, she went again. She called first at Vi's lodgings and was persuaded to wear a shimmy dress belonging to her friend. It was red, not her colour, but fitted her beautifully. The Astoria was crowded with summer visitors and the band played ragtime. After two drinks her head began to swim and she agreed to Vi's suggestion that she take her wedding ring off and slip it into her purse.

Three men came along and asked to sit at their table. Vi smiled and nodded. A big, good-looking man slid his arm around the back of Vi's chair and talked to her intently, so Sarah was left to talk to the other two. She smiled at a thin young man with dark hair and an expression that reminded her of someone but he looked downwards, studied his shoes, then went to buy another drink. The third man, older, with grizzled greying hair shouted after him to bring one for himself and Sarah and beamed at her.

'You on holiday, love?'

'No. I live here.'

'You're a lucky little girl, then. It's lovely here. I come every year.'

He told her about his job. She drank the drink he had placed before her. It wasn't sherry, but she decided she liked it. She had another and when he pulled her up to dance with him she did not demur. They both found it extremely funny when she fell over his feet. Voices grew louder, and blurred into the music, as the musicians worked themselves into a frenzy playing the latest and noisiest dance tunes.

Sarah raised her glass to Vi and winked. This was better than sitting at home opposite Cissie and listening to the clock tick. Later she lost sight of Vi and was on the dance floor doing something called the 'Bunny Hop' with the grizzled man, who was called Frank. Later still, she was outside the dance hall and leaning against a wall with Frank kissing her. The evening air was chill after the frenetic, sweaty atmosphere inside. She shivered and pressed against the warm, comfortable bulk of her partner.

'That's right, lovely,' he said in a hoarse voice.

His hands closed about her waist, drawing her even closer to him. She could feel the powerful muscles in his legs pressing against her.

'Jesus, you're really beautiful, you know.'

She closed her eyes and sensations new to her, hot and languorous, rippled through her body. He kissed her again and, as her mouth relaxed and parted beneath his, he thrust his tongue deep into her mouth.

She recoiled and the muzziness in her head retreated momentarily. She became aware of the rough wall against which Frank was pressing her, and the realisation that her skimpy dress was being drawn above her hips as his hand groped at the fastening of her camiknickers.

'Stop it!' Her voice sounded thin and harsh. She beat at his shoulders. 'I never meant . . . please . . . stop!'

'Come on, girl. Don't be a spoilsport.' He grabbed at her hair, pulled her head back and kissed her again.

She gagged as his probing tongue once again forced its way into her mouth.

'No!'

She brought her hands up to his face, scratched him. He swore. She closed her eyes despairingly as he forced her back, even harder against the wall. Then the weight of his body was removed from her. She opened her eyes. The thin young man was there. He pulled at his friend's arm.

'Pack it in, Frank. You're frightening the lady.'

The glare died from the older man's eyes. He straightened up and rubbed his hand across his face.

'I didn't . . .' he mumbled.

'It's all right. Come on. Let's go.'

Sarah shakily smoothed down her dress and gave the newcomer a hesitant smile.

'I'm very grateful,' she said. Her smile faded as she saw his expression.

'There's a name for women like you,' he said.

He leant forward and whispered in her ear, then he turned and followed his friend out of the alley. Sarah pressed her hands against the wall and tried to control the shivering in her legs. Her head ached and she thought of the thin man's face again. Of course, she remembered now, Jim would have looked rather like that if he had lived.

She pushed herself from the wall and walked slowly home. She washed herself and hid the red dress beneath the bed. When Victor came in she pretended to be asleep. Next day she washed the dress and posted it back to Violet. She never went to the Public Baths again.

Chapter Twenty

When her mother-in-law returned home promptly from Sunday Evening Service and slammed the front door behind her, Sarah raised her head from her book and sighed. She knew the two seemingly innocent incidents meant trouble. Cissie always stayed on after church for a chat with her fellow worshippers. It was the only time she left the house except to shop and church was, therefore, the social event of her week. Also, Cissie *never* slammed doors, merely closed them quietly and carefully.

One look at Cissie's face as she entered the kitchen confirmed Sarah's fears. The old woman's features, always hard, were set in a mask of ice. She marched across the room to the table, removed her hat and jabbed the hatpin into the brim. As she did so, she threw a look of such antagonism towards Sarah that it was plain she wished the pin had reached another target.

Oh Lord, thought Sarah. She braced herself for the expected assault with a feeling of dismay. As the years had passed and the two women shared the house, the husband, and the child, a state of truce had imperceptibly developed. It was tactically understood that they could never be friends but, for the sake of Eddie and Victor, a form of neutrality was observed. It was now obvious hostilities had recommenced. Cissie went straight into the attack.

'Mr and Mrs Edmunds saw you yesterday!'

'Did they?' Sarah's voice was cool but her thoughts were savage. *They would!* Of all their neighbours, the Edmunds were the couple to run and tittle-tattle to Victor's mother. 'I was only playing with Eddie. A four-year-old boy needs to enjoy himself, to have some fun.'

'Fun! Is that what you call it? Ida Edmunds said you were tearing about the park, screaming and yelling with a pack of noisy boys at your heels. She said,' Cissie quelled the tremble in her voice, 'you had a feather stuck in your hair!'

Sarah bit her lip. 'It wasn't a feather. I'd just tied my belt around my head.'

Cissie threw up her hands in disbelief. 'What are you – demented or something?'

'No. Of course not. It was just a game. The boys wore feathers. We were playing Cowboys and Indians, see?'

She knew Cissie wouldn't see. Cissie would never understand how the tight repressive life Sarah was forced to live in this bleak house stifled her. How the quiet, 'so-obedient' figure of her son dismayed her. Eddie was a little *boy*, he should play and laugh more. *She* should laugh more.

Generally, Sarah could restrain such thoughts. Unleashed, they made her miserable but, occasionally, they escaped. Yesterday had been one such occasion. After days of rain the sun had appeared. She had taken Eddie to the park. They had been walking along a path when a group of youngsters had surrounded them. They had been eight or nine years old with dirty, rosy faces and home-made bows and arrows. She had looked at them and loved them, for they reminded her of her own childhood. She had allowed herself to be captured, then she had entered their game, whooping and chasing through the trees unmindful of the disapproving stares of the matrons seated on iron benches nearby.

'Come on, Eddie,' she had shouted. 'Join in.'

And Eddie had trailed after her, ill at ease. She had embarrassed him. She knew that now.

'I thought Eddie would enjoy it,' she said.

Cissie glanced about her. 'Where is he? It's almost his bedtime.'

'He's round at number 20. It's the little girl's birthday and her parents bought her a puppy. Eddie was wild to see it. It's all right,' she hastened to add, 'I was just about to go and collect him.'

'A dog.' Cissie was further displeased. 'Sometimes I think you deliberately do things to vex me, Sarah. You know all dogs have fleas.'

She paused, but Sarah was silent, fighting down the wave of dislike and resentment she felt for her mother-in-law. So Cissie reverted to her original grievance: 'Don't you *care* what is said about you? You're Victor's wife. And you're not a young girl anymore. Don't you want dignity, respect?'

'Not particularly.' Sarah stood up. 'Not from people like the Edmunds, anyway. I want . . .' She flung out her arms in what she knew Cissie would regard as a wild theatrical gesture: 'I want a little fun and happiness. I want to hear people laugh more and I want Eddie to behave like a small boy and not a middle-aged man. I want . . .' she paused.

'Me out of the way, I suppose,' said the old woman, her voice dry and expressionless.

Sarah turned towards the door. 'I'll go and get Eddie,' she said quietly.

Cissie Manvell died in 1929. Sarah returned from a trip to the library to find her sprawled on the scullery floor, a bar of Sunlight soap clutched in her stiffening hand. The steam was still rising from the copper. Sarah stared down at her feeling no grief, no anger, nothing. Finally, she stirred herself. She closed the old lady's eyes and tugged at her skirt so it laid decently about her legs before going next door to summon a neighbour. She was glad Eddie was at school. The six-year-old was fond of his Granny.

It was generally agreed Mrs Manvell had a grand send-off. Naturally, she had kept up her insurance payments for this very occasion. No matter how hard times were, it was important to have a good funeral. There was no 'new-fangled' motor car for Cissie's last journey, but two black horses wearing mourning plumes. Back at the house, after the funeral, the neighbours ate and drank, avidly watching the principal mourners with inquisitive eyes. Victor Manvell was stone-faced as usual. And to think how his Ma had slaved for him. Poor Cissie, she never did get over the shame of his hurried marriage. And that wife of his, never did a hands'-turn in the house. Only the one child, too.

Sarah never knew Victor's feelings about his mother's death. He was called from the theatre immediately but, by the time he arrived home, his mother was laid-out decently upon her bed and the doctor was there.

'Instantaneous,' said the doctor. 'Never knew a thing.'

Victor had gazed down upon the dead woman, then brushed past the doctor and his wife and left the house. When he returned he set about the trappings of death with an impassive face and Sarah dare not put her arms about him to comfort him. Victor knew too well what she had thought about his mother.

It was strange without the old woman. Once the funeral was over Sarah began to feel deliciously free. It was *her* home now. Victor gave her the house-keeping money. She could do the shopping, cook, rearrange the furniture. She comforted Eddie whom she found snivelling on the stairs.

'Don't cry. She was an old lady. She'll be happy in Heaven.' She suppressed an hysterical laugh as she pictured Cissie Manvell, dourly scrubbing the floor of Heaven, insisting it wasn't clean enough.

'Don't cry, Eddie. Maybe we can get a dog for you now.'

Victor came back from work to find Sarah had stripped the heavy net curtains from the windows.

'But people can see into the rooms now,' he protested.

'Let them,' she replied. 'It's such a dark house, Vic. Let's try and make it more cheerful.'

Another day, he arrived to find the furniture piled into the passage and Sarah, a dab of paint on her nose, painting the parlour.

'White paint will show all the dirt.'

She glowered at him and kept on painting.

'You've missed a bit, there.' He pointed. She threw the brush back into the pot in a temper.

'Well, you help me then.'

'No, no. You want it doing, you do it!' He stalked into the kitchen. She'd been too busy to get his tea again. He sighed. He missed his mother. Many a time he entered the house expecting to hear her dry voice: 'Have you wiped your feet?' Sarah didn't notice whether he had wiped them or not. He missed his good meals and the old, regular routine. And Sarah was forever buying flowers. He attempted to remonstrate with her.

'Oh,' she replied. 'Don't nag, Victor. They were selling them cheap at the market. Almost giving them away, they were.'

'You'd do better spending a bit more on decent grub,' he said one day, stung by her irritating good humour and the fact that his dinner was over-cooked again.

Sarah's face sobered. 'I'm sorry. It doesn't taste very nice does it? I do try.'

He pushed a grey-looking potato around his plate. 'You know my stomach's been playing up lately. I can't eat this.' He moved the plate aside. 'Beats me. I give you more money than Ma had and you still can't produce a decent meal!'

Sarah banged a pot on to the table. 'If your Ma had given me a chance to cook things now and again perhaps I would have learnt to do things the way you like them,' she flared.

Victor glared at her. His eyes held a light that inwardly made her tremble, but she stood her ground. One of these days, he was going to hit her, but she'd not kow-tow to him. Anyway, she knew Victor, he loathed arguments.

He pushed past her. 'You can throw that muck out. I'm going for a drink.'

She sat down at the kitchen table after his departure. The trembling in her stomach gradually subsided. She sighed as she surveyed the unappetising food. Poor Victor, he'd got a bad bargain with her. She was a rotten cook, she had a bad temper and she had come to the conclusion she was cold by nature. There was no Cissie Manvell in the next room now, but they slept together very rarely. When they made love, she laid acquiescent beneath him, her mind dwelling on anything other than what was happening. It was better that way. She no longer raged within herself after he had finished. But she supposed it was a bit disappointing for him. Not that he would ever tell her. She rose and put the kettle on for the washing up.

Later that afternoon, someone knocked on the door. Sarah removed her apron and went to see who it was. The tall, red-headed young man grinned at her.

190

'Guess who, Sarah?'

She stared, then exclaimed: 'Arthur, it's our Arthur, isn't it?' She beamed at him, then glanced at his companion, a beautiful blonde girl expensively dressed in a wrapped-round coat of télé-de-Négre gaberdine with embroidery down the front.

'Come in.' She ushered them into the parlour thanking her lucky stars she had redecorated.

'This is Beryl, my wife.'

Sarah stared open-mouthed at her brother. It was years since she had last seen Arthur and in her mind he had remained a sniffly, whining little boy. When had he changed into such a smart, well-spoken gentleman?

He took a cigarette case from his pocket and opened it, offering it to Sarah.

'Do you smoke?'

She shook her head and he turned to his wife. 'Here you are, darling.' Beryl took one and Sarah jumped up to find some matches, subsiding into her chair again when Arthur produced a cigarette lighter. Beryl reminded her of one of the elegant creatures Redvers Linford had brought to Hammond House. She had almond-shaped brown eyes and a creamy skin. She looked quality.

'How long have you been married?' Sarah asked.

'Just a couple of weeks, actually.'

The couple looked at each other and laughed. 'We met in Aix-en-Provence.'

Sarah nodded. She knew that Arthur travelled extensively with his employers.

'I'm private secretary to the old boy now.' Arthur knocked cigarette ash on to her new hearth rug but she dare not reprimand him. 'He's given me three weeks' holiday so I'm introducing Beryl to the family.' He cleared his throat.

191

'We've visited Florence. Her husband seems a bit of a dry old stick but they do very well together.'

'Oh, yes.' Sarah didn't know what to say. This elegant man seemed a million years away from the boy she had grown up with. A thought struck her. 'Would you like to stay; for the night, I mean?'

'No, thanks. We're on our way to see Mam . . . Mother.' Arthur corrected himself. 'So we thought we'd drop in to see you. We don't come up north very often.'

Sarah looked at the clock. 'Well, you'll stay for tea and meet Victor and my son, Eddie, won't you? In fact, I'll have to pop up the road to meet Eddie from school in a minute.' She stood up. 'Make yourself at home.'

She went through into the kitchen, feverishly calculating what extra luxuries she could afford to buy for tea. Arthur followed her.

'Don't mention anything about home, Sarah,' he whispered hurriedly. 'I've told Beryl we had a bit of property in Swaithdown, see, before the miners' strike and that there's still a bit of money put away.'

'But Arthur,' Sarah was horrified, 'as soon as you get there she'll realise you were lying.'

'Maybe not, at least – not straight away.' Arthur's expression, half bravura, half shame-faced, made him seem more like the lad she remembered. 'I told her most of it went after Pa's accident. Well – I had to tell her something. Her old man's place is in Ireland and I gather he's worth quite a bit. I had to pretend we had *something*, Sarah, otherwise she might not have taken me; and I *do* love her.' He put his head on one side and grinned at her.

She shook her head. 'Well, good luck to you. Only I wouldn't like to be in your shoes when she realises the truth.'

Dance Without Music

She went off to fetch Eddie and do the shopping. Teatime was less of an ordeal than she anticipated. True, Victor retired into his shell and Eddie was struck dumb when Arthur aired some of his French expressions but the young couple were so obviously wrapped up in each other nothing really mattered.

After their departure the house seemed flat and quiet. Eddie, who had settled on a rabbit for a pet, instead of a dog, went out to pick some dandelions and Victor read the paper.

Sarah fidgeted. She wanted to talk. 'What did you think of them?' she said at last.

'All right.' Victor was not going to be drawn.

'Do you think we're alike, Arthur and me? I know he has red hair, but even so . . .'

Victor lowered his paper and considered: 'He doesn't sound much like a Yorkshireman. You'd think he came from down south.'

Rightly suspecting his remark to be a criticism, Sarah frowned, but her husband continued his line of thought.

'Still, he's lively – like you.'

'Am I lively, Vic?' Sarah was surprised. 'I know I've got a bit of a temper.'

'That's all right. I quite like it when you get all fired up.'

Sarah was even more surprised. Victor, noting her expression, fell silent and retreated behind his paper. Then Eddie dashed into the room. His hands were full of dandelion leaves and he had a smaller boy in tow.

'I'm going to feed Snowy, Mam. Can Stanley come to see the new hutch?' Sarah nodded and the two boys disappeared again. She looked about her. The kitchen looked reasonably cheerful now. It never got much sun, of course, but the new tablecloth and curtains brightened it up

wonderfully. She stood up and walked behind Victor's
chair. His hair, she noticed, was starting to go grey. It had
taken him a whole week to build the new rabbit hutch but
then, when Victor did a job, it was always done well. On
impulse, she draped her arms about his shoulders and
kissed the top of his head. His body stiffened a little, then
relaxed.

'What's that for?'

'Nothing. I just felt like it.'

'Go on with you. You daft woman.'

She ruffled his hair, then moved away. It was time she
brought the washing in from the yard. By the doorway, she
stopped and smiled. He was hidden behind his paper but
she heard him whistling softly through his teeth.

Chapter Twenty-one

By the early thirties Sarah stopped buying flowers, even cut price ones from the market. Unemployment figures soared and the recession hit everyone, not only the jobless.

Victor, handing over a depleted wage packet, explained: 'We're playing to half-empty houses. Oh, the boxes are usually taken, there's still plenty of wealthy holiday-makers but it's the others: the orchestra stalls and the pit are practically deserted by mid-week.

'I didn't realise things were that bad. The Lyric won't close will it, Vic?'

He sighed and rubbed his chin. 'No. It won't come to that, but we've all agreed to take a cut in pay until things settle down.'

Sarah looked worried. 'I told Eddie he could go on the hiking holiday. The one the church committee organised. Shall I tell him we can't manage it?'

'No. Let the lad go. It won't cost too much if they stay at youth hostels. There's one thing I've thought of, Sarah. It's something you could do.'

'You'll let me look for a job!'

He made an impatient gesture. 'No, not that. It's the artistes at the theatre; they are always grumbling about their scruffy digs and the price they pay for rooms. What if . . .?'

'They come here!' Sarah's face brightened. 'That's a grand idea. I'd enjoy the company and we'd make money. Why didn't we think of it before?'

'Your cooking wasn't good enough.'

'Oh, you.' She laughed then looked thoughtful. 'I'll spring clean the back bedroom tomorrow.'

Her first paying guest was the Grand Coram. He was a quiet, pleasant gentleman, but he was a ventriloquist and his dummy made Sarah's flesh creep. It was so lifelike. She could never bring herself to go into the bedroom to clean when it was propped up against the door. Norman Evans stayed for three weeks. A kindly man, he kept Sarah in tucks of laughter when he did his Fanny Fairbottom impression for her. She thoroughly enjoyed the company of her 'paying guests' and if Victor and Eddie would have preferred their normal, quiet routine, they made no complaint. Times were too hard to sniff at good money.

Sarah's favourite lodger was a man called Ronald Barrasford. When the tall, thin bald-headed gentleman arrived on her doorstep he spoke with such a cultured accent she was afraid their home would not suit him. He announced, however, that everything was 'capital' and proceeded to make himself at home. He played the Lyric three years running and each visit he stayed with the Manvells.

Sarah soon lost her awe of Ronald and he became her good friend. On his first evening with them she had taken into the front parlour, where the lodgers' meals were served, a plate containing a thick wedge of Yorkshire pudding covered in rich gravy. Returning shortly afterwards, to retrieve the plate, she found him patiently waiting for the accompanying meat and vegetables. Blushing, Sarah explained the Yorkshire way was to eat the pudding by itself, and he thought that most amusing but agreed it was a good idea.

Ronald, a much-travelled and well-educated man, recognised in Sarah a quick intelligence and a receptive mind. They had long conversations together. Books were his passion and he invited her to read any of his collection.

Sarah looked along the row of books, Dickens, Trollope and Hazlitt.

'But they're classics,' she protested. 'I'll never understand them.'

Ronald smiled and pressed into her hand a copy of *Emma*. 'They're about people, my dear. Try them. Give them a chance.'

So Sarah's horizons widened. Victor bought her a wireless set and she listened to classical music as well as enjoying songs by Ivor Novello and Noel Coward. She still enjoyed the friendship of Maisie and they regularly visited the cinema. Sometimes Sarah felt guilty about spending money on entertainment but, she and Maisie agreed, eightpence was well spent to enjoy the spectacle of Claudette Colbert in *Cleopatra*.

Maisie was shocked by news of the Abdication. 'His poor mother,' she said to Sarah. They were enjoying a cup of tea in Sarah's kitchen. 'She'll never get over it. And poor George. He stammers, you know. He'll just hate being King.'

'Umm.'

Sarah looked pointedly at the clock. Maisie was a dear, but she'd been going on for almost an hour. 'I'll have to start Victor's tea soon.'

'Still,' Maisie's chest rose in a gusty sigh, 'say what you like, there's no denying love. Like he said, "he can't go on without her".'

'Oh, rubbish,' replied Sarah, rudely. 'He's just running away from his responsibilities.'

Maisie looked at her sorrowfully. 'You don't understand, Sarah. You've never experienced a grand passion.' She saw the frown on Sarah's face and struggled to her feet. 'You needn't keep looking at the clock, I'm going now.' She donned her coat in dignified silence but as she reached the door she relented.

'See you next week? There's a George Raft picture on.'

Sarah nodded. 'All right, Maisie, I'll call round for you.'

Left alone Sarah felt restless. She switched on the wireless but it was a Brahms concert, so she switched off again. The silence in the house pressed in on her. Eddie was late back, but then, he was growing up fast and often away on his own business. She climbed the stairs to the bedroom and looked at herself in the mirror.

'You're getting old, my lass,' she said to her reflection. Then she laughed and stuck out her tongue. 'But not as old as Wallis Simpson.'

'You're never reading poetry?' asked Victor as they lay in bed that night.

'Yes.'

'Good God, why?'

Sarah turned over the page. Victor looked at her intent expression, her pert profile.

'It's late, love,' he said. 'Switch the light off.'

She put down her book with a sigh. As she put her head on the pillow he slid his hand under her nightdress.

Afterwards they were silent, isolated in their own thoughts.

I never really have her, thought Victor, not all of her. He kicked irritably at the bedclothes tightly tucked in at the bottom of the bed.

Sarah was drifting in a kaleidoscope of memories, feelings and desires. She remembered Jim's face that day by the river at York, she thought of Eddie's baby hands clutching at her neck. Fragments of the poem she had read twisted with the pangs of discovering her first grey hair. She wished she could think of something different to serve for dinner tomorrow. She drowned in the river of sleep.

Chapter Twenty-two

'You shouldn't have done it, Mam. I'll not work in an office. I'd hate it! I want to work on a farm.' Eddie's normally pale face was flushed with defiance as he faced his mother. 'Mr Lawrence promised me. Soon as I left school, he said, I could work on his farm.'

'Eddie!' Sarah was horrified. 'What's got into you? You've never mentioned farm work before.'

'You never asked.' The boy's lip quivered but he stared straight at his mother. 'I'm sorry but it's the only thing I want to do and I'm going to do it.' And, moving with careful precision, he left the room.

'You never asked.' The words hammered in the silence. No, she never had. Oh, Eddie, why was there such a gap between them? Had they ever been close? As a baby he had preferred his Granny. Once at school he had become totally self contained. How often had she met him, hugged him to her and questioned him about his day. Always, he had eased away from her, a look of embarrassment, almost distaste, upon his face: 'Nothing, Mam. Nothing has happened.' Until finally she had stopped asking.

She rounded on Victor. 'You heard him. Say something!'

'Like what?' He lowered his paper, a wary look in his eyes.

Why was he always reading that blasted paper?

'Go and explain to him. He doesn't know anything. He's so young. Why on earth does he want to go farming?'

Victor cleared his throat. 'It was you who took him to Swaithdown.'

'So it's my fault is it?' She sat at the table and drummed a tattoo with her fingers.

Yes, he had enjoyed visiting his Granny Armstrong and running wild in the fields. He'd been a different lad there. Two years ago, during Pa's final illness, she had been glad when her old friend, Lucy Smailes, now Lucy Lawrence, had taken him off her hands during the day.

'Let him come up to the farm,' she had urged. 'You can help your Mam then without worrying. And a young lad doesn't want to hang about a house of illness.'

She turned back to Victor. 'It's a good job Jack and Lucy aren't here now. I'd give them a piece of my mind.'

'Come on, Sarah. Calm down.' Victor folded his paper. 'It might not be a bad thing.'

'Bad thing! I get him a good job in an office – do you know how much he was going to get paid? – and instead he wants to wade about in mud looking after animals.'

'Listen to me, will you?' Victor's voice had acquired a sharp edge. 'If you spent more time reading the papers instead of those posh books of yours,' he waved her to silence, 'you'd have realised there's going to be a war. Think about it, Sarah. When it starts, and it will, it might go on for years and years. Where will Eddie be then? Choking in a bloody trench, more-like, same as I did.' He breathed heavily. 'I'd not wish that on any lad, least of all a lad of mine. If he's working on the land he might miss it. They'll leave farmworkers alone. Miners, too, I don't doubt.'

'You really think there's going to be a war?' Sarah's temper faded.

'Sure of it.'

'But he's not even fifteen yet.'

'Three years soon pass, Sarah. And they'll take the young ones first. Remember the last time.'

Sarah remembered. 'I thought there was never going to be another one,' she said heavily.

Eddie was surprised and pleased when his mother raised no further objections. He left school in July and Sarah travelled to Swaithdown with him.

'I'll not come to the Lawrences' with you,' she said as they said goodbye outside Mary Armstrong's house. She gave a rueful smile at the expression of relief on his face. 'I'd like a letter now and again though.'

He nodded.

'Do I get a good-bye kiss then?'

'Aw, Mam.' He frowned then suddenly stepped forward and gave her a violent hug. 'I'll be fine, honest.' He gave her a wide grin and trudged off carrying his case. Comforted, she went back inside.

'He looked happy enough,' she said to her mother.

'He'll be fine.' Mary Armstrong leant back in her chair. 'Lucy and Jack are a nice couple. Anyway,' she chuckled, 'he might do better than you realise, Sarah. They only have their three lasses and they've taken a real liking to Eddie. Who knows what might happen?'

'He's really set on farming.' Sarah looked across at her mother. 'I'm sure he'll be popping over to see you, Mam, in his free time.'

'I'll enjoy that. I get a bit lonely on my own.'

Sarah glanced away. For her mother's sake she had been glad when her father breathed his last. For as long as she could remember Joe Armstrong had been quarrelsome drunk or maudlin sober. The last two years of his life he had become senile, talking incoherently and wandering off getting lost. Yet Mary had looked after him and humoured him, coaxing him to eat and struggling to help him in and out of his chair and bed.

'I know what you're thinking, Sarah.' Mary's voice was quiet and low. 'But I do miss your father so much. We were married a long time.' Her lips began to tremble and she felt in her pocket for a handkerchief. 'He wasn't even that old, you know. It was just the accident.' Her voice broke on a sob.

'Don't, Mam.' Sarah was appalled. Mam never cried. She went and knelt at her mother's side. She cradled her like a child as the tears ran down Mary's thin cheeks.

'Oh, Sarah. If only you could remember your Pa before the accident. He was such a handsome man. No one could touch him for looks.' She sniffed and mopped her eyes. 'I'm all right now, love.'

She patted Sarah's hand. Her face was still soft with memories . . . 'He was always laughing, fooling about. My mother thought he would make a terrible husband. She said he had no sense of responsibility and would never settle down. But she was wrong. He worked so hard for us and was so proud of you all. I tell you, Sarah,' she looked into Sarah's eyes, 'the first fifteen years of our marriage I wouldn't have swopped places with the Queen herself.' She sighed. 'I had hoped you would find someone like that, love.'

Sarah experienced a feeling of pain mixed with anger. All these years her mother had struggled with poverty and a drunken husband and yet she felt pity for her – Sarah.

'Victor's a good husband, Mam.' She spoke the words through lips which felt stiff.

'I know that. He's a good man and I think a sensitive man but he's not the one I would have picked out for you. Eh, Sarah,' Mary shook her head, 'you were the bonniest lass for miles round and such a madcap. You needed a strong man all right, but one that could match you in your love of life. I used to be so fearful for you. You seemed to want to grab the whole world and hold it in your hand. And you can't, love, as you have found out.'

'I didn't want the whole world, Mam.' Sarah had lowered her head. 'I just wanted people to care for me, and you know . . .' her voice broke. 'They never did.'

Mary's voice held bewilderment: 'Sarah, why do you say that?'

The pent-up frustration of years broke through. 'I was pushed off to York, wasn't I. Why did *I* have to go? All those years . . . you knew I hated it, but I wasn't allowed home.' She gave a bitter laugh. 'Bonny, you say; much good it has done me. Victor, well,' she shrugged, 'I can't explain, but things have never been really good; and Eddie, he couldn't wait to get away from me. I was never close to Florence and Arthur and I never had a chance to love Harry. There was only our Jim.' She stopped short, blinking back tears.

'Oh, Sarah!' This time it was Mary who drew close to her.

'I'm sorry, Mam. I never meant . . .'

Mary rocked her back and forth. 'Hush, don't be sorry. You'll feel better now. We must talk, Sarah.' She rested her chin on Sarah's dark curls. 'I've always loved you; although I didn't always understand you. I suppose I talked more to Florence because she was straightforward and didn't fly off the handle all the time. Oh, you had such a temper, Sarah, and then I got cross and tired, but I always loved you.'

Mary sighed. 'I can't fuss people, even those I love. I'm just not made that way, whereas you, it was always hugs and kisses you wanted. As for York,' she stilled her rocking motion for a moment, 'don't you remember anything about when you were ill that time?'

Sarah shook her head.

'Perhaps it's for the best.' Mary stared into space for a moment. 'I can only tell you there was a good reason for you leaving, Sarah. I'm sorry but that's all I can say. I didn't want you to go and,' she put her face against that of her daughter, 'I honestly never knew until later that Blanche was such an old bitch!'

'Mother!' Sarah had never heard her mother swear before.

They both laughed.

'What a couple of wailing willies we are.'

Mary pressed her soft cheek against that of her daughter then straightened up. 'Well, that's cleared the air a bit. We'll have that cup of tea now, shall we?'

Eddie had been away a month and Sarah couldn't find enough to fill her days. The theatre was presenting a local review so she had no lodgers and it was pointless cooking proper meals for Victor because he ate so little. He had no appetite, he said, and his stomach hurt.

'Go back to the doctor's,' she told him. 'Maybe you need some different kind of medicine.'

'I've had bottles of the stuff already. It's no good. Anyway, he says the pain's due to nerves so the medicine won't help.'

'You've got to stop worrying about work, Victor. The houses have been better these past weeks, haven't they?'

'They have and that makes it worse.' Victor sighed. 'The

house manager was talking to me today. He says when the war starts most theatres will be closed down.'

'Oh, Lord!' Sarah noticed he said 'when' and not 'if'. For the first time she fully appreciated the reality of the conflict before all of them and her legs felt strangely weak. She moved towards a nearby chair, then changing her mind, marched towards the sink and proceeded to scrub at a perfectly clean pan.

'Well, that settles it, Victor Manvell. I'm going to get a job. I'm sick of doing nothing and if the Lyric closes we will need the money.'

She would brook no argument. Times had changed. It was 1937. Plenty of married women worked nowadays. Next day she dressed with care and went to call on Maisie.

'Victor's okay about you coming back, is he?'

Maisie sounded dubious.

'You know what he's like. He will look down his nose but if I go home with everything fixed up, he'll grumble then agree.' Sarah looked about her at the new furnishings. 'Things have certainly changed in here.'

'I should think so. It's been a long time, ducks.' Maisie grinned. 'Think your mental arithmetic is up to it?'

'Of course.'

Sarah continued her inspection. The bar of the Flower in Hand had been newly painted and in place of the old drawer for the takings there gleamed a smart till. The old fittings had been ripped out and, best of all, the smelly spittoons had disappeared.

'Wonder you haven't put a carpet down,' she commented.

'What – with the spring tides, we get!' Maisie chuckled. She put her head on one side and assessed Sarah's appearance. 'Leif wants to attract a better clientele and we all know a pretty barmaid brings in the custom.' She sighed with envy. 'Do you know, Sarah, you've a better figure now than you had when we first met. It's not fair. No one would believe you had a grown-up lad.'

'Do I have a job then?'

Maisie nodded. 'Yes. There's room for another pair of hands and even if the war does start I reckon drink will be the last thing the blokes will give up. Or nearly the last,' she winked.

After Sarah had gone, Maisie sat for a moment reflecting on the past. It would be good working with Sarah again. Her husband called through from the back.

'The brewery dray's here, love. How much mild do we need?'

'Just coming.' She did not move immediately. She was still thinking about her friend. There was something about her that was hard to put into words. She thought deeply, then nodded. She'd got it. Virginal, that was it. Sarah had a virginal look about her. Stupid really, seeing how she had a grown-up son and had been married years but, nevertheless, it was the right word. What a waste! She'd always said Victor Manvell was the wrong man for her, but would she listen? All those wasted years, stuck with him and that moaning mother. Good job she kicked the bucket when she did! Still, maybe it wasn't too late; after all there were a lot of people calling in the Flower in Hand these days. That chap yesterday, lovely smile he had and twinkly eyes. She'd try and find out more about him. A Cheshire-cat smile lit her broad features. It did not disappear even when Leif shouted again, more irritably this time.

'Maisie!'

'Coming.' She went to sort out the brewery men.

Chapter Twenty-three

It felt strange to be back at the Flower in Hand and working once more with Maisie. There were times when Sarah felt she had been transported back through time; that she was a young girl again, writing to Alice, wondering how the Linford family were getting on – particularly Martin Linford – and learning how to pull a pint of beer. She smiled, remembering the glasses half full of froth she had passed to dismayed customers. But those feelings soon passed. Maisie was now Mrs Svenson and a reformed character. Leif was a good-natured, good-humoured man and Sarah rejoiced in their genuine, if matter-of-fact, happiness. Alice had stopped replying to Sarah's letters many years ago so all links with her life in Harrogate had gone. The pub itself was a much pleasanter place in which to work, although Sarah, now pulling pints with great efficiency, wished the improvements had included more fans to extract the pall of cigarette smoke which hung permanently in the low-ceilinged bar.

This particular evening the smoke really stung her eyes for the room was packed. A special Gala Fireworks Display was to be held on the beach and, as always with a free show, it seemed everyone had turned out for the occasion. Sarah wished it would hurry up and start and then the pub would empty. When the door swung open to admit yet more people, she sighed before moving forward to serve them. She brought a pint of beer and a gin and tonic for a young couple then looked enquiringly at the next customer: 'Yes?'

He did not reply immediately. She saw he was good-looking and neatly but casually dressed in a sports jacket and flannels. He had a tanned face and thick, springy blondish-brown hair. In his late twenties, or early thirties, she guessed. He stared at her.

'Yes?' she said again. 'What can I get you?' She was aware her voice trembled slightly and she was annoyed.

He blinked.

'Sorry.' He rubbed his chin and grinned at her. 'Half of bitter, please.'

She turned to get his drink, acutely aware he was watching her every movement. Yet his gaze did not offend her. His eyes were the brightest blue, startling in his brown face. A seaman, she guessed, but definitely not one of the local fishermen. When she handed him his change his fingers brushed against hers and a shiver ran through her body. She retreated to the far end of the bar and feverishly polished some glasses which did not need polishing. But when she saw Maisie had approached the man, she moved nearer to hear the conversation.

'Decided to come and see the fireworks after all?'

'Sorry?' The stranger seemed disinclined to talk to the landlady. He was still glancing in Sarah's direction.

'The Gala! I mentioned it the other day when you called in.'

'Oh – yes.' He drained his glass and glanced again at Sarah.

'Oh, you need a refill. Sarah!'

Sarah approached them with wary footsteps.

'See to this gentleman, love. I have to go through the back.'

'The same?'

'Yes, please.'

What stupid, stilted conversation. Yet the silences between the words seemed to Sarah to be full of whispers. She pulled the beer so clumsily, she spilt some.

'Sorry.'

She wiped the glass carefully before placing it on the bar in front of him.

'It's all right.' He smiled, his well-shaped mouth parting to show white even teeth and it was as if she recognised that smile. His hair needed cutting, there was a tiny piece curling beneath his right ear. Sarah looked away.

'Are you in Branswick on holiday?'

He shook his head. If only he would stop *looking* at her.

'No. A relative of mine has died. My only relative as a matter of fact; my auntie, she brought me up. I've come to sort through her effects, decide whether to sell her cottage, things like that.' At last, he looked away from her. He stared down into his glass, sighed, picked it up and drank. 'Sad business. That's why I called in here. I felt the need for some company. Mind you, I didn't reckon there'd be so *much* company.'

'There's always a lot of visitors around this time of the year, but tonight we have the locals as well. They've all come to see the fireworks.'

'And they'll be worth seeing.' Maisie had joined them. 'Our councillors are a stingy lot but at least they pay out for a couple of really splendid Fireworks Galas during the season.'

She paused: 'I know,' she nudged Sarah, 'crowd's thinning out now. Why don't you get your coat and go along with this gentleman to watch them? It's not much fun if you're on your own.'

'Oh, I couldn't. There's all the glasses to wash and anyway,' Sarah hardly dared to look at him, 'we don't know each other.'

'Rubbish!' Maisie laughed, fatly, 'me and Leif can do the glasses. Go on, it's only along the road. You'd like some company, wouldn't you, sir?' She glanced at the man.

He looked from her to Sarah. 'There's nothing I'd like better,' he said softly.

Outside, and walking side by side towards the harbour they were silent amidst a buzz of noise and activity. Groups of sightseers crowded the pavement and children, excited about being out so late, played tag between the adults.

At last, Sarah spoke: 'Look – over there.' She pointed out a cleared space where scaffolding supported the larger set-pieces. Dark figures scurried about, flaring torches held in their hands. The expectant crowd fell silent and waited. Then a chorus of 'Ooooos' sounded as the first rocket soared heavenwards and exploded in a shower of coloured lights.

There were screams of delight from the youngsters and a nearby toddler, overcome with excitement, burst into tears. Another rocket soared and Catherine wheels flared into life, illuminating the darkness, outlining the ghostly shapes of tied-up fishing smacks bobbing on the silent water.

Amid the noise the man turned towards Sarah. He caught her elbow and swung her round to face him.

'I'm John,' he shouted. 'John Saul.'

She gazed up at him, her breathing quick and shallow, like that of a baby.

'Sarah,' she replied.

'I know.'

He threw back his head and laughed, then he took hold of her hand and her fingers curled in his palm like an anemone. The crowd sighed and swayed. There was the smell of cordite in the air and clouds of smoke drifted over the spectators. The gigantic set-piece, a model of the Crystal Palace, leapt into life.

Sarah began to cough.

'More smoke here than in that pub of yours,' John shouted, and she began to laugh in between coughing, and then to hiccup. He pulled her to him and they clung together, laughing and choking as the crowds began to break up and drift away.

'Let's walk along by the shore,' he suggested. 'Give you time to get your breath back.'

She nodded, wiping the tears from her eyes and trying to catch her breath. As they walked by the water's edge the noise receded, and they listened to the soft wash of the waves and watched the moon ride the high clouds without speaking. Finally, Sarah stopped.

'I must go,' she said.

'I'll walk you home.'

'No.'

'But I must.' He caught hold of her hand. 'You *know* I must. You felt it too, back there in the pub. You know I must see you again.'

'No, it's no good.' Her voice was dull. The magic had died, as ephemeral as the fireworks. 'I'm married.'

She pulled away from him and ran clumsily through the soft, dry sand, towards the slipway. He watched her go, his face serious.

'You don't get away that easily,' he murmured.

When St Hilda's Church clock struck two, Sarah was still awake. She moved towards the edge of the double bed, to a cooler section of the sheet and away from Victor's warm, recumbent body. If only she could control the thoughts whirling through her brain, she could sleep. It was so stupid. She must be coming down with a fever or something. That man, that perfect stranger, how could he affect her so? She would refuse to go and serve him if he came in the bar again. If he persisted she would tell him she had a grown-up son. That should put him off. Why, she was years older than him. Why on earth had Maisie encouraged her to go to see the fireworks with him? She stared into the darkness. Why did she feel so *alive*? It was as though every nerve in her body was tingling. She had *never* felt like this before. Oh, plenty of the customers had flirted or tried to flirt with her but she had never felt the slightest interest in them. Why, oh why did she feel like this now? Wide-eyed she gazed into the darkness.

John Saul placed the pile of letters and photographs with the other papers in the cardboard box ready for the bonfire. There – that was the desk cleared. He glanced at his watch. It was two o'clock. He was crazy to tackle this job now but he might as well. He couldn't sleep.

Sarah, Sarah . . . where do you live? You'll be lying with your husband now. He forced his mind away from that picture and looked again at the printed evidence of his aunt's life. The programmes of the concerts she had attended, she had loved music. There were old knitting patterns there, recipes and lots of photographs.

On impulse, he picked out one of himself as a self-conscious lad of seventeen, striving hard to appear nonchalant as he leant against a cigarette kiosk in Marseille. He slipped it in his pocket. It was there, he remembered, he had first gone with a woman. It was a long time ago but he had never forgotten her. She had been much older than him, but she had initiated him into the mystery of love-making with infinite patience and tenderness. He smiled ruefully at the memory. He had returned to his ship boasting of the beauty who had bestowed favours on him only to learn she was a well-known whore. How shocked he had been, how innocent. Yet now he remembered her with affection. Since then there had been quite a few women. His shipmates commented upon his successes.

'Tell us the knack,' they would say.

How could he explain there was no knack? The truth was, he genuinely liked women. He liked the toughness which lurked beneath their apparent fragility, the way they stayed and coped with messes that men would run away from. The way they kept families together and put their kids and their men before themselves. And tonight Sarah had told him she was married.

He pushed back his chair and walked restlessly round the room. It had been many years since he had lived in Branswick and now his auntie was gone there was nothing in the town to keep him. He would put the cottage up for sale, he decided. No point in keeping it. He was never in one place long enough to need a house of his own. Already he was eager for the feel of a deck beneath his feet.

Yes, he would sell the cottage. War was coming, that was for sure. There would be an even greater need for experienced seamen in the coming months. He listened. It was so *quiet* here. With his auntie dead there was no one to really care what happened to him. But that was best, wasn't it? No grieving widow for him, if the worst happened. Funny, all the women he had loved, and he *had* loved them, but never one he had loved enough to marry. The girl tonight, no – not a girl, a woman. He guessed she was a little older than he was. She was just . . . so beautiful. Her dark, silky hair, her full curving mouth . . . He swore softly; what the hell was he doing, mooning over a married woman in the early hours of the morning?

The sound from the church clock was dying when Leif Svenson awoke suffering a bad attack of indigestion. He sat up in bed, belched and rubbed his chest. No, it was no good, it wouldn't go away by itself. He heaved himself out of bed and padded off to find the bicarbonate of soda. When he returned, his wife was sitting up in bed, squint-eyed with sleep, resembling a small Buddha.

'Do you have to make so much noise?' she complained.

'Sorry,' he belched again. 'Indigestion,' he explained.

'Serves you right,' she rubbed her eyes. 'Too much beer.'

'That's not fair!' He thumped into bed beside her. 'I only had two pints. It was more likely to be that rabbit pie.'

'Well, that's as bad.' She rolled up her eyes, heavenwards. 'Whoever eats rabbit pie for supper?'

'I was hungry. Great stack of glasses to wash, floor to sweep, barrels to check. Anyway, I've been meaning to ask,' the bed creaked as he turned towards her, 'what was that business with Sarah?'

'I don't know what you mean.'

'Yes, you do. You wanted her to go off with that fair-haired young chap. I'm not stupid. But why, for God's sake?'

'Oh, I don't know.' She pleated the corner of the sheet. 'I feel sorry for her. She's never had any fun. She's stuck in that dreary house with Victor. She never goes anywhere. And she's not getting any younger.'

'So you think her getting involved with another man is a good idea? Honestly, Maisie.' Leif shook his head in disbelief. 'I thought you were her friend!'

'I am. Oh, Leif, don't you see? This chap won't stay

here, so it can't get too serious. Yet you can tell he's smitten with her. And he's so good-looking *and* nice mannered. It can't do any harm. Sarah needs *cherishing*. You've only to look at her to know she's never, well, you know, enjoyed sex. I said that Victor Manvell wasn't right for her. And yet, I know her, she's full of love to give. I want her to know what it *can* be like. Like you and me.' She leant forward allowing her husband a good view of her breasts. 'You don't begrude her that, do you?'

'Nooo.' Leif was looking in the direction she intended, but he floundered on. 'Sarah's a more complex person than you or me, Maisie. I should leave well alone. You might be helping her to a load of grief.'

'Oh, get on with you,' muttered Maisie comfortably. She put her arms around her husband's neck and proceeded to make him forget all about his indigestion.

Chapter Twenty-four

'You were restless last night, Sarah,' Victor looked up from pouring a cup of tea.

'Yes, I know. It was so hot.' Sarah watched her husband butter a piece of toast. 'I went to watch the fireworks yesterday. Maisie let me off early.' She waited. Would he ask who she had gone with? Or why Maisie had allowed her to leave work early?

He did not. He gulped down his tea and stood up. 'I'll have to dash. Change-over day, you know. The scenery isn't packed yet and they're on about wanting an extra garden scene next week: can I fix up greenery, fairy lights and lanterns?' He shook his head ruefully, yet smiled as he said, 'You won't see much of me these next few days, I'm afraid. Perhaps it's a good thing you went back to work after all.'

She smiled but did not reply. After he had left the house she began to wash the breakfast dishes but her hands slowed and she stared out of the kitchen window. John Saul. A strong, plain name. He hadn't said where the cottage was. She wondered if it was near to the Flower in Hand. She wondered if he would come back again.

'Look at the place, it's half empty. What's the good of having a good night when the next evening it's like a tomb?'

Sarah looked at Leif with astonishment. Her employer

was usually so mild tempered it was surprising to hear him so irritable. He caught her look and shrugged, rubbing his chest. 'Keep getting indigestion,' he explained. 'Damned painful.'

'He eats too much.' Maisie poured herself a stout. 'But he's right about tonight. I hate it when it's quiet. Makes it seem like hours to closing time.'

'Listen to her.' Leif pulled up the trap door behind the bar. 'It's not me that's getting as fat as a pig,' he shouted, as he disappeared down into the cellar. 'I'll put another barrel on. The last hour might be busy.'

Sarah fervently hoped so. She always felt more tired when she was standing there with nothing to do. At least, that's what she told herself. The truth was, she had been on tenterhooks ever since she walked into the bar. Every time the door opened, she jumped, but it was never him. Maisie spoke, and she jumped again.

'My goodness, you are nervy tonight. What's the matter with you?'

'Nothing.'

Maisie was wearing the look that Sarah didn't like, speculative and yet lazy, the way a cat sometimes looked when it was playing with a mouse. 'Well, you certainly look pretty. Is that blouse new?'

'Of course not, I've had it for ages.' She had, but she wasn't going to tell Maisie this was the first time she had worn it. The door swung open and she jumped. It was only one of the men from the fish pier but she was glad to move forward and serve him.

At last, it was time to give the bar a last wipe, cover the pumps with a clean teacloth and go home. She stepped outside the pub and took a grateful gulp of the sea-scented night air.

'Sarah.'

He had been standing by the railings fronting the beach. He crossed the road and walked up to her.

'I was hoping you wouldn't come,' she said.

'Were you, Sarah, honestly?'

She thought she saw his lips crease in a faint smile at her silence.

John had spent a restless two hours walking up and down Foreshore Road. Three times he had approached the Flower in Hand and three times turned away. Then he had positioned himself opposite the building and waited for closing time. When she finally came out and he saw the pale oval of her face in the rapidly gathering dusk, he had almost turned away. Her face had looked so . . . pure. He fought a losing battle with himself. He would probably bring her nothing but trouble, he admitted it. Yet even as he did so, he was walking towards her.

'I *had* to see you again, Sarah. Is that so wrong?'

'It could be.' She spoke in a whisper.

'Oh, for goodness' sake!' He stopped, put his hand on her shoulder, forcing her to turn and face him. 'Don't look so worried, so serious. My God, we've hardly exchanged two words and yet you're looking guilty.'

He felt her moving away from him and he tightened his grasp. His words came quickly now, tripping over each other. 'Very well, I admit it. I'm attracted to you and you know it. But you've told me you're a married woman, Sarah, and I accept that. I won't do anything you don't want me to do. I'll be leaving Branswick in a few days. Surely, it wouldn't do any harm just to *see* me?'

She was staring up at him but her expression was unreadable.

He hurried on: 'I need to talk to someone, Sarah. I've spent the last week sorting out the affairs of an old lady I loved deeply. She was my last living relation. It's a strange feeling, Sarah, being completely on your own. I've been rattling round town, knowing nobody, feeling miserable, then I saw you and immediately, there was this *bond*. You felt it, I *know* you did! Please meet me, just for a couple of hours.'

She hesitated and he saw the little frown-lines appear between her dark eyebrows. He realised he was gripping her shoulder hard enough to hurt her and hastily released her.

'All right,' she said. 'I will see you. I'll meet you at noon outside the Marine Café. It's just along there.' She pointed to where the café was, then looked up at him. Her eyes were bright now and totally trusting. 'Now please, let me go. I must go home.'

He stared after her, confused at the depth of his own feelings. He had spoken the truth, he did need to talk to her. And he wanted to watch her face as she talked back to him. He wanted to see her really laugh. She didn't seem to laugh much. She was such a small woman it made him feel he wanted to cherish her. He crossed over the road and leaning over the railings stared at the quiet sea.

He wouldn't hurt her. If she spoke fondly of her husband tomorrow, seemed happy, he would leave it at that. He would somehow subdue the desire he felt for her and he would leave Branswick.

This time it was different. Oh, he'd had affairs with married women before but they had been, he searched for the right word, more worldly. No one had got hurt; at least, he brushed his hand over his mouth, he didn't *think* they had

222

He hoped he hadn't hurt anyone. He wouldn't hurt Sarah, he wouldn't.

'So your Auntie Ethel brought you up?'

'Yes.'

He watched her fill his teacup. They were on their second pot of tea.

'She was a hard old girl but she was fair, brought me up right. I suppose she loved me in her own way, but she never showed it. Once she knew I was set on going to sea she got me into the sea training school, did all she could to help me.' He sighed. 'I remember her seeing me off on my first trip. I was away over a year and she must have missed me, she was getting on then, but she never let on.'

'And since then, you've been all over the world?' She smiled at him. There were faint shadows under her eyes and a string of blue beads, matching her eyes, around her slender throat.

He swallowed. 'Yes.'

'Don't you ever get sick of the sea?' She leant forward. The dress she was wearing was demure in style but the movement caught the material, pulled it tight across her breasts. 'And think about settling somewhere?'

He put down his cup with clumsy fingers. 'Not really.' He cleared his throat. 'Just once, I worked in Canada for a year. I liked it there, but things didn't work out.'

He paused. 'Sarah?'

'What is it?'

'We're all right in here, are we? I mean, I don't want to make things difficult for you. Your husband . . .'

'Oh, no.' Her face cleared. 'Victor never comes below the Bar. Anyway,' she gave a half-rueful shrug. 'He's practically buried in his work in the theatre at the

223

moment. There's a new show starting and he is very busy.'

'I see.' John's voice was gentle. 'Tell me something about yourself. You've listened to me long enough. Have you children?'

'We have a son. Eddie's grown up now. He's away. He works on a farm. We don't see him much.'

The flat tone of her voice told him many things. He touched her hand.

'If he's on the land, he'll probably be safe when the war comes.'

'Oh, don't talk about that.'

'No. You're right.' He beckoned to the waitress. 'This next hour we'll talk about happy things. Did I see a fun fair along by the harbour? Let's go there.'

'It's not much of a fun fair,' Sarah told him as they walked along being careful not to touch in any way. 'Same old rides and stalls every year. The council keep on about closing it down.'

'Oh, it will be great; it's years and years since I went to one. Come on, let's enjoy ourselves!'

He paid his sixpences at the entrance and caught hold of her hand as they went into the Hall of Mirrors. She did not pull away. They went into every booth and on every ride and as they did so, he saw her become a child again. The Fat Lady made her sad.

'The poor thing,' she whispered. Unconsciously, she linked his arm.

He smiled to himself.

'You're too soft-hearted, Sarah. She probably weighs seven stone and is stuffed with pillows.'

'And you're a cynic,' she retorted and pinched his arm before running over to try her luck on the penny machines.

'We can do better than that,' he said when she mourned

the failure of the mechanically operated 'grab' to pick up a tinselly brooch for her. He steered her over to the shooting range and won a prize.

'Oh, John. It's beautiful!'

It was a small glass globe on a stand. Within the globe was a little world, a windmill, a river bank, a swan sailing on blue water. She inverted the globe, shook it, and a snow-storm whirled round and round.

'Thank you,' she said. She looked at him, her lips half smiling, the globe clasped to her breast.

'*You're* beautiful,' he said. He drew her, unresisting, past the swing boats, the large roundabout where luridly painted horses tossed their manes and flared their nostrils as they pranced and pawed their way on a never-ending journey, and into a secluded corner behind a tent which, according to the faded notice outside, housed the remains of a mermaid.

Gently, very gently, he placed his finger beneath her chin and tilted up her face towards him. Softly he kissed her forehead, her nose, the line of her jaw. He could feel her trembling. He moved to kiss her mouth but she made a small sound, a kind of whimper. Immediately, he stopped. He put his arms about her and held her. He could feel the shivers running through her. In truth, he was trembling himself. He had *never* felt like this before. He shut his eyes. The sounds of the fair seemed muffled yet the real world was so close. He could smell the aroma of toffee apples from a nearby stall. He moved his foot slightly and heard something snap beneath his heel. He saw it was the stick of a paper Union Jack some child had discarded.

'You'll see me again, won't you, Sarah?' he asked quietly.

'Yes.'

225

Her voice sounded small and scared. They left the fun fair and walked along the shore. They went hand in hand. John saw a man at one of the crab stalls watching them and he glanced down at Sarah wondering if she had noticed. The man would know her. If she had noticed, she didn't say anything. She remained silent so long, he became worried.

'I've made you unhappy, haven't I? I'm sorry, I didn't mean to.' The smile she gave him was so luminous, he was shocked.

'No, no. Don't say you're sorry. I'm happy, John, really happy.' She bent to pick up a shell from the sand. Studying it intently, she said, 'Where's your cottage?'

His heart leapt in his breast. 'Close by the harbour. St Michael's Close. Do you know it?'

'Oh, yes. I often walk down there.' She threw the shell into the sea and watched a wave bear it away.

'I'll tell Victor that Maisie wants me to work more hours. It will be all right.' The sun was hot but she wrapped her arms about herself as though she was cold. 'Victor trusts me, you see. It'll be quite safe.'

He moved to touch her but she shook her head.

'I'd better get home now. No, you stay here. I'll see you tomorrow,' She paused. 'One o'clock in the Esplanade Gardens, near the pond with the statue of Pan. Do you know it?' He nodded.

'You're sure, Sarah?'

'One o'clock,' she repeated.

As John retraced his steps, his mood of elation ebbed. 'You'll have to watch it, my son,' he cautioned himself. 'Things could easily get out of hand here.'

Then he remembered the feel of her in his arms and his heartbeat quickened again. She was his, he knew it! He started to run along the firm sand fringing the sea. A couple of youngsters, paddling, glanced at him curiously as he pounded past them, his head back. Oh, it was good to be alive. He stooped to pick up a stone and hurl it far out to sea.

'Hurrah!' he crowed.

The stone narrowly missed a seagull floating on the swell of the waves. Its powerful wings opened and it left the water and flew high into the sky, its raucous shrieks sounding notes of discord in the calm, blue expanse.

Chapter Twenty-five

The garden bench upon which they sat was backed by a mass of late-flowering phlox and the heady perfume emitting from the flowers added to their already strained emotions.

'I shouldn't have come,' Sarah repeated. She laced her fingers together in a vain attempt to stop them trembling.

'But you did. You knew all along that you would come and so did I.' John leant forward. 'Stop this, Sarah. You're tearing yourself apart!'

'But I can't believe it's happening!' The look she gave him was almost hostile. 'It must be easier for you. But I'm married! When I'm with you, it's wonderful, but then I go home and everything is as it was, and I look at Victor reading his paper, eating his meals and I know this is all madness.'

'It's not madness.' He shrugged: 'It's fate, it's . . . oh, I don't know what it is, but don't you feel it's meant to be? The moment I saw you, Sarah, I knew!' He stopped talking and looked at her averted face. 'Please look at me, Sarah.'

He waited, but she stared stubbornly at her clenched hands.

'Well then, I must leave.'

Her dark lashes swept upwards then and he saw the gleam of tears in her marvellous eyes.

'No!'

'I have to. I can't hang about here, seeing you but not

allowed to touch. Have you any idea of the strength of my feelings for you, Sarah?' He groaned and buried his face in his hands. He felt her fingers timidly touch his hair. He straightened up and gave her a shame-faced smile.

'I'm sorry. I'm not behaving very well, am I? But I want you so much. I want to kiss you.'

He pulled her to him and kissed her so fiercely she made a sound of protest. An old lady, walking past with her dog, tut-tutted audibly and pulled away the corgi which had stopped and was sniffing with interest the foot of the bench. The movement brought Sarah to her senses.

'It's still madness, John.' She spoke unsteadily.

'Yes, it is.' John's face was tense with emotion. He stood up and held out his hand. 'It is madness to stay here when we feel as we do.'

She hesitated. A small cloud passed over the sun and the sudden coolness made her shiver but she looked up into his eyes and smiled. She reached for him and their hands joined.

John raised himself on one elbow and looked at Sarah, marvelling at her loveliness and the feelings she had aroused in him. She lay naked beside him, sprawled in the wonderful abandonment of satiated passion. He looked at her smooth-rounded breasts tipped with coral-coloured nipples, her slender waist curving softly into womanly hips, and her shapely legs tapering down to fine ankles and delicate high-arched feet. His gaze returned to her face and he watched the slight flare of her nostrils as she breathed and the faint violet shadows beneath her closed eyes. Feeling his gaze, she stirred and opened her eyes. Her expression was peaceful and serious. She reached up to him and touched his face.

'I never knew,' she said.

He rolled towards her and stopped her words with a kiss. He was absolutely certain he would love this woman for ever. She had come to him, shyly, yet with implicit trust and he had realised, with awe, that she was entirely unversed in the arts of love. And so he had wooed her gently, blessing in his mind all the women who had taught him skill and understanding of a woman's needs. He had restrained his own passion, stroking and kissing her body. But then she had moaned and trembled under his touch, arching her body towards him until, finally, he could wait no longer. He had entered her and, as their entwined bodies had merged and moved in perfect harmony, he had cried out in triumph. He had been right. They were made for each other. Then he had stopped thinking of anything as they reached the rapture of perfect consummation.

'I was too quick,' he said. 'I'm sorry.'

'Oh, John.' She laughed and traced her finger around the shape of his mouth. 'You made me feel . . . wonderful.'

She shivered and a concerned expression crossed his face.

'You're cold,' he said. 'Just a minute.'

'No,' she protested, but he stood up and crossed the room, snatching a vividly coloured silk shawl from the chair upon which it was draped and handing it to her. Then he went to the fireplace and, striking a match, lit the fire which was already laid in the grate. He turned to look at her again and his eyes darkened. She had pulled the shawl about her shoulders. The soft folds of blue and gold enhanced the colour of her eyes and the darkness of her hair.

'It's beautiful, John.'

'I brought it back from India, a present for my aunt. She never really liked it. I think she thought it was slightly wicked.'

She narrowed her eyes and stroked the silk with her

231

fingers, saying with a laugh in her voice, 'Does it make me look wicked?'

He caught his breath and moved towards her, smiling slightly as he quoted:

> 'Would you like to sin
> With Elinor Glyn
> On a tiger skin?'

'John!'

She gurgled with laughter and he grinned in sympathy at her expression. All her doubts and tension had fled and she was radiant with happiness. She looks about eighteen, he thought.

'Don't tell me you've read that terrible book, *Three Weeks*?' she said. 'Is it from that you learnt how to love a woman?'

'I have read it, as a matter of fact.' He grinned. 'But no, it didn't teach me anything about love.' He reached out to stroke her hair. 'All I want to do is to make you happy, Sarah. And my instinct tells me how to do that.'

He smoothed back her tumbled curls. The expression in his eyes was warm and loving. Her laughter stilled as he kissed her, but her eyes remained smiling as they came together once more. And this time their loving was full of sunshine as they teased and touched each other. Until, finally, feeling her hands tighten on his back and her breathing become thin and ragged, he lifted her closer to him and rejoiced in her sweetness as their two bodies became as one.

Afterwards, they lay together watching the firelight flicker, busy with their own thoughts. Then Sarah sat up.

Dance Without Music

'John – may I ask you something?'

'Of course.' His body tensed slightly.

'Why on earth did you read *Three Weeks*?'

'Oh, Sarah!' He put his hands behind his head and laughed. 'On a long sea voyage, darling, you read anything you can lay your hands on. I've read westerns, adventure books, history books, everything Dickens wrote, mystery books by Dorothy L Sayers, horror books, Bram Stoker's *Dracula*, for example . . .'

He suddenly reared up over Sarah, his lips drawn back from his teeth in a demonic snarl. 'Let me kiss your neck, my proud beauty!'

She shrieked and threw a cushion at him. They collapsed together in a gale of laughter.

'Oh, John. I wish we could stay here always.' The laughter fled from her eyes. 'What you said about leaving?'

'Hush.' He pressed his fingers against her lips. 'Don't spoil things.'

'But we have to. This isn't real!'

'God – don't say that.' He pulled her closer to him and readjusted the shawl about her shoulders, his fingers marvelling at the silkiness of her skin. 'Right now, I feel more alive, more real than I have ever felt in my whole life.'

'That's what I mean. "Right now"; yet in half an hour I must leave here.'

'You'll come back, Sarah – tomorrow?'

The flatness in her voice had alarmed him. He couldn't let her go now.

'Tomorrow, no.' She half-smiled at his expression. 'Tomorrow Victor is home all day,' she explained. 'But I'll come here the day after.'

She looked away from him and around the room. 'It's a lovely cottage, John. You could put pots of geraniums on

233

that low window-sill. They would look just right with the white walls.'

'I'll get some.'

'But I thought,' the frown was back between her eyebrows, 'you said you'd put the cottage up for sale?'

'I was going to, then I met you. Oh, Sarah, don't look like that. Now what have I said?'

'You knew,' she said. 'You knew all along that I would come here, make love with you.'

'I *hoped*, Sarah. I hoped. Do you blame me for that? Look at me, tell me you're sorry. You can't, can you?'

'No.' She kissed his cheek and then his mouth. 'But what shall we *do*?' she murmured.

'Let's stop agonising, Sarah. Christ, we've picked a hell of a time to fall in love.'

He left her to place another log on the fire, then returned and sat in front of her, taking hold of her hands.

'I hate to mention it here, but war is coming.' He stroked her fingers as he felt her start. 'God knows what's going to happen in the coming months. Let's just be glad we found each other. Let's live day by day and not think too much about the future. I'll stay on here at the cottage. We'll meet when we can. Please, Sarah, say you'll do that?'

She raised his hands to her lips and kissed them. 'All right, darling. I'll try.'

They stared into each other's eyes then she glanced at the clock on the mantelpiece.

'But I must go now.'

He watched her move about, collect her clothes, dress. He watched as she combed her hair, frowning a little at her reflection in the mirror. It amused him how unselfconscious she seemed despite his regard. She walked across the room to collect her bag and it seemed to him she moved in an entirely different way. The tenseness in her body had gone and she carried an aura of awareness of her own feminine sensuality and ability to love.

'Sarah.'

'Yes.'

'If anything happens; if Victor says anything or, oh, I don't know,' he shrugged, 'if you just can't cope, come straight here, to the cottage.'

'I will, love.'

She blew him a kiss, opened the door, and was gone.

He rose, dressed, and brought out a bottle of Scotch from a cupboard. He poured a drink and sat by the fire, staring into the flames.

He knew she'd cope. She was that kind of woman.

What special magic did she possess that affected him so strongly? She had been gone less than half an hour yet he felt the urge in him to possess her again. How many years had she been married? What kind of man was she married to? Holding her, loving her, he had sensed *years* of anxieties, loneliness and frustration leave her body. Would Victor, his lip curled at the thought of that name, even notice the change in her? Probably not. What the hell had the man done to deserve her? Well, damn him! He half hoped Victor *would* notice, then she could come to him.

He rose and poured another drink.

'I've got some good news, Sarah.' Victor's heavy features brightened into a smile.

'Have you, love – what is it?' Noticing her husband's lined face and rapidly greying hair, Sarah felt a familiar pang of guilt and pity.

'We've just heard for definite, the Lyric's staying open, whatever happens. The boss says people will need cheering up when this bloody war finally gets started. We'll be booking revues mostly and we'll give continuous performances.'

'I'm glad for you, Vic.' Sarah spoke sincerely. She knew how Victor had dreaded the thought of the closure of the theatre.

'There's one thing.' Victor looked sheepish. 'Mr Benson feels there should be someone handy, to keep an eye on the place should we get any bombing raids.'

'Oh Vic – the war hasn't even started yet!'

'No, but you have to think ahead. Anyway, there's a nice little flat attached to the theatre and it's empty right now.' He paused. 'It really is nice, Sarah, so I said we would probably move there. What do you think?'

'I don't know.'

For six months now, Sarah hadn't known what to think. She veered from despair to joy in a matter of minutes. She was married to a good man who was not in the best of health and she was deceiving him. She was terrified Victor would find out about John, not for herself but for him. She endured agonies of loathing when she imagined her son or her mother knowing of her infidelity. Then she thought of John and the times they spent together and beneath the torments of shame and indecision ran a calm clear spring of joy.

'Sarah?' Victor watched her, a puzzled expression on his face.

She prevaricated: 'I never thought you would want to leave this house, Victor.'

He shrugged. 'Well, you've never really liked it, have you? And the flat would be handy for work.'

'Yes – it was always your Ma's home, rather than mine,' she said.

'Then you agree?'

She nodded and he gave a relieved smile. 'There's a proper bathroom. No more running across the yard in the rain, eh? I'll go and tell Mr Benson now.'

'But you haven't had your tea.'

'I'll get a sandwich. I don't feel hungry.'

She saw he was holding his right hand pressed against his stomach and she experienced another pang of guilt.

'Oh, Vic – why won't you go to another doctor?'

He shook his head and left the room without replying. Left alone, Sarah closed her eyes and wondered what to do. The question of whether or not to move slipped out of her mind completely. It was the question of what she should do about the two men in her life which occupied her waking hours. She thought of her last meeting with John. How his face had tightened with jealousy and frustration:

'You have to choose, Sarah. Him or me – you can't have both!'

John, John! Just whispering his name made her body tingle. Each time they met their loving reached new heights. And afterwards, that was almost better. She had realised with delight, that they were friends as well as lovers. They laughed together and never ran out of things to talk about. She could *never* give him up. Dear Lord, why didn't she just go and live with him as he was always begging her to do?

Then, unbidden, her mother's face formed in the blackness behind her eyelids. She couldn't leave Victor. Mam had never ducked out of her responsibilities. How could she?

The days grew longer and the last of the cherry blossom scattered from the trees. Her brother Harry called to see her. He had joined the Royal Navy three years ago, and Sarah thought how good looking he was, smartly attired in his uniform. He had received his new posting but he couldn't tell her where he would be. When he went for his train she walked with him to the station.

'Take care,' she said. He may be almost six foot tall but he was still her baby brother.

'I'll be all right.' He laughed. 'Ready for a bit of excitement, I'm sick of kicking my heels in dry dock.'

'Write to Mam.'

He pulled a face. 'I hate writing letters, but I'll send postcards if I'm able.' He swung his kitbag on his back. 'Anyway, the rest of you will be okay. Florence is safe in the Midlands and Arthur's landed himself a good job in London.' His expression was half-admiring, half-scornful. 'Just 'cos he can speak foreign languages; trust him to land a desk job. No overseas for him.'

Sarah made no comment. Mam had told her on the quiet that the lass Arthur had married had turned out to have less money than he did but they were still together and, as far as she knew, happy. She waved the train away and walked home in dreary mood. Vic would be at the theatre tonight so she could meet John but he had been so quiet lately. She had a terrible feeling he was going to leave Branswick.

A dozy bee bumbled its way around the bowl of fragrant pinks which stood on a low table beneath the bow window. Sprigged curtains stirred in the evening breeze and the distant hoot of a trawler leaving the harbour reminded the couple of the world outside.

She stirred. 'I must go soon.'

'Not yet.'

John was stretched out on the sofa, his hands idly stroking her hair as she sat, curled up, on the rug beneath him. He bent towards her and kissed her.

'Come back to bed with me first.'

'John – you're insatiable!' She shook her head. 'Haven't you had enough of me?' she teased.

'Never.' He kissed her again and his hand slid inside the open neck of her dress brushing against her nipples. She drew in her breath and sat upright.

'No, John. I can't. Victor . . .'

John's face clouded and he moved away from her. 'Ah, Victor.'

With a swift movement he bent towards her again and imprisoned her wrists in his hands. 'How much longer, Sarah? Don't you know how much I need you?'

'I know.' She bowed her head. 'But Victor needs me too. If I leave him he has no one.'

Still holding on to her wrists, John pulled her up to sit beside him. 'I understand how you feel, darling – but think; look at what's happening. Within a few weeks, maybe, we'll be at war! There may not be much time for us. We can't waste it. We should be together now.'

Sarah's face looked troubled. 'Don't talk like that. There's still a chance things might improve; Chamberlain said . . .'

'No.' His voice was harsh. 'There'll be war and everyone will be involved this time. Herr Hitler wants the whole damned world under his heel. We can't sit back and let him get away with it. They'll be crying out for soldiers and,' he paused, deliberately, 'experienced seamen.'

'Don't!' Sarah pulled her hands free and clapped them over her ears. 'I don't want to hear. Men, you talk of nothing but war. I'm here now, and we are happy together. Don't spoil it!'

'But don't you see, Sarah. That's what I want, our happiness, and I can't bear you leaving, going back to him. How

239

can you? After we have been doing this . . . and this . . .' As he spoke, he kissed and caressed her and her treacherous body betrayed her.

'Please John, you mustn't . . . Oh, God.'

He eased her gently down on to the rug and they lay together side by side. She moaned softly as slowly and with infinite delicacy and expertise he brought her to new heights of passion.

During August Sarah and Victor moved to the new flat. Like a schoolboy with a new toy, Victor listed for Sarah all the advantages: 'Sorry about the entrance steps but look at the kitchen, good, isn't it? And the living-room's really big. We'll have to get some new curtains.'

Seeing his pleasure in the flat Sarah realised he was finally shaking off the last vestiges of his years of domination by his mother. How could she blight his happiness? Yet she had promised John that once the place was set to rights and Victor settled so close to his beloved theatre, she would face him with the truth.

'Come on, lass. Show some enthusiasm!'

She forced a smile. She bought material and made the new curtains but a week after they were hung, black-out was enforced and the colourful prints were hidden from view. When war was finally declared on 3rd September, 1939, it came almost as an anti-climax.

Eddie came through to inspect his parents' new home. He had grown broad and strong, although he would never be tall. He brought with him two dozen fresh eggs, a side of home-cured bacon and a message from his grandmother.

'When are you coming through to see her, Mam? She asked particularly.'

'Soon, I'll be through soon. She's all right, isn't she?'

'Oh, yes. You know Gran.'

Yes, thought Sarah. Mam will never change. She will face the fact of war and Harry being on active service as phlegmatically as she faced Pa's accident and Jim's death.

'I want to buy a present, Mam. For a lass.' Eddie's face turned pink and he shuffled his feet on the hearth rug. For a moment, Sarah forgot her worries. She laughed, then turned the laugh into a cough. Not for the world would she tarnish the blooming of first love.

'You've got a girlfriend?'

'It's Mavis, you know – Mr Lawrence's middle daughter.' Eddie examined his fingernails critically. 'We're going to a dance, after Harvest Festival, and I thought I'd buy her something. Just a small present,' he added hastily.

Sarah enjoyed her son's visit. It stopped her thoughts whirling about like a cageful of birds. John was away for a few days. He had made up the crew on one of the trawlers. To think things out, she suspected.

She stood on the doorstep to wave Eddie off.

'Got the brooch for Mavis? Oh, and your gasmask, of course.'

'This daft thing?' Eddie hitched the strap of the case up on to his shoulder. 'They'll be no use, you know. Gerry's developed a new kind of gas, called arsine. One whiff and we'll drop like flies.'

He gave her a cheerful grin and marched off down the road. She watched him, grateful that he apparently entertained no ideas about joining up. Not for him the head-strong exhilaration many young men felt about the prospect of 'going to war'. Eddie's life was working the land and he would continue in the regular, slow rhythm of the country-side relatively undisturbed by the fury and drama of the wider world. She was glad it was so. She suddenly remembered the conversation of so many years ago with Martin Linford. She wondered how he was feeling now.

Turning to go indoors she noticed a familiar figure come round the corner of the road. Her hand went to her neck. She watched as John came towards her.

It was strange to see him in working clothes. She noticed his face was unusually sombre and dark shadows were etched beneath his eyes. He needed a shave. When they had first met and loved, he had smiled a lot. Her heart smote her as she realised what she had done to him. Why should she decide his need of her was less than that of Victor's?

'I'm sorry to come like this, but I have to see you.'

She touched his sleeve. 'It's all right. Will you come in?'

He shook his head and she knew his sensitivity would not allow him to enter that area of her life she shared with her husband.

'Can you make it tonight, Sarah?'

She nodded.

'I'll see you about eight o'clock, then.'

He touched her cheek then turned away. She went indoors, closing the door behind her quietly. It was important, something to do with their life together. Finally, and quite simply, she made her decision. She looked across at a photograph of Eddie on the sideboard. She hoped one day he would understand and forgive her. Would Victor ever forgive her? If he did not, then that would be a burden she would have to bear. Because she was going to John.

He was waiting for her. He had bathed and changed but the lines of tiredness remained about his eyes. She went to him and placed the palms of her hands on either side of his face. 'I've missed you so much.'

He kissed her with tenderness and love but his expression was abstracted and she felt a pang of anxiety.

He spoke, almost brusquely: 'I've been to see the port recruiting officer, Sarah. They need seamen for special duties.'

She gaped at him. A coldness crept over her. 'What does that mean? Oh, John – you haven't joined up?'

'Not really. It's not like joining the army; not even the navy. They want us for the patrol service, mine-sweeping, mainly.'

'Mine-sweeping – but that will be terribly dangerous!'

'We *are* at war.'

She sprang to her feet. The feeling of coldness within her was replaced by hot anger.

'Why rush into things? The war's just started. Are you so keen to get killed?'

'No, but we're needed *now*. The Germans have laid magnetic mines, Sarah. Women and children have been killed. Anyway, I'm qualified to do the job and there will be fewer rules and regulations involved.' He gave a half-rueful grin. 'If I hang about here, I'll probably end up drafted into the Royal Navy.'

At the expression on her face, his grin faded. He came and put his arms about her. 'I'm sorry. But it's something I must do. I can't explain.' His arms tightened about her. 'I don't want to leave you but I'm going crazy, Sarah. I have to go to sea again.'

He rested his chin against the dark cloud of her hair.

'Remember the first time you came here and I said, "let's live from day to day"?' Well, I can't any more.'

He stepped back to look at her face. 'Ironic, isn't it? I was the one who could handle emotional entanglements, but you took me out of my depths, Sarah. I can't handle this one, anymore. I *hate* your Victor, do you know that? I hate his guts. You say you love me, but you won't leave him. I can't understand that.'

She tried to speak but he checked her.

'No, let me finish.'

He gave a wry smile. 'I've been rehearsing this speech, Sarah, so hear me out. When I first met you, I was charmed by you, I wanted you. Now that's happened to me before. No,' as again she tried to speak he waved her to silence. 'But now you're a part of me and I thought you felt the same. I'm sorry, I can't understand how you can stay with *him*. Do you love him more than me?'

'Oh, John. How can you say that? You know I don't. But I've been married to him so many years and he needs me.'

He shrugged. 'Well, it's immaterial now. I'm leaving to report for duty in two days.'

At her exclamation of pain, his expression softened.

'It won't be too bad, Sarah. It really isn't that dangerous. Most of the time it will be plain boring. Honestly. I'll be watching a float bob up and down. It's just like fishing, really. And on this job, I'll get back here fairly regularly.'

He took her in his arms again. 'I'll always love you, Sarah. Don't think I'm giving up on our chance for happiness. Once this lot's sorted out I'll make you come with me. I'll sell the cottage and we'll go out to Canada. It's wonderful there. You'll love it.'

He kissed her cheeks, wet with tears, and cajoled and comforted her into acceptance, but Sarah knew he was veiling the truth. Mine-sweeping was dangerous. He was risking his life and he was going away without knowing she had decided to come to him. If she told him now he would believe she was saying it in order to keep him with her. With bleak acceptance, she knew she had left her decision too late.

Chapter Twenty-six

John wrapped his frozen fingers round the mug of steaming cocoa. He had never been so cold in all his life. If he survived the war, he thought it would be the bitter winter weather of 1940 he remembered rather than his rare encounters with Germans. He took a gulp of the scalding-hot liquid. Ah, that was better. Like all the food and drink on board ship it tasted of paraffin, but the heat was a life-saver. As the warmth from the cabin penetrated his frozen body he shucked off his coat and grinned across at the bald-headed Yorkshireman watching him.

'I'm getting a taste for this stuff, George. We drink so much of it we'll be saying no to a good pint of bitter when we get ashore.'

The man drew on his pipe. 'That day'll never come, lad. Not as far as I'm concerned.' He lapsed into his habitual silence. George was not noted for his conversation but as a seaman he was without parallel and his shipmates counted themselves lucky to be serving alongside him.

John rubbed his eyes. The hours on watch searching for mines, particularly in the weather conditions now prevailing, had made him feel dazed, almost drugged. 'Boring', he had told Sarah and he had spoken more truly than even he had realised. Yet you could never relax your vigilance. A touch from one of the small, sinister globes washing so silently on the heaving surface of the waves and you were a goner. He thought longingly of Sarah. Those snatched wonderful hours in his cottage seemed a million years ago. He surveyed his present surroundings. The squalid, tiny cabin was sweaty and steamy and blue from the haze of George's pipe. He ran his hand over his unshaven chin. His mouth felt like blotting paper.

Sarah used to bring flowers to the cottage; often wild flowers she had picked on her walk across the cliff top. He closed his eyes and tried to recapture the pungent, earthy smell of marigolds. He smiled and felt in an inner shirt pocket for the photograph she had given to him. It was crumpled and he smoothed it flat with an oil-stained finger.

'I never bought you flowers, did I?' He spoke to her silently. 'And you love them so much. When this lot's over, I'll buy you the biggest bouquet I can find.'

'That your lass?'

'Yes.' John showed his photograph to his companion.

'My, she's a right beauty.' George cleared his throat and knocked out his pipe. He felt under his fisherman's guernsey and produced a picture of his own.

'That's my Missus.' He regarded the picture fondly. 'And that's four of our five lads.' With a stubby finger he pointed to the tallest young man: 'That's Steve. He's a mechanic in the Air Force.' He chuckled: 'Odd one out, you might say. Rest of 'em are at sea; Alec's in the Royal Navy and the other three are in mine-sweepers, like me.' He sighed and looked hard at the photograph. 'It's Edith I worry about. Sitting at home, waiting . . .'

John looked at the picture. George's wife was a bonny, plump woman with grey hair. She smiled proudly out of the photograph surrounded by her family. He felt a lump in his throat.

'This bloody war,' he was saying when there were shouts from above. The two men looked at each other.

'That's the look-out.'

They snatched up their coats and rushed on deck. Once there, the cold took John's breath away. The shrouds of the ship were festooned with icicles and the seamen, moving swiftly yet purposefully to their allotted stations, resembled Eskimos in their hooded duffel coats. John climbed half-way up to the bridge companion. The Lewis guns were mounted, one on each side of the bridge. Jock, a five-foot-one-inch-tall Scot from Aberdeen, clapped him on the arm.

'Action Station, laddie. It's an Aircraft Alarm.'

John peered about him but the snow squalls rendered the poor light even worse. The sky was overcast with low cloud, but now he could hear the drone of twin aeroplane engines. The sound was over by the starboard bow. His heartbeat quickened. He concentrated his gaze on the lightest patch of cloud which was moving about four hundred feet above the sea. He waited. The sound droned on, then slowly grew less and finally died away. A long expulsion of air sighed its way from John's lungs. His tense fingers relaxed.

'Probably one of ours,' said Jock laconically.

'Sounded more like a Heinkel to me,' John replied.

'Well, it's gone. So that's that.' A mixture of relief and disappointment sounded in the Scotsman's voice. But the next minute tension returned. A man had moved to the port side. He shielded his eyes with his hands, then shouted: 'Hey – what's that?'

Through the drifts of snow John saw the figure of their skipper through the window of the wheelhouse as he swung round, his glasses to his eyes.

Then came another shout from the port side. 'Floating object on the port bow. It's a mine!'

The skipper must have rung down to the engine room, thought John, because the throb of the engines ceased. He stared into the water but could see nothing. The deck hands were gesturing and pointing and one had a rifle. Another snow squall bore down on the ship. John strained his eyes. There it was! He opened fire with the Lewis gun and a spray of water shot up, hiding the mine from view. The ship was rolling. It was difficult to focus on the spot. He fired again. There was a flash then an ear-shattering explosion.

'We've got it.'

Jock gave the thumbs up to John. There was a wide grin on his face.

'We got the bugger.'

There was a ragged cheer from the deck hands. Then someone 'hushed' them, waving his arms about to silence them.

'For Christ's sakes, be quiet!'

That was the skipper, bawling at them. The cheers died away. The men stood silent, the falling snow turning them into marble statues. The plane was back. John had been right. It was a Heinkel. It appeared from a low cloud and dived low over the ship. The air gunner opened fire and as the deck was raked with machine-gun fire the men dived for cover.

'Bloody hell!' Jock, from his position behind the Lewis gun, grasped his left arm above the elbow and watched the thick blood drip sluggishly from his fingers. 'Where did that come from?'

'Watch out!' John snapped. 'Here it comes again.'

The Heinkel climbed, turned and came straight for them.

'Where's the bloody Spitfires?' groaned his companion, nevertheless forcing his injured arm to move and preparing to fire the Lewis gun. 'It's on its own – it's a raider.'

John had read about these planes. They flew alone, dodging among the clouds like a guerrilla dodging among rocks and bushes. The raiders cruised just above the lowest cloud bank, spotting their potential victims from several miles away. After attacking, they would dart away again, giving the RAF Coastal Command no chance of catching them.

'Jesus.'

This run was even worse. Instead of machine-gunning, the raider released a salvo of high-explosive bombs. One exploded under the counter of the ship, another shattered the starboard side of the bridge.

John was blown off his feet by the explosion. He landed on the deck with a thud which knocked every bit of breath from his body. He fell amongst a tangle of splintered glass, beams and wires. Clouds of steam from burst pipes mixed incongruously with the fluttering snowflakes. Nearby he could hear some poor devil screaming, but John himself felt very cold and very peaceful. So this is it, he thought. He tried, without success, to move his arm to retrieve Sarah's photograph then remembered he had left it in the cabin. He sighed. It didn't really matter. There was another explosion. The ship reared up then slid, silently, beneath the waves. The two photographs, one of Sarah and one of the older woman surrounded by her family, whirled about with the rest of the flotsam and jetsam, then gently they, too, sank, drifting downwards into the darkness of the sea.

Sarah had thoroughly enjoyed the Ginger Rogers film, but when the house lights went up and the Wurlitzer organ launched into *Run, Rabbit, Run* she nudged Maisie.

'I'll have to go now,' she whispered.

'Oh, I wanted to see the shorts and the news.'

'That's all right. I'll see you tomorrow, at work.'

Sarah left Maisie lustily singing *Roll out the Barrel* and went from the warmth of the cinema into the freezing street. She shivered and pulled her coat collar close to her throat. Few people were in evidence; the drifting snow made travel difficult. A youth selling newspapers sheltered in a shop doorway. As she drew level with him she heard him shouting: 'Tragedy at sea! *Arctic Star* lost! No survivors!'

He blinked as a white-faced woman loomed up before him, pressed a coin into his mittened hand and snatched a paper.

'You want some change,' he said, but she had gone. He put the two-shilling piece in his pocket, a self-satisfied smile on his face.

Sarah fumbled her way into the flat. The short winter day was already fading. She switched on the light, spread the newspaper flat on the kitchen table and read the headlines. She beat with her hands on the black and white newsprint. No, no, no. It couldn't be! She would have known. He said he would be all right. He couldn't die. He couldn't! She slumped into a chair. Her grief kept her immobile, frozen into stone.

About an hour later, Victor came in. He glanced at her, went quickly to draw the black-out curtains, then came to her. She looked through him, her eyes burning holes in her expressionless face.

'Come on, lass. Come on.' He placed a heavy hand on her shoulder. She blinked, a faint look of puzzlement animated her dull features. She raised her eyes to his.

'You knew?'

'Yes.'

'How long?'

'Almost as soon as it started.' He spoke quietly with an air of resigned bitterness.

'You bastard!'

He stepped back in surprise as she flew at him. Her features were contorted, her lips drawn back from her teeth. She clawed at his cheek before he recovered sufficiently to imprison her hands and subdue her. She shook her head from side to side and laughed wildly, hysterically: 'You knew all the time. I could have gone to him. We could have been together.'

He shook her. 'Stop it, Sarah. Stop it.' He pulled her to him, wrapping his arms about her and holding her tight. For a moment longer she struggled, then her body went limp and harsh, dry sobs shook her frame. Victor smoothed back her hair with his hand.

'I couldn't lose you,' he said. His voice was unsteady. 'I kept thinking something might happen. I was prepared to share you rather than lose you altogether.'

With a tired, tired gesture she moved to free herself from him. His arms dropped to his side. She stepped back and they stared at each other.

'I just want to be left alone now, Victor.' Her voice was flat and full of fatigue.

'I know.'

He watched her move towards the door with leaden steps.

'Sarah.'

She stopped, without looking at him.

'I've never made you happy. I know that. I suppose we never should have married, but we did and we must make the best of it.' He swallowed hard. 'It's not been easy. I hated him, you know. I would see that look on your face. You never looked like that for me. I've wished him dead many a time, but now . . .'

She fumbled for the door handle like a blind person, then she said: 'I can't say I'm sorry because I'm not. No matter what I feel now I can never wish it hadn't happened.'

She left the room. He heard the floorboards creak and her hesitant footsteps cross the bedroom. Then there was silence. He strained his ears for the sound of weeping, but there was nothing. He rubbed his eyes. They felt gritty. Then he looked down at the newspaper lying on the table. With a savage gesture, he snatched it up, tore it in half and threw the pieces across the room.

Chapter Twenty-seven

One fine April evening, Victor bumped into Maisie.

'How's Sarah?' The handbag Maisie hitched up on to her shoulder was made of real leather. Maisie had moved up in the world. She was a member of the Ladies Licensed Victuallers Committee and a respected member of Branswick's business community. In essence, however, she remained the same old Maisie. She stepped in front of Victor making it difficult for him to pass her. She was sure he blamed her for what had happened and indeed, sometimes she blamed herself for Sarah's unhappiness, but she still believed Sarah and John had been made for each other.

'She's all right.' Victor moved to walk round her, but she caught hold of his sleeve.

'Come on, man. Tell me the truth. I haven't seen her for ages and I can never get a reply when I call round to see her. Go on, Vic. Tell me. I just want to know how she is.'

Victor's hard expression softened. He saw the genuine concern in Maisie's face. 'She's not too good,' he admitted.

'In what way?'

He frowned and looked down the street. 'We can't stand nattering here.'

'Then walk along with me.' She laughed. 'I'm well thought of now, you know, so your reputation's safe.'

They moved together down the street.

'I don't know how to explain.' He thought for a moment, then said, 'She sees to the flat, cooks the meals, things like that. She's calm and friendly and she doesn't cry, at least not when I'm there.'

He stopped suddenly. 'It's awful. It's like living with a ruddy ghost.' He gave Maisie a bewildered look. 'You know Sarah. There was always something she was enthusiastic about, or something she hated. God, I used to loathe it when she got a new bee in her bonnet, the way she went on and on . . . but now, I'd give anything to get a flash of temper from her.'

'She needs something to take her out of herself.' Maisie rubbed her chin and looked up at Victor. 'You know you're all right, Victor Manvell,' she said unexpectedly.

He looked uncomfortable.

'I've always thought you were a real misery guts but you're all right. I realised, when I first called round, that you knew about Sarah and John Saul and I was worried. But you've stood by her and now, today . . .' She paused. 'You must love her a lot.'

Embarrassed, he glanced at his watch. 'I'll have to go.'

'No. Just a minute. I've thought of something.' Maisie's eyes gleamed. 'It's just the thing. Why didn't I realise before?'

'Think of what?'

'You know I've been voted on to the Child Welfare Committee? Oh well, maybe you don't. It doesn't matter.' She hitched up her handbag again. 'We've got twenty-five kids arriving on Saturday. They're from Hull.'

She frowned at his look of incomprehension. 'It's like the London evacuees. They're kids from poor homes and Hull's had such a pasting recently, we decided to give them a holiday. They are coming for three weeks. It will give them a change and their parents a rest. I'll allocate one to Sarah. That will stop her mooning about.'

'Just a minute. I don't know . . .' Victor was undecided. 'I don't think she's up to coping with a youngster right now.'

'Of course she can. Always good with kids, your Sarah. It will keep her busy and it's only for three weeks.'

Swayed by her conviction, he agreed. He watched her hurry away down the street and his stomach tightened as he anticipated Sarah's possible reaction. Still, he thought, any kind of reaction would be preferable to the blankness in which they were now living.

'You've what!'

Sarah stared at him in disbelief.

'I said we would take one.'

She laughed; a harsh, disbelieving laugh. 'I never would have believed it of you, Victor, letting Maisie manipulate you like that. Don't you know she likes playing games with people. And you fell for it! And don't pretend otherwise. Since when have you wanted your precious peace and quiet disturbed by a slum kid?'

'It's only for three weeks, Sarah.' He answered her quietly. 'You may have forgotten but there's a war on and these poor kids have put up with nightly raids. You used to like the thought of a challenge but you've changed haven't you? In fact,' his voice dropped, 'sometimes I'll swear you are beginning to sound like my mother.'

She turned and slammed out of the room. He sighed and picked up his paper. At least he had succeeded in forcing a reaction.

When the doorbell rang on Saturday, Sarah answered it. Victor had disappeared half an hour ago.

'Mrs Manvell?'

'Yes.'

The woman ticked a name on the piece of paper she held, then pushed forward a young girl. 'This is Dorothea Bellows. Dorothea, this kind lady will look after you.' She glanced from one to the other, smiled weakly and retreated at a walk so fast, it threatened to turn into a run at any moment.

Sarah and the girl stared at each other then Sarah stepped back.

'You'd better come in,' she said.

Was this the half-starved waif she had been led to expect? Dorothea was a large lump of a girl. Her bulging, pale cheeks suggested she lived exclusively on potatoes and suet pudding, her mouse-coloured hair straggled untidily over the dirty velvet collar of her too-tight jacket and her eyes were unpleasantly bulbous and a strange greeny colour.

'This way. Do you want something to eat?'

A spark of animation lightened the girl's dull features. 'It's nice in here,' she said. She went over and patted the feet of a brown and white china spaniel which was placed by the hearth, then wandered over and fingered the chintz curtains at the windows.

'We've not got proper curtains,' she said. 'Just brown paper and an old blanket we tag across for the black-out.' She scratched her head vigorously.

Sarah's heart sank. She stared at the girl. 'Whereabouts in Hull do you live, Dorothea?'

'Close by the docks. Mind, it's a good job we don't have anything nice 'cos they'll be blown to kingdom come before long, I expect. And you can call me Dotty,' she offered. 'Me Mam called me Dorothea, out of a soppy romantic book.' She shrugged her fat shoulders. 'Must have been a real disappointment for her.'

She looked at Sarah, a gleam of amusement in her eyes. 'Can we have chips?'

'Yes, why not.' Sarah was conscious of a faint feeling of warmth towards the girl. She picked up a brown paper carrier bag.

'Is this all you've brought with you?'

'Yes.' Dotty laughed. 'Nearly brought me bucket and spade, but they said the beach was probably mined.' She grinned. 'Just my luck. First trip ever to the seaside and the bloody beaches are mined.'

'She's twelve,' Sarah told Victor when they had finally persuaded Dotty to retire to bed.

'She looks about fifteen,' protested Victor, thinking of Dotty's thick body and the speculative look she had given him on his arrival home.

'I know, she knows an awful lot for a twelve-year-old. I'll have to get some shopping in. I hope's she brought her ration book, she does eat a lot. Oh, and Victor,' she lowered her voice, 'she keeps scratching her head. I'd better get something for head lice.'

'Hell.' Victor was appalled. 'I didn't reckon on this, Sarah. Shall I contact Maisie? Tell her to send her somewhere else?'

'No, don't do that. I quite like her.' The beginnings of a smile curled round Sarah's mouth. 'She's quite a challenge.'

The tense feeling inside Victor eased. It was going to be all right. A light had come back into Sarah's eyes. She had joined the world of the living again. He smiled to himself, then actually laughed as, raising his hand to scratch his head, he caught out Sarah in the self-same action.

'Put the chemist at the top of your shopping list,' he said.

* * *

'You're an amazing girl. Do you know that?'

'I know.' Dotty nodded complacently.

They had walked along Burbank Crescent, past the grand houses perched high on the cliffs above the town and were now seated on a grassy bank overlooking the wide sweep of the bay. The terrible winter had finally given way to a spring dramatic in its loveliness. They had passed gardens bursting with glowing daffodils and, where they now sat, shy primroses starred the sweet-smelling grass and high above the seagulls swooped and cried. Dotty laid back with a sigh of contentment.

'It's real nice here,' she said. 'I won't half miss it.'

'You can stay a bit longer, if you like.'

'Honest?' The girl sat up. 'You really mean it?'

'I wouldn't say it if I didn't mean it.' Sarah smiled at her visitor.

'Wow, that's really something!'

'What is?'

'You really do like me.'

A crease formed between Sarah's brows. 'What do you mean?'

'Well, I know I'm kind of odd. And I can make people laugh.' Dotty picked a piece of grass and chewed on it. 'But it's a bit like the monkeys at the Zoo. You can soon get tired of them.'

'Dotty!'

The girl spat out the grass and smiled kindly at Sarah. 'It's all right. I know I'm kind of a freak. I mean,' she cast a glance at her body. 'Look at me!'

Sarah had been quite convinced her capacity for feeling had died months ago and her heart was merely a pump, pushing the blood around her body. Now she knew differently.

'Looks aren't everything. You're clever and sharp and very amusing. People will always want to be with you.'

'Yes, I know.' Dotty rolled over on to her stomach and gazed reflectively out to sea. 'I don't particularly want to be good looking.' She flicked a glance at Sarah. 'You're getting on a bit but you're bloody beautiful and you're not happy, are you?'

There was no answer.

Undeterred, Dotty continued her line of thought: 'I reckon looks can be a handicap. My Mam's pretty. She's stupid too. She's always at the pictures dreaming of Clark Gable. She buys crummy paper flowers and pretends we have a nice home.' She gave a short laugh. 'Maybe it's better that way. She can look at me and pretend I'm pretty, pretend me dad loves her and this bloody war's just a bad dream. Maybe she's right, but that's not for me. I don't day dream.'

She watched a gull hover above them. 'I am clever, you know; especially with figures. I'm going to get a really good job one day and have my own place. I'll have proper furniture; proper wood, not the bloody matchstick stuff like we have.'

Sarah listened to this strange girl. She almost felt the younger of the two. She brought up her knees and rested her chin on them. 'Won't you be lonely on your own?'

Dotty shrugged. 'I dunno. Maybe I won't be on my own, but if I am, I'll survive.' She looked slyly at Sarah. 'Lots of married people are on their own really, aren't they?'

Sarah's cheeks grew hot. 'I don't know what you mean.'

'It's not just you and Victor,' said Dotty, encouragingly. 'It's most people. I mean just look at you both. You're nice people. You've made me real comfortable and Victor is ever so kind and considerate, but you're not really,' she frowned thoughtfully, 'easy with *each other,* are you? Maybe it's 'cos you're different types.' She gave a wry grin. 'He should have picked someone like me. Someone who doesn't expect much.' She heaved a sigh. 'It's just the same with me Mam and Dad. I think marriage is a bloody silly idea really. I suppose it's just better if you're going to have kids. But it gets boring, doesn't it? And women go moony about romance and blokes couldn't care less.' She knocked a fly off her plump, bare knee. 'Your Victor's not a bad sort though, thinks a lot about you, I can tell.'

'Don't be silly,' Sarah jumped to her feet. 'Vic's a good husband but we've been married years and years. He spends most of his time at the theatre, he always has.'

'I wonder why,' mused Dotty as she brushed the grass off her skirt before following Sarah's hurrying figure.

That night Sarah watched Victor as he bent over the table, his head close to the mousey locks of Dotty. The girl was struggling to solve a mathematical equation and he had stopped to help.

'See, it goes this way.' With the stub of a pencil he drew various diagrams on a piece of paper.

'Yes, I see.' Dotty's eyes lit up with admiration. 'Where did you learn all that?'

'I use equations in my work,' he explained. 'We have to adapt measurements for the stage, see?' He straightened up and ruffled Dotty's hair before moving away.

Sarah was surprised at the look on the girl's face. Then Dotty saw Sarah watching her and the look changed to one of faint hostility.

She's jealous of me, Sarah thought with a shock. She's got a crush on Victor. How ridiculous.

Over the next few days she found herself studying her

husband. How could a young girl find Victor attractive? Why, he was almost fifty.

He came into the kitchen when she was ironing. 'Have you done my blue shirt yet? Oh, good.'

She watched as he pulled his working shirt over his head. His back was lean and well muscled, his stomach flat. Ironically, his stomach pains had almost ceased and he was eating more, but he would never be fat. Perhaps, mused Sarah, the doctor had been right about his nerves.

'What's up, Sarah?'

'Nothing, why?'

'You keep looking at me.'

She laughed: 'Can't a wife look at her husband?'

'You never have before.'

'No. I haven't.'

He reached across to take the clean shirt and she felt a strange stirring within her as he brushed against her arm. He had made no attempt to touch her for so long. Before John, she had never experienced sexual yearning, but his expert loving had awakened within her a deep sensuality. She was shocked at her own feelings. She felt she was betraying her love for John. She stared at Victor, her face a mixture of emotions.

'Sarah, what is it?'

She did not reply.

'Sarah?'

He moved towards her. God – he couldn't believe it. She wanted *him*. His legs shook and he tried to steady his breathing. He must be careful. He had spoilt things so many times. But it had been so long.

He held her and kissed her; gently.

She sighed and ran her hands along his bare shoulders.

'Come on,' he said.

'Where?'

'Upstairs.'

'But the ironing, and Dotty might come back.'

He reached out a hand and switched off the iron. 'She's gone on the trip, remember. Won't be back for ages.' He took her hand and led her upstairs.

He tried so hard. He subdued his own passion, all the feelings he had held down so long. He watched her face, saw it slacken, felt her body relax and brought her to fulfilment before he took her. Then they were together and he was happy. She said his name. Her eyes had been closed and he wondered, but no . . . she said *his* name and opened her eyes and smiled at him.

'Jesus!' he said and the word was a prayer and not a blasphemy.

Later, she said: 'You'll be late for work.'

'Bugger the work,' he replied.

'Oh, Victor, I never thought I would hear you say that.'

And they clung together and laughed until tears poured down their faces into their open mouths.

Later still, he stirred, reluctantly. 'Better go,' he said. He dressed, then sat on the bed next to her.

'That other business.'

She opened her mouth and her eyes darkened.

He shook his head. 'I'm not asking anything. I just want you to know. It's gone.' He looked down, smoothing out her fingers. 'A lot of it was me. I can't . . .' he stopped.

'Go on,' she said softly.

'Oh, hell!' He pressed her fingers until they hurt. 'I love you. That's all.'

'It's enough.' She reached up to him and kissed his mouth. 'I love you too.'

And because she meant it, she felt a great sadness.

Chapter Twenty-eight

Dotty tugged at the leather strap which opened the train window. She stuck her head out and looked down at Sarah.

'Ta-ra, thanks for having me.'

'It's been a pleasure. Any time you want to come through and see us, you'll be welcome.'

Dotty nodded. She fumbled in her pocket. 'Here.' She handed Sarah a piece of paper. 'It's my address.'

She ducked her head, embarrassed: 'You said you'd write.'

'I will.' Sarah read the address: '43 Dagger Lane. Sounds very dramatic.'

'When the pubs chuck out it's usually fists not daggers!'

The guard blew a whistle and walked along the train, slamming shut the open doors.

'If you're in Hull any time, come and see me.' Dotty clutched the top of the window. 'Anyone will tell you the way. We're in dockland. Ask for the Land of Green Ginger.'

'Another exotic name!' Sarah was doing her best to keep the farewell light. Dotty would hate either of them to become emotional.

'It's not. Just mucky old warehouses mostly, but some-times, when the wind's right, you catch a smell of the spices and things.'

The train began to move and Sarah walked and then ran alongside.

'Bye, love. Hang on to those plans of yours. This war can't last forever.'

The quietness, the emptiness of the flat brought about in Sarah the sensation of being outside her own body. She took off her coat and paused as her heart began to beat violently. *No,* she would not allow herself to slip back into her former despair. She switched on the wireless and tuned in to *Itma.* As Mrs Mop's familiar voice asked: 'Can I do you now, sir?' Sarah's lips turned upwards in a smile. She unpacked her shopping. She had been lucky today. The butcher actually had meat to sell. She must keep busy.

When Victor came home, he raised his head and sniffed appreciatively: 'That's not Spam!'

'No, pork chops, would you believe?'

'Smashing.' He glanced at her, then stared: 'What have you done to your hair?'

'It's a new style. It's called a "Victory Roll". Do you like it?'

'Very smart.' He put his head on one side. 'But I prefer it loose, like this.' He moved across to her and pulled out the hair pins.

'Oh, Victor,' she protested. 'It took me ages.'

'But now you look younger.' He put his finger under her chin and tilted her face upwards. 'I guess it sounds stupid, but coming home I remembered Dotty was going today and I felt excited; like we were on honeymoon and it was our first time together.'

She smiled. 'I don't think that's stupid.'

'Let's act like newly-marrieds, then.' He kissed her.

'But the meal,' she parried him, half-heartedly.

'Food's not what I need right now.'

After they had made love he lay with his head on her shoulder and she stroked his hair. She felt gratitude and love that he was big-hearted enough to forgive and forget. She also felt sorrow, for all the arid, wasted years; and she felt pain because, sweet though their loving had been, she knew she would never again experience the passion she had shared with John.

'What are you thinking?' asked Victor.

'About Dotty, she'll be home now.' Sarah answered honestly. She was thinking now about Dotty. *She* had known, at her tender years, that life was not perfect.

'Is that all?'

She gave him an affectionate prod. 'I was also thinking it was a terrible waste of good pork chops.'

Spring turned into summer. Dotty wrote to them. She was top of her class in maths and she had spring-cleaned the house. Then an air raid had flattened half the street and everything was covered in bloody dust again. Still, she was all right. She sent her love and two kisses for Victor.

'That girl's got a crush on you,' Sarah told him.

'Rubbish!'

'It's true. Oh, and I've received a letter from Mam. She wants to know if I will go through and see her.' Sarah chewed on her fingernail. 'It's her birthday in July and she wants as many of the family as can to visit her. She says she has something to tell us.'

'You'd best go, then.'

'Sure you don't mind?'

'Of course not. It will do you good and it's time you visited your Mam again.'

*   *   *

Mary Armstrong looked at the group of people crowded in her kitchen, and found it hard to realise they were her children. Arthur was doggedly struggling through the last piece of birthday cake.

'All right, Arthur?'

'Fine, Mam. Fine.'

Mary sniffed. It was a terrible cake but the best she could make with the ingredients available. Her son flicked a crumb off his smart grey suit. Little Arthur – his stockings had always bagged round his skinny legs and he'd worn patches on his britches. She looked in vain for the child in his smooth city face and failed. Arthur could speak three foreign languages now and had a job he couldn't talk about. He also had a pretty, ice-cold wife he adored, but no children. Mary suppressed a sigh.

Her gaze travelled on to Florence and her husband. Again, no children. Poor Florence, three miscarriages and a still birth before they'd given up trying. Still, they had their teaching and their music. How old they looked, like Darby and Joan sitting there. She shook her head. Harry had his arm around his wife. Mary felt her heart lighten. They were fine. Harry's broad shoulders were set off to advantage by his naval uniform and he looked proudly at his rounded robin of a wife. Betty was eight months pregnant and she had confided in Mary she hoped they would have at least four children. Harry would give her grandchildren, if he was spared. She sent up a secret prayer to the Almighty.

'Shall I make some more tea, Mam?'

'Yes, please, Sarah.' She watched her daughter as she moved across the room. Something had happened to Sarah. There were fresh lines about her eyes and mouth. Mary's heart ached in sympathy. But a mother must wait to console a child that had become an adult, until invited to do so. And Sarah had coped with her pain. Her mouth was still tender and her eyes held serenity. Mary took the cup of tea from Sarah with a murmur of thanks. She hoped she would be able to talk with her before the visit ended.

'I'm giving up the house,' she announced abruptly to her children. Their faces registered shock.

'But, why, Mam?' Harry's deep voice broke the silence. 'You've lived here all your married life.'

'Maybe it's time I had a change then.' She took a sip of tea, allowing time for the announcement to sink in. 'Anyway, I'm lonely here.'

'You never let on.' Betty's soft brown eyes held a look of distress. 'Why don't you come and live with us, Mam. Harry's at sea such a lot. I'd love your company.'

'No, love. Although thank you for offering; I've always sworn I would never live with my married children.'

'What are you planning?' asked Sarah in a quiet voice.

'I'm moving in with Eliza Fenton.'

'Fenton!' Arthur pulled a face. 'Why, Mother? She's the last person I would have thought . . .' his voice trailed away.

'Eliza and I will do very well together. She's on her own, too, and although she's as bright as a button she's terribly plagued with rheumatism.'

'You have to look after someone, don't you, Mam?' Sarah smiled.

'Eliza's good company. It will suit both of us.' Mary appealed to them: 'I'm not going far; just to her house. Her place is a mite bigger than this. But I thought I'd get you back here just one more time in your old home. The house isn't mine, as you well know, so there's no trouble there. But,' she paused, 'there's a few things I would like you to

267

have. I'll give them to you before you all leave. There, that's all.' She waited for comments but no one spoke. She rose from her chair and began to clear the table.

'I'll do that, Mam.' Florence took the dishes from her hand, and Mary looked at her youngest daughter.

'Sarah.'

'Yes, Mam.'

'There's something I want to show you. Come upstairs with me.' The two women climbed the stairs leaving the other members of the family to speculate on the proposed change. In the bedroom Sarah watched her mother bend down and attempt to pull a suitcase from beneath the bed.

'Here, let me do that.' The case retrieved, Sarah placed it on the bed.

'Remember it?' Mary spoke softly.

Sarah stared at the battered brown suitcase.

'It's Jim's.'

Her mother nodded. 'I couldn't bear to see it after he died but now, I want you to have it.'

Sarah sat down beside the case and ran gentle fingers over the clasp. 'Are you sure?'

'There's little enough in it. I haven't much to give any of you.' Mary sounded embarrassed. 'But I knew you would want this.'

'Thank you.' Sarah hesitated, then pressed the spring; the locks flew open.

The two women looked inside the case. There was an exercise book. Sarah picked it up, glanced inside, then replaced it in the case hurriedly.

'It's some kind of diary,' she said. 'I'll read it later.'

Mary nodded. 'Look.' She picked out a yellowing programme. 'It's for a concert. Can't think where he got this from.'

'Don't you remember?' Sarah leant forward and took the programme from her mother. 'Just before he was ill, he went to a concert with a friend.' She read out an item from the programme.

'*Cavalleria Rusticana* by Pietro Mascagni. Fancy Jim liking things like that!'

Mary shrugged. 'Jim was interested in everything and everybody. Remember how his pals teased him because he liked poetry?'

'I remember.' Sarah picked up a tattered book of verse and smiled as she turned over the pages. The book had obviously been bought from a second-hand book stall. It was dog-eared and falling apart, yet her brother had marked special passages with pieces of paper rather than deface the already shabby book. Just like Jim.

'Listen, Mam.' She read:

'When the green woods laugh with the voice of joy
And the dimpling stream runs laughing by;
When the air does laugh with merry wit
And the green hill laughs with the noise of it.'

She cleared a suddenly husky throat. 'How he loved the country, Mam.'

'Aye.' Mary stood up, her face set. 'And most of his life he was stuck down that mine.' She turned away: 'I'm off downstairs, Sarah. Coming?'

'In a minute.' Sarah was turning the pages of the book. It was as if her beloved brother stood before her for a moment, his thin, sensitive face smiling at her. The book opened at another page marked with a paper insertion. Across the top of the bookmark, written in fading pencil, was written one word 'Sarah'. She looked at the page: 'He that lives in hope, danceth without musick.'

'Oh, Jim!'

She placed the book on the bed and crossed to the window. All she could see were rows and rows of grimy houses marching their way towards the pithead. From here you couldn't see the farmlands beyond nor the wild and beautiful moor but Jim had treasured the knowledge of their existence.

Working in the bowels of the earth he had still perceived the beauty of the world. Yet his innate wisdom had told him that life, of necessity, must be composed of darkness as well as light. How eager he had been to take up the challenge.

She returned to the bed and picked up the book, holding it to her heart. So many years since Jim had been denied his chance at life but it seemed to her that he was speaking to her now. She bent her head.

'I'll dance for you, Jim,' she promised.

Chapter Twenty-nine

When Sarah returned home, Victor sensed a change in her. She was less quick to anger and more thoughtful in speech. Some of her earlier vivacity had disappeared, yet she was obviously content. Victor was delighted when once again she showed an interest in the theatre. She came to the shows, waiting in the stalls at the end of the performance until he had finished his work, and they would return home together.

The war occupied everyone's waking thoughts, yet the life of Branswick itself went on relatively unchanged. A seaside resort on the east coast was of little interest to the Germans. Occasionally, a few unused bombs would be jettisoned over the town as the Jerry planes left the English coastline, but little damage was done. The women, unless they had husbands or sons on active service, were more preoccupied by the amount of time they had to spend queuing for food and annoyed when their families grumbled at being served with carrot flan twice a week.

Victor was happy. He often felt guilty about it, but there you were! He had Sarah and he had the theatre. If only they could win the war and his stupid stomach would settle down, he would ask for nothing more. And so, when Sarah confided her news to him one frosty spring day in 1942 he was dumbfounded.

'You can't be!'

She nodded, her eyes twinkling.

'But . . . you can't be.'

'It's still possible, you know.'

He blushed. 'I realise that. It's just, well . . .' He rubbed his chin. 'I thought you had reached that time of life.'

She pulled a face. 'Charming! I tell my husband he is going to be a father again and he tells me I'm too old. I'm only thirty-eight.'

'Oh, Sarah!' The shock was wearing off. 'That's wonderful news. It's just, I never imagined. Do you feel all right? Should you be resting?'

'I feel fine,' she reassured him. 'The doctor says I'm perfectly healthy and there shouldn't be any problems. He did say it was a long time since Eddie . . . Oh!'

She bit her lip, a rueful expression dawning on her face. 'Eddie! Will he be dreadfully shocked?'

He hugged her. 'Let him be,' he declared. 'He's grown too solemn by half.'

Sarah dropped her head down on to his chest to hide a smile. Victor did not realise that Eddie was exactly as he had once been. He was going steady with Mavis Lawrence now and though, to Sarah, the courtship seemed dull and prosaic, it seemed to suit all those immediately concerned. Eddie, it had been agreed, would eventually take over the farm from the Lawrences.

'I suppose he will find it strange, having a baby sister when he's twenty,' she murmured.

'How do you know it will be a girl?'

She smiled. 'I just do.'

Diane Manvell was certainly the bonniest baby ever born. Victor was absolutely convinced of it. For a start, she was the image of her mother. When she was four weeks old he pushed the pram round to the back of the Lyric and showed her off to his workmates. The stagehands took off their caps and scratched their heads when he left them. Vic was going soft in the head, they agreed. Sad thing to happen to a man.

He doted on the child. He would sit and nurse her for hours, examining her tiny fingers and stroking the fine dark curls wisping around her delicate skull. Sarah, watching him, could hardly believe this was the same man who had been so cold and awkward with his first child. Poor Eddie. She was glad he was not often at home to remark and comment upon the difference. He came through for the christening, of course. He was godfather and stood up with a smiling Betty, already pregnant with her second child, and a beaming, speechless Dotty, as godmothers.

Diane was so contented. She spent hours lying in her cot or her pram staring into space or playing with her toes. The months sped by and overnight, it seemed, she was an enchanting toddler. It was then that the first finger of fear touched Sarah's heart. Diane was almost *too* good. She seemed to live in a world of her own. Sarah gazed at her baby's tea-rose skin and straight sturdy limbs and was comforted. No, her child was perfect. Why, she had walked at eleven months although she still made no effort to talk. How stupid of her to worry over some intangible feeling while every day she read in the papers of the dreadful suffering of millions. Ashamed, she pushed her worry to the back of her mind.

Then something happened which brought her doubts and fears rushing back. She had taken Diane shopping for some new shoes. On the way home they bumped into Maisie so they stopped and talked. Diane was bored. She fidgeted and pulled at Sarah's hand.

'Be a good girl,' said Sarah. 'Mummy won't be a

minute. Oh – My God!' Her eyes opened wide in horror.

Diane suddenly pulled free from her mother's grasp, grinned a cheeky grin, and ran as fast as she could towards the edge of the pavement. A red, double-decker bus had just rounded the corner.

'Diane!' screamed Sarah at the top of her voice. Leaving behind the lumbering, puffing Maisie, she sprinted after her daughter. She reached her just before she stepped off into the road.

'You bad girl!'

She caught hold of the child and jerked her backwards then, as Diane turned towards her, she smacked her leg. As Diane opened her mouth to howl, Sarah stared white-faced down at her. In the split second her daughter had turned and looked at her, Sarah had seen surprise and confusion on her face. She didn't hear me, Sarah thought. She crouched down and pulled her child into her arms. She hugged her fiercely. When Maisie panted her way up to them, Sarah put her dread into words: 'She didn't hear me, Maisie. I shouted at the top of my voice and she never heard!'

'Rubbish! Of course she heard, it was the shock, that's all. Enough to make anyone act deaf, or daft. You come home with me for a cup of tea. That will put you right again.'

Obediently Sarah accompanied Maisie home. She listened to her friend chatter as she filled the kettle and found a biscuit for Diane, who had completely recovered from her scare.

'Look at her, the little pet. You're as right as rain, aren't you? Can't think what your Mummy's worrying about.'

Sarah watched Diane stuff the biscuit into her mouth and beam at Maisie. Her friend's reassurances did nothing to quieten her fears. She watched Diane closely. After finishing her biscuit the child went to the window and, climbing upon a chair, gazed through the glass. Maisie had a whistling kettle.

When the water boiled, the shrill shriek made Sarah jump, but Diane never moved.

'Enough to make anyone act deaf' Maisie had said. What if Diane was deaf?

'I have to go, Maisie.' She spoke through lips stiff with anxiety. 'I have to talk to Victor. I've thought before that there was something strange about Diane's behaviour, but today has proved it. We have to think of what to do.'

Maisie placed a cup of tea before her. 'Have this first.' She stared at Sarah, a solemn look on her face. 'I still think you're jumping to conclusions, love. There's probably nothing to worry about at all. If I were you,' she screwed up her face in concentration, 'I'd not mention anything to Victor yet. You know how he dotes on the child. He'd worry himself to death about it and that wouldn't do his stomach much good, would it? No,' she sighed. 'If you're really worried take Diane to the doctor's. See what he says first.'

The doctor was noncommittal.

'Difficult to judge in a child so young, Mrs Manvell. There does appear to be some hearing problems, but just how bad they are I'm not qualified to say. She's certainly a happy child, a credit to you.' He looked over his glasses at Diane who stared back at him.

'Mobility's good.' He hesitated. 'You say she's made no attempt to talk yet?'

'No.' Sarah's eyes dilated and she covered her mouth with her hand. 'Oh God, if she's deaf – does that mean she won't be able to talk?'

'I didn't say that. There are a great many tests yet to be done.' The doctor took off his glasses and tapped them on the desk in front of him. 'I'll refer you to Mr Cobham at the hospital. You'll have to wait, probably about a month, but you're lucky really. Mr Cobham is one of the best men in the country in this field. Leave it with me. You'll receive an appointment in due course. In the meantime, we'll continue with our own tests to find out the extent of the damage. Make an appointment for next week with the receptionist.

'Thank you, Doctor.' Sarah's voice held a bitter note. She picked up Diane and walked out of the room.

'We're lucky, Diane, do you know that?'

Diane laughed and patted her mother's face.

'No, of course you don't. You couldn't hear him!'

What to tell Victor? *When* to tell Victor? Sarah found it impossible. She ached to share her burden of fear and despair with him but, seeing his face light up every time he saw Diane, she prevaricated. Then his stomach trouble flared up again and she decided to keep her secret until after her visit to see the specialist.

Worry always made Victor's stomach pain worse. He was working as hard as ever at the theatre and refusing to hand over the more physical jobs to others. In truth, the staff at the Lyric was comprised of elderly men and some women; the war had seen to that. Sarah thought Victor was also worrying about Eddie. Since he had moved to the Lawrences' farm Eddie had become increasingly remote from his parents. During the past year he had only visited them twice and the first occasion was the day of Diane's christening.

When Sarah thought about Eddie she felt angry. He should be more thoughtful, particularly when he knew his father did not enjoy the best of health. She thought back over the past years. Eddie had never been the kind of child to kiss and cuddle but, surely, he must have known they loved him? They had supported him over his decision to go into farming and every week Sarah wrote to him, telling him about their life and asking about his intended wife and their plans for the future.

Well, she shook her head, Eddie would have to come round in his own time; but she knew Victor missed his son and she hoped he would visit them soon.

She looked at the clock. There was still an hour before Victor would be home. She went to the cupboard and brought out some toys.

'Diane.'

Diane took no notice. Sarah picked up a box of bricks and went to sit beside her child. She touched her on the shoulder and Diane looked up.

'This is a brick, pet. A *brick*. Try and say "brick" for me.'

Diane watched her mother's mouth intently. Sarah gave her the brick and she smiled and hurled it across the room.

There was something about hospitals that made Sarah's flesh creep. The antiseptic smell was awful, and the green-coloured walls depressing. The reception area consisted of row upon row of tubular chairs upon which the patients waited. A man seated near Sarah felt in his pocket for a cigarette but seeing the nurse gesture towards the 'No smoking' notice he sighed and slouched gloomily in his chair. A moment later his thin frame was racked by a bout of coughing and the nurse smiled, a thin-lipped 'told you so' expression on her face.

Diane wriggled on her knee so Sarah set her down on the floor but retained a grasp of the skirt of the new blue-sprigged frock the child wore. At fifteen months her daughter was a picture. Attracted by her cornflower blue eyes and bouncy dark curls several people stopped to talk to her. Diane enjoyed the attention, bestowing her wide smile on all who approached her.

Sarah glanced round at the few posters adorning the walls. They gave details of special ration books for expectant mothers and warned that 'Careless talk cost lives!' Pity they haven't got a few flowers about the place, she thought. That would brighten things up a bit. She changed her position on the chair. How much longer must they wait?

The nurse, busily writing on stacks of buff-coloured files, answered the telephone. She replaced the receiver and rang a hand bell. Everyone jumped, aroused from their lethargy.

'Mrs Manvell – Mr Cobham will see you now.'

Sarah stood up and, leading Diane by the hand, followed the directions given to reach the Department of Audiology, where she found the appropriate room and knocked at the door. After a few moments she was asked to enter.

Mr Cobham consulted his notes.

'Sit down please. Let me see, your child, Diane, is fifteen months old?'

Sarah nodded and held Diane firmly on her lap.

'You've seen your own doctor and the doctor at the clinic, is that correct?'

'Yes. The doctor at the clinic gave me some leaflets. He seemed to think Diane's,' she paused, 'difficulties were caused because I may have contracted German Measles during the pregnancy.' She bent her head and smoothed back her child's hair. 'I never realised at the time; I vaguely remember not feeling well and staying in bed for a couple of days and I had a rash for a few hours. I'm not even sure if it *was* German Measles.' She paused again, expecting the specialist to speak, but he waited, his hands steepled together as he sat behind his desk and listened to her.

'Dr Seymour, at the clinic, said her hearing was seriously impaired. He suggested lip-reading classes, but said there was very little to be done.' A tremor sounded in her voice.

'Well, I'd better examine her.' He stood up and taking a chair placed it in the centre of the room.

'Right! Would you sit here please and put Diane on your knee, but don't touch her. It would help if you kept your arms by your side and stayed perfectly still. It's amazing how much unconscious direction a child picks up from its parent.'

Mr Cobham pressed a button and a nurse entered the room.

'I shall test Diane for a high and low range of sounds found in speech, Mrs Manvell. Please remember to keep as still as possible.'

Half an hour later he dismissed the nurse and gestured Sarah to return to the chair by his desk. His eyes looked sad.

'I'm sorry. There is little I can add to Dr Seymour's diagnosis.'

Sarah stared at him without speaking. Diane, tired of the strange, grown-up game, was struggling and whining to be free of the constraint of her mother's arms. Mr Cobham picked her up, sat her on the carpet and gave her a pencil and a few sheets of paper to play with.

'She's a beautiful child, my dear.'

'But you can't help her?'

'There is no cure for nerve deafness. However, great strides are being made nowadays. There are special teachers for the deaf, special units and schools.'

'Will she ever be able to speak?'

His silence was her answer.

The full horror of the situation exploded inside Sarah. She had pinned her hopes on this man. There was nowhere else to turn. What kind of life would her child have? And Victor, how could she tell him? Would he blame her for keeping the truth away from him so long?

'There *must* be something you can do,' she cried.

'We'll get a hearing aid for her. That will amplify the small amount of sound she can hear. You'll be put in contact with a teacher. You can work with her and implement the lessons at home.'

Sarah was leaning forward, a strained look on her face. 'Tell me everything you can, Mr Cobham. My husband and I will do anything at all if it helps Diane.'

The specialist smiled. 'I'm pleased to see your reaction, Mrs Manvell. So many parents seem to give up when they hear what I have told you. But there's always hope. We are learning more every day and, of course, because we have diagnosed her handicap early we can get to work immediately.'

'The name of these special schools; is there one in this area? Could I receive training to show me *how* to help her?'

Mr Cobham's smile became wider. 'Diane is fortunate in her mother,' he said.

He pressed the button again. 'Nurse, inform the appointments clerk my schedule will be running approximately twenty minutes late. Oh, and bring two cups of coffee.'

Diane lagged behind her mother as they walked through the gates of the hospital.

'Come along, darling.' Sarah spoke automatically. Then she stopped. Diane couldn't hear her. She couldn't hear the traffic as it rumbled along the road, nor the sound of the dog barking in the distance. She never would. She picked up her baby and hugged her. Diane would never hear a bird sing or a friend laugh. She would never hear her mother's voice. The tears trickled down her face and Diane, solemn-faced, patted them away.

Chapter Thirty

The time had come to tell Victor the truth. Sarah prepared a meal and anxiously waited his arrival. He was late home. Some minor disaster at the Lyric had demanded his attention. Just as he walked through the door Diane started to scream.

'My goodness, have we got our own personal air raid siren?' Victor scooped Diane from her chair and jigged her up and down in his arms. This action normally had her giggling in a moment, but Diane was tired and querulous. She screamed louder.

'I'll see to her, Victor. You sit down and eat.'

'No, no. You've had her all day. I'll take her upstairs and try and get her settled. She's all ready for bed, I see.' He smiled at Sarah and carried Diane upstairs. Sarah heard him say: 'Now, young lady. You must have had a bad day to make you so cross.'

Sarah felt the tears scratch the back of her eyes. He would know soon enough. She re-lit the oven and placed his meal inside to keep warm.

After twenty minutes Victor was back.

'She was a little devil tonight,' he said. 'Wonder where she gets her temper from?' And he chuckled. Standing behind Sarah, he slid his arms about her waist.

'Sit down, love,' she said. 'I'll get your dinner.'

She placed it on the table before him. 'Afraid it's a bit dried up.'

As Victor picked up his knife and fork the door slammed.

'Who on earth is that, at this time?' Sarah's question was answered when their son appeared in the doorway.

'Eddie. Oh, it is good to see you.' Her former harsh thoughts about him forgotten, Sarah flew to hug him.

Victor stood up, still clutching his knife and fork, a huge grin on his face.

'Sit down, lad. Do you want something to eat?'

'No, I'm all right, Dad.'

Eddie extracted himself from his mother's embrace. 'I'd love a cup of tea though.'

'Of course.' Sarah rushed to put the kettle on, then sat down to gaze at her son. 'You're looking very well. Smart, too.'

Eddie fingered the lapel of his jacket. 'Ah, well, I'm over on business, see. Jack's been negotiating a deal over some sheep and he's sent me to check things out with the solicitor. Now I'm marrying Mavis, he says he wants me to learn more about the financial side of farming.'

'It's Jack now, is it?' teased Sarah. 'Not Mr Lawrence.'

Instead of smiling, Eddie reddened. 'I'll not be getting anything I haven't earned, Mam. I've worked damn hard for the Lawrences and he knows I'll run the farm properly in due course.'

'I know you will, Eddie. I was only joking.'

There was an awkward pause then Victor said: 'You'll stay overnight, Eddie? There's a spare bed made up and we want to hear all about your wedding plans.'

'Well, I hadn't reckoned on . . .'

Sarah interrupted him. 'Of course he will. You've no idea,' she said, staring hard at Eddie, 'how your dad's been pining for a "man-to-man" talk with you.' She had not missed the flash of disappointment on Victor's face. 'All he has nowadays is two women to contend with.'

Eddie shrugged. 'All right. I'll have to be off early in the morning though.'

Victor beamed at him. 'Speaking of women,' he said. 'You should have heard your little sister an hour ago. Screeching like a banshee, she was, but she calmed down for me. Didn't she, Sarah?'

'She did.' Sarah answered him quietly. She had observed the flicker of impatience that passed over Eddie's face. Could *that* be the trouble? Eddie was jealous of Diane? She suddenly felt very tired. Then she stood up and crossed to where Eddie sat. She bent and embraced him.

'Oh, it's so good to see you, Eddie. But I'm going to leave you two men together now. I've had a busy day and I'm tired. I shall be up at the crack of dawn tomorrow, so we'll have plenty of time to talk before you leave. All right, love?' she looked at Victor.

'Of course. You do look a bit tired now you mention it. You go up. I'll see to things down here. Now then, Eddie, what's this deal and how did you get on with Jack's solicitor?'

Sarah closed the door quietly behind her. She would have to tell Victor about Diane tomorrow.

At six o'clock Sarah was up and about. After her tantrum of the night before Diane had slept in, so the kitchen was quiet when Eddie appeared. Sarah picked her words with care.

'I know Jack and Lucy Lawrence have been good to you, Eddie, but don't forget us, will you? You must have seen how happy your father was last night when you

283

came. You'll try and get through more often, won't you?'

'It's not easy, Mam.' Eddie picked at his breakfast. Sarah had given him the sausages she had meant for Victor's tea. 'There's always so much to do on the farm.'

Then, catching sight of his mother's reproachful face, he sighed. 'I'll try,' he said and with that, Sarah had to be content.

Victor was down to see Eddie away and shortly afterwards he left for the theatre. Sarah knew she must keep her secret for yet another day.

Years later she was glad she had.

Victor collapsed at work. His friends brought him home and carried him up the stairs to the flat.

'Just dropped, missus, like a stone,' volunteered a scene-shifter, circling his cap in his calloused hands.

'Didn't you get a doctor?'

The man cleared his throat and glanced about him as if looking for somewhere to spit before recollecting his surroundings.

'Vic's had stomach trouble for years, ain't he? Doctor's done nowt for him up to now. No, we reckoned on getting him home and in bed. He'll be all right again in a couple of days.'

Sarah was not so sure. Victor's face held a ghastly hue and his breathing was rapid and shallow. She felt his forehead. It was so cold and yet he was sweating.

'Will you stay, just for a moment,' she begged of the men, who nodded reluctantly. She glanced at Diane who slumbered peacefully on the sofa, snatched up her purse and raced down and into the street. There was a telephone box on the corner. With shaking fingers, she dialled and dropped the coins into the slot.

'Yes, Mr Victor Manvell. Please ask the doctor to come immediately.'

The men were itching to go, so she thanked them, watched them leave then went to sit by Victor. Half an hour passed and still the doctor had not come. Victor seemed to be dozing. She crept from the bedroom and watched by the living-room window.

'Sarahhh . . .'

She ran back. Victor had pulled himself up in bed. He put his hand out towards her, a look of astonishment on his face. He gagged, then gurgled as a rush of bright blood gushed from his mouth. Sarah cried out. For a moment, she couldn't move. With fascinated horror she watched the white bedcovers turn crimson as the blood poured from him. Then she ran to him, cradled his head in her arms. His blood covered her clothes. He retched, tried to speak.

'No, no,' she cried. 'Don't talk.'

The doorbell rang. Oh God, she'd left the latch down. It rang again.

'It's the doctor, love. I have to let him in.'

He plucked at her arm.

'I *have* to get the doctor!'

She pulled herself free of him. As she ran for the door a thin wail came from the living-room. Diane had awakened. She slammed the bedroom door behind her. Diane must not see! God, how could she leave him?

Ignoring her child she rushed down the stairs; they were never-ending. She fumbled with the door. The doctor was looking at his watch, an abstracted expression on his jowly face. He looked up and his face changed. She stepped back as he walked past her, and put her hand upon the door for a moment. Thank God, the responsibility had passed from her. Then she took a deep breath and followed him upstairs.

Diane was stretching and rubbing her eyes.

'Mummy won't be a minute, darling.'

Sarah went back into the bedroom. Victor was slumped in the bed. The doctor bent over him. Blood seemed to be everywhere. She could hear it, dripping on to the floor.

'Too late, I'm afraid.'

The clipped unemotional voice cut through her horror. The doctor straightened up, made as if to draw the sheet over Victor's face then, with a look of distaste, refrained from doing so.

'He must have been in a terrible state,' he said. 'Why didn't you call me sooner?'

Then, seeing her face, he caught hold of her and pushed her from the room.

'My baby's awake.'

Sarah half fell on to the sofa and, ignoring Diane's cries of protest, strained her fiercely to her chest.

'I'll get hold of a neighbour, and ring for an ambulance. There'll have to be a post mortem, I afraid.'

She heard his footsteps retreat and began to tremble. They would take him away. She should go to him, sit with him. But she remembered the blood. It wasn't Victor any more. She rocked backwards and forwards. She couldn't go in. She was a coward! Victor had been her husband for over twenty years. He had married her reluctantly; they had been strangers for so much of their married life, but then he had loved her and she had learnt to love him. He had given her Diane.

Diane! Her whimpers were developing into full-scale screams. Sarah forced herself to her feet. She took Diane across to her playpen and put her in there, surrounded by her favourite toys.

'Be a good girl for Mummy,' she whispered.

She rubbed distractedly at her arms which itched. She frowned. The blood was drying on her skin. She put her hand over her mouth and ran to the bathroom. The cold water revived her, but she knew she must go into the bedroom to fetch clean things. She dragged her way back. She tried desperately to think of Victor, to go over to the bed, but she couldn't. She grabbed some clothes from the wardrobe and ran. Diane's cries drummed in her brain as she stripped off her dress and pulled on a clean skirt and a sweater.

It seemed a great effort to lift her child up and carry her back to the sofa. Mercifully, Diane's cries subsided. She put her thumb in her mouth and sobbed intermittently. Sarah closed her eyes and leant back. Something hard clinked against her hip. She realised she was wearing one of Victor's sweaters. She put her hand in the pocket and brought out his cigarette lighter.

Then the grief hit her. Victor was *dead*! And she cried, great sobbing cries; because so many of their years together had been wasted and because the past three years had been so good. She cried for Victor, who would never see his beloved daughter grow up; and for herself, because she knew she would never find a man who loved her more.

Sudden death invoked such activity. Victor would have been embarrassed by all this attention, thought Sarah. She watched the faces come and go.

The doctor, hushed voice, took her pulse and tut-tutted: 'Your husband should have visited me regularly, Mrs Manvell.'

'He did.' She rubbed tired eyes. 'You told him he had a nervous stomach.'

The doctor passed his hand carefully over his head. His

pink scalp showed through the sparse, arranged, grey hair.

'The last visit was eighteen months ago – a long time. The post mortem showed a gastric ulcer. Mr Manvell suffered a severe gastro-intestinal haemorrhage.' He shook his head.

'He'd been feeling much better.'

Sarah shut her mind to the doctor's words. Behind his concern she sensed a throb of fear. Did he think she was going to sue him? That wouldn't bring Victor back.

Mr Benson, the owner of the theatre, was a dried-up old gentleman with a piping voice. He reminded Sarah of a gnome.

'One in a million, Vic. God knows what we'll do without him. Knew everything about the Lyric. How we shall miss him.' He patted her hand and thrust an envelope into it. 'Vic was sensible. I'm sure you are well provided for. Still, that might help. We're putting a piece in the programme about him. He would have liked that.'

He stopped by the door. 'Oh, don't want to rush you but the flat goes with the job, you see. We'll need a new stage manager pretty quick, so if you can make arrangements . . .'

His last remarks stunned her. The flat was her refuge. It meant much more to her than the house in which they had spent most of their married life. In the flat they had been happy.

She'd think about it later, the insurance agent was knocking on the door.

'I'm sorry, Mrs Manvell. I did try and tell your husband. After all, he was quite a bit older than you. Still the policy allows a small amount of money after the funeral expenses are paid, and you have your son.'

Eddie, uncomfortable in his best clothes, was staring at her with Victor's eyes.

'I'll do what I can, Mam, but it's difficult. Yes, I know I'm doing well, but the farm swallows the money. We've invested all our spare cash in new equipment lately.

'Yes, of course I'm upset but let's face it,' a flash of coldness in his eyes, 'Dad was never really *that* close to me, was he? Not like he was with Diane. Both of you were quite happy for me to leave home at fourteen and a lot of years have gone by. We're going ahead with the wedding. Makes sense doesn't it? Arrangements made, and I have to think of Mavis. Look, I've brought you a couple of rabbits I've caught. Help out with the rationing a bit, won't it? Can't stay, Mavis is expecting me back tonight.'

Eddie, Eddie – were we such bad parents? I played with you, cuddled you when you fell down. But you never cried, did you? You don't cry now. Oh, Eddie!

She wandered into the kitchen. The limp bodies of the rabbits lay on the draining board, their eyes glassy in death. She touched their soft coats and saw the blood. Oh God, she retched into the sink.

'Maisie, good of you to call. There's a couple of rabbits there, Eddie brought them. No, honestly, I don't want them. Yes, I know you'll help if you can. Yes, there will be lots of things to see to, particularly packing up to move from the flat. But *please* leave me on my own just now.'

At the funeral, more faces. Victor's workmates, good men, inarticulate and uncomfortable in their best clothes, but with genuine distress in their faces; neighbours, not many. They had few friends. Dotty, through on the early train, her face plainer than ever, patched and blotchy with grief. Poor Dotty, her first love and her first death, ironically not in bombed-out Hull but here, in quiet Branswick. Mam, seeing to everything. Increased pain to see Mam starting to stoop and shrink a little. Mam, smiling, humming to

Diane – some old tune about a cat called Felix. And Harry's ship posted missing; no information.

Maisie: 'That's the last of the tea, ducks. I'll let you have some of mine. Nice thing when you can't have a cup of tea. This blasted bastard of a war!'

'I'll look after her, Mrs Armstrong, don't you worry. And little Diane. No trouble, honestly.' Maisie put the older woman's case on the train and stood back.

'She'll be through to see you before long but I reckon she needs a bit of quiet right now. And she has the baby, that will help.'

She waved her arm in farewell then stumped from the station.

A good woman, that. Been through it too but it hadn't made her bitter. Maisie sighed. Poor old Sarah, she didn't have much luck. Now, if John Saul had been alive . . . She pushed the thought out of her mind. He wasn't, and it did seem a bit unkind to be thinking such thoughts just after Victor's funeral.

It started to rain. Blasted weather. The puddles she splashed through made dirty patches on her legs. Not that it mattered, she thought, looking at the drab utility stockings she wore. Even with silk stockings the clumsy wooden-soled shoes she was now reduced to wearing made her legs look terrible. Maisie was proud of her legs. No matter how fat the rest of her got, her legs were on a par with Betty Grable's, plenty of men had told her so.

She entered the Flower in Hand, shook her swagger coat and hung it up to dry before going through to the living quarters at the rear of the building.

'All right, love? Got settled?'

'Yes thanks.'

Sarah was playing with Diane. Maisie noticed, with pleasure, that her face looked less strained.

'It's really good of you to take us in. It won't be for long, you know.'

'Bless you, I'm glad of the company. The staff run the bar now and Leif's a good husband but he's not much in the conversation stakes. His head's either in a newspaper or glued to the wireless.' She shivered. 'I'd rather not hear about the war but he wants to know everything that happens.'

'Most men do.'

'I had a bit of luck on the way home. Alec Lambert saw me near the pier. He gave me some fish.' Maisie's shoulders shook with soundless laughter. 'Said it was in memory of good times now past – but don't tell Leif! Still, it's nice when your old mates remember you. I had nothing to put it in so I wrapped it in my scarf. Expect it will pong of cod for the rest of its natural!'

She heard Sarah laugh with a sense of satisfaction. Cheering up, that's what she needed.

'Time's getting on, Maisie. Can I help with the tea?'

'Well, there's some spuds to peel.' She glanced at Sarah. 'You've a bit more colour today, love. Feeling better are you?'

'Yes, I am. Diane helps there. You can't sit feeling sorry for yourself when a child's involved.' Sarah cut up a potato and dropped it into the pan of water. 'I've got an awful lot of thinking to do, Maisie. Now Victor's gone, there's only me to look after Diane.'

'But there's no hurry. You've had a terrible shock. If you start rushing about now, you're liable to collapse or something.'

'I know.' Sarah smiled at her friend. 'I promise I'll take

things easy for a couple of weeks. I just wish I could sleep better. Every time I close my eyes I see Victor . . .' She swallowed hard. 'There's one thing, Maisie, he never knew about Diane being deaf. I'm so glad about that.'

'Oh, don't use that word.' Maisie looked uncomfortable. 'I still think it could be temporary. You know how some kiddies have squints when they're little and then they grow out of them. Maybe it's something like that?'

'No. It's nothing like that. Diane is deaf.' Sarah put down the potato she was peeling and faced Maisie. 'It's pointless kidding ourselves.'

Her face expressionless, she went on, 'It's hard, Maisie, and no doubt it will get harder. Poor Diane – can you imagine what it must be like. I try to. I lie in bed and think about it, but I can't really imagine it. You must have noticed how she's changing, her temper tantrums, the way she seems so . . .' she searched for the right word, 'elusive. I think it's because she is growing, and she gets frustrated. But how should I handle her? How can I explain things to her without words?'

'I still say you're exaggerating, Sarah. Of course she screams. She misses her daddy.'

Sarah's eyes filled with tears but she blinked them away. 'We both miss him, but it's Diane's future that concerns me now. You've been so good, Maisie. Staying here has been a godsend but I must plan. I need a job and somewhere to live, but first I need to find a way to help Diane. I need to learn about the kind of school she should go to and the lessons and treatment, if any, she should have. There's so much to know and I don't know anything. I'm scared . . .'

She bowed her head and Maisie hurried across to her.

'Don't, Sarah. We'll help you. But don't be in such a rush. It will take time.'

A bleak smile flitted across Sarah's face. 'Time is one thing Diane hasn't got. Every day she's falling behind children who can hear. But she's going to live a normal life, Maisie. Somehow, she's going to learn to speak. I'm determined on it. It's a big world and Diane's not going to live on the fringes of it. She's going to be *in* it!'

Chapter Thirty-one

The man in the corner seat of the train compartment stared at his newspaper. With one part of his mind, he noted Lord Mountbatten had succeeded Lord Wavell as Viceroy of India; with the other he pondered over the woman seated opposite him. He had seen her before. He was sure of it. But where? He lowered his paper and risked a second glance. Good! She had rested her head against the padded headrest and closed her eyes. He stared. She was worth looking at. Not a young woman by any means but damned attractive. Now, why did he feel that stirring of memory?

Her skin was creamy and flawless, but there was a fine network of lines traced about her eyes and mouth, a touch of silver in the dark hair which was swept simply back from her broad forehead and caught loosely at the nape of her neck. He looked at the winged eyebrows showing so strongly against the pale skin and the full mouth held in a controlled line, even though she was resting. He frowned, almost remembering, then she stirred and he retreated behind his newspaper.

The headlines spoke of the 'Cold War'. Churchill had been right about Russia. Look what happened to poor little Czechoslovakia. He folded the paper and as he did so the woman sat up and opened her eyes. He blinked.

'Sarah?' he queried. Then he repeated her name more confidently: 'It is, isn't it – Sarah Armstrong?'

Her look was startled, but no recollection showed on her face.

'I *thought* I knew you, then when I saw you properly, with your eyes open . . .' he stopped, suddenly shy. Then 'It's me, Martin Linford.'

She looked at him curiously, then a tinge of colour showed in her face and she smiled.

'Of course. I'm sorry, Martin Linford. I didn't recognise you.'

Her voice had changed. It was lower than he remembered yet very distinct and the north country burr had disappeared.

'Well, it's not surprising. How many years is it, Sarah?'

She laughed and shrugged. 'Too many.'

'But it doesn't *seem* it. At least, not to me. I've often wondered what became of you. Remember the first time we met and you sent me round to the tradesman's entrance?'

'Oh, don't!'

She pulled a face and he chuckled at her expression of mock horror. Animation livened her face, made her look more like the girl she had been. He was surprised at the rush of interest and, yes – warmth – he felt.

'Tell me, do you still live in Harrogate? You're married, of course.' He looked at her left hand, resting gloveless on her lap, unadorned save for a plain gold band.

She hesitated and he sat back in his seat, abashed.

'I'm sorry. I don't mean to be rude but I am pleased to see you again.'

Her face resumed its slightly remote expression, but she answered him politely enough: 'Are you usually interested in people you haven't seen for, let me see, it must be nearly thirty years?'

'No.' He leant forward again. 'But that time in Harrogate was a strange time for me, Sarah. I was so unsettled, wondering what to do with my life; but I could talk to you. I've never forgotten that.'

'Yes, I suppose I was quite useful.' There was an ironic twist to her lips. 'But then you sorted yourself out and went off to London.'

'Yes.' He shifted in his seat but gazed at her steadily as he went on: 'I never said good-bye to you, did I? I never bothered to write or find out what kind of job you went to, but,' he gave an impatient sigh, 'I was young, Sarah, and selfish and slightly arrogant.'

She studied his face, then smiled again but this time it was unforced, a smile of friendship.

'That was a generous statement, Mr Linford, but not necessary. I was just a maid, after all, and young and perhaps too impressionable. I found your attention hard to handle.' She laughed. 'The staff were sure you had designs on my virtue!'

'Oh dear, I'm sorry. Please call me Martin, not Mr Linford, it sounds so formal.' He smiled back at her and there was a silence which lasted a little too long until Sarah spoke again.

'If you really want to know, I was married. I'm a widow now. I have a grown-up son who has just made me a grandmother, and a beautiful daughter who is almost seven years old.' She looked down and pleated the skirt of her smart grey costume. 'A large age gap but I love them both dearly.'

She looked up. 'What about you, Martin?' She stumbled slightly over the name.

'I'm a widower, so we're both in the same boat, Sarah.' A shadow crossed his face. 'I have no children, unfortunately. I lead a busy life. Nowadays I spend a lot of time in London but my work brings me to the north regularly and I own a small property here.'

'Your mother and father?'

He shook his head.

'Oh, I'm sorry.'

'They had a good life. Mother died shortly after Father. You know how these old couples are.'

She nodded.

'And what about your family?' he asked. 'It was a large one, as I remember.'

'Not really, not in our village.' She smiled at him. 'My father died many years ago, but the rest of them are fine. I'm returning from a visit to my mother. She has just moved in to live with my youngest brother Harry and I was a little concerned. They have three boisterous children you see. But I needn't have worried. She's absolutely in her element and so happy.'

Again the contours of her face rounded into a look of youth and the blue of her eyes deepened into the colour of hyacinths.

They were silent, she lost in her own thoughts, he watching her face. The train whistle sounded, making them both jump.

'It's quite incredible, meeting like this.'

She nodded. 'Yes. Even more incredible that you recognised me.'

'Why? You haven't changed that much, Sarah.'

'You think not? I have really.'

'Then I'd very much like to get to know the new Sarah. Do you think we could meet again, talk over old times?'

'It's a nice idea, Martin. But I think not.'

'Then, give me your address.'

The train slowed down and Sarah looked through the window. 'Oh Lord, we're nearly into the station. I must rush.' She jumped up and attempted to lift her case from the rack.

He swung it down for her.

'Thanks. I must be quick. If I'm delayed here, I'll miss the bus to Oaklands and then I'll have to wait for ages.'

'But you can't just go, Sarah.'

The jolting of the train threw her towards him and he caught hold of her elbows to steady her. She smelt of green woods, tantalising, mysterious and cool.

'I have to. Sorry.'

She opened the door and looked back at him. 'It's been lovely meeting you again, but I think we'd better leave it at that, Martin. We're completely different people now and we can't go back.'

She hesitated, then jumped down on to the platform.

He leant out of the window and watched her slim figure hurry towards the exit. A moment later the train started. He stared into space a moment, then smiled. 'Oaklands' she had said.

'Well, Sarah,' he murmured. 'We'll have to see . . .'

The old green Austin clunked noisily as it swung into the driveway leading to the house. It had been raining but now the sky was clear and Martin wound down the window to admire more clearly the daffodils swaying in clumps beneath the trees. The oaks which lined the driveway and gave their name to the house were sprouting fresh young leaves and he slowed when he spotted a grey squirrel race along the branches. He loved the smell of the earth after rain. It was at times like these when he wondered why he spent so much time in London. Yet he loved the city, too, despite his sad memories. The scars of the war were beginning to fade. The gaunt, bombed-out ruins still stood as bleak reminders of the past years of hell, but a new feeling of optimism permeated the air. It was a time for new beginnings.

He followed the winding road and came upon a group of children scattered across the drive in front of him. They ranged in age from about five to twelve and were dressed in variously coloured mackintoshes and wellingtons. He slowed the car and watched them deliberately jump into the puddles, sending sprays of water into the air. They were too busy to notice him, so he gave a short, loud warning blast on the car horn. Rosy, laughing faces turned to view him and, like a flock of sheep, they scattered right and left. All except one – a slender figure in a poppy-coloured mac skipped blithely onwards in the exact centre of the drive. An older girl ran up and tapped the younger child on the shoulder, drawing her to one side. As Martin eased his car past them, the older girl waved and nodded.

'Sorry, she didn't hear.'

The girl spoke in the toneless voice of the deaf.

Martin flapped his hand in acknowledgement and nodded. Then his expression altered as he looked into the face of the younger girl. It was Sarah, but a Sarah younger than he had ever known her. He felt a lump in his throat and he stepped on the accelerator and left the two figures behind him as he approached the house.

Matron awaited him. 'Pleased to meet you at last, Dr Linford. I've heard so much about you and your work. Please come in.'

She led him across the cool hall. It smelt of beeswax and a faint perfume which he presumed came from the huge bunch of daffodils standing in an earthenware jug on an oak side table.

'What a lovely place.'

'Yes, we're very lucky. The school was originally a manor house. We've done our best to retain the ambience of the place. Of course, many of the rooms have been converted to classrooms, bedrooms etc, but on the whole, we've managed well, I think.'

She pushed open a door leading to a sitting-room.

'We'll have coffee, shall we, before I take you round and introduce you?'

'Lovely,' Martin said, appreciatively. Because the room was painted in pale green, it seemed to extend and flow into the garden which could be seen through the french windows. He sank into a chintz-covered armchair and gave a sigh of pleasure.

'Ah, Betty.' Matron took the tray from a pretty teenager in a flowered overall who had timidly knocked on the door and entered. 'I expected Sarah to bring this?'

'She's helping the little ones, Matron. They'd got all wet and they are due at Mr Hanson's lesson in a minute.'

'That's all right, then.' Matron dismissed the girl and, pouring out the coffee, handed a cup to Martin.

'Sarah's my treasure, Dr Linford. She came as housekeeper four years ago, but, now, I really don't think I could function without her. She's a most unusual woman. I'm sure you will be most interested to meet her.'

Martin sipped his coffee without replying but his eyes held an alert look.

'She came to see me desperate for a job. Any kind of job, she said. She had a small child, a girl. Beautiful little creature, but unfortunately almost completely deaf. Sarah wanted her to become a pupil here. Well, I had my misgivings. It doesn't always work, you know – pupils, staff and all that. Anyway, she convinced me it would work and it has, beyond my wildest imaginings. Officially Sarah's the housekeeper but really,' Matron gave a somewhat nervous laugh and sipped her coffee, 'I sometimes think she knows more about audiology and the education of the deaf than some of my teaching staff.'

'You mean, she helps with the children, Matron?'

A blush coloured Matron's thin cheeks. 'Not in an official capacity, of course. That would break the rules. But yes, Sarah Manvell is a valued member of staff.'

'That's interesting.' Martin continued in a noncommittal voice: 'You see, I knew Sarah many, many years ago. She was Sarah Armstrong then.'

'How strange. Of course, she would have been just a young girl, but when you meet her again I'm sure you will see what I mean.'

'I look forward to it.' Martin placed his cup and saucer on the table. 'Now, it's time I met the children and the staff.'

The school impressed Martin. He noted that the teachers taking the mixed-ability groups – children with varying degrees of deafness – handled their charges with patience and skill and the atmosphere seemed happy and free from strain.

'We try to keep the pupils in small units but as you know,' Matron sighed, 'in the end it always comes down to finance.'

· He nodded without speaking.

'The little ones are in here, Dr Linford.' Matron paused, her hand on the doorknob. 'As this is a residential school, you will appreciate there are difficulties. We have a new little boy who is dreadfully homesick. We are doing our best to help him settle down, but he has virtually no communication skills, which makes it very hard.'

The small, ginger-haired youngster was huddled in a chair near the window, weeping softly.

Martin's face stiffened. 'Things should be different,' he spoke almost savagely to the Matron. 'I don't mean to imply places like this are wrong; you do a fine job, but separation from their parents traumatises young children. We need more peripatetic teachers. I keep telling them in London. Put in home teachers, involve the parents more and there is no reason why fifty per cent of these children should not attend normal schools in due course. How can we expect society . . .!' he paused when he saw Matron's startled face and smiled ruefully. 'Sorry, favourite hobby-horse of mine, I'm afraid.'

He stood aside and motioned to her to precede him into the room. As they entered, the girl he had seen skipping down the drive went over to the new boy. A concerned look on her face, she reached out and put her hand on his shoulder. The boy shook her off.

'That's Sarah's daughter,' whispered Matron.

Martin nodded. He watched the girl as she tapped the boy on his chest, then with rapid movements of her hands attempted to converse with him. The boy shook his head, then looked at her, reached out and touched her face. Martin smiled. He heard a sharp indrawn breath behind him and looked round, straight into the angry face of Sarah.

'What are *you* doing here?'

Matron blinked at the decidedly unfriendly voice of her housekeeper. 'This is Dr Linford, Sarah. He's . . .'

'Excuse me a moment, Matron.' With an apologetic look, Martin caught hold of Sarah's arm and propelled her into the corridor.

'This is unforgivable, Martin. Just because we met on the train . . .'

He interrupted her. 'Give me a chance to explain.' He raised his hands in a deprecating gesture. 'It isn't what you think. I would have explained on the train, when you mentioned Oaklands, but there wasn't time.'

'I don't understand.'

Rapidly, he explained: 'I'm visiting all the schools for the deaf in this area. I'm a paediatrician, Sarah, with special reference to work with hearing-impaired children. The government wants to streamline facilities to assist education techniques for deaf children. I have to inspect schools and write reports. I had no idea you were involved in any way until you mentioned Oaklands. Then,' he shrugged and smiled. 'Very well, I admit it. I rearranged my schedule so I could visit now rather than waiting for the autumn. Is that so terrible?'

'A specialist in audiology.' She averted her face. 'Oh Martin, what I would have given to talk to you four years ago.'

'I know.' His look was compassionate. 'Matron told me about your daughter. She says you are marvellous with her.'

'She's called Diane and I'm not marvellous, she is. She's so intelligent, Martin.'

'I believe you. Also kind-hearted. I saw her mothering the new boy in there. She looks like you, Sarah.'

She flushed. 'I'm sorry I was rude. Now you've explained things, I am glad to see you again.'

'Good. But now I must get back to Matron. She must think me a very strange character.' He hesitated, then, 'I'll be here about ten days, Sarah, and then I'll be reappearing from time to time to check out certain things. I hope we manage to see each other a little. We're both busy, I know, but perhaps one evening? I'm staying at the White Hart and so far as I can see, the meals are really good, despite the usual shortages.'

'I don't know, Martin. Let me think about it.'

'All right. But don't forget, will you?'

He was smiling as he retraced his steps towards the classroom and the waiting Matron.

Chapter Thirty-two

For the first few days of his visit it unsettled Sarah to see Martin about the place. She would tend to her usual tasks, supervising the girls with the laundry, planning the meals, wheedling extra eggs from the man who delivered goods twice weekly from the nearby town, then she would turn and see him. It gave her a jolt; reminded her, in fact, of those far-off days at Hammond House. But she quickly realised things were not the same. Life had changed both of them.

Physically he was not so different. His formerly fair hair was now silver-grey in colour and his face was thin and lined, but he was still slim and moved quickly around the classrooms and the corridors. Two days after his arrival she showed him around the gardens and made a small sound of protest as he outpaced her.

He had turned to her, a smile starting in his grey eyes as he said: 'Still having difficulty keeping up with my long legs, Sarah?'

It was good to see him smile. He did so rarely and only, it seemed, for her or the children. She tried to remember how he had been in Harrogate. Surely, not so guarded and impatient as he was now. She heard two of the teaching staff discussing him. They thought him sarcastic and censorious.

'Know what he said to me? Why didn't the children get

out on more trips? I ask you! Doesn't he know how hard
pressed we are, just to keep them working? Wonder if he's
ever tried his hand at actually *teaching* children like these?

'He was on to me about the need for more efficient
audiograms. The man talks of nothing but work. I'll be
glad when he's finished here. I don't think he has any
human feelings.'

But Sarah knew he had feelings. She saw him with the
young children, stooping to adjust the piercing whistle of a
hearing aid, sitting in a corner with a pathologically shy
young boy painstakingly discussing trains and even, when
he thought himself unobserved, giving a piggyback ride to
an excited five-year-old. What a pity he never had a family
of his own, she mused. When he asked her again to dine
with him, she accepted his invitation.

The White Hart had an air of unapologetic decayed
splendour. Sarah had passed the hotel many times, but had
never been inside. There were holes in the red carpet cover-
ing the entrance hall and the huge gilt mirrors were spotted
with age, but when she saw the still-elegant dining-room
and glimpsed through a door an imposing billiard room,
she was glad she had dressed with care in her one formal
evening dress.

'You look very nice,' said Martin as he led her to their
table.

'So do you.'

Martin was the kind of man who looked his best when
dressed formally. His dark, beautifully cut suit showed off
his tall, spare frame to perfection.

'Shall I order?' he asked.

Sarah smiled to herself. He seemed almost nervous.
Whether it was on her behalf or his own, she was not sure.

'Yes, please.'

As he studied the menu she sat back in her chair and surveyed the room.

'It's terribly grand, Martin. The education board must regard you as a person of importance.'

'Not really, you should see some of the places I stay in. It's just that this hotel is the nearest to the school. Oaklands is somewhat isolated, you know.'

'I do know.' A quick frown creased her brow. 'That's the only thing I have against it. It *is* a good school. Diane's making excellent progress, but I wish she could mix with,' she hesitated, 'normal children more. I hate that word,' she went on, 'but you know what I mean.'

He nodded, his expression serious. 'Of course I do. One of my main ambitions is to get more hearing-impaired children into ordinary schools, but there are immense problems.

'Ah,' his tone lightened. 'Here's the waiter.'

He ordered, then sat back in his seat with a sigh of pleasure. 'No more shop talk now. Let's enjoy the meal.'

It was a meal to be enjoyed. To add to the pleasure of eating real steak, Sarah savoured the peace of the setting. It was so long since she had eaten away from the noisy school dining-hall. Martin, too, ate heartily.

'Don't know how these country places manage it,' he said. 'The restaurants in London can't produce half the stuff that out-of-the-way spots like this one do.'

Sarah tapped her nose, her eyes twinkling. 'Black market,' she whispered.

'Really?'

'Well, it makes sense, doesn't it? This farmer has a pig, this one lamb, or free-range hens; there's a flourishing barter system goes on.'

'Benefits of the country, eh?'

'Well, you should know. You have a place somewhere around here, you said?'

'Yes.' Martin pushed his chair back. 'If you've finished we'll have coffee.'

Coffee was served in the bar, an intimate, oak-panelled room with cricket memorabilia displayed on shelves around the walls.

'The meal was lovely, Martin. I did enjoy it.'

'Yes, it was good.' He stirred sugar into his cup. 'I don't suppose you get many chances to eat out?'

Sarah laughed. 'Not many chances to get out, period. But I don't mind.'

'Matron said you have been at Oaklands for four years. Your husband must have died when Diane was very young?'

'She was just a toddler. After Victor died, it was hard. I moved about, different jobs, different places to live, but all the time trying to find out what I could do to help her. It was the best day of my life when Matron gave me the job at Oaklands.'

'Poor Sarah.' He put out his hand to touch hers, but she avoided his touch and picked up the coffee pot.

'Like some more?'

He shook his head so she refilled her own cup.

'I'm happy now,' she said, reverting to their conversation. 'And Diane's happy too. There's really nothing I would change.' She waited a moment, but he was silent so she continued: 'But what about you?

'Oh, nothing special.' He pushed his coffee cup away from him, 'I realised eventually that I *did* want to be a doctor. I always wanted to be one really, but Redvers put me off.' He made a gesture of distaste. 'All my brother's interested in is money. I wanted to contribute to the wellbeing of mankind, or rather, the wellbeing of children; very philanthropic of me, wasn't it?'

She frowned. 'Why sound so bitter?'

'Because life is never simple. There's always a person, or a committee, or some nameless financial power to block things, to tell you it's just not possible. Anyway,' he fiddled with his coffee spoon, clinking it against the side of the cup, 'I specialised in work with deaf children. Everyone insists that being blind is the worst possible handicap. It is dreadful, of course, but in deafness there is this terrible lack of communication, as you well know.' He threw her a brief smile. 'It's all very boring, I'm afraid. I became a workaholic, and was on my way to crusty bachelorhood when I met Claire.'

He sighed.' 'Look, let's leave it, shall we?'

'If you want.' Sarah wanted very much to hear about his wife but she sensed his reserve.

'I'd better be getting back,' she said. 'It's quite late.'

He stood up. 'I'll bring the car round to the front.'

On the drive back they were silent. The roads were quiet and the moon-painted landscape slid by as if in a dream. Sarah looked at Martin's face as he concentrated on his driving. It was strange being alone with a man whom she had once known and yet now was virtually a stranger. It was strange being alone with a man. Surrounded by children, her sole object in life Diane's welfare, she had forgotten the arts of being feminine. Yet, she told herself, she needed no arts with Martin for, if she wanted to know him better, she wanted him only as a friend. She smiled. He was so pleased to have met her again. Did he still think of her as the little maid and his confidante? If so, he was in for a rude awakening. She had learnt a lot in the past few years. She felt a tiny thrill of excitment as she realised she looked forward to showing him how much she had changed. Nothing must disturb her life at Oaklands, Diane's future depended upon it; but it had to be said, a life of work and more work with no distractions was boring at times.

The car wheels crunched on the gravel of the drive up to the house and she jumped. She had not realised they had reached their destination.

'I really enjoyed tonight,' said Martin as he switched off the car engine. 'Evenings can pass slowly when you're staying alone at a hotel.' He turned towards her and she tensed a little.

'I'll have to leave next week but I wondered?' he paused. 'This coming Sunday I thought I'd visit my cottage. It's in easy driving distance, only about thirty-five miles from here. Would you like to come, and Diane, of course?'

She considered. 'Sunday, you said? I think that could be arranged. And Diane can come?'

'I'd like her to come with us. It would be good for her.'

'All right. I'll have to clear it with Matron of course, but there shouldn't be any difficulty. I have a lot of time due to me.'

'That's marvellous. If I don't see you before then, I'll pick you up at about nine o'clock.'

'Right. Thank you for a lovely evening, Martin.'

She got out of the car and closed the door, giving him a friendly wave. She watched him drive away then entered the house. There was no need to turn on any downstairs lights, the moon shed its gentle light for her. She prepared for bed and as she brushed her hair, she hummed a little tune, a popular love song.

As the car bowled along the country lanes, Martin outlined to Sarah his plans for the day.

'Beverley first,' he said. 'We'll take a look in the Minster;

there's some lovely, comical wooden carvings which Diane will love, then we'll have lunch.' His eyes twinkled, 'I want to show off my attractive companions.'

Sarah put her arm about Diane's shoulders. The child was fidgety with excitement.

'Martin thinks we look pretty,' she said, facing her daughter and speaking slowly and distinctly.

Diane laughed and nodded. 'Mar-tin', she struggled a little but the word was distinguishable, 'like us?'

'I do,' agreed Martin, fervently.

Sarah had taken pains with her appearance. She wore a smart pleated skirt and a dark blue jumper which matched her eyes exactly. Diane also wore a pleated skirt, but her jumper was yellow and complemented the brightness of the spring day.

'It must be lovely to be able to drive,' said Sarah, as they sped onwards.

'It's easy to learn.' Martin shot her a sideways glance before once again concentrating on the twisting country roads. 'I'll teach you, if you like?'

Sarah did not answer immediately, then she said: 'You are much too busy. What about all your travelling?'

'I'm sure I could fit it in somehow.'

After exploring Beverley and eating lunch they headed for the Yorkshire Wolds. They parked the car and admired the gently undulating landscape before them then went for a walk to stretch their legs. The grass was springy beneath their feet and enamelled with pink-tipped daisies and the odd, shy primrose.

'I'd forgotten how lovely it all is.' Impulsively, Sarah linked arms with Martin. 'Thank you for bringing us.'

'It's my pleasure.' He nodded to where Diane ran about in front of them. 'She seems to be enjoying herself.'

'Yes. It will do her good. She works so hard, sometimes it's easy to forget how young she is, how important it is for her to play.'

'It's quite hot, isn't it? Let's sit down for a minute.' Martin flopped down and, after a moment's hesitation, Sarah sat beside him. The grass smelt sweet and high above them, a skylark soared.

'I really had forgotten.' She picked a daisy and twirled it round absently.

'Forgotten what?'

'This, the outside world! Everything is so contained at Oaklands. Apart from visiting my family, I haven't left it often during the past four years.'

'I mean it, you know.'

She looked at him, bemused. Martin was staring at her, an intent expression on his face. She was annoyed to feel the blood mount in her cheeks.

'Mean what?'

'I could teach you to drive.'

She laughed, relieved. 'What on earth for, Martin? I could never afford a car.'

'You might.' He waved his hand towards Diane who was running back to them clutching a bunch of primroses. 'It would give both of you a break from the school and you can pick up an old banger for a few quid. Think about it. I'll be backwards and forwards to Yorkshire for the next few months and I'd enjoy teaching you.' He stood up then, brushing the grass from his clothes. He put out his hands and pulled Sarah up beside him. She looked at him but his expression was inscrutable.

'Thanks,' she replied. 'I will.'

'Right, young lady.' Martin reached for Diane as she raced up to him, and swung her round. She squealed with pleasure. He set her carefully upon the ground and kneeling before her enunciated: 'Now I will take you and Mummy to see my house.'

Sarah warmed to him as she saw the trouble he took with her child. Diane had no misgivings in his company. She even took his hand as they returned to the car. Sarah was ashamed to feel a pang of jealousy. For years she and Diane had been partners against the hearing world. They had struggled through hours, days, weeks of hard frustrating lessons, at times almost hating each other but now Diane was beginning to triumph over her disability. Sarah chided herself. She should rejoice in the widening of her daughter's world. That, after all, was what they had been working for.

Chapter Thirty-three

They drove past a cluster of cottages and an old farmhouse before bumping along a shady lane to stop in front of a secluded cottage. The small garden was lush and green and overgrown.

'Coming in for a cup of tea?'

'Of course. I'm dying to see inside.'

He opened the front door and they entered directly into a tiny sitting-room. The furniture was old fashioned and homely and the copper kettle standing by the fireplace and the colourful hooked rugs on the floor gave the place brightness and warmth.

'The kitchen's the larger room,' said Martin, leading Sarah and Diane through a low doorway. 'In here.'

'What a beautiful oak dresser,' said Sarah, running her hand over the wood and looking about her with undisguised curiosity.

'Yes. Some of the pottery is quite good, too. It seems old-fashioned things are once again becoming fashionable.'

He filled a kettle and lit the gas ring on the cooker. 'We had gas laid on when we bought the place,' he said quietly.

Diane tugged at his jacket. 'Up?' She pointed towards the narrow wooden staircase winding up to the next floor. She rested her hand on her chest: 'Me – up?'

Martin nodded and tugged her hair affectionately.

'There's nothing she can hurt herself with,' he said to Sarah.

In a swirl of pleats, Diane vanished upstairs.

'Are you sure, Martin?' Sarah asked. 'I mean, if you have private things . . .'

'No. It's all right. There's nothing here of my wife's. We never actually managed to spend much time here.'

He averted his face and in the silence, Sarah felt, rather than saw, the rigidity of his still figure.

'Would it help to talk?' she said gently.

'No . . . yes.' He turned and sat down in one of the straightbacked wooden chairs.

'Yes.' He spoke more decisively. 'I would like to tell you about her, Sarah.'

Sarah sat down near to him.

'I was over thirty when we met, quite old, really. She was twenty-two.' He stared into space then blinked and, shame-faced, smiled at Sarah. 'Sorry.'

She touched his arm lightly. 'Go on.'

'We met here in Yorkshire. Surprisingly, because I was working in London and she was, too. She was American, but her mother was British and she had been brought up on tales about England. She came over to study medicine. She was on a tour and we met in York. I was attending a conference.'

He started as the kettle boiled and a hiss of steam disturbed the silence.

'It's all right.' Sarah moved to turn off the gas. 'I'll make the tea, you carry on talking.'

She moved about quietly, finding the tea caddy and setting out three cups and saucers as Martin stared down at his clasped hands, the words now tumbling out.

'We hit it off straight away. She was a bit like you, Sarah.' He gave a brief smile. 'Not in looks, she was blonde with brown eyes, but she had a way of looking at you with her chin stuck out. She was stubborn too.'

Sarah raised an eyebrow but made no comment. She opened one of the cupboards and found a tin of condensed milk and a blue sugar packet.

'It was like in the films. We fell wildly in love.' He gave a shaky laugh. 'We married two months later. Her parents were none too pleased, I can tell you, but Mother and Father loved her. They couldn't help themselves.' He swallowed. 'Everyone loved her. We were so happy, we decided to get ourselves a place, here in Yorkshire. We were working in different hospitals, the hours were awkward; we must have been crazy.

'In the holidays we came up here and searched about until we found this place. We could afford it. I was earning decent money and Claire insisted on putting in a nest-egg she had been left by some old aunt.'

Sarah placed a cup of tea before him. He took the cup with an abstracted expression on his face. Sarah wondered what Diane was up to. She was very quiet. Should she fetch her down? No. She decided not to. It was obvious Martin needed to talk.

'We weren't in a rush for children. Claire finished her training and wanted to practise. That was fair enough and although I was older – well – I wasn't that old.'

He took a sip of tea and stared down into the cup. A shadow seemed to creep across his features.

'The war started, then came the Blitz. I wanted her to leave London but she wouldn't. I told you she was stubborn. She was a good doctor and as time went on, doctors were needed more and more. It was a hell of a time. We were working day and night. Then she found she was pregnant. It wasn't the best moment, but we were both delighted. I finally persuaded her to come up north. The night before she was to leave, we went out to celebrate. I was determined to take her somewhere special. God, it was so wonderful, having something to celebrate.'

He looked across at Sarah, his features haggard.

'You can't imagine what it was like, Sarah. No one can, unless they experienced it first hand. Night after night, those poor mangled bodies brought into the hospitals; men, women, children.' He replaced the cup on the saucer with an unsteady hand. 'The ones that did recover often had no home to return to.'

'Martin, don't . . . not if it hurts so much.'

'I want to tell you, Sarah. I couldn't speak about it, before.' His voice was low and even. 'She wore her favourite dress. It was greeny-blue. I was so happy. I'd always wanted a child. I'd taken her to the best place I could think of – the Café de Paris.'

Sarah put her hand to her mouth.

'We were dancing, when I heard the noise. Then there was darkness and screaming; such awful screaming. At last someone got the lights working and I couldn't find her. Jesus, I'd been dancing with her and I couldn't find her. Then someone realised I was a doctor. They kept on at me: "Doctor, over here. Doctor, attend to this poor devil." All I wanted to do was find her. I remember one man, out of the band, I believe, I saw to him. Then I was tearing at the chunks of masonry. I thought I was going mad, Sarah. Then I saw it, a scrap of greeny-blue.'

The low monotonous voice ceased. He covered his face with his hands.

Sarah pushed away her cup. The condensed milk had made the tea sickly sweet. Her stomach heaved. Compassion showed on her face as she watched Martin, but she made no move to touch him. The lancing of a wound was, of necessity, painful and personal.

Diane came downstairs.

'Mum-my, you come.'

Sarah shook her head. 'Not now, pet. You go into the garden and play.'

Diane watched her mother's lips carefully, then nodded. She turned towards Martin, but when Sarah shook her head and laid her finger on her lips she shrugged and ran outside.

Martin raised his head. 'I'm sorry.'

'Don't be. I'm honoured you told me.'

'I couldn't talk to anyone about it, you see. Mother and Father were so cut-up, and in little over a year they were dead too. Redvers I hadn't seen for years, he went over to America to live in 1933. I'm afraid I was bitter and full of self pity. "Why me" I thought.'

He managed a wry smile. 'If I hadn't been so self absorbed I would have realised practically every family in London was experiencing similar traumas. Anyway, I'd had enough of London. I went into the Army and ended up in Burma. Remember my original convictions, Sarah?' He glanced at her. 'I still think I was right. But this last war was different. Pacifism would never have stopped Hitler. And at least I was a medic. But it was still ghastly, a different kind of killing there.'

'Poor Martin.' The tears came into Sarah's eyes then as she thought of the young man in Harrogate, so against the idea of war. She stooped over him and put her arms about him, and then she thought of John, that wide grin of his that could turn her heart within her breast and she wept for all of them.

'Come on, Sarah, this won't do.' He cleared his throat. 'What's got into the pair of us? We're supposed to be enjoying a day out.'

He rose and holding her by the hand drew her towards the window. 'Where's that daughter of yours?'

She blinked and sniffed. 'Over there.'

Outside, Diane's dark head was bent over the flower beds. She looked up, waved, and held up a plant for inspection.

Sarah made an effort to inject a lighter note into her voice. 'She's liable to pull up more flowers than weeds.'

'It doesn't matter. The whole place is a bit of a shambles. There's a couple who call in once a week. Mrs Holland gives the cottage a tidy-up and buys groceries in for me if she knows I'm coming and her husband does any maintenance and keeps the garden tidy.'

Martin's face was still sombre. 'It's stupid hanging on to the place really but, deep down, I don't want to part with it.'

'I shouldn't sell it until you feel absolutely certain you want to.' Sarah spoke in a noncommittal voice. She felt sick again and cursed the condensed milk. 'Of course, once you've finished your work you probably won't have any reason to return to Yorkshire?'

Martin turned towards her. The shadows had lifted and his face had relaxed into its usual quizzical expression. 'I shall always want to spend some time here. I find I have an affinity with all things northern.'

She gave him a suspicious glance but he had already turned away and gone outside to join Diane.

Sarah waited quietly in the sunny kitchen. She listened. Did the ghost of a blonde American girl sigh wistfully in the stillness? She heard only the chirping of a bird perched in a tree close to the open window and shouts from Martin as he played with her daughter. She shook her head at her strange fancies, washed and dried the cups and saucers and went outside to join them.

Chapter Thirty-four

'Pull on the rope, Gordon. Harder!'

Sarah waited, her hands supporting the canvas then, when nothing happened, she muttered something rude under her breath and crawled, rear-end first, out of the tent.

'Come on, boys. You should . . . Oh!' Looking down at her were Mr Allen, head of the teaching staff, and Martin.

'Morning, Sarah.' Mr Allen turned towards Martin. 'I suppose you already know our housekeeper, a lady of many talents?'

Mr Allen smiled as he spoke but Martin's face was blank as he replied: 'Yes, we have met.'

Miserably conscious of the disreputable, paint-spotted slacks she wore and her turbaned head, Sarah sat back on her heels and rubbed her nose.

'The boys needed help to put up the tent,' she explained.

'Yes. Well,' mirth was threatening to overwhelm Mr Allen, 'shall we get on, Dr Linford?'

Martin nodded and turned to follow the teacher. As he passed Sarah he bent down and hissed: 'You've just rubbed dirt all over your face.' He winked at her, then resumed his impassive expression and hurried after Mr Allen.

Sarah gazed into space for a moment then grimaced and turned her attention towards the group of boys chuckling behind their hands.

'Come on, you lot. I'm not doing it all on my own. Fetch the mallet.'

After lunch she saw Martin again.

'That's a distinct improvement.' He eyed her plain blue dress with approval.

She frowned at him. 'Why do you do it, Martin?'

'What?'

'Be so stiff and unfriendly with the staff.'

'Do I?' He sounded surprised.

'Of course you do. You must know they don't like you very much.'

'That's their prerogative.'

'You see! You're doing it to me now.'

'I don't know what you're talking about.'

'This morning, Mr Allen saw the funny side of things and so did I, even though I felt a bit of a fool. You did too, I know, but you're so formal and correct everyone else feels they have to be like that as well.'

He rubbed his chin. 'I suppose I can be a bit forbidding. I'm not like that with the children, am I?'

'You know you're not and you're not like that with me.'

'Ah, well,' he smiled. 'You're different. For one thing, you tell me off.'

Suddenly embarrassed, she looked away. 'I didn't mean to be rude.'

'No. You did right. The trouble is, I've spent the last few years talking to boards of governors, civil servants and lecturing. My social life has been non-existent and I suppose my small talk has just dried up.'

'You don't need small talk, Martin. Just be interested in people.'

'Like you are, you mean. Some of us don't find it so easy.' He gave her a sly look. 'I'll try if you'll help me.'

She looked puzzled. 'What can I do?'

'Well, I'll be leaving for London in a couple of days, but I intend coming back here in a fortnight. Will you let me take you out again? Perhaps you could introduce me socially to some local people – what do you say?'

'Oh, I don't know.' Her voice was dubious: 'We don't have many social occasions around here.' Then she began to smile. 'There might be something,' she said. 'I'll see what I can arrange.'

The village social committee were impressed and honoured when the important doctor who was visiting Oaklands came to their beetle drive. Mrs Jackson ran back to her house to fetch some of her best china teacups when she heard who he was. He was a nice chap, they agreed, but a bit quiet. Reg Hughes disagreed. 'He chatted to me all right,' he told his friends afterwards at the local pub. 'We talked about fishing and farming. But I don't know.' He shook his head. 'For a clever doctor he wasn't very bright. Thought main farming round here was sheep! "Pigs, man," I told him, "ninety per cent of t'farming is pigs." Think he'd have known that, wouldn't you?'

They agreed his education left much to be desired but also felt that he seemed to have enjoyed himself. He had two pieces of cake with his cup of tea, in one of Mrs Jackson's cups, of course. It was fitting, really, that he won first prize in the raffle.

Sarah had doubled up with suppressed laughter as he went up to collect the prize. His look of horror when presented with a ghastly salmon-pink wash jug and bowl would stay with her forever. But heroically, he had pasted a smile of thanks on his face and spoke a few appropriate words.

Frances Anne Bond

'But what shall I do with it?' he asked her as he struggled to fit the jug and bowl into the back of his car.

'Don't worry. We'll put it in the kitchen garden and grow parsley in it. Oh, Martin, your face . . .' and Sarah went off in peals of laughter again. 'I haven't enjoyed myself so much for ages,' she finally said, breathless and spluttering.

'Well, if that's your idea of a social event, Sarah, *I'll* fix up our next outing. Say you agree. It's only fair I have my revenge.'

'I suppose so. But what about your work? We can't keep gadding about like this.'

'It is work. I'm speaking at Danes Burton next Friday. A new annexe has been added to the school there, especially for the teaching of deaf children. I've promised to take part in a fund-raising meeting to buy more equipment. If you come with me, I'll take you to the pictures in Ripon afterwards.'

Sarah agreed. She was interested to see Martin as he went about his public duties.

The body of the hall was packed with members of the public and the platform with local and civic dignitaries. Sarah took a seat on the end of a row of hard-backed chairs and watched Martin shaking hands with the mayor, who was resplendent in his chains of office.

There was a speech of welcome and introductions by a nervous little man who was difficult to hear and then Martin stood up. After ten minutes Sarah had a lump in her throat. Adopting a low-key start, he began to describe the advances that were being made in the teaching of deaf children. He detailed specific technicalities, then forgot his notes and, his thin face blazing with enthusiasm, launched into vivid descriptions of how rewarding life could be for

326

those children who had sufficient up-to-date equipment
and dedicated teachers. He completely won over his audience and sat down to loud applause. Sarah clapped until her
hands tingled.

Then came the questions.

A worried-looking little woman wondered if her hearing-
impaired son would ever be employable. Someone asked
about the latest hearing aids and then a stout, fur-coated
woman stood up. She realised, she said, that a great deal
could be done for *some* children with hearing difficulties
but, surely, she paused, pouring money into education for
severely deaf children was a waste? Little could be done for
such children. It was a handicap to be accepted and lived
with.

Martin rose to answer, then paused before saying,
'There's someone in the audience who is better equipped to
answer this question than I am.' He looked straight at
Sarah.

She froze. Surely he didn't expect her to stand up and
speak. There was a silence and heads turned in her direction, then a buzz of whispered conversation as nothing happened. Somehow she stood, legs quivering like jelly, and
began to speak. Her words came haltingly at first and a tide
of humiliation crept over her but then she glanced at the
questioner and saw a look of boredom on her face and a
fierce rage flared up inside her. Rage at Martin for putting
her in this position and rage at people like this ignorant
woman, who knew *nothing*, nothing of the hours, years of
struggle necessary to help a deaf child to speak.

Her voice strengthened, and she told them: of the tantrums to be faced; the despair and the tiredness; and of the
flashes of triumph and exhilaration at each small step of
progress. She told them for Diane and for all the children at

Oaklands, and when she had finished and sat down again there was a silence and then a wave of applause and shouted promises of donations from all parts of the room.

She heard nothing else of the meeting. When it finished she filed out with the rest of the audience and waited for Martin in the lobby. Several people approached her and congratulated her and she inclined her head and smiled and said something in reply. She waited as he came through the door and walked up to her and then she exploded.

'How could you! I could have died in there. That awful silence when everyone waited for me to stand up and speak.'

'But you managed. You managed very well.'

His voice held a tone of detached interest. She could have killed him.

'I shall never forgive you.'

'Oh, calm down, Sarah. Do you know we've raised one hundred and fifty pounds over the estimated target? You helped do that.' She bit her lip. She still seethed with rage but it now seemed petty to rant on about her embarrassed feelings when the children had benefited so much.

'But I could have made a complete mess of it, Martin. I was terrified. When I began, did you hear how I stuttered and stammered? I've never felt such a fool in my life.'

He grinned. 'I felt just as big a fool at the Beetle Drive, and you just laughed.'

Her look was hostile. 'That's ridiculous. How can you compare the two things?'

'Because it's true! Don't you see? No matter how assured we are in our own little world, it's frightening to step into another. But we must do it, otherwise life's a very tame affair.'

'I still think you were unkind,' she muttered.

'I suppose I was. But I knew you would cope splendidly.' He stared down at her and raised his hand in a sort of salutation. 'And I was right. I think you're a woman who could do anything, Sarah.'

A tremor sounded in his voice and she looked at him in surprise. As their eyes met, she almost flinched. His were so alert, so probing. It was as if he could read her innermost thoughts. They stood, locked in silence, until the caretaker of the hall walked through, noisily jangling a bunch of keys.

'Sorry, thought everyone had left. I have to lock up now.'

Martin withdrew his gaze from Sarah's face and blinked. 'That's all right. We're just going.'

He took Sarah's hand and tucked it firmly under his arm as he guided her out of the building. It was just as well he did so, she walked as if in a daydream.

He unlocked his car and they got in. They were half way to Ripon before they spoke again.

'You're starting to worry me, Sarah. You're not usually so silent. Do reassure me you're not in shock. The experience of public speaking hasn't rendered you dumb, has it?'

The half teasing, half serious voice reassured her. He was still the same old Martin. She relaxed.

'I still haven't got over it,' she said. 'But if we raised that much money and I helped in a small way, then I'll forgive you.' She smiled at him. 'Where are we going next?'

'Well, I thought we'd have a bite to eat and then go to the cinema. I looked it up in the paper and they're showing *Casablanca*. Have you seen it?'

'Yes.' She fell silent again for pain flooded her body. *Casablanca* was the first picture she had been to see after John's death. Maisie had persuaded her to go. Do you good, she had said. Sarah was in a state of dull acceptance at the time so she had accompanied Maisie and watched the screen with disinterested eyes. Then the war-time sentiment, the moving romantic element of the story had penetrated her reserve, awakened her agony and, muttering excuses, she had left before the end.

'Something the matter, Sarah?'

'No, no. I'm all right.' She glanced now at Martin. The late afternoon sun was warm and he had removed his tie; the open neck of his shirt revealed a tanned skin. He looked much better now than he had when they had met on the train. Working in the country obviously suited him. His shirt sleeves were turned back and she saw his forearms were covered with dark blond hair. She looked away.

John, she thought, and tried to remember his beloved face but she realised, with a touch of panic, that time was blurring her picture of him.

'Sure you're all right? I suppose I was a bit of a brute letting you in for that ordeal at the meeting.'

Martin's grey eyes showed nothing but friendly concern.

She smiled at him affectionately. 'Perhaps a little tired.'

She put her head back, closed her eyes and concentrated on remembering John's face, but the only image she could conjure up was the love in his bright blue eyes. She sat up again and looked through the window of the car. The sun, dipping low in the sky, created a dazzle on the glass. It seemed to her that the colour of the sky blended with the blue of her lover's eyes. She raised her hand and rested it against the car window. What would John have thought of her speech this afternoon? But the Sarah he had known would not have made that speech. The tears blurred her eyes and she spread out her fingers on the glass, a symbolic gesture of farewell. The last vestiges of bitterness over his death ebbed from her. She would never forget their love, but John belonged in the past, and she must look to her future, with Diane. She could live, she thought, without love. Life held other good things: friendship, laughter.

She turned to Martin. 'Really, I'm fine,' she said. 'I'd like to see *Casablanca* again. The first time I didn't manage to stay to the end.'

Chapter Thirty-five

During the next four months Martin Linford called at Oaklands frequently. Sarah wondered what his superiors in London thought of his many visits.

'I hope you're not giving the impression there's something wrong with the place,' she protested one day.

'Not at all. My remarks are most favourable. Anyway, the report's not due until December so I'm well on schedule. Steady on, Sarah – ease off the gas a little.'

They were in his car. Bowing to his persuasion and her own secret inclination, Sarah was learning how to drive. She found the experience exhilarating and Martin said she was a natural.

'Glad to find there's *something* you still can't do,' he had said. 'You've come a long way since Hammond House.'

'I should think so.' She had looked at him, a twinkle in her eyes. 'I'm a mature woman of the world now.'

He had merely smiled in reply, but there was something lurking in his eyes which both thrilled and alarmed her. Constantly she reminded herself, a pleasant friendship, that's all she wanted.

'Hey – stop daydreaming. You'll have us in the ditch.'

'Sorry.' She returned her attention to the road. The corn had been cut and the air was heavy with the scents of late summer.

'The leaves will be turning soon,' she said. 'People are often sad at the thought of autumn, but I love it. If the fates are kind, it can be so beautiful.'

'Like you,' he said, his voice low.

'What?'

'Turn off here. Go on, Sarah, please.'

Shakily, she followed his directions and the car stopped on the side of the road close by a rustling copper-beech hedge.

'Now, Martin, why . . .'

He put his arms about her and kissed her. Momentarily, she succumbed to his embrace. His body felt good, lean and strong. It had been so long. Her head began to spin; she turned from him and pushed him away.

'Don't do that!'

'Why?'

'Because we're not . . . we're *friends*.'

'I know we are. But perhaps we could be something else?'

His light grey eyes were bright and she felt a pang of uneasiness. Were there sparks of anger there?

'I don't want there to be anything else, Martin. I thought I made that clear.'

'So that's why we've spent hours together, walking, talking. You've enjoyed my company, haven't you?'

'Yes, you know I have. But as a friend!'

'You haven't always given out that message, Sarah. There have been times, when we've shared a joke, enjoyed a meal together and you've looked at me a certain way.'

'That's not fair, Martin.' She clenched her hands on the steering wheel of the car. 'I've never purposely done such a thing.'

He moved away from her, but his intent gaze never left

her face. 'And that's the only way you see me, as a friend?'

'Yes.'

'Then I apologise. I've obviously misinterpreted certain things. I could have sworn you felt more than friendship. I certainly do.'

She felt angry, confused. He was spoiling everything. 'I'm sorry too. This summer, the outings we've shared together, they've been good for both of us. I don't want things to change.'

He was silent and the flicker of anger inside her grew stronger.

'*Why* must you want more? Oh, Martin,' she sighed, took her hands off the wheel of the car and gripped them tightly in her lap. 'I might as well tell you.' She took another deep breath. 'For years my marriage was unhappy and then I met someone. We had an affair, but it was much more than an affair, we truly loved. For the first time in my life I realised what love meant. It was so wonderful. Yet at the same time there was guilt and worry and pain. Later, when it was all over I knew I never wanted to go through that again and,' her voice was almost inaudible, 'I never shall.'

Martin was staring straight in front of him. 'What happened?'

'He was killed in the war. Victor and I sorted out our life. Strangely enough, the last years were the most happy.'

'I see.'

She looked at him. His face was impassive. 'Do you? Will you settle for friendship then? It's a very important thing.'

He leant over and turned on the ignition key. His face was taut and a nerve jumped in his thin cheek.

'I don't know, Sarah. The past doesn't concern me but

the future does. I think it may be impossible for me to keep regarding you as merely a friend.' He glanced behind them. 'You'd better pull out. This isn't the ideal place to park.'

During the ride back to Oaklands their conversation was stilted. Twice Sarah stalled the engine and muttered awkward apologies. Conscious of Martin's unsmiling face she felt tense and miserable. She lurched to a nervy, undignified halt outside the school and stared with unseeing eyes at the mass of purple and white Michaelmas daisies flowering at the side of the building. By his action today, Martin had ruined everything. He would probably go back to London and it was possible she would never see him again. Perhaps that would be best.

Diane must have been watching for them. She came running down the steps to greet them. Sarah watched as Martin stepped out of the car, without a word to her, and went to meet her daughter. Diane, what about her? Would she understand if Martin went away and never returned?

She watched them together and a frown gathered on her face. Martin was conducting an animated conversation with Diane, using sign language. Sarah switched off the car engine, slammed the door behind her and stalked over to them.

'Please don't do that, Martin.'

He looked surprised. 'Do what?'

'Don't sign to her.'

His expression of surprise turned to hostility. 'That's unfair, Sarah. You use sign language all the time when you are speaking to her.'

'I use it in teaching; when I am trying to explain a particularly difficult concept or new word. If you use it in ordinary conversation she'll become lazy. You know she must try and speak as much as possible. She *has* to live in a speaking world.'

Sarah was conscious of Diane's worried expression as the child tried to follow their rapid speech and, irrationally, she heard her own voice become increasingly belligerent.

'Of course I know.' In contrast, Martin's voice was cool and dispassionate. His expression was now positively unfriendly. 'I was explaining to Diane that I have to go away to finish my work. I have told her I will write to her and I will come and see her again when I can. That is a fairly important concept, I'm sure you will agree?'

Sarah had the grace to blush. 'I'm sorry. Martin . . .' she stepped towards him and touched his arm.

He gave her a brief smile then bent down and gave Diane a hug. 'It's all right. I'll be in touch. Look after each other.'

He turned, ran down the steps and drove away in his car.

'Bummy?' Diane's face was forlorn. Sarah forced a smile on her face.

'It's Mummy, pet – not Bummy. And come on, we'll be late for tea.'

'I thought Doctor Linford would have visited again before now.' Matron polished her glasses and replaced them on her nose. 'Have you any idea when he will be coming, Sarah?'

'Not really.' Sarah kept her voice noncommittal. 'I suppose he's hard at work finishing the report.'

'Yes. But he did mention some new post-aural hearing aids . . .' Matron tut-tutted. 'It's most unlike him to forget.' Through thick lenses, she peered at Sarah. 'You look somewhat pale, my dear. Not working too hard, are you?'

'Not at all.' Sarah picked up a pile of sheets. 'I just have to change the beds in the blue dormitory, then I'm off duty. I might have a rest then.'

'Good. But why don't you go for a walk instead? It's a beautiful day and you don't seem to have been out much recently.'

Matron adopted an arch expression. 'Of course, you can't pursue your driving lessons at the moment, but you should get some fresh air. It's November next week, remember – we can't expect many more days like this one.'

Sarah left the room without replying. Matron was behaving more and more like a mother, and it irritated her. For heaven's sake, the woman was only about four years older than she was and yet she was trying to organise Sarah's life as she did her pupils'.

She climbed the stairs to the dormitory. The room smelt musty. The children had left the windows tightly shut. She opened them. That was better. The heather would be purple on the moors now, the sheep standing heavy in their thick coats. She sighed. She missed the outings in the car. She missed Martin, too. What a pity he was not content with friendship.

Quickly she tidied the room; picking up sandshoes from beneath cupboards, washing and reassembling toothmugs and toothbrushes in the bathroom and spreading sweet-smelling fresh linen on the small beds.

Diane would be moving into this dormitory at Christmas. She was seven years old now, already long-legged and skittish as a young colt. She was going to be taller than her mother. Sarah smiled as she thought of Diane. The realisation of her deafness had been a devastating blow, but now Sarah was confident her child would hold her own in life.

She left the dormitory and climbed the narrow staircase at the back of the house which led to her own small room. She closed the door with a sigh of relief.

It was good to be alone. She knew she had carved her

own special place in the affections of the pupils and most of the staff in the school and she enjoyed the feeling of friendship. The school had been good to her and she hoped she had repaid her debt of gratitude. Yet there were times she wished she had more privacy. For instance, she knew the staff were curious over her relationship with Martin; Matron in particular, since she knew they had been acquainted many years ago. She had made a point of telling Sarah that Dr Linford seemed much happier and relaxed since his first visit to the school.

'Such a lonely man,' she had commented. 'Nice to see him smiling more.'

Well, everyone was lonely at times.

She put her hands to her head and released her hair from the confines of the hairpins. It fell loose about her shoulders, thick and glossy. She slipped off her cotton overall and donned a silky dressing-gown. She was tired. She would lie on the bed and rest. The old-fashioned window had small squares of stained glass across the top and Sarah idly watched as the daylight streamed through the glass and painted pink and blue patterns on her cream-coloured counterpane.

She had received two letters that morning. One was from her mother. Mary Armstrong sounded happy, but her writing was becoming increasingly thin and shaky. Sarah frowned. The thought of anything happening to her mother was unbearable. At least she was with Betty and Harry. Mary had looked after Betty during the long months when Harry had been 'missing', before they heard he had been picked up from a life-raft by a German E-boat and interned. Now the two of them looked after Mary. The letter from Dotty had been a surprise. They corresponded at Christmas and birthdays, but Sarah hadn't seen her for over a year. Dotty still had her ambitions. The last time Sarah had met her, she had just been promoted to head receptionist at a large hotel in York. Sarah had hardly recognised the self-assured young woman who had taken her out and bought her lunch. Now Dotty had written to say she was thinking of getting engaged. Arnold was a chef at the hotel. A good one; Dotty had underlined the word *good*. She also stated they would not marry until they had enough money to set up in a place of their own. 'Marriage wasn't in my plans,' Dotty had written, but she was confident they could be happy.

'Happy.' The pink and blue patterns blurred as Sarah's eyes closed. Why did people assume their right to happiness? Contentment was more to be aimed for, a tranquil, even existence. No earth-shaking highs meant no depths of despair – much more sensible really. She slept.

The knocking awoke her.

'Sarah.'

It sounded like Martin's voice. She must have been dreaming.

'Sarah.'

It was Martin. She sprang from the bed, pulled her gown closely about her figure, belted it and opened the door. Her face was soft and dreamy from sleep.

'Can I come in? It's all right. Matron knows I'm here, she sent me up.'

'But I'm not dressed.'

'So?' He pushed past her. 'I am a doctor, after all.'

Acutely conscious of her upsurging emotions and her dishevelled appearance she stood by the door.

'Please, Martin, I'll see you downstairs, in a few minutes.'

'No.' He sat down in an easy chair by the side of the bed and looked at her. 'I've often dreamt about waking up next to you; this is the next best thing.'

Colour flared in her cheeks. 'Please go.'

'No.'

His eyes had darkened to a smoky hue and his steady gaze disconcerted her.

'Then I will!' she said.

'No you don't.' As she turned to leave the room he sprang up and caught hold of her. 'Not until you've heard me out.'

She stared down at her imprisoned arm. 'Please let me go.'

'In a minute. Have you thought about me, Sarah, during these past weeks?'

She looked up at him. 'Of course I have.'

'Really thought, I mean. I've thought about you, all the time. I'm not losing you, Sarah. I don't know why you won't face it, but all those years ago, there was *something* between us then, and there is now. You can't deny it.'

'That was another life. We were so young.'

'And now you think we're too old, is that it? I don't think we are.' He pulled her close to him and his hand brushed against the curve of her breast as her dressing-gown gaped open.

'Is that all you want?' She jerked her arm free and her eyes flashed contempt. 'You want to sleep with me?'

He frowned. 'Of course I do. I rather hoped you wanted me, too.'

He waited but she did not reply.

'You're a desirable woman, Sarah. You must know that. But that's not all I want. I want you to marry me.'

She blinked incredulously and stepped back against the

wall. 'Don't,' she cried. 'You're making it worse!'

He stared at her.

'Don't you see, Martin? I could love you, but I mustn't. I've been on my own too long. I fought hard to get here and now I'm happy at Oaklands and so is Diane. I don't want that to change.'

'But it doesn't have to.' At her words, his face lightened in relief. The words poured from him. 'I know how important this place is to you. Oh, I do love you, Sarah. At first, I was just intrigued. I wanted to see how the youngster I remembered had grown up. But I think all the time a little voice inside told me our meeting again was important. Then I got to know you all over again. Why do you think I wanted to teach you to drive? I've worked it all out. You've seen how I must travel about the country,' he shrugged. 'That can't be helped. But if we married, the cottage could be our base. Diane could continue her lessons here and when I was able to come north we could be together. And I'd make sure I came often.'

'You've really planned it all out, haven't you?'

He swore softly under his breath at the flatness of her voice.

'I could go on being a housekeeper and you would be in London. A strange marriage that would be.'

'I think it could be a good marriage. I love you and I love Diane. So think about her, don't you think she deserves a father?'

'That's not fair.'

'Are you being fair?'

She shook her head. 'It's crazy, Martin. All right, I've changed, learnt a lot of things, but I could never fit into your world and you know it.'

He grabbed her hand and gripped it so tightly she cried out but he made no apology.

'For God's sake, Sarah, you're not a housemaid now,

you're a perceptive, intelligent woman. At least, I thought you were.'

Stung by his words, she retaliated: 'And you're a well-known medical specialist travelling the country, lecturing and attending conferences. What use would I be to you?'

'But you would!' He shook his head in frustration. 'I lecture about what you have actually experienced, Sarah. Surely you can see that! As Diane becomes older and more independent, and that will happen sooner than you realise, you could travel with me. You have *lived* with the difficulties I can only speak about. The knowledge you have gained could be invaluable and you could help countless other parents to cope with their problems.'

Her eyes widened and Martin gave a smile of relief as he saw her expression change. But then his smile faded as her lips set in their former stubborn line.

'I still can't marry you. I never shall.'

His grasp slackened. He released her. 'Then I'm wrong and you don't care for me at all.'

She swayed a moment then wearily, like an old woman, moved away from him and towards the bed. 'I've nothing left to give, Martin. Anyway – I'm bad luck, to everyone I have ever loved –' she sighed. 'Please leave,' she said.

'But that's stupid. You . . .'

She interrupted him, her voice now firm and even. 'I won't change my mind.' She glanced at the clock, ticking on the bedside cabinet. 'I'm due downstairs in fifteen minutes and I would like to be alone now.'

'Do you want to be alone for the rest of your life, Sarah?'

She bowed her head.

He rubbed his hand over his burning eyes and left her.

* * *

The children made a circle around the room. They were in pairs, hand in hand with their partners and their faces brimmed with mischief. The autumn sun, slanting through the large window, gilded the plain wooden floor and brightened the chalked self-portraits which hung on the walls.

Sarah switched on the microphone next to the gramophone and placed a record on the turntable. When the music started, Simon, the ginger-headed boy, missed the opening bars of music so she crossed the floor to take his hands. The children enjoyed their dancing. Sarah knew that music to them sounded more like humming, but she also knew the vibrations were absorbed into their bodies giving them a sense of rhythm.

She moved her hands. 'Listen.' She marked out the tempo: 'That's right, one-two-three, one-two-three.'

The door opened, she turned and a flash of anguish crossed her face as Diane broke away from her partner and ran towards the man framed in the doorway.

'Mar-tin, come, dance with me.'

He took her hand and allowed her to draw him into the group of children.

Sarah raised her voice so he could hear her above the music. 'I thought you'd gone.'

He shook his head. 'I needed to think. I went back to your room. I thought perhaps if I wrote something down for you to read, later . . .'

She gave a hopeless shrug then looked at the small boy who waited patiently. 'I can't talk now. Anyway, we've talked enough.'

'Just one thing, Sarah. Look at me and tell me you don't love me.'

She bent her head, unable to meet his eyes.

344

'I saw this on the table in your room.'

From his pocket he produced a battered old book. 'I picked it up and the pages fell open here.'

He stepped closer to her, showed her. He watched her face as she read. The music stopped and the children bobbed about them, watching them.

'It's Jim's book, my brother,' she said slowly.

'Yes. I remember.' He put his arm gently around her slim shoulders. His face was serious.

'Read it out, love.'

One of the older children ran over to the gramophone, turned over the record and replaced the needle. The music began.

In a low voice Sarah read: 'Love bade me welcome, yet my soul drew back.'

She looked up at him.

'You're contrary, Sarah Armstrong, and you're stubborn, but I never thought you were a coward.'

'Oh, Martin.'

Her face, so strained and controlled in expression, softened and smoothed into surrender. Her eyes became luminous. The corners of her mouth turned up into a smile and her body relaxed in the circle of his arms.

He kissed her briefly, then more leisurely, and hugged her.

'We'll probably have some terrific rows,' he said happily.

Someone giggled and, remembering, the couple drew apart.

'You should be dancing, children,' reproved Sarah, but for some reason she found it impossible to assume a stern expression. Diane, her eyes huge with astonishment, took hold of Simon's hand and whirled the boy away.

. Martin listened to the music then sketched Sarah a bow: 'May I have the pleasure of this dance?'

She hesitated. 'I can't dance,' she replied.

'Oh, I think you can.'

He kissed her again and, in the middle of the children, they began to dance.

'See,' he said. 'It's easy when you know how.'